HORTUS DIABOLICUS

HORTUS DIABOLICUS

Further Twisting Tales of
Menacing Flora and Malignant Fungi

Edited by Chad Arment

COACHWHIP PUBLICATIONS
Greenville, Ohio

Hortus Diabolicus, edited by Chad Arment
© 2022 Coachwhip Publications

Cover image is from a 1925 news article on the Mindanao 'octopus-tree.' Back cover image is from an 1893 news article depicting a 'vampire vine' from Nicaragua. Both were presented as alleged undescribed species, but no physical evidence corroborates such claims.

CoachwhipBooks.com (print) / Coachwhip.com (epub)

ISBN 1-61646-525-5
ISBN-13 978-1-61646-525-4

Contents

PHALAENOPSIS GLORIOSA

Edgar Wallace
(writing as John Jason Trent)

Two men sat over their liquor and cigars in the big library of Driscoll's country place. It was a chilly evening in April, and the great pine logs which blazed on the hearth before them and threw tremendous lightings over the books, paintings, and heavy ebony furnishings of the apartment scarcely served to dissipate the chill of the unused room.

To the right, three long French windows looked westward over acres of lawn sweeping down to the broad river, while to the south the view was shut off by dense masses of evergreen shrubbery, supplemented by vines and creepers which had flung their festoons of delicate leafage in every direction across the windows. A great elm standing guard at this corner of the house tossed its branches to and fro in the spring wind and tapped nervously on the nearest window.

The house, in spite of its wealth and beauty, impressed one with a sense of loneliness. A dwelling reflects the daily life of its tenants in the same intangible way that a man carries the reflection of his life writ large in face and person; and this stately room had the air of one who has looked on his dead and stands appalled and desolate. From the more distant parts of the house came the occasional creak of a board or the slam of a shutter in the wind, and at each fresh noise the elder of the two men turned a face full of ill-concealed uneasiness in the direction of the sound. At last the other tossed the ash of his cigar in the fire and turned to his host.

"Bob, old fellow, what's the matter with you? You're as nervous as my grandmother! Is it a ghost or delirium tremens that is freezing your young soul? Speak out man, what is it?"

Driscoll, thus addressed, rose, and going almost stealthily to the two doors leading out of the room, slipped the massive bolts across into their, sockets; then he came back to the fire, poured out some liquor, drank it, and pulled his chair near to Larcher.

"Larcher, you and I have been out together for big game. The tiger skin there tells one story, this leopard's skin beneath our feet another, but I have brought you here to-night to help me kill or capture the most devilish thing that ever walked the earth. You, because you are the one man whose brain and nerve and muscle I can trust."

"Good!" said Larcher. "Is it man or beast?"

"Not beast, yet scarcely human," replied the other, "but I must go back and tell you the story of this accursed thing that has come upon the place. You know what a hobby my orchid houses have long been to me, and you have heard me speak of the difficulty I have had in getting a capable foreman to minister to my favorites. The run of these fellows know merely the few common commercial varieties, and my interest has always centred in the rarer species. Six months ago I was in such despair over my collection that I had almost decided to give up their culture entirely rather than suffer the constant disappointment of having successive importations die on my hands, when, in response to my advertisement in the Herald, there walked into my office one morning a fellow who seemed exactly the one for the place. I couldn't tell his nationality exactly, but his bronzed face bore out his statement that he had spent many years in the tropics, collecting orchids for one of the big English importing houses. Details were soon adjusted between us, and it was arranged that he was to come down here and begin work at once. I inquired if he had a family, and he replied that he had a wife, who would come down here with him the next day.

"As he rose to leave the office, I said: 'One thing more, Hearston. I hope you are up in growing Phalaenopsis Gloriosa. They are my favorite orchid, and I have a special house of them out there.' Larcher, at mention of the orchid's name I could have sworn that the fellow turned green under his tan. He caught at the chair back as though to steady himself, and answered oddly that he thought he could do nothing with them, and then added, as though he had said more than he had meant to: 'They are the most difficult orchids in the world to bloom in captivity, sir.' I smiled at the conceit of the orchids as imprisoned wild things, bade him good morning, and forgot the incident for the time.

"Well, they went down the next day, and were soon established in the pretty little cottage on the slope of the hill near the greenhouses. I went down some weeks later, found everything running smoothly, and Hearston introduced me to his wife. You know that since Mollie died, women have rather gone out of my life, and I am not easily impressed with a pretty face, but I shall never forget the exotic beauty of that woman.

"Whatever doubt there might be about his nationality, hers was unmistakable. She was pure, high- caste East Indian; you know the type, tall, slim, with exquisite features and eyes of midnight witchery. I thought as I looked at her that she had the same subtle atmosphere of mingled spirituality and splendor that my orchid blooms possess. She spoke no word of English, and stood beside Hearston as we talked, eyeing him with a world of pathos in

her dark, unfathomable eyes. It was plain to see that she
adored her husband from his footprints upward. You remember the handsome collie dog I had here, a beautiful
fellow, who lived up to his ideals in a way to shame most
humans. He had always been slow to make friends with
strangers, though devoted to the old servants on the place.
He came bounding up to us as we stood there, and to my
surprise, ignored me to fawn at Mrs. Hearston's feet, leaping upon her with the utmost affection. 'Your wife has
made a friend worth having,' I remarked to Hearston. The
man smiled and assented, and the subject passed.

"We spent the rest of the day going through the greenhouses together, and I found that I had made no mistake
in my man. Such a knowledge of orchids, of their native
conditions of growth and climate, and such a stock of East
Indian lore was a revelation to me.

"The greenhouses have been altered and enlarged considerably since you saw them last; the chief addition being
an immense circular house at the foot of the range. Here
I have gathered thousands of fine plants of Phalaenopsis
Gloriosa. Instead of the usual equipment of benches I had
a number of trees on the place cut down and sunk in the
ground at irregular intervals from each other, on all sides
of the house, and the orchid plants were then wired to
them from the ground up, interspersed with ferns imbed-
ded in moss. Great palms were planted thickly round the
trees, and hundreds of orchids were suspended by wire
from the roof. The whole effect was that of a bit of tropical jungle. In spite of all my care they had never done
well, and I was anxious to have, my new foreman's advice
on the subject.

"Rather to my surprise, Hearston's wife accompanied
us on our rounds, but when she came to the floor of the
Phalaenopsis house, she drew back pale and shuddering.
He spoke some rapid words in what I suppose was her

native tongue to her, and she turned and sat on a stool in
the shed outside. He murmured some apology to me about
her being tired, and followed me into the house. Before
communicative, the man grew oddly quiet and nervous.
We were there some five minutes, and in that time he
never took his eyes off the slim little figure in the shed
beyond. I could get nothing out of him about the culture
of the Gloriosas, and attributing his evident embarrass-
ment to his ignorance on the subject, we returned to the
other houses. That night I went back to town.

"I am going into all this wearisome detail, Larcher, in
the hope that you, with your years of experience in India,
and your knowledge of the Oriental character, may be able
to see some glimmer of dawn in the darkness of the mystery that followed."

Larcher nodded, eagerly, and Driscoll continued:

"Six weeks passed, and Hearston's reports were uni-
formly satisfactory. At the end of that time I received a
curious letter from him. It was a request for a couple of
private police to patrol the place night and day, and the
man urged haste as though oppressed with terror. We are
too far off the turnpike here to be often troubled with
tramps. Still I felt that my new foreman had deserved my
confidence so far, and I took steps that afternoon to en-
gage a couple of men for watchman's duty. The next day
was Sunday, and still a bit worried by the unusual tenor
of Hearston's letter, I took the afternoon train and came
out here. I had neglected to wire anyone of my coming, so
there was no trap at the station to meet me, and I walked
the mile to the place in a bleak February twilight that
seemed to deepen in perceptible gradations.

"As I came down the curve of the drive and round the
southern corner of the house, I paused, struck by the
beauty of the view. Great crimson clouds were banked up
on the horizon as though rolled up by a stupendous fire,

while streaks of sullen red shooting almost to the zenith flung their sinister reflection on the river and the lawns. I had never seen the place take on such a lurid unearthly beauty, fit setting for the tragedy to come. The group of dwarf Norwegian pines at this corner of the house stood out against the angry sky like some exquisite tracery, and while I stood admiring their symmetry and grace, a branch not twenty feet away from me swung back and—a face looked out.

"A hideous face, such as one might conjure up in the nightmares of a fever, a yellow, square Mongolian face, seamed with a thousand wrinkles, and every seam a sin. Larcher, I saw that face as plain as I see you now. For the space of three seconds I stood still, looking straight at that grinning mask, hypnotised, perhaps, by those beady glittering eyes gazing into mine. Then the branch dropped back into place, and I, released from the spell cast over me, darted forward to the spot where it had been. It had vanished like a dream. I searched among the bushes for half-an-hour or more, but finally gave up in despair, and went into the house.

"I took occasion, while old Mrs. Mayhew was serving my dinner, to question her guardedly on the subject of tramps or strangers on the place. She told me there hadn't been a stranger seen on the place all the winter. That some of the servants had been commenting on the fact only the night before. This made Hearston's letter more inexplicable than ever, and after dinner I sent for him, intending to have a plain talk with him on the subject. He came in answer to my summons, and I jumped at sight of the man's face. White and haggard, with a certain hunted fierceness in his eyes and a restlessness in his manner which changed him utterly. I felt that the situation rose to its feet, and explained itself as a bad combination of man and whisky. I never strike a man when he's down, or preach temperance to a convalescent drunkard, so I ignored Hearston's apparent condition, told him of my receipt of his letter and the arrangements I had made for the patrolling of the place.

"'They must be quick, Mr. Driscoll,' Hearston broke in. 'They, must be quick. For God's sake, sir, get them over here at once!' He came up to me in his excitement and laid his hand on mine. I shivered at his touch; it was so cold. His eyes blazed into mine in passionate eagerness, and then I saw my mistake. It wasn't drink that had changed the man; it was sheer, clear, cold, blue terror!

"'Hearston,' I said, 'there is something wrong here on the place; I want you to tell me frankly what you fear.'

"Before the fellow had a chance to reply the night was broken by a succession of sharp yelps like an animal in pain, followed by a shrill scream, and on the sound the man beside me dashed through the door and out over the verandah. I followed him almost instantly and ran out of doors. There, ahead of me, Hearston was running over the lawn to his cottage, as though he had been shot from a bow. I followed him as rapidly as possible, marvelling at the speed with which he crossed the ground, and a second later I came up to him bending over his wife lying in a dead faint on the verandah of his cottage. A shadow lay at the woman's feet, and as I bent to see what it was, a pitiful little moan came up from the darkness.

"Someone brought a lantern, and by its light I saw, my collie Donald lying there, his bright fur all matted with blood from a murderous knife-wound in his side. His beautiful, faithful eyes turned up to mine as I knelt beside him, then glazed as the little life went out. Together we lifted Mrs. Hearston, and, carrying her into the house, laid her upon the bed. Hearston, wild with excitement, bent over her, begging me to do something—anything. In a few minutes she recovered her consciousness, but relapsed at sight of us into a state of helpless hysteria.

They both seemed too near the verge of collapse to give me any information as to what had occurred.

"Hearston was walking to and fro like a crazy man, wringing his hands, while his wife lay laughing and sobbing uncontrolledly. The dog's death showed me that something serious was on foot on the place, and, feeling that they were probably not safe in the cottage by themselves, I proposed to Hearston that he and his wife come up here for the night. He assented with eagerness, and they came up to the house with me. Mayhew put them in a room on the ground-floor which had at one time been used as a sort of spare room when the house was crowded. It was in this wing, but on the other side and facing the greenhouses. I saw them comfortably installed, told Mayhew to see that Mrs. Hearston had everything she needed, and bade them good-night.

"I sat long over the fire that evening, trying in vain to puzzle out Hearston's behavior, and the cause of my dog's death. It all depressed me more than I can tell you, and I was filled with a miserable, presentiment of evil, try as I might to shake it off. I must have sunk into a sort of a doze before the fire, for I dreamed a curiously vivid dream. I was out on the lawn in the moonlight, pursuing a baffling shape which fled from me, eluding me ever as I gained on it, and which kept giving out yelps like the dying cry of the dog.

"Faster it fled, and I faster, with that curious rapid increase of momentum peculiar to dreams, till at last I had him by the shoulder. He turned in my grasp, and I saw again the hideous yellow face outlined against the shrubbery, and an appalling scream shot through my brain and brought me to my feet. I knew that I had dreamt the rest, but I could have sworn that the scream was real. I rushed to the door and flung it open. The hall lay dark and silent. I threw open a window thinking the sound might have come from without, but the grave could not be quieter; and cursing my nervous imagination for the fright that it had given me, I turned in and went to bed.

"The next morning I woke early, and eager to clear up in the daylight the wretched business of the night before, I sent Hendricks over to Hearston's room to tell him I wished to see him as soon as possible. The fellow came back and said he had knocked repeatedly on Hearston's door, but couldn't rouse him, and in that instant all the vague horror of the night before returned to me. The room had two long French windows in it like these, opening out on the north verandah, so I sent Hendricks out on the porch to reconnoiter from the outside. He returned, almost immediately this time, to say that one of the windows was wide open, and he had looked in. The room was in confusion, Hearston and his wife were gone. It came to me that they might have risen early and gone back to the cottage, so I sent Hendricks for the third time to deliver my message. A third time he came back to say that they were not there. I went myself to the cottage. It was just as we had left it the night before. I hailed one of the gardeners on his way to work. 'Have you seen Hearston?' 'No,' he answered; 'perhaps he is in the greenhouses.'

"'Perhaps he is,' I said; 'we must find him. You and Hendricks take the first house and I'll take the second, and we'll go through alternating.' I started on my tour of the houses, calling Hearston's name aloud in my eagerness to find him safe, and shake off the deepening conviction that I should find him otherwise.

I reached the Phalaenopsis house at the foot of the range, still calling, opened the door and started to go in. The masses of greenery made the interior seem dim to me after the morning sunlight; but as I closed the door I saw something coming towards me out of the forest twilight of the place. At first I thought that it was Broughton's

Great Dane—the dog is over here half the time—but it rose upright, upright and gibbering, lunged at me through the shadows of the green! I leaped to the door and crashed it behind me, and the thing fell against it heavily, and rolled over on the floor. It was Hearston; Hearston with snow-white hair and eyes of flame! Hearston, and he was mad—mad!"

"And the woman?"

"No trace! If the earth had opened and swallowed her she could not have disappeared more utterly. We captured Hearston after a terrible struggle; there was nothing to be elicited from him. Every inch of this place has been searched and searched again, and still, no trace! And, Larcher, It seems a trivial thing, a weak and empty fancy, and yet—"

"Tell!"

"Since that night when that mysterious horror happened, those Gloriosas seem to have taken a new lease, of life! Great sprays have started from every plant and hang laced and interlaced like some strange web on every side. Buds developed, but they do not bloom! A month ago I said to the man in charge—'To-morrow will see this house white with blossoms.'

"He looked at me curiously. 'So I thought, sir, a week ago.'

"'They were not sufficiently developed, then,' I answered.

"'Yes, sir, just as they are now.'

"'Why, man, they couldn't be,' I cried! 'look at them, they are just ready to burst open.'

"'As you say, sir,' he answered; reservedly.

"'But you don't agree with me?' I asked.

"'No, sir, they were just like this ten days ago; one would say, sir, they were all ready to bloom, but—that they were waiting for something!'

"It is true! I have watched them ever since. The whole place is full of a dismal, haunting oppression that I cannot shake off or banish. An indescribable terror hangs over it, and I never want to see it again.'

Larcher rose to his feet, his face alight with excitement, and stood with his back to the fire looking down at Driscoll.

"And the motive, the clue, the explanation to it all? What do people say? What do they think?"

"Everything and nothing! A woman is made away with—by whom? By Hearston, himself, some say: Bah! The man loved her. She had no fear of him. There was a third person whom they both feared—the face in the pines."

"The other men on the place?"

"Are above suspicion! They all room together in quarters over the carriage-house, and were all there that night. They say that Hearston was a good fellow and devoted to his wife; that she was with him in the green-houses every day, and that he never seemed content unless she was close beside him. Further, it was brought out that in the ten days preceding the occurrence Hearston had seemed strangely excited and nervous, but perfectly sober and sane, and, note this, that there had been no tramp nor suspicious character seen on the place since Hearston had come on it."

"Did you tell the police of the face you had seen?"

"I did. But no one else had seen it; I had no tangible proof that I had, and the consensus of opinion seemed to be that it was the result of overstrained nerves."

"What has become of Hearston?"

"He is, or rather was, till two days ago, in the lunatic asylum, the tower of which you can see just over the trees, to the west of the place. It's about three miles distant. They said from the first that his condition was quite hopeless. When they took him there he was almost uncontrollable; then he sank into a sullen silence difficult to break. Two days ago I received word from the superintendent

that Hearston had burst the heavy iron bars at his window
and escaped. They begged me, if I had any knowledge of
his whereabouts, to inform them at once, and added that
they were watching my place, as it was likely that he would
seek his home.

"I came down here immediately, but so far, have had no
sight of him. Yesterday afternoon I grew lonely and nervous. I had been in the house all day, and, thinking a little
exercise would do me good, I strolled up the drive to the
gate. It was almost dark when I turned to come back, and
I couldn't help glancing sharply through the shrubbery as I
passed along. I had on an old pair of tennis shoes I found
in my room here, and the soft soles were almost noiseless
on the gravel roadway. And as I walked it seemed to me I
heard a sort of swish, swish, as of someone moving through
the bushes to my right. I drew my revolver, and gradually
slackened my speed, that whatever it was might pass me.

"The movement in the bushes slackened, too, and I
knew that I was being watched. I walked on till we came
to a place where the shrubbery lining the road was thinner
than usual, and, wheeling suddenly, I plunged through
the bushes in the direction of the sound. As I wheeled, so
did the intruder, and put such distance between us that I
could but faintly make out a tall supple figure in the robe
of some dark stuff, wound round the waist with a scarf.
I had hoped to find it Hearston. But it wasn't he, for the
man glanced around just before he disappeared, and I saw
again the villainous yellow face, and the beady eyes! I ran
after him, discharging my revolver as I ran, but the shots
went wild in the gathering night, and for a second time he
eluded me. This morning I sent you a wire. You are here.
That is all."

"Driscoll, you say the face you saw in the shrubbery
was grinning? Did you notice anything, peculiar, about
the teeth?"

Driscoll sprang to his feet with a smothered oath. "Larcher, you have seen it! Where?"

"I haven't seen it, Bob, upon my word!"

"Then how did you know that it hadn't any teeth? At least, just the two incisors, at the angle of the jaw, long and yellow like a wolf's fangs! How did you know the one thing I omitted to tell you?"

"Sit down, and I'll tell you. It's a bit of a story I haven't thought of for years," answered Larcher, lighting a fresh cigar. "By the way, since you confess so frankly to carrying a gun, I may as well unload myself of my armoury. I never stay in civilisation long enough at a time to accustom myself to going without a weapon. I'll lay it here on the table, if you don't mind. Well, you remember that I went out with the British East India Geographical Commission some seven years ago, and you will remember, further, perhaps, that our chief mission at that time was the exploration of some of the tributaries of the Mekhong River. The British Government has ploughed India with its army, and harrowed it with its civil service, till it is surprising that there should be a wild spot left; but there are still great stretches of territory unknown and almost impenetrable, where the weeds of native custom flourish in rank luxuriance. There is probably no place on the habitable globe, under the nominal control of the civilised nation, concerning which so little is known as the valley of the Mekhong River. Immense forests, centuries old, stretch unbroken for hundreds of miles, hiding in dank, impenetrable morass and jungle, the wild, fierce people who inhabit them.

"We struck the Lam-nam-si River at its junction with the Mekhong, and started off to follow it to its source. We had not been out more than three days' march when we began to hear of tigers, and I determined to leave the party at Menatkong and browse round the neighborhood a

bit to see if I could get a tiger skin or two. I expected to
join the others about a week later at a point agreed upon.
They protested that my life wouldn't be worth a farthing,
alone in that country; so I compromised by taking Haranya Vatani, a native, who accompanied the party as guide
and godmother. The first day we were disappointed in our
game, and found ourselves at dusk, with a tropical storm
on our track, near an isolated native village.

"It was the only place for miles around that offered human habitation and a shelter from the storm, but in spite
of that Haranya tried to steer me past it. This only made
me curious to see it, so I took the rudder in my own hands,
and we stayed over night there. We were civilly received,
for Vatani's fat face is a sort of general ticket of admission
to that part of the universe; but the next day, the worst of
the storm being over, one of the inhabitants tipped Vatani
the wink that it would be more tactful if we would move
on, and we, accordingly, did so. After we left the place,
Vatani told me the cause of our scant entertainment. The
name of the village is Kong-Satru. You know, doubtless,
that practically all the Gloriosas come from there."

"No, I thought they came from Panom-Pehn; that is the
place mentioned in the invoices."

"That is the river-port where they are packed for ship-
ment. They are stolen from the forests around Kong-Satru
by sturdy adventurers, who evidently have little love of
life, and shipped by stealth and night down the Mekhong
to the sea. The forests on the hills around Kong-Satru are
the most magnificgnt imaginable, and teeming with this
variety of orchid. A native, Haranya said, would much
sooner think of selling his children than a plant of the
Gloriosas, which are indescribably sacred to them. These
people mix their religion with the culture of the plants in
a manner at once horrible and grotesque. The flowers are
cared for by a band of native priests, who to the thousand

other Oriental ideas, add one more, the most gruesome of them all.

"They say," and Larcher leaned across the table towards Driscoll and gazed meditatively out into the night as he continued: "They say that the orchids must have blood, human blood, and so it happens just before the plants' blooming season, the priests select a victim from among the inhabitants of the village for this sacrifice."

"And then?" asked Driscoll, as Larcher paused, still gazing past him out of the window, sunk in reminiscence.

"I was thinking of the night Haranya told me this tale, sitting in a little tent in the midst of the jungle, not 30 miles from Kong-Satru, with the tail of the storm lashing round us, and Vatani shivering with fright lest he be overheard in the telling; in India it is neither polite nor healthy to discuss your neighbor's religion."

"And then?"

"And then, on the day of the feast of the flowers, which was the festival our presence interrupted, on that full moon of April, when I unwittingly grazed Death, there is high carnival in Kong-Satru, and the priests take the victim to the forests above the town—and feed the flowers!"

"And then?"

"'And then they bloom!' said Haranya, 'and not until then!' The priests are a vile-looking lot, with yellow skin like parchment, their teeth not gone as you describe, it, but the four front teeth blackened so that at a distance they are invisible. There is a large Chinese element in these priests, if they are not indeed full-blooded Mongolians, which marks them off from the rest of the Aryan population."

"And you think that Hearston's wife—"

"Was doomed to the sacrifice! That Hearston was in the neighborhood gathering Phalaenopsis, and either had seen her before, or met her while she was trying to escape; that by his knowledge of the country he succeeded in getting her to some sea-coast town where they shipped for England. Then they came here and lived content, till the fanatic face rose up at her elbow, inexorable as fate. I think myself that those priests must have some hypnotic influence over the people; you heard the girl's cry when he came to her that night? How else did he awe them to the submission and silence that followed?"

"I see it now. It must have been the priest, too, who killed my poor collie."

"Do not lament the dog, Bob; he died trying to defend the gentle soul who had been kind to him, and no death could be nobler. I think that the priest has the girl in hiding, hypnotised; he is waiting for, the hour. It has struck! This is the full moon of April, the day of the feast of the flowers. If the girl is to be saved, it must be now. We shall have an able ally."

Driscoll sprang to, his feet. "Who?"

"Hearston! He is tracking the priest; I have been watching him at it the last half-hour."

"Where?"

"There! See! The gaunt figure crouching in the shadow of the pillar on the porch! At first I thought he was the priest; and laid my gun handy; then he moved a bit, and the moonlight fell on the white hair and asylum garb. Depend upon it, Driscoll, Hearston, too, has seen that face from his prison windows and the iron bent like tin beneath the maniac strength that gathered itself and passed out to slay. See! He is watching something that is moving across the lawn from south to north. I can tell that, from his movements. It can be nothing else but the priest. Look, he is rising! Are you armed? Then come."

Leading the way, Larcher noiselessly unlatched the window and passed out on the verandah, Driscoll following. The man in front of them crept cautiously forward from the shadow of one tree to the next till he reached a clump of shrubs commanding a view of the great stone staircase which terraced the hill beside the greenhouses. He paused here, watching the stairs intently. Larcher and Driscoll at a little distance did the same.

"He's lost him," whispered Driscoll; but Larcher shook his head. A moment later the priest glided out of the bushes fringing the stairway, almost at the bottom of the hill. For an instant the supple figure stood out in the full moonlight, black against the whiteness of the stonework, listening; then, apparently satisfied, he beckoned, and a slender white figure crept out and after him as he opened a door and disappeared. In an instant Hearston was making his way down the steps, the others following as before. There was no hesitation or undue haste in his movements; as silently and relentlessly as the tide laps up the shore, so did he cover the space between himself and the priest. He reached the door of the Phalaenopsis house and melted into the blackness of the wall. As the door opened a low monotonous sing-song chant struck the ears of the two outside.

"Chinese, by all that's holy? Bob, he is worshipping the flowers!"

A second later they had reached the door and looked in.

It was a weird scene! Lofty trees towered sheer to the height of forty feet or more, covered with the delicate green of ferns among the darker shades of the orchid plants, while thousands of sprays of half-open flowers filled the house with a subtle and exquisite odor.

The priest stood in the centre of the house, his back to the door. He had cast off his robe, and, naked save for a loin cloth, was swaying to and fro in a sort of religious ecstasy, his arms extended towards the flowers above him, and chanting as he swayed. At his feet knelt the woman, white, unseeing, tranced!

Behind him, mute and terrible, crouched Hearston, waiting for the instant of his spring.

"Hearston's unarmed!" breathed Driscoll.

"Yes, like a gorilla! Let be! The quarry's his."

At last the priest paused in his chant and the moment came. Hearston reached out with his left hand, caught the bolt of the door, and shot it home with a crash that shook the house. It was challenge and ultimatum in one, and at the noise the priest swung round and faced his death!

He flung one arm aloft, in what almost seemed like a gesture of command; but, as he did so, Hearston's embrace went round him like a hoop of steel, crushing him in with slow, resistless force. The Mongol would have been a match for a heavier man in a poorer cause, and he writhed in Hearston's grasp, making frantic efforts to release himself, till the mighty muscles rolled under the yellow skin like the coiling and uncoiling of a cobra. A frantic tug at the loin cloth and his free arm flung upward, a curved knife in his grasp, and twice it fell in abortive strokes which glanced off Hearston harmlessly.

The men outside flung themselves against the barred door with a force that splintered the glass in the upper half, but the bolt held. Larcher reached, in through the splinters that remained, pushed back the bolt, and the two rushed in.

Suddenly, in one last supreme effort, the priest raised himself to his full height, almost lifting Hearston off his feet. Again the light quivered along the knife as it rose and fell, and as the priest sank backward, dead, he carried Hearston with him, the knife lodged in his back.

Driscoll bent over the prostrate forms, trying in vain to unlock Hearston's fingers still knotted round the priest. A cry broke from the lips of the girl beside them, and the men both turned and looked at her. She was standing gazing at Hearston in pathos unutterable; the cry that had escaped her was the long, low Indian wail for the dead. Larcher stooped, and with practised hand drew out the knife, then turned.

"Do not mourn," he said to the girl in her own tongue. "He will live, since you have come back to him."

And as he spoke Hearston released his hold on the priest, and turned and held out his arms to the girl. The flame had died out of his eyes—the man was sane!

"Driscoll," cried Larcher, in a curious toneless voice, "look up, look up at your orchids, they think they are going to be fed!"

Driscoll straightened himself from surveying the priest and looked about him. He went white as he gazed and threw a steadying hand against the nearest tree.

Multitudes of great white flowers swayed on every stalk, crisp, new blown! Wide open, each petal distended and with eager stems, as happier flowers turn to the sun, they craned their faces towards the dead priest on the floor.

THE TREE THAT EATS

Brew Molohan

"Here is something that will interest you, Fletcher," I remarked as I picked up the morning paper. "Listen: 'At the orchid exhibition yesterday a superb specimen of the *Epidendrum vesillaria* was purchased by Lord Southwold for fifteen hundred guineas.'"

Fletcher yawned. "Serves Southwold right," he said. "I offered it to him three months ago for five hundred, with a guarantee that it was the only one of its kind in the country, but he wouldn't accept."

"Oh! was it you who found it?"

"Yes; it formed one of the collection I brought from the Malay Archipelago last year."

"You were very successful over that trip, weren't you?"

"Fairly. After all expenses were paid I made about twenty thousand pounds."

"Twenty thousand pounds!" I ejaculated in amazement.

Fletcher smiled wearily. "Seems a lot of money for three years' work, doesn't it?" he replied. "But you must remember that if the pay is big the risks an orchid-hunter runs are correspondingly great. Cutting his way through tangled forests, wading through stagnant swamps, always on his guard against savage beasts and still more savage men, the orchid-hunter earns every penny of his money; and if

27

he has an experience such as I encountered on that trip no monetary reward can repay him for the danger he runs."

"You had a striking adventure?" I remarked tentatively.

Fletcher looked at me for a moment in silence, then he said quietly, "I have not told the story to a living soul in this country, because it is so much outside the bounds of probability that nobody would believe it; but that it actually occurred this will bear witness;" and he slowly removed a wig from his head.

"Why," I exclaimed, "I didn't know you were bald!"

The few remaining hairs were cut close to the head to admit of the wig fitting closely, and, to my astonishment, the scalp was dotted all over with bare patches varying in size from a pin-head to a shilling. On examining these closely I saw they were covered with new, delicate skin, and from their appearance it was evident that the old skin had been torn away at a comparatively recent date.

"Curious sight!" remarked Fletcher as he replaced his wig. "Makes me look like a Dalmatian dog! Say, let's have lunch here, and over it I will tell you the story, although I don't think for a moment that you will believe it."

The Explorers' Club is noted for its cuisine, and we ate slowly, enjoying to the full the good things provided by Felix. When the coffee was placed on the table Fletcher lighted a cheroot and settled himself comfortably in his chair.

"When," he began, "I started for the East four years ago it was with a fairly definite idea of the country I meant to work. My previous experience of orchid-hunting had taught me that the more out-of-the-way the district the more valuable, as a rule, is the orchid, and I determined to strike away from the beaten track altogether, and explore some of the little-known valleys in the interior of the huge islands which stretch from Singapore to Australia.

"Hiring a sampan manned by a Malay and two China-men, I touched Sumatra, Java, and Bali, and then crossed over to Celebes, where I met with a fair amount of suc-cess. I then determined to visit Borneo and explore the unknown interior of that island in the hope that, if I escaped the attention of the head-hunters, I might be able to acquire some new specimens.

"As you are aware, Borneo is about three times the size of the British Isles, and although Sarawak and a strip of the north coast are comparatively civilised, the great bulk of the island, with the exception of the country in the immediate neighbourhood of the Dutch trading stations, is absolutely unexplored. It consists of huge forests, the haunt of the dreaded tiger and the no less dreaded orang-outang, where the merry sport of head-hunting goes on to-day as it did hundreds of years ago, and where a chief's claim to renown depends mainly on the number of heads strung to his roof-tree.

"When I arrived at Mendawi, the Assistant-Resident (who happened to be an old college chum of mine at Bonn) engaged a trusty headman and five Dyaks to accompany me on a lengthened excursion into the interior.

"A word as to the Dyaks. The inhabitants of Borneo have acquired a bloodthirsty reputation in consequence of their propensity for head-hunting; but, apart from this little peculiarity, the race possesses many estimable quali-ties. Head-hunting is simply a custom arising out of their intertribal wars; and a peculiar feature about the Dyak is that, although glorying in the number of human trophies that he can hang round his dwelling, whilst he is in your service you can absolutely rely on his fidelity, his honesty, and his bravery.

"My plans were to follow the Mendawi River to its source and thoroughly explore the tributaries that formed

its headwaters, in the hope that a systematic search in
the deep tropical valleys would reward me with some new
specimens. The party consisted of myself, the two Chi-
namen Lung and Kling, the Malay Ali, the Dyak headman
Rayut and his five companions; and although the sampan
was large enough to carry us comfortably, I took another
boat for exploring the smaller rivers and streams.

"On the fifteenth day after leaving Mendawi we sighted
the range of mountains that runs through the middle of
the island. The weather hitherto had not been oppressively
hot; but now a sudden burst of heat set in, and—the river-
banks being lined with forest—there was not a breath of
air to temper the sweltering rays. For four days we paddled
up this reach, and the intensity of the heat was such that
during that time the evaporation from the river wetted me
like a continuous rainfall as I sat under an awning in the
stern.

"When on the twentieth day an opening on the right
bank showed where a tributary fifty yards wide ran into
the main river, we gladly paddled in there for shelter. The
trees on each side met overhead and afforded relief from
the scorching rays of the tropical sun.

"The trip, so far, had been uneventful, and it was
just before turning into this creek that I first made the
acquaintance of the orang-outang—the wild man of the
Borneo forests. We were paddling close to the bank, when
Rayut, who was in the bow, made a significant click with
his tongue. His companions ceased paddling immediately,
and he pointed to the branches of a large tree that over-
hung the water. '*Mias!*' he whispered.

"I saw the foliage move, and, looking closely, made
out an indistinct shape descending from branch to branch.
Just underneath the tree, and half-embedded in the soft
mud, was something which I at first took to be a large

log, but which on closer inspection proved to be a croc-odile following the movements of the branches with that interest with which every creature, tame or savage, views a probable dinner.

"Suddenly there was a fierce roar, and the *mias* leaped from the tree right on the back of the crocodile. The sau-rian, realising for the first time the nature of the dinner that he had expected, lashed his tail savagely, and, plung-ing violently, endeavoured to unseat his rider. Failing in this, he snapped round viciously, trying to seize his antag-onist with his cruel jaws. This was what the orang waited for. As the crocodile opened his mouth he suddenly seized the upper jaw, and, planting his feet at the back of the head, with an incredible effort actually wrenched the jaw from its socket with such force that we could distinctly hear the cracking of the bones. A convulsive slash of the tail sent the mud flying in a shower; and the orang, after holding the jaw back to the shoulder for a few minutes as if to satisfy himself that his enemy was no more, seized an overhanging bough and quietly drew himself into the tree.

"I had a good view of the monster, and should judge that he was not less than six feet in height; the arms and body were much longer in proportion than the legs, and a mat of thick brown hair falling over the upper part of the face gave the beast a peculiarly ferocious appearance.

"The creek was comparatively cool when contrasted with the river outside; and, as it promised favourably, I determined to leave the sampan near the mouth and ex-plore it in the small boat, accompanied only by Rayut and Bati, a wizened old Dyak who had been a noted head-hunt-er in his time.

"At daylight next morning we started and paddled along this highway, which, always of the same width, maintained a sluggish, even way through the heart of the forest. The

hot, damp atmosphere was peculiarly favourable for the
growth of those trees that the orchid loves to feed on; and,
there being no necessity to hurry, we searched the forest
in the neighbourhood of the creek as closely as possible.
The result exceeded my most sanguine expectations, and
I was fortunate in securing some choice specimens of the
Bulbophyllum, one of which was quite new.

"My method in searching was to land Rayut on one
bank and Bati on the other, where they proceeded parallel
to the creek at a distance of about a hundred yards, whilst
I paddled the boat and called out from time to time to
direct them.

"It was on the fifth day that I noticed a marked disin-
clination on the part of the Dyaks to enter the forest, and
if by any chance I omitted to call they both came running
to the banks. As cowardice is an uncommon trait in a
Dyak's character, I was at a loss to understand their conduct, and asked Rayut what he was afraid of. He hung
his head in confusion, and on my repeating the question,
answered, 'Bati, oh chief! says this is the country of "The
Tree that Eats."' 'What does he mean?' I asked in astonishment. 'It is the Evil Spirit of the forest, oh chief!' he
whispered, 'who is angry when men approach his village.'
'What nonsense!' I replied with disdain. 'Rayut, you are
only fit to dig in the fields with women!'

"The taunt cut him deeply; and, not without a certain
dignity, he replied, 'Oh chief! why does this river run on
and on and yet not become smaller as we approach its
source. It is because this is the country of the great spirits,
and, being mortal, we are fearful of incurring their anger.'

"Next day proved, as I had suspected for some time,
that the creek was a huge canal constructed in days gone
by, when, as may be seen by the huge monuments that are
occasionally found in the depths of the forest, the Malay
Archipelago was inhabited by a highly civilised race. We

had been gradually approaching higher ground, and now arrived at a spot where the canal had been cut across the face of a hill. The depth of the cutting was considerably more than one hundred feet; and, noticing at one point a break in the forest that lined the banks overhead, I climbed to the top. A tornado had worked havoc amongst the trees, levelling an avenue a couple of hundred yards wide, and through this opening I looked down on a small valley running straight in front of me between lofty hills.

"From the situation of the valley, lying as it did between mountains which would deflect the tropical heat, I conjectured that it was a likely spot for the production of the object of my search, and made up my mind to explore it thoroughly. One new specimen would repay the time and trouble ten times over.

"Calling the Dyaks to my side, I pointed to the valley and explained that I had reason to believe that a search there would probably be successful. It was evident from their bearing that they were not enamoured at the prospect; but afraid, I suppose, that I might taunt them with cowardice, they said nothing, although I could see that they were horribly uneasy.

"With some difficulty we made our way down the mountain, and at the foot struck a stream which apparently followed the course of the valley. Confident from the appearance of the trees that our quest would not be in vain, I followed the stream.

"Rayut touched me on the shoulder. 'Oh chief!' he said earnestly, 'venture not farther into the valley. There is death in the air.' 'Rayut,' I replied angrily, 'you are a coward. I shall tell the great Dutch chief to send you into the ricefields with the women.' He ground his teeth at the insult. 'I am not afraid of anything that lives, oh chief!' he replied; 'but this is the abode of the Evil Spirit. However, we are your children; do with us what you will.'

"I strode on once more, the two following closely behind, and we had traversed about half the valley when
Rayut again touched me. I turned sharply, to find him
pointing through the trees; and, looking in that direction,
I saw traces of a clearing showing through the forest. We
instantly turned towards the spot; and, as the steps of all
the inhabitants of the forest tend towards the few open-
ings that are to be found here and there, we approached
the edge of the trees with caution.

"The enclosure—or enclosures, for there were two,
each a few acres in extent—was in shape exactly like the
figure 8, and we had struck the lower one about thirty
yards from the neck. I was examining the trees all round,
when suddenly Bati, with eyes starting out of his head,
pulled me violently back, pointing at the same time to
an extraordinary tree that grew right in the centre of the
passage between the enclosures, and which, owing to the
intervention of some foliage, had escaped my notice.

"Picture to yourself a dirty-green pillar—which afterwards proved to be hollow—twenty feet in circumference,
and cut off evenly at the height of thirty feet from the
ground. From the top, however, rose a circle of whip-
like branches somewhat similar to those we see on wil-
low-trees, each fifty feet long and gradually tapering from
a circumference of six inches at the butt to a fine point.
These almost touched the forest that, running in on each
side, formed the neck of the enclosure, and were without
a vestige of foliage, but curious circular discs of varying
sizes studded the lower side of each.

"But what drew my eyes like a magnet, and made my
breath catch with a gulp in my throat, was that on a stump
which projected sharply from the trunk at the height of
about six feet from the ground grew the most wonderful
orchid that it has ever been the lot of man to behold.

"It was almost the shape and size of an umbrella, but no words of mine can even feebly convey the marvellous colours which, as I gazed entranced, slowly changed their hues before my very eyes. What a minute before had been a brilliant scarlet was now changed to a deep blue; this was succeeded by a bright green, to give way in its turn to a beautiful orange, each coming up at the side and slowly extending over the whole face of the flower. I gazed enraptured at the wonderful display, lovingly thinking of the sensation this tropical jewel would create in far-away London, when suddenly my attention was caught by a movement in the clearing beyond, and I glanced up, to see a deer walking through the upper enclosure in the direction of the passage. Its course carried it just by the orchid, which suddenly became a veritable kaleidoscope of changing colours, at which the animal gazed as if mesmerised.

"To my unspeakable horror, as I gazed at the marvellous display I suddenly saw the snake-like branches, which a moment before had been growing vertically, suddenly bend downwards and encircle the unfortunate animal. The deer struggled violently, giving vent to great sobbing snorts of terror, but a couple of the arms enveloped its neck and quickly strangled it, and, to my utter horror, I saw the body slowly lifted from the ground.

"Thinking that it must be a fantasy of the brain, I turned to my companions. Bati had sunk to the ground, his face covered with his hands, whilst Rayut was peering over my shoulder, the eyeballs standing clean out of their sockets, his face the colour of dirty ashes, and the spear dropped from his nerveless grasp.

"I looked again, to see the deer lifted higher and higher—that ghoulish orchid, its work done, changing colour slowly as before. Up, up, the body was raised, and it was horribly uncanny to mark how every arm of the tree arranged itself to the best advantage to lift the weight. Those on the near side of the tree enveloped the body, whilst the opposite branches bent right over, and, entwining themselves round the others, lifted the carcass until it was held at the extremity of their length high above the trunk; then they bent inwards and lowered it slowly into the hollow interior.

"I am not ashamed to say that as the deer disappeared spasms of icy coldness ran through my body, and I trembled all over with sheer fright. The utter gruesomeness of it and the sudden realisation of the danger I had escaped absolutely paralysed me, and I could only gaze with horrified fascination at the unnatural monstrosity.

"Presently my self-possession returned, and with it that covetous feeling with which every orchid-hunter beholds a new specimen. Besides, I felt a certain self-contempt for having given way to the momentary panic in the presence of my followers, and I stood there revolving various schemes for obtaining possession of that wonderful flower.

"Suddenly an inspiration came and I saw a possible means of success. Turning to Rayut, I said sharply, 'Rayut, you are a woman!' He turned a look of horrified reproach on me. 'You are a woman,' I repeated, 'and to show you how little a white man fears your Evil Spirit I shall cut that orchid and carry it way.'

"The man passed his tongue over his parched lips, endeavouring to speak; his companion lying inert as a log.

"I took a step into the clearing, when Rayut with a convulsive effort flung himself in front of me. 'Oh chief,' he gasped, 'do not approach The Tree that Eats! Be warned by the fate of the deer.'

"My blood was up; and, pushing him aside impatiently, I walked to a spot where I was just outside the reach of those diabolical arms. The horrible monstrosity knew of my presence immediately. The snake-like branches bent towards where I stood, swishing stealthily to and fro in their effort to reach me, and the surface of the flower was transformed into a veritable rainbow with flying colours.

"Returning to the Dyaks, who had partly regained their courage on seeing me unscathed, I explained the plan I had formed. We had passed a troop of large monkeys feeding on a mangosteen-tree as we came up the valley; and, returning stealthily, I shot one, which we carried back to the upper enclosure. Here I explained to Bati that he must push it within reach of the branches when I had taken my station on the other side near the orchid. I hoped that whilst the arms were all engaged lifting the body I should be able to run in and chop away the stump on which the flower grew, Rayut standing by to warn me of danger.

"Bati threw the body towards the tree; in a moment the branches bent and seized it, and, waiting until they were all engaged, I jumped in and struck at the stump. A stream of black liquid shot out as the hatchet sank in the leathery-like substance; and as I hurriedly raised my arm to repeat the blow Rayut shouted, 'Fly, oh chief; fly!' I jumped immediately, but was just an instant too late. The ends of three of the branches had settled on my head as I sprang; and, although the momentum carried my body forward, those diabolical arms, stretched to their full length by the weight, held my head and the upper part of my body a few inches off the ground, the discs burning the scalp like so much molten lead.

"Fortunately I did not lose control of my senses, though flashes of living fire seemed to shoot through my brain, and I shouted to Rayut to grip my legs. This he did immediately, pulling his hardest, so that my head was suspended just beyond reach of the other arms which snaked madly to and fro in their efforts to reach me, and failing by a matter of inches.

"In a curiously impersonal manner I called to Bati to grasp one of my legs, and then, advising them to find a firm grip for their feet, I gave the order, 'One—two—three—pull!' With a superhuman effort they dragged me free, leaving three-quarters of my scalp adhering to the discs. I collapsed then, and remember no more until I found myself on the sampan returning to Mendawi, where my friend the Assistant-Resident nursed me back to health again.

"That happened nearly two years ago; but even now at times the fascination of that wonderful flower overcomes me, and I feel that one day I will return to that tropical valley. If I am successful the orchid will cause a sensation such as the botanical world has never known. If not, another will have been added to the number of the victims of that mysterious horror—The Tree that Eats."

THE DEVIL PLANT
Lyle Wilson Holden

It was the last straw! Injury upon injury I had borne without a murmur, but now I determined to revenge myself upon Silvela Castelar, let the cost be what it would. His malevolent influence had pursued me since early boyhood, and it was he who caused every fond hope of my life to turn to ashes before its realization.

Long ago, when we were boys in school together, his evil work began. We were both of Spanish blood, and both, having lost our parents in childhood, were being educated by our respective guardians at one of the famous boys' schools of England.

Nothing was more natural in the circumstances, than that we should become chums and room-mates. However, it was not long before I began to be sorry that I had entered into such close relationship with him. He was absolutely unscrupulous, and soon his escapades won him an unenviable reputation among the other students, although he always managed, by skillfully covering his trial, to stand well with the authorities of the school.

Before many weeks had passed, a particularly heinous outrage, which he had committed, set the whole school in an uproar. It could not be overlooked, and a strict investigation was started.

What was my horror to discover that his devilish ingenuity had woven a web of evidence which thoroughly
enmeshed me within its coils! There was no escape; I was
dismissed in disgrace from the school, and in disgrace I
left England. The notoriety I received in many of the leading papers of the Kingdom made it impossible for me to
enter another school or to obtain any honest employment.

I came to America, working my passage over upon a
cattle ship. The years that followed were hard ones, but by
sober industry I forged slowly ahead until, at last, I had
bright prospects of becoming the junior partner in a large
business house in Baltimore.

Then my evil genius appeared. Silvela obtained employment in our company, and by his devilish cunning
soon made himself well liked and trusted.

Then one morning, a few months after he came, it was
reported that a large amount of money had been stolen
from the firm. Again a network of circumstantial evidence
pointed indisputably in my direction.

I was arrested and brought to trial. The evidence not
being entirely conclusive, the jury disagreed, and I was set
free; but my career in America was forever blasted.

As soon as I could close up my affairs, I buried myself
in the wilds of Australia, where I began life anew; Fortune
was kind to me and I prospered. Under another name, I
became a respected and honored citizen of a thriving new
settlement

Then the crowning blessing of all came when I won the
love of the beautiful Mercedes, a black-eyed, olive-hued
immigrant from my old province of Andalusia. Then, indeed, I was at the threshold of Heaven! But how short was
my day of bliss!

Four weeks before our wedding day Silvela Castelar suddenly entered our settlement. It is useless to dwell upon
that wretched period. Sufficient to say that this hellborn

fiend again worked his diabolic sorcery, and Mercedes was lost to me forever.

The report came to me that Silvela, for the first time in his life, loved with a fierce, consuming passion, and that Mercedes soon would be betrothed to him. Then it was that I vowed by all that was holy that Silvela Castelar should pay in full his guilty debt, even though, as a result, my soul should sink into stygian blackness.

Why do I write this! Because I take a grim pleasure in telling of my revenge, and because I want the world to know that I had just provocation. I am not afraid. Life or death—it matters little which is my portion now. When this is read I shall be far from the haunts of men.

Silvela Castelar thought I was a fool. It suited my purpose that he should continue to think so. I treated him as a bosom friend, and he, poor idiot, thought I never guessed that he was the instigator of the ruin which drove me from England, wrecked my business career in America, and in the end left me desolate, without hope of ever enjoying the blessings of love.

So, while we smoked, read, or hunted together, I brooded upon my wrongs, and racked by brain for some method by which I could accomplish that which was now the sole absorbing motive of my life. Then chance threw across my path the instrument of my vengeance.

One day, while I was wandering, desolate and alone, through a wild and unexplored part of the country, I came upon one of the rarest and at the same time one of the most terrible species of the vegetable kingdom ever discovered. It is known as the octopus plant, called by the natives "the devil tree." When I saw it my heart gave a throb of exultation, for I knew that my search was ended; the means by which I could accomplish my purpose was now at hand.

Silvela and I had but one passion in common—an intense love for botanical investigation. I knew that he would be interested when he heard of my strange discovery, and I believed that his knowledge of the plant was not sufficient to make him cautious. On the evening of the next day but one, as we sat smoking, I broached the subject.

"Silvela, in the old days you used to be considerably wrapped up in the study of plant life. Are you still interested?"

"Somewhat," he replied, and then his eyes narrowed craftily. "I exhausted the interesting possibilities of most of the known plants of the world a number of years ago. Lately I have found 'the light that lies in women's eyes' a subject of greater interest."

I could have strangled him where he sat; but a lifetime of trouble has taught me to conceal my feelings. I betrayed no emotion.

"I'll venture that there is one plant which you have never studied at first hand."

"What is that?" he asked, with mild curiosity.

"A plant," I continued, "found only in the most inaccessible places of the earth. Probably it could be seen only in the wildest parts of Sumatra or Australia, and then scarcely once in a lifetime."

He was now thoroughly aroused.

"What is the family of this wonderful shrub?" he asked. "I have a dim recollection of having heard of it Let me see—isn't it called—"

"The devil tree by the natives, by others the octopus plant, "I broke in. "But I have heard that the name is somewhat of a misnomer. It is said that it is rather a tree of heaven, for it distills a rare and delicious nectar which has a wonderful rejuvenating power. At the same time it intoxicates in a strange and mysterious manner, causing him who drinks to revel in celestial visions of love and

radiant beauty. Instead of leaving one depressed, as is
the case with alcohol, it is said that the impression lin-
gers, the face grows younger, and he who sips is actually
loved by any of the female sex whose eyes look upon him.
Indeed, I have heard that if our countryman, Ponce de
Leon, had gone to the South Seas instead of to Florida,
he would have really discovered the fountain of youth for
which he sought."

I looked at Silvela. His eyes were sparkling, and he was
breathing quickly; I knew I had found his weak point.
His was a dreamy, half-superstitious nature, and my words
appealed to him strongly.

"Ah!" he exclaimed. "Would that I could see this marvelous phenomenon and sip of its celestial juice!"

"It could be done," I replied, hesitatingly, "but it would
involve some hardship and considerable danger."

"Did you ever see one of these plants?"

"Yes; not two days since."

Silvela sprang to his feet, with a Spanish oath.

"Dios mio!" he cried. "Rodriguez, why did you not tell
me? When can we start to find it?"

"Softly," I admonished. "I told you there was danger.
Haven't you heard that this devil's plant has been known
to gorge itself upon human flesh?"

"The wild story of some frightened native," he scoffed.
"Take me to it and nothing shall prevent me from testing
the fabled powers of its juices. Stop! Did you not drink of
this delicious nectar?"

I shook my head sadly.

"No, I had no wish to try. Why should I seek to become
young in body when my heart is old within?"

"You were afraid," he sneered, "afraid of the trailing
tendrils of this plant devil."

"Have it that way if you wish," I answered indifferently.
"However, if in spite of my warning, you still persist in

wishing to see this strange freak of nature, I will do my best to guide you to it; but, I repeat, the way is long and difficult, and you had better leave this cursed thing alone."

"We will start in the morning," he asserted decisively, as he arose to leave.

I said nothing more, but, alone in my room, I laughed like a devil at the success of my ruse.

Next morning the weather was squally and tempestuous, and I was afraid that the fire of Silvela's enthusiasm would be burning low. But I also knew that opposition would be fuel to the flame.

"I fear we shall have to postpone our journey," I remarked, when he appeared.

If Silvela had any doubts as to the advisability of our starting out that morning, they vanished at once.

"Nonsense!" he rasped. "It is fine weather for our purpose."

"All right, my friend," I replied. "Remember, though, that I advised against going."

"The consequences be upon my head," he rejoined. "Come, let us be on our way."

Our path was strewn with difficulties, and we progressed but slowly. At times the wind howled and whistled across the wild spaces with a sound so mournful that it sent a shudder through me. The heavens were murky, and low, dark clouds raced across the leaden sky as though fleeing from some scene of horror. Great rocks impeded our progress at every step, and their grotesque forms seemed to leer at us evilly as we passed. At length Silvela paused and mopped his brow.

"Come," I exclaimed, "you are tired and exhausted. The day is declining. Let us go back."

Silvela hesitated, and there was an instant in which I was afraid he would take me at my word. Then he straightened, and his chin set determinedly.

"No. We have come far; we will continue to the end. Lead the way."

"So let it be," I returned grimly. "We will continue to the end."

I thought a tremor passed over Silvela's sturdy form and that his face paled slightly, but he turned resolutely and followed me as I pushed forward once more.

It was late in the afternoon when we approached the end of our journey. The clouds had become less dense, and the sun, hanging low upon the horizon, gleamed through with a sullen glare. The whole western sky bore the appearance of curdled blood.

At length I led the way around an immense rock, stopped, and pointed to the north. There, but a short distance ahead, stood the ghastly plant.

It was, in appearance, like a huge pineapple about ten or twelve feet in height. From the top sprang the broad, dark green leaves, trailing downward to the ground and enclosing the plant in a kind of cage.

Inside these leaves, at the top of its bulky body, could be seen two round, fleshy plates, one above the other. Dripping constantly from these was a golden, intoxicating nectar, the fatal lure that tempts the victim to his fate. Surrounding these plates were long green tendrils or arms like those upon an octopus. A slight pressure upon one of these disks would cause the serpent-like tendrils to enfold the victim in their deadly embrace, while the sweet fluid rendered the poor wretch oblivious to danger until it was too late.

Silvela stood for a moment silently looking at the strange plant at which I pointed.

"It is an uncanny sight," he muttered, and a shiver ran over his body.

"Uncanny it is, indeed," I replied. "I, for one, have no desire to make a closer acquaintance."

"You were always ready to show the white feather," he derided scornfully.

I did not openly resent this; I could bear insult for a little while longer.

"Silvela," I said, "Let us leave this dreadful plant alone. I implore you to return with me now. You have seen this horrid thing, why should you care to test the legendary power of the fluid which it distills?"

"Because I love," he replied in a dreamy voice, "and I wish to be loved beyond all men. If it be, indeed, the fountain of youth, what danger can deter me from sipping its miraculous juice?"

"Then I will say no more. Drink, then, of the fabled wonders of this tree of destiny, and may all the joy and all the happiness to which your life entitles you, come to you as you drink the nectar that drips in golden drops from its heart."

Silvela darted a quick look at me from his dark eyes, as though half suspecting a hidden meaning in my words. Then he stepped quickly toward the ominous plant.

"Careful!" I cautioned, "Do not touch the long, green tendrils. There is where the danger lies, for they might tear your flesh."

Silvela stood for an instant close beside the trailing arms, his eyes glowing with a half insane light. His face was flushed with the passionate fire that surged through his veins. To his susceptible mind I know that it was the crowning adventure of his life. I could tell that his heart was pounding, from the throbbing arteries of his throat. His lips were moving, and I strained my ears to catch the sound.

"For Mercedes!" he murmured, and stepped between the hanging tendrils.

Another moment's pause, and he bent down to the fleshy plates in the heart of the plant and drank long and deeply of the golden juice. Dreamily he closed his eyes, and, leaning forward, I could faintly catch some of the broken accents that came from his lips.

"Ah, love, my only love!" he murmured, "See, beloved, the angel faces—celestial voices coming near—sweet, how sweet—the unearthly light of elysian fields—ah, the heavenly perfume—the surging of the eternal sea!"

With folded arms, I stood and waited. Lost to all else save the delights of his entrancing vision, every faculty, every sense deluded into happy quiescence by the chimerical phantasm, he did not note the tremulous vibrations which ran through the whole mass of the horrible plant.

Slowly at first, and then more quickly, the long, sinewy palpi began to rise and twist in what seemed a fearful dance of death. Higher and higher rose the dreadful arms, until they hovered over the unconscious form of their victim.

Once I pressed a little too closely, and one of the awful, twisting tendrils came in contact with my hand. I sprang back and just in time for so deadly was the grasp of the noxious arms, that the skin was stripped from my flesh.

Slowly, but surely, the octopuslike arms settled about Silvela's body. One of them dropped across his cheek. As it touched the bare flesh a tremor ran through his frame, and he suddenly opened his eyes.

It was only a moment until he was fully awake to the horror of his position. While he was reveling in dreams of paradise, the grim arms of the death plant had enclosed him in their viselike clasp, and I knew that no power upon earth could make them relax until they opened to throw forth the dry husk—the dead skin and bones—of their prey. Already they had so constricted his chest that he could breath only in short, panting gasps. His terror-stricken eyes sought my face.

"My God, Rodriguez!" he cried in a terrible voice.

The arms gripped him closer. He gasped out a word, *"Help!"*

"Silvela Castelar," I said, with quiet bitterness, "You are beyond all human aid. I could not help you if I would. Once within the grasp of those awful arms, I would be as helpless as you. Remember at every step of this fatal journey I warned you, but at each warning you grew more determined. Three times you have brought ruin upon me; the third time you left for me nothing in life, but I was resolved that you should not enjoy what I had lost. Silvela, tonight the debits and credits of your account with me stand balanced. Across the page of the book of life I write the words, *'Paid in full!'*"

He heard me through. Then, as he realized that hope was gone, shriek after terrible shriek burst from his frenzied lips. In his terror and despair, he struggled in a madness of desperation; but every movement caused the embrace of the ghastly arms to tighten upon his body.

With a sick heart, I turned from the awful scene and plunged forward on my homeward path. As I passed around the great rock from where we had first glimpsed the fatal tree, a last heartbreaking wail reached my ears.

"Mercedes! Mercedes!"

Like the last cry of a lost soul hovering over the abyss of Gehenna, it shrilled in vibrating terror through the air, echoing back from the ghoulish rocks, and then died away into the silence of the approaching night.

A faintness seized me, and I shivered at the touch of the chilling breeze which sprang up as the sun sank, blood-red, below the horizon; and my heart was as cold as my shrinking flesh.

Sunshine or shadow—it is the same to me now. But in recompense for my shattered life, I shall carry with me always, the vision of Silvela's distorted form writhing in close embrace of the devil-tree's snaky arms, in my ears there will ever ring the echo of his last despairing cry of, *"Mercedes!"*

FUNGUS ISLE

Philip M. Fisher

I

Even as I crawled up the gently sloping beach, gasping and sobbing with half strangled lungs seeking to retch out the burning water and gulp in some life-giving air, I sensed something uncanny in the low-lying hedge of scrub before. It did not give me fear—my fears had come with the first roaring swoop of the typhoon, had vanished when the schooner struck the barrier reef and time for action came. Even the wandering thought of sharks had not restored them. And now, with solid land beneath me, fear was the emotion furthest away.

As I toiled on I admit I gave the feeling but little actual attention. My voluntary thought was of other things: My shipmates, the loss of the *Emerald Spray*. I found myself, in choking, water-quenched anathema, cursing the fate that had so malevolently pursued us ever since our discovery, months back in the scorching barrens of West Australia, of the petrified log whose heart had glowed with the pulsing greens, crimsons, and blues of fire opal. I looked bitterly back on shattered dreams of wealth, revenge, and of recovery from the blackguards who had fled with our treasure through these ill-known waters for their haven in degenerate Macao.

Yet, still would this subtle sense persist. And soon, it
seemed, I must regard it. Something must be above me
there, something. Else why to my unusually blunt percep-
tions should come such sense of eerie menace?

I scrutinized the black fringe before me intently as I
crept on. My salt-burning eyes could make out no movement there. And besides what moving thing, animate or
inanimate, could compel that atmosphere of vague dis-
trust? I knew where we were just before the typhoon had
blown up. There were islands by the hundreds scattered
under the southern coast of New Guinea; many of them
unexplored. But all known were the same, all of coral
origin, protected by barrier reefs, and crowned with wind-
bent coconuts. All were the same with nothing on them
to fear but loneliness; no serpents, no beasts, no human
beings. And this—this land was but another islet in the
chain.

I found myself striving to put aside this peculiar unease that was growing on me. I insisted now that it was
foolishness; that there were other and more important
questions. Douglas Gordon, whose tortures and canteen I
had shared in our search for the block of crystallized fire
that had promised life comfort to us all. He had been in
the bows, clinging to the stay, and his was the first cry
just before the hope-ending crash. Had the smothering
torrent of solid green that roared over us then swept him
to his death? The leader of our little party, skipper of the
crushed schooner that the dying storm must now be merci-
lessly battering out there on the coral heads, Jim Dowell,
what of him? And the Kanaka boy, faithful slave. Once
in the quieter lagoon they had been safe; all could swim,
and well. But had they fought down the outward seas and
broken through?

These were the questions, these were the important
things just now. Not the disquieting sense that beyond

that nearing black mass of vegetation, and within it—yes, and of it—there lay a strange and waiting menace. Not that, I did persist. My friends. Water. Food. A boat—for continuing our chase. Revenge. To glory again in the mystic beauty of the stone—to touch again, in full possession, our fortune.

I dragged my eyes away, and scanned the wide spreading beach. Even under the black and cloud flung sky its ghostly surface would betray another man. But the pale sands showed not a single darker object, no moving thing. I crawled on.

Then, quite suddenly, I stopped.

I repeat that I do not know why. I have read of charging soldiery coming to sudden involuntary halt—then, after a screaming shell had all but burned their faces with its wind, press on. They had been brought to a full stop warned by some unconscious perception of danger—and so, I must suppose, had I.

I stared before me. Crept a dozen yards forward. Paused again.

I did not fear. I repeat: there was nothing to fear. Common sense insisted that there could be nothing to fear. And yet I stopped there on my knees, and stared.

In the back of my mind began a whisper. It tried to explain a simple cause for part, at least, of the feeling that was on me. I groped to catch the words, to understand it. It was so simple, so obvious. Yet strain though I might, I could not comprehend. And in exasperation I cursed a dumbness I could not overcome.

Then, as I stared, I heard myself speak, with a kind of half laugh.

"Funny. Where are the coconuts?"

I gave a grunt of humor again—it did sound idiotic. Yet now a more discerning eye swept up and down the black fringe before me, to right and left. Not a palm in sight. The voice at last—clearly.

"Every coral islet in the South Pacific is fringed with coconut palms. Why isn't this? Every one of them. Why not this?"

The impenetrable blackness above me, the smooth, warm sand beneath, the sea at my back, and before me—mystery. The shadowed hedgelike growth, but not one single towering palm. And the storm from the sea fiercely determined to push me on. The wind?

Came another whisper. Another interpretation for my feeling, another solution based on common sense. This wind, trying to urge me forward—yet up there, but a dozen steps, not a sound. No thrashing rustle of torn foliage, no screaming rub of branch. Yet there was vegetation. I could see differences in it now; shapes, pillarlike. But not a sound of swishing leaf.

"That *is* funny," I said aloud. "Damn funny."

I started to crawl on, but the impulse died as I put out a hand. I cursed my folly, yet decided to hang the wind, anyway, and sleep the night out where I was.

First, though, another look up and down the sands.

My heart gave a great leap. I rose to my feet unsteadily and wildly whooped. Answer shrilled at once, and a figure lifted and came slowly to me. A welling of thanksgiving tore at my throat.

"Doug! You came through."

Silently he gripped my hand. Then his eyes left mine and he glanced to the shelter of the growth. Then back at me.

"I've crawled along that stuff for a quarter mile," he said in a low voice. "I wanted to get somewhere out of this wind."

My fingers clenched about his arm.

"Why didn't you go behind the trees, Doug?" I demanded in a whisper.

He turned and stared again. Then shrugged his shoulders, gave a short, dry laugh.

"I—I don't know. Just didn't, I suppose." He paused a moment, then quickly countered: "Why didn't you?"

I pointed, stiff armed, and even to me my words still sounded like those of a child.

"Where are the coconuts? Where are the palms? And why doesn't the wind make a noise of some kind among that stuff?"

He grunted again. And this time did not laugh.

"I move we camp right here," he said. "Right here. We both need sleep."

II

But I found that I could not sleep. And despite the fact that I had but just been shipwrecked, my body was not by any means exhausted. The typhoon had come up with hardly any barometric warning, had caught us beating through Torres Straits, that broad, though treacherous, channel between the great island continent of Australia, and that last unexplored land of mystery, the steaming man-killing green of New Guinea.

The three of us, with the Kanaka lad, had done our best to take in the canvas, but the rushing madness of the storm had won out. Two hours perhaps had we scudded, under bare poles, swept ever and ever to the north. Then, even as Douglas Gordon, clinging in the bows, had cried his warning of land ahead, we had struck. Came the short struggle with great avalanching seas, the comparative peace of the lagoon, then the beach.

No, I could not sleep. I was not weary enough for that.

I lay there in the smooth coral sand, and stared up at the clearing skies, and wondered about things. And most of all, I wondered now about this sense of uncanniness that had sifted into me as I crept up toward the black line

of vegetation that was ahead. That growth had called me
so at first—called me when I waded through the shallows;
there, just ahead, I would find shelter from the stinging
wind. And then, as I neared—it repelled. As I lay there I
felt working into me, body and soul, the feeling that it
would not be shelter. Something—I could not name it—
menaced there. A voice within me warned against seeking its refuge. Insisted that it would not give refuge, but
something else.

The wind died, and but for an occasional swift
sand-scattering ruffle, left a growing peace in which the
eeriness somewhat dimmed. I began again to call myself a
fool. It had been the blackness of the night, the desolation
of shipwreck and loneliness, and the simple fact that this
island was not adapted to the natural growth of palms.
That latter was exceptional, true, yet it had worked upon
my imagination. And that the wind made no noise in rushing through the low scrub, but added to the natural unease
of a black and stormy night. It was all nonsense. I was a
fool.

And yet, how about Doug?

He certainly had sensed something. What had he said:
that he had crawled along the stuff for a quarter mile,
looking for shelter? Why had he not entered the stuff?
Wasn't that shelter?

This was not like him. Long had I roamed the seven
seas with Douglas Gordon, many the tight hole in which
we had found ourselves; yet never had I seen him in a predicament which he had feared, or, discovering doubt within himself, given that doubt voice. But now—why had he
glanced askance at the black fringe above us? Had he not
sensed, too, that which I had felt?

If he had, then the thing was not the result of my own
environment stimulated imagination. No, then there was
something else?

Suddenly I found myself stiffening, my body quite tense.

An odor—a dank, peculiarly pungent odor—was in the now quiet air. A strange odor, thick, almost tangible, and heavy, as though of a miasmic gas settling close to the ground because of its own damp weight.

This could not possibly come from the sea. It could not drift down upon us from the clouds above, nor yet percolate up through the coral sands. It could have but one source. The vegetation that crowned the low rising land above us.

And yet, if this were a coral island—I seized a handful of the sand beneath me. Yes, its rounded, slick-coated grains were of disintegrated coral, unmixed with the sharp silicate particles from a rock-bound coast. The sudden newer doubt as to the land upon which we had been thrown left me; the storm had not driven us so far to northward as the mainland of savage New Guinea. We were on a coral island without doubt.

Yet coral islands do not ordinarily contain marshy land. And only from a dank, steaming morass could such a peculiar odor emanate. The belief that something here was far from the usual began again to strengthen.

I glanced at my old companion. He was limp in the sand, arms thrown wide, eyes closed. I wondered if he slept, yet hesitated to whisper to him. If he were finding peace in unconsciousness after his trial of the last few hours it were the last thing to do to awaken him. No, I must at present keep my thoughts to myself.

The odor persisted.

And now, too, with even the fitful puffs of the passed storm exhausted, it took on a certain warmth.

This, in itself, was not unusual.

In these equatorial seas, the heat of the sun is literally soaked into the land areas as it is into the blue waters

themselves, and by night as by day the earth gives forth
soothing comfort to one's recumbent form.

And to the stimulation of this warmth, as well as to
the torrential downpour, the fertile land responds, giving
birth to that lush and overwhelming tropical vegetation
so astonishing to men of more temperate climes. Man,
white man, quickly falls beneath its rhythmic impulse.
Heat and moisture first forced life itself in times primeval.
And tropical heat and tropical moisture, now that man is
man, double his every bodily process. He comes to early
maturity, his own seed bursts forth into bloom with results alarming even to the accustomed mind. Seasons are
blended into one ebullient springtime, and before he is
aware of it, he has come to manhood, the fruit of his own
flesh is matured about him, his own decay brings him back
to elemental disintegration. Heat, moisture, the tropics
are a forcing house for living organisms.

Yet, the sand was warm beneath me. This miasmic
odor was warm and moist to my nostrils. And lush, alive,
it tasted to me. Alive, and—I felt an involuntary thrill
pass through me—it, too, seemed to menace. It smelled
of growing things, but of things growing too quickly. Of
life developing in its highest intensity, of animate things
that, with their own life force, their own will to grow and
mature and decay, threatened with almost a premeditated
malignancy all other animate things, all other forms of
slower developing life than their own.

All this I sensed. And the sensing of it had no calming
effect. The very fact beyond all others, perhaps, that this
warm, moist odor had a lulling effect upon my nerves and
body, did most to expand my growing apprehension until
it tingled in every fiber.

Why had the wind made no sound in the vegetation up
there? The eternal silence of it, the waiting silence, the

silence that was so sure of its own power that in its very silence lay its threat!

I was becoming vastly uneasy, I had to admit. I did not like it. I dared not sleep.

The sky was sweeping clear, and the brilliants with which it was bespangled were outthrust ready for a plucking hand. The lagoon, peaceful now, glowed with a super-phosphorescence lately lashed into being by the elements in conflict. The moon had risen behind me and the beach spread to the water's edge like a sheet of ghostly silver, though I myself yet lay in shadow.

I was still prone upon my back, with hands beneath my head, struggling to keep awake despite the influence of the strangely drugging odor, when my restless eye was arrested by a movement above the gleaming coral far down the strand to my right. I watched it at first rather absorbedly, and with a feeling of relief, wondering what it might be. Some sea fowl, I decided, preying on other living things lately cast upon the beach. I grunted and relaxed.

Quickly, as in answer to my movement, came a grip, hard upon my arm. Then Doug's voice, tense with wonder.

"Clarke! What—what do you make of it?"

I swung about upon my stomach—and felt again the strength of menacing mystery.

The full moon was peering over the island at us, yet had not cleared completely the fringe of growing stuff above. And the shapes it blackly lined were shapes such as I had never dreamed of before.

No—there were no gaunt rising, gracefully bending, palms! No sharp crested tangle of tropical grasses, no wreathing tendrils of vine, against the silver glowing face of the curious satellite.

Instead, upon the sand itself, sharp outlined, lay a solid wall of black. And from this wall soared strange, unheard-of forms; rounded trunklike forms that ended not

in branch or leaf, but in egg-shaped, caplike heads, black,
too, against the brilliant sky. Some of these, where the
moon cut low, were but a few feet above the dense thicket
below, others rose to perhaps three times the height of a
man. Some were body thick; others, and these sometimes
bent as by the weight of the bulbous tops, appeared no
larger though than my own right arm. Some, also, stretched
clean cut against the moon. Others seemed distorted with
nodular swellings that presented the appearance of horrid
plant disease.

But all—all, rising more or less pillarlike, swelled out
at last into a heavier top, grotesquely shaped: the heads of
gigantic asparagi, the semblance of an ovate sphere, others
of an umbrella shape that, in its significance, brought my
heart leaping.

The rays of the moon were luminously dissipated just
where these forms broke from the black beneath. And ever
and ever again wraithlike ghosts would tear way from this
heavy lying mist and, clinging for a moment as though reluctant to sever themselves from the dense mass of it, drift
vanishing away like the shrouded spirits of a seance.

Then would come, with renewed strength, the warm,
moist odor, stealing down upon us as we stared in unbe-
lief.

I sniffed again, almost without thought. Musty it was,
as if a warning, pregnant, fallow, a thing vital and fecund
with a staggering regenerative force. And overwhelming in
its impression yet held as in waiting. As though, suddenly released, this power to grow would submerge even us
in its life force, suck us dry for its own sustenance, rush
our own bodies into some devastating supermaturity that
could only end in decay and horrid death. The odor of it
sank into my senses, and for the first time I really feared.

The pressure of Doug's clenched hand upon my arm
had not been lessened as we lay thus upon the sand, rigid,

eyes hypnotically held on those weird black silhouettes
against the silver moon and the glittering sky. And I believe that at least ten minutes passed, before either of us
thought to speak—or could. The sight was so utterly unbelievable. It stupefied. I know that I myself had no con-
secutive thought. I could not think. I could only wonder
and stare, with something like the prickling of primeval
fear proceeding up and down my spine.

"What—what do you make of that?"

Thus came Douglas's first words, and almost in exact
repetition of the exclamation with which he had startled
me from my contemplation of the fluttering thing down
the strand. I suddenly found loose tongue.

"Heaven knows," I whispered back. "Nothing like anything I've ever seen before."

"You—you notice that peculiar smell—kind of heavy;
like mold?"

"And warm? Damp? Steamy—"

"Like a drug?" he whispered. "Yes. I've been lying here
trying to think what it was. I still don't know. But it certainly has something to do with that stuff above there,
and the mist that is beneath. Clarke, I confess it, the
thing doesn't appeal to me at all. I've been in some funny
places—but—" His hand tightened, and rising to his knees
he pointed toward the face of the moon. "There's something else."

Well above the peculiar vegetation, and at some distance from us, had suddenly risen a flock of flopping,
batlike creatures. They were flying about with no apparent
motive or destination, weaving in and out among themselves with slowly beating wings, dipping, swooping, fluttering high again, now in compact body, then in scattering
disorder, almost as though in aimless play. Not a cry came
from them. They winged against the face of the moon in

absolute silence, a silence as uncanny as that grimly waiting growth just before us, and from whose depths they had
come.

Then, as though by command, they suddenly dropped
from our sight.

Recollection of things I had seen in other South Sea
lands flashed before me.

"Flying foxes!"

But Douglas shook his head, though his hand now left
my arm.

"No. I've seen them flying almost like that; but once
in a while at least they'd let out a chirruping squeak. It's
something else." His whisper came tense again: "I tell
you, Clarke, I don't like this place at all. Not even a coc'
palm! What the devil'll we eat, or drink? And this sickening smell, thick. Why, it almost seems alive! Like a living
thing that's seeking us out to do us harm."

I felt again the pricklings run over my skin. He had
sensed the menace of the thing as surely as had I.

A gentle puff of wind came to us then, and the odor,
doubly strong, swept mist-clad upon us. I had just raised a
hand to cover my mouth and nose, when I felt, rather than
heard, a gentle swishing behind me. Almost immediately
something seemed to alight and creep clingingly upon the
back of my neck.

With an oath which I heard echoed from Douglas, I
swung about and struck with my open hand.

Whatever it was fluttered beneath, then fell away.

And on the sands beside me, twisting and turning in
vain attempt to take to the air, was what seemed at first
glance to be a strangely shaped bird. I scrambled to seize it,
and my very touch apparently spelled its death. For a hand-
size sector of the unbroken wing came off between my fingers, and the mutilated body shivered, wilted, and lay inert.

Then again I felt the weird sense of uncanny things about me. The piece of wing at which Douglas and I stared was not feathered, nor was it the leathery membrane of a bat. No; it was thin and smooth and covered with an almost microscopically furry substance. And the foot-long body on the moonlit sand was not that of any bird or animal I knew. Feelers—the body of an insect. And my companion's own startled whisper gave the thing its name.

"A giant moth!"

Then we stared again into each other's eyes in silent question.

That fluttering swarm of things we had seen against the moon—had they not been the same? And the creature I had noted slowly beating along the sand—that must have been this very one.

A peculiar thought took hold of me as I again examined the wing in my hands. It had broken off so easily. That were hardly natural. The wing of a moth fresh struck down does not crumple at a touch; it is of more substantial material, has more strength. Yet this—I took the edge of it between my finger and thumb. It broke off at my least effort. I raised my eyes to Douglas Gordon.

He was watching me intently, and now he took the thing from me and with his own hands deliberately broke off a corner of it. Then his glance sought the fantastically shaped growth rearing, up to the spangled sky—he sniffed at the thick air again—dropped his gaze upon the wing stuff he held.

"Breaks up at a touch," he whispered uneasily. "At the lightest touch. Like—like—that's it, like a thin rolled sheet of yeast. In Heaven's name, how does it live? How—"

He broke off sharply, mouth open, swung back staring to the shadows above. And though he had asked a question, I did not answer. I could not.

From the black depths of the island had arisen a cry that made my blood run cold. The first sound. Low at

first, then rising higher, higher, higher, the cry reached a
point where its vibration seemed to become rhythmic with
that which I felt in my own body. Then, quite suddenly, it
turned to a sobbing diminuendo moan, as of hopelessness
and despair. Down, down, down it fell—until we strained
to hear. We strained, every nerve, but the hidden shadows
were become as silent as before, as darkly mysterious, as
menacing, as evil with the now even doubled feel of malignant life force that with deadly will and diabolic artifice
was reaching out for us, and ever drawing, drawing us in.

III

The cry was not repeated. And to tell the truth, although
I, too, with Doug, stared into the tangle of strange black
shapes beneath the rising moon, and strained every nerve
to listen, something within me was saying over and over
again, insisting that I did not want to hear that cry again.
Had it been clear call of anything normal in our lives, this
peculiar insistence would have had no effect. I would have
wanted then to hear it so as to place it in its proper cate-
gory of known things. It would have been the call of some
night bird; or of a startled monkey, perhaps, or of a man
himself, on some nocturnal hunt.

Of course, I must admit, I was still filled with the
uncanny feel of this lonely bit of land. The silence of it,
the misshapen vegetation, the soporific odor of the warm,
heavy mist, the great moth to which death and decay had
so quickly come at our veriest touch, the flutter of a myriad of its fellows, black against the moon—and then, this
cry. Of utter woe, despair, and of horror, too. A cry not
more of the fear of death than of dread of a living death
from which there could be no escape. Yet it was not so
much the hopelessness in it that struck me, as the peculiar lack of real vibration in its wavering notes. It was, in

a certain sense, rhythmically harmonious with the taut vibration then in my own body, and yet it did not present to my mind, as well it must have to the mere mechanism of my ear, the sense of a physical impact. Furry. That was it. As though the sound had come from an organ pipe that was lined with fur. At once the logical answer leaped before me: a pipe lined with fur, or a throat with—mold.

The train of conjecture following this idea so filled me that when Douglas suddenly again gripped my shoulder and pointed down the silvered beach to a dark object moving there, I felt no further apprehension. I watched the thing approach. It seemed to stagger, wabble in its gait—fall—then rise and continue on. Its distance prevented even vague surmise as to its shape, yet on it came in that oddly awkward stumbling.

Then suddenly the grip on my shoulder relaxed, and with a muttered cry Doug left me and ran toward the thing. And I, in a spasm of fear, and with a glance at the silent rising stuff above me, took to my heels after him.

And a moment later I found myself with an arm about the skipper of the little schooner, Jim Dowell, half fainting as he recognized us.

We must have slept. I know that the sun was well above us when first I perceived in that gentle struggle for consciousness that precedes awakening, that something was wrong. The perception gradually became two. The first of these was the natural one—there was no motion about me; the sea was not underfoot; something had happened to it, for the schooner's motion was gone. Then I remembered. I was on solid earth. With a rush came the second feeling— distinct, clear, as I opened my eyes. Something—I could not tell what, nor whence came the sense of it—something was watching me.

I flung myself about, and caught a fleeting glimpse of movement in the vegetation above us. Just a glimpse, and so vague a one that I almost doubted. Then, for the first time, I saw what manner of vegetation that was, and my involuntary exclamation of wonder and disbelief brought my two companions to their knees.

The blackness of the night before had given no idea of the color of the growth above us. Yet deep-rooted within all mankind, I suppose, is the firm belief that all growing things must necessarily be green. Or at least, if not inevitably green in the individual plant, at least verdant in the general aspect of growing things in the mass.

Yet here—it was perhaps the lack of fresh green life that so astounded me, so bewildered. Fresh green betokens normal life. It means clean life. It gives the appearance of everyday life under a beneficent Nature. Secure life—and a right one. . .

But here there was no such green.

The panorama before us was a horrid futuristic conception in ugly splotched colors—purples, yellows, browns, vermilions, and hideously mottled green grays. The mass of it repelled. The eye was tormented, the senses appalled. The colors were monstrous, loathsome—as though reeking with the deadly poison of an unclean and obscene living malignance.

And the shapes of these horrid growths were now in the light of day familiar, awfully familiar, staggeringly so.

The lower hedgelike mass of the stuff, stretching from one curve of the upper beach to the other, had been a black wall under the shadows cast by the moon. Now it showed itself the edge of an earth-covering bloat, consistently of one hideously painted purple, a purple that seemed slowly to pulsate, to watch the three of us human beings as we stiffened on the sands and stared. Just above the oily-looking smoothness of its upper line it was spined

and folded and serrated with masses of splotched vermilion and poison orange, slick surfaced crimsons, and dull
brick reds. And above this soared greasy coated trunks of
leprous, gray spotted yellows. These trunks rose to various heights, the greatest of them arising to perhaps three
times the height of the tallest man of us. And they terminated in the nodular caps we had seen silhouetted against
the moon the night before.

Deeper in the island, we could make out huge fanlike
objects, fluted like deep-sea shells, and whose brownish
purple was as repulsive to the eye as their size was stupendous. To the right, also, and creeping toward us over
the creamy cleanness of the coral sands, stretched long
tendril-like things that seemed like the leathery feelers
of gigantic starfish, vermilion, and spotted with the yellow
grays again—unclean. Dipping down toward our staring
trio, leaning to us on its attenuated stalk of streaked and
greasy yellow, one great egg-shaped head peered at us not a
dozen feet away, its purple spotted surface a great all-seeing
eye, an eye that thought, that calculated, that menaced.

I glanced at the white sun above us, and to the pure
coral sands beneath our feet. They were the only natural
elements about us, the only clean things. That growth—no
wonder I had sensed the uncanny when I had crawled up
the beach in the blackness of the night before. No wonder
I had felt repelled when I would have sought shelter from
the dying typhoon. No wonder Doug had crawled for a
quarter mile, not daring to enter the black growth at his
very side because something deeper in him than voluntary
thought had warned him.

The warm, damp odors of the night, the wraithy mist
under the rising moon, the sense of a life that menaced, of
living things of such swift growth, such absorbent vitality,
such relentless devotion to that teeming vitality—no wonder we had felt it as a presence. These haunting shapes, by

their very gigantic familiarity becoming each second more awful, lived, and the life in them was so strong that they seemed to think and to threaten all other life that their own might be the more secure. I found myself shuddering at what might have happened had we entered its depths— and at that moment Douglas Gordon's voice broke the silence, hoarse, choked, unbelieving.

"Fungus! A forest of giant fungus growth. Good Heavens!"

Captain Jim's muttered oath followed.

And I turned to find him rubbing his forehead with the back of one hairy hand. I do not know what started my heart to beating then. Yet beat it did, indeed, and a surge of genuine alarm rushed to my throat for the first time since the wreck of the *Emerald Spray* on the jagged coral head of the outer reef.

Then my eyes flashed to the face of Douglas Gordon. Paused there a moment. Then back to Captain Jim.

And my own hand went uncertainly to my own forehead, furtively rubbed. My heart beat again, as I held my hand before my eyes. The palm of it was slightly browned from contact with my face.

I stared at it, then to the faces of my companions. And I saw that their eyes had followed my own, their glances slowly bending first upon my own face, then upon the others'.

"Covered with the stuff," I gasped. "Covered with it. What can it be?"

My eyes went over Doug's shoulder to the fungus growth behind him. Then to the green-brown scum on my hand. I lifted my hand to my nose.

"The same smell," I muttered. "The same."

Doug was the first to recover himself.

"And that fungus growth! Humph! I don't think we need be alarmed, fellows. Toadstools, puff-balls, any fungus, you know. During the night, while we slept and the wind fell, it drifted out and settled upon us. Spores from that fungus. Like from a mushroom, you know. Spores, that's all."

Gradually I felt my apprehension depart. Well I recalled certain grammar school experiments. The head of the toadstool, or the mushroom, cut off from the stem, set down upon a sheet of glass or white paper. And in the morning the delicate print of its gill-like under part traced in the fallen spores.

"Naturally." I nodded. "But it got me for a moment. This heathenish place—uncanny. Never can tell what might happen, you know. I thought—"

I came to an abrupt halt. I really did not know what I thought, or had thought. The alarm had made itself felt. That was sure enough. It had come upon me with a heart-jolting sense of danger. Impressed itself upon me even as the uncanny feel of the dark fringe of growth before me had impressed itself upon my consciousness as I crawled toward it in the night.

Jim Dowell dipped his head toward me, his wide blue eyes staring into mine.

"Just what did you think?" he demanded in a low tone.

I shook my head.

"I don't know," I muttered again.

For a moment Captain Jim stared, then slowly turned toward that mammoth and horrid colored fungus growth above the sands.

Then with a grunt gave word to the first practical suggestion since our casting upon this strange bit of land.

"Last night," he said, "I saw something flying about in the moonlight. And I'm hungry and thirsty. The first thing we must find is water. I move we explore a bit."

IV

Reaction came then to us all. It was quite evident to me that the soporific exhalations from the giant fungus, warm, damp, insinuating, had had much to do with the sleep that had gripped us until the sun, risen high toward tropic noon, scorched our nerves into wakefulness. And I knew that I was very thirsty and hungry as well. Yet there was, however, something unaccountable about this thirst. I had taken in some salt water while in the crashing breakers of the reef, and later during my swim to the ghostly line of the beach. I had experienced thirst, too, on the semidesert regions of West Australia, when we had searched for, and found, the fabled block of fire opal. Yet now there were none of the torturing symptoms of thirst.

I needed water badly, but my lips were not cracked; they were smooth to my tongue—almost feeling as though spread with camphor ice. And my tongue itself, and the roof of my mouth, had nothing of dryness. Yet my body craved water, overpoweringly demanded it.

I do not believe that I was wakefully conscious of my mouth and lips being in this condition. Yet I do recall now that thus they felt—as though oiled with some taste-less oleate fluid or rubbed with some tasteless theatrical grease. But I could not have explained this then. I thirsted, but something about even that thirst was not normal.

The call of my stomach for food, however, was the call of old.

We decided to go together and explore the beach for any depression through which water might flow to the sea. We knew, of course, that the ordinary coral atoll has no flowing streams. But with the uncanny vegetation of the land only too present, other peculiarities might easily be.

"So profuse and gigantic growth of fungus can only argue plenty of fresh water," declared Douglas. "And with such an amount of fresh water in the place we ought surely to come upon some of it flowing into the sea."

We had grunted that our sentiments were the same, and plodded down the beach to our left.

Not a dozen steps away we came upon a brownish object lying in the sands. We paused a moment, looking at it, for nothing dark had been upon them during the night. Then I saw the two depressions made by Doug's body and my own, and at once the things came to us.

"The body of the moth!" exclaimed Doug.

Jim Dowell looked at us quickly, blue eyes wide again. "The moth?"

I told him of our visitor of the night before, and stooped for the body. But even as my hand was about to touch it, Doug seized my arm.

"Don't!"

I straightened up in some surprise.

"I wouldn't touch the thing, Clarke," Doug said. "It was gray last night, remember. Even in the moonlight there could be no mistake; it was gray. But now—look at it."

The foot-long body was hardly gray now. Brown it had appeared as we approached it, but upon closer examination the brown was slightly greened, and blotched here and there with leprous yellow. I shuddered. Thank Heaven, I hadn't touched the thing! It was covered with a scumlike mold.

Furtively my hand went to my forehead and face again, and as we plodded on I rubbed the skin until, in the white hot rays of the overhead sun, it tingled and drew.

The beach curved ever to our right, and still we came upon no running dip in the glistening sands. And the thirst was growing upon us. I licked my lips again, and found them still as though lately rubbed with grease paint. Yet my body demanded water, water—and my throat was getting dry. Yet, strangely enough, my tongue did not thicken, and the roof of my mouth was smooth.

"What's that?"

Jim was pointing down to the water's edge, where there appeared a great mound of brownish green, set off clearly against the emerald crystal of the waters of the lagoon.

"Rock! Seaweed!"

The words came from all three of us, and unmindful of the beating of the sun, we raced down to it. For seaweed meant crabs in these latitudes, and crabs were food, and food was life.

Yet disappointment met us with her hard, rebuffing hand.

"Fungus!" exclaimed Doug disgustedly. "Just a great mass of fungus. Hell!"

"It's water I want," grunted Captain Jim. "If I don't find it soon on the beach, I move we break through the stuff and look for it inside."

For some reason neither Douglas nor I made answer to that last suggestion. And something bade me hasten my step to keep abreast of the others. Break through that stuff and look for water inside? I wasn't so sure that I wanted to crash through that low crawling mass of purple bloat. The idea of my bare foot crunching through up to my knee into the hidden flesh of it made me shudder. No, until absolute necessity demanded it, I would place these feet of mine where I could see.

Then Captain Jim gave a whoop.

He had led us straight up the sands from the mass we had examined at the water's edge, and between the weird fungoid forms was a break in the purplish ground mass. The ground dipped slightly, too, and in the tiny depression crept lichenlike growth, too brilliantly orange in color for beauty, and seeming to my rather stimulated imagination to be the tentatively outthrown pickets of the strange life behind it.

For a moment we looked at each other, standing in that dip beneath the soaring forms. I think each of us well knew what was in the others' minds, yet we knew too that if we would live we must go within.

Doug coughed slightly, then, with his eyes on mine, nodded.

"Jim ought to know," he said quietly. "Last night, cap'n, just before we were put to sleep by this stuff, something from inside here made its call. I can't tell you what the cry was like, except that I never heard anything just like it before. It didn't exactly frighten us, either, Cap'n Jim. But there was something to it that"—Doug shrugged his shoulders—"that made us feel that something had gone wrong with the thing that made it. I don't know if you get me, but that's the way it sounded. Something had gone wrong—hopelessly wrong."

Doug turned and his eyes sought the horrid colored depths. "Just thought you ought to know, that's all."

Jim Dowell made no answer.

Yet we stood there some moments before any of us made a move.

Beneath our feet was the lichenous mat of glaring orange, vermilion, running from beneath that purple, crimson mottled, bloated mass that, knee high, lay like a spreading quilt, covering the ground itself in all directions as far as the eye could carry. To our right, within hand reach, stretched a brown mottled trunk of dirty yellow. This rose to the height of perhaps fifteen feet, and there spread out into the umbrella shaped head of a giant toadstool. The gills on the under part of this head were close tightened, and but for the fine radial lines tracing

the contracted lips might have been a smooth uncut surface, of a light and greasy green, like the underside of a
fish.

To the left was a widespread fan, as wide as the stretch
of a tall man's arms, and as high as a man might reach—
purple at its base, shading to a green spotted purplish
brown at its rounded edge. Where it burst through the
bloated cover at our side, small tongues of the orange stuff
ran out, as though eager for the light, avidly, lustfully,
pursuing its own desire for unhindered life.

Before us ran the depression itself, crowded upon all
sides by the purple undercarpet with its oily, leather appearing surface, and overbent by huge, heavy-topped forms
of musty toadstools. More fanlike growths, strange shapes
noduled in uncouth cactus form, queer mounds of grayish
white, some of a single leprous hue, others mottled with
the greenish brown of mold. Perhaps a dozen paces up the
depression the sun broke through upon a large, waist-high
bowlder—gray green.

The scene was not one to give confidence to men in love
with life, clean life of clean sea and clean air. And I confess
I did not care to follow up between the purple bloatings
bordering the vermilion-tongued depression. But we must
have water, and surely such a dip in the ground and such a
break in the growth could but argue that in times of storm
the water drained thither from the interior of the island.

Douglas himself gave an oath, and started forward.

Then before we knew it something swooped overhead, and
we were drenched with a suffocating mass that had fallen
upon us from above.

Coughing and choking, we broke out to the beach for
air. And looking back, I saw that the great toadstool had
bent its head almost upon our own, and discharged a cloud

of brownish spores from its suddenly opened gills. My heart had almost stopped beating, and the sense of uncanny menace seized me again with greater strength as I saw the great umbrella head suddenly raise back to its full height, and watched the gills themselves slowly, lap by lap, close until the underside of the thing again was like the belly of a fish, oily smooth.

We found our breath at last, and cleared our throats and eyes and ears of the clinging spores. Then Doug looked again into our eyes.

"Fellows," he said slowly, and as though weighing his words, "the thing did that deliberately."

For a moment there was silence.

Then Captain Jim guffawed—a bit too loudly.

"Nothing but a damned overgrown toadstool! Faugh! Coincidence. We just happened to be there when it burst with ripeness. Come on!"

V

Water we must have. But as I looked up at that motionless giant fungus, hardly daring to believe that but the moment before it had bent to us and let go its choking cloud of seed upon our heads, I felt that, once discovering that water, we must make all haste to take our fill and return to the sun-swept beach again. And Jim Dowell gave voice to my thoughts.

"Rush it, fellows. Up the creek bed."

Rush we did.

And I, in my greater desperation—or, perhaps, more tumultuous imagination—took the lead. A dozen paces up the depression I came upon the bowlder-like thing, and, not thinking, dropped a hand upon it and vaulted.

The next moment I had crushed through the thin crust of what had seemed solid stone, and head and shoulders deep, was choking in a mass of damp, clabberlike substance.

Doug and Jim dragged me forth and cursed me for my
foolhardiness, sympathizing the while for the accident. I
shook off the clinging pulp of the giant puffball and followed on.

The depression twisted and turned, and each bend gave
glimpses of newer and stranger forms of fungus life. Each
moment, too, the warmth increased, and the steamy dank-
ness of the heavy exhalations of the strange life surrounding us settled deeper and deeper in our lungs.

Great man-thick trunks soared fifty feet into the air
here, trunks warted and noduled with masses of parasitical
fungi. Huge fluted fangs of leather-surfaced brown spread
on either side of us. Giant puff-balls loomed beside us
like gray-scum surfaced balloons at anchor on the purple
bloated earth. Things spread out in poison-splotched yellow greens like enormous fungoid octopi, lying in wait
with their thousand-warted suckers to trap the unwary and
take his life that their own might rush on to completion.
But the path itself, save for that first obstacle, was smooth
spread before us with its carpet of brilliant vermilion and
orange.

Here and there the sun glared through and the colors
would clash in hideous contrast, the vapors disappearing,
and now again would come the slow, silent burst of a vast
umbrella head, and the thick air would cloud with suffocating brown.

On we rushed. And at last came a half-strangled cry
from Doug, who now led, and Captain Jim and I flung ourselves upon our knees beside him and plunged our heads
beneath the clear waters of a fungus surrounded pool.

The risk we took in doing that!

When I think of it now, I can see how men of usual
good sense may needlessly throw away their lives. We made
no test of that water. We thought of nothing else but that
it was water. We believed it must be fresh; and even the

poisonous looking growth teeming about the pool did not give us thought that the waters, even if fresh, might be polluted. We threw ourselves upon our knees, dipped our burning faces into the clear fluid of that tepid pool in a fungus forest, and drank.

It was Jim, I think, who gave the first cry.

I looked up and saw him, still kneeling, slap at something upon his neck; saw him dip his face again and drink. Then felt something light, yet clinging, touch my own neck. Reached back one hand and brushed. The feeling departed. I dropped my hand again to the lukewarm waters that were so grateful—the sense of something touching my skin came again. Tingling, yet coldly so, coldly—like back there on the vermilion trail—the giant puff-ball.

With a loud yell of alarm I started up, and flung my hands back to my shoulders and neck. Tore them away, and my hands were full of a grayish fungus growth. A mass of the stuff seemed to be enveloping me. I gave another yell, and saw with horror that Jim and Doug were struggling with a foggy cloud of it even as I was.

Jim's cursing began to rend the silent air, and I heard Doug muttering as he strove to fling the suffocating frondlike stuff from about him.

"The trail! The trail!"

Jim this time.

I looked frantically about the. The trail! "Where the devil is the trail out?" Jim's voice rose to almost a shriek.

And I felt my own heart misgive me as I seized a mass of the now warming, puttylike stuff that seemed to grow even as I tore it from my eyes, my face. Warm, warmer now—with the quickening chemistry of life!

The trail—the entrance to the pool! Where—

The fungus walls had closed in about the place, were slowly thickening before my eyes—growing, sending out new shoots, pulsating with avid, eager life—life begotten of the white hot sun and steaming tropic rains. A life that rushed forth, madly demanding more life; life that thought, that sensed, that knew, that menaced—

A shadow cast over us, and raising my eyes I beheld three great umbrella heads bending over. Even as my eyes were cast up upon them, their great gill lips opened as if by concerted action, and again came the drench of suffocating brown spores.

I heard Doug's voice, half choked, desperate.

"To your right, Clarke. To your right, Jim. Break, break now—or you never will."

It rose to a crescendo of horror at the end—Douglas Gordon crying out with horror—with fear. I fell, tripped by a great spongy mass that seemed to grow out of the very earth. I stamped it down, and other stuff grew, unfolded, shot upward to and about me in puttylike fronds, clinging, warmly now, thrilling my skin with the feel of their resistless life energy; their will, their will to live, and their determination to add our lives to their own.

Another shadow above. Another silent descent of a great spore cloud. Another gasping curse from Jim or Doug, I could not tell which.

"To your right!"

Soft, clammy warm; so easily pulled off, destroyed, torn asunder—yet growing, growing, enveloping us, throbbing with life, determination—another cloud above, overshadowing all. With a last desperate effort I struggled to my feet, I tore away the gray stuff that clung, ever growing, to my face, eyes, nose—and crashed with all my remaining strength through the thick of the walled mass to my right. One great sobbing moment, and the sun shone down again on a hideous motley of poisonous color and giant forms. I was free.

But Doug. And the captain.

Back there. And I—I alone. I plunged back, only to be thrown against the purple bloating that walled the little depression as two gray-shrouded, uncouth figures broke through into the clear.

"Clarke! Clarke!"

One of the figures turned as if to go backhand I caught it by its horrid arm.

"Doug! I'm Clarke. I'm all right, Jim!"

"Thank God! All here. To the beach."

Ah, the cleansing action of the clear salt water of that beautiful emerald lagoon!

I cannot tell you how we rushed into it, threw ourselves down into its limpid cleanness. The stuff broke up, dissolved to mere shreds of itself. Salt, salt water—it seemed that the fungus stuff found a sole life-destroying element in the salt water of the sea. We bathed in it frantically, rubbing the last bits of the foul growth from our skins.

We breathed deep, but found ourselves choking with gray froth in our nasal passages, our lungs, our mouths. Desperately, one by one, we plunged into the deeper part of the lagoon, and, despite the spasmodic effort of a reluctant nature, deliberately breathed in the cleansing fluid. Then would a companion, gasping for breath against the choking fungus developing in his very lungs, haul us out and cast us strangling and gagging upon the glistening coral strand. Then he would fling himself into the sea, and in turn be dragged out, and belly down, drain himself of the cleaner element and gulp, in great convulsive heavings the pure, life-giving air.

In another fear now we threw ourselves back into the lagoon and even as we had gulped of the fresh waters of the treacherous pond far up that twisting color-clashed glade, gulped now of the salt. But at last we deemed our

bodies saved, and we relaxed in the scorching sun, forget-
ful of the burning that was sure to follow, only grateful for
its purging warmth and light.

A dread weakness took us, and in that weakness we
cared not what might come against us from out of the sea.
It at least was clean. That hot, lustful, fungoid life was not.
Here, we knew we might have a chance for life, a fighting
chance, and if death were our lot at least we might expect
that it, too, would be clean. But back there—

Two things, however, must be spoken of. First—it was
Doug who brought up that.

The Kanaka boy—what of him?

"He jumped with me," volunteered Captain Jim.
"Jumped with me in the ruck of it out there. I hollered to
him to keep close to me, but the little devil could swim
like a fish and I've no doubt he reached the beach long
before I did. Lord knows I was slow enough."

For a moment there was silence: Then Doug again:
"Good God!"

The words were not a profanation. They were more a
prayer, and I think Jim and I both knew well enough what
Douglas Gordon feared. No lashing sea could have beaten
the brown lad down. He must have reached the lagoon; he
must have reached these very sands. Yet we had not seen
him, nor any trace. What else then might we expect?

Minutes passed in which we drew in the grateful air
which now with the coming of the night stirred in gentle
motion.

Then Captain Jim spoke again.

"We must get off this island. But to get off we must
have two things, something that will bear us up in the
water, and something to eat and drink."

"Heaven forbid drinking at that pool again," I muttered.

Captain Jim raised himself on one elbow.

"Yet water we must have, my boy. And, food. But what to eat—what to drink—"

He raised himself again, inquiringly, his face grave in the moonlight.

"Coming down the beach this morning, did either of you see any drift from the schooner? Wood? Oars? Chests? One of those little pontoon rafts we got in Sydney? Anything?"

Slowly we shook our heads.

The only things upon the beach had been the body of the giant moth lying near where Doug and I had slept in the sands, and the huge mound of fungus not a hundred yards from where we now lay. Nothing else.

And Captain Jim echoed again our thoughts in monotonous repetition.

"We must get off this island. We must get off."

Then we stiffened, staring at each other in suspense and question.

From far in the interior of the fungoid forest above us had come again that strange unearthly cry. Again, the lonely, hopeless, sheer horror of it quickened our hearts, yet chilled the leaping blood in our veins.

Low at first, then ever rising higher, higher, higher, the weird cry came to a crescendo pitch that cut every nerve. Then, with disconcerting suddenness, it droned away in a sobbing diminuendo moan, a dying echo of hopelessness and utter despair.

Down, down, down it fell—until we strained to hear.

Then the black depths, with the moonlit monster silhouettes ranging above, became as silent as before, as darkly mysterious, as menacing, as deadly with its waiting malignant life force as we had found it when we fought that very life force by the pool.

VI

Despite our weakness we could not think of sleep. We lay
there in the sands staring back upon black forest, from
the depths of which had come that cry. Twice now we had
heard it, Doug and I. We knew now that the first had
been no nightmare, no horrid fiction of our imaginations.
Something lived within those horrid depths, something
besides the giant gray moths, something other than the
silently waiting and diabolic fungus.

"Animal?"

Doug's wondering voice questioned the stars above.
And I found that I could say neither yes nor no. We were
animals, we humans, and the strenuous demands of that
life within the island—and island it surely must be—had
all but made our animal bodies its own. How could that
cry have come then from anything of the animal kingdom?
But could it be of vegetable origin? Of fungoid? That, too,
could not be answered with a simple yes or no.

Captain Jim's words, coming in answer, and yet not in
answer, to Doug's query, brought again the desperateness
of our situation.

"It cried out, at any rate. It must be different from
anything we've seen so far. And anything different might
mean something that will save us."

"How do you mean?" I demanded, rolling over so as to
face him.

His answer came in one word.

"Food."

Again we relapsed into silence.

Food, indeed—and water.

Without thought my tongue ran along my lips, and
then came the consciousness that now they were dry and
cracked. And I was thirsty. I recalled that earlier in the
day when first we had set out to search for water the call
for fluid had been just as strong, but my lips, my mouth,

my throat, had not been dried. No. Instead they had felt as though smoothed with grease paint, camphor ice. Now— now that sensation was gone.

I started—the salt water I had drunk to kill the crowding fungus growth that would have choked me! It had cut the greasy feel, and it had cut, later, the fungus itself. Had that first smoothness been but a result of the spores drifted upon us during the night? Had it? If it had, then—

I found myself repeating, too, in dulled monotony:

"Fellows, we must get off this island. We must get off this island. We—we're threatened. Our lives, our bodies— we must get off this island."

"How do you feel now?" demanded Captain Jim.

I shook my head.

"Like a rag, eh? Well, my boy, no one wants to get off this filthy spot any more'n I do. But we've got to find something to get off on, don't we? And we've got to have some strength before we can even search. Sleep now, that's the dope. Come morning, we'll search for some wreckage from the *Emerald Spray*—go clean around the cursed island. Something'll show up, sure. But now, take it easy and sleep."

The advice was good.

I grinned weakly at him, and murmured a response.

But no sooner had I settled myself for sleep than my skin prickled once more as that weird call came again from the depths of the island.

I sat up instantly, turning my face to the interior. And Doug and Jim, I noticed, were not behind me in apprehensive movement.

Again came the call. And even before it dropped to the final sobbing wail there arose above the forest a veritable cloud of the great flapping moths. Once more under the moon they waved in and out, up and down, in inexplicable play in the now breathless night. Perhaps ten minutes passed as we watched, eyes hypnotically held upon the moon-touched gray of them. Then, as if by preconcerted order, they dropped back into the black mass from which they had arisen.

With another grunt Captain Jim turned back and wriggled to a more comfortable position in the coral bed.

But Doug himself was the one who mentioned the fear they had suddenly brought to me.

"May they have a pleasant night's rest," he said; then added with undue emphasis: "And stay right there for the rest of the night."

"Right!" The ejaculation burst with vehemence from Jim.

Somewhere in the night I began to dream.

A great cloud of those huge gray things had winged their way from the center of the island. Their horrid-eyed leader saw us, indeed they seemed to have risen again from their black retreat for the very purpose of seeking us out, and steered the mass of them our way. Over our recumbent sleeping forms they fluttered and dipped and rose and dipped again, watching us, making sure, gaining strength in numbers, and in will. Then, as one, they had descended upon us, covering our bodies completely with their yeasty wings, crawling over our skins, seeking, feeling, rubbing.

We struggled against the suffocation of their mass. The musty smell of dank mold choked our lungs. It became insufferable. We began to struggle. To fight even as we had fought back there by the pool. And like that devilish fungus, leaping forth into hot breathed life even as we ripped and tore and fought, they broke beneath our effort, crumbled to nothing, vanished—only to be replaced by countless hordes of newer things, leaping up in full life and body from the broken remnants of the old.

The weight of them. The overpowering odor of their moldy foot-long bodies . . .

I flung out my arms in a last frantic effort to throw them off—and found myself lying on the open sands of the beach, with the glittering diamond points of the blue-black sky staring in cold wonder down upon me. I glanced over to my companions. Beneath the white light of the moon their chests rose and fell to the deep breathing of sleep. I was a fool. I had been dreaming.

And yet—something, something was now right about us.

Something was close upon us. Watching us. Had even noted my wakening movements, and retreated somewhat. Yet, retreating, still watched—and thought. Watched and thought, and—I felt it uncannily—did *not* fear.

I sat bolt upright with a jerk. And would have cried out but that my tongue cleaved to the roof of my mouth.

Between us and the great mound near the water's edge a hundred steps away stood a group of figures. Upright they stood, even as men, and I found myself counting them as I stared. Five—five; yes, certainly, there were five of them.

Not twenty paces away from us they stood, and though the moon gave no hint of white upon the faces of them, I knew that they were intently watching us.

For some minutes I sat thus, petrified, staring at the five figures and feeling their own stare upon me. A gentle breeze had again arisen, and the lulling *lap-lap* of waters on the beach brought me finally to a sense of reality. This was no dream. Here was the beach, spreading silver to right and to left. Above was the dense black of the fungus forest. Below, not a step away, the flashing waters of the clean lagoon. Overhead were the same old stars, and at my side Douglas Gordon and Captain Jim.

And these things that watched—no, certainly they did not fear; but neither did they menace. Just stood and watched. Pity? Was it *pity* I sensed in their distant regard?

I whispered softly. "Doug. Jim."

My companions did not show by word or movement that they had heard me. Evenly their deep respirations showed their sleep.

I called again, a bit louder, and from the tail of my eye saw the five figures retreat a step toward the dark mass behind them.

"Doug. Jim!"

Had they not awakened then, I believe I should have given a veritable bellow. The feeling that I was alone with that staring quintet out there was not calming in its effect.

Silently then I pointed.

And Doug and Jim froze even as had I.

Then, slowly, came a gasp from Jim.

"Whew-w-w! What the devil—"

He started to his feet, and Doug and I were instantly at his side. All the exhaustion of the earlier night slipped from me. If this were to be the end, I was ready for it. These things before us were alive, and alive with animal life, not fungoid. And if fight we must now, the odds were not so bad, and the struggle would at least be clean. Blood against blood.

Yet, these things did not menace.

The five of them retreated another step, then gathered together, heads close bent.

"Show 'em we're peaceful. Raise your arms up and hold 'em so," whispered Doug tensely.

At our motion the figures seemed to stiffen once more. Then the heads went closer. Thus a moment, and now one of the figures stepped a half dozen paces nearer to us.

Grotesque, that figure was. Upright like a man, and yet in the moonlight surely no man had so appeared before. The face should have stood out milk-pale in the silver light, and its features clear. Some grace, too, there would

have been some trimness of form. But this creature had
none of these. The face turned upon us was of the same
weirdly mottled cast as the rest of the body, and the latter
itself was neither trim nor shapely. It seemed peculiarly
broken in outline. Distorted. Uncouth. Broken. Things—
things hung upon it, dangled from it, crusted over it, like
a thing unclean.

Unclean! The thought rushed to me, and I felt my raised
arms tremble. Unclean, even as the fungoid stuff had been
upon us when we had torn from its menacing life force in
there by the pool.

"Quiet," cautioned Doug.

The creature came closer.

It, too, raised one arm, and slowly waved it to and fro.

But a couple of fair leaps' distance from us, it came to
a halt, half turned as though ready to flee at our slightest,
hostile move. And then we could see the full horror of its
body, and I knew that the mold I had smelled in my dream
of the cloud of great gray moths had come veritably from
these.

Legs, body, and arms were ridged and mottled and
fringed with funguslike growths—ghastly, splotched green
and gray in the moonlight. The head itself was a huge
modular mass of the same gruesome hues. And of features
it seemed to have none; though from somewhere in the
fungus crusted face of the thing shone two deep-set eyes,
the only part of the creature that appeared alive.

I heard Jim's quick, indrawn hiss as we stared.

Then came a movement in the lower part of the face of
the thing, and in a low, monotonous, furry-soft voice it
spoke. We shook our heads. It spoke again, and the same
sounds seemed repeated.

In startling contrast boomed Captain Jim's voice.

"No *sabe*. Say it again."

The creature took one step back, and repeated. Then raised its arms again in a beckoning movement.

Jim turned to us. "Does it want us to follow? Shall we go?"

Doug's voiced sentiments were my own.

"I certainly am not going to lie here in the sand while those things are around. Yes. Go ahead."

We took a step forward. And the creature nodded its awful head, and turned away, stepping slowly and silently toward his fellows and the hill-like mound of fungus near the lagoon. Shortly he turned and glanced at us, raised his arm, still beckoning, and went on.

In wondering silence we followed. The others joined him, and walked on in a compact group until in the very shade of the mound.

There the first creature raised his arm, and signaled us to stop. Then he pointed to the great mass, then to himself, and then to us. Back to the mass of fungus again. And began to talk once more in his peculiar, furry-throated, monotonous tones.

"What does it mean?" demanded Captain Jim, turning to us, his wrinkled brow contrasting oddly with the light of half fear in his eyes.

We shrugged our shoulders.

Doug stepped forward toward the stuff. He raised his arm and elaborately pointed at it.

"You mean that?"

The great mottled head of the thing nodded eagerly.

"What about it, then? What's it to us?"

The peculiar voice came again, pointing once more to the fungus mound, to us, to his fellows, back to the mound.

"Hanged if I know what he wants," exclaimed Jim. "Something about that stuff there."

With a sudden thought coming to me, I stepped quickly toward the mound to examine it. But no sooner was I close upon it than all five creatures leaped in a line between it and me and began to claw eagerly at the fungus growth on the surface. I jumped to them to help. Instantly one of them emitted a short cry and seized me by the arm.

The damp, clinging touch of the creature filled me with a spasm of fear. I swept at the arm that had reached to me, and to my horror it seemed to break beneath my blow—break and a crustlike bit of ridgelike excrescence upon it fell to my feet.

At once the five of them turned and fled toward the blackness of the forest and disappeared within its shadows.

Then, once more, came that awful call.

VII

Watch and watch we stood for the rest of the night, judging the hours by the passage of the moon.

But before falling back into my hollowed resting place I went to the lapping waters and scrubbed my hands and arms and face. Rubbed and rubbed, in feverish regard for thoroughness, my left hand and forearm, for with it I had touched the creature. That contact had been unclean.

The others watched a moment in silence, then one by one, and without word or explanation, they also laved themselves in the purifying salt water of the lagoon.

Toward morning Doug awakened me with a touch. The moon was overcast with a single black cloud, and we were soaked in the drenching downpour of a tropical squall. He nodded as I lay back, for a moment, arms spread wide, mouth open.

"Take your time, Clarke. Let it soak in. This rain may save our lives."

We awakened Captain Jim. He, too, stretched so that every part of his body might be cleansed now from the sticky salt. He, too, lay face to the storm, mouth open, drinking in hungrily the great heavy drops of fresh water. Then the beach was flooded with silver again, and the silence fell, like a pall.

From the fungus growth above us came a breath of the warm, mold-rank mist, drifting along the sands, spreading out, all seeking. Thus it covered the strand for a moment, then, with a counterwhip of breeze from seaward, disappeared.

So the others lay them down again, and I took over the watch.

Clear thought came to me as I paced the smooth coral sands, and traced again the events that had put us in this predicament.

The long search in the semi-desert land of western Australia, the search impelled by that whispering hearsay drifting so tentatively, yet so persistently, through the public houses of Melbourne. The half jocular suggestion that Doug had made.

"Let's get the stuff, Clarke."

Then, with the romance of the thing covering all doubt with its veil of glamour, a serious desire to follow up the insistently recurring rumor. Then the search, and finally the discovery of the great petrified log in the heart of which we had come upon the solid block of glowing fire opal. How we had clasped hands over it—the light of fortune in our eyes.

Then the long, careful, conveying of the precious stone. The report that our success was known at Melbourne. Our decision to change our point of destination to Sydney. The ambuscade when not twenty miles from that port, and the theft of our fortune.

Our search for clews. Then the certainty that the half-caste, Point-Five Markleigh, with his company of cronies in crime, had sailed with the opal in the stolen schooner, *Black Moth,* for that haven of all thieves, all treachery, all degenerate vice, Macao.

Two weeks later our own schooner, owned by Captain Jim, shoving off through the twisted harbor of Sydney in pursuit.

And now—this.

My thirst had departed, but I was filled now with a great hunger. I recalled my boyhood days, mushroom hunting in the pasture land of the hills behind our town. And I found myself staring up at the fungus of the island—somewhere I had read that there were nearly eight hundred known varieties of mushroom, the greater proportion of them edible. Surely, somewhere in that fecund growth would be some fungoid that we could eat. Its sustaining powers might be weak, yes. But anything was better than nothing, and a filled stomach gives at least the feel of coming strength.

Those great moths—must eat. The horrid manlike creatures—must eat. Both lived; both must be sustained by some kind of food that grew in that weird and fearsome forest.

My pacing drew me closer to the long, narrow hill of the fungus stuff on the beach. The things had led us to it; obviously that had been their intention. Intention argues the power to think. And they had spoken. I shuddered. Were they men, or were they, like the moths, half fungoid? The way that fringing ridge had sloughed off the thing's arm at my first slight violence!

But why had they come to us? Come with such obviously peaceful intentions? Pointed out the mound there? Torn at its lower surface with their moldy, handlike paws? Then, at my touch, fled for the shelter of their uncanny retreat?

The stars were retiring now, and the silhouetted forms peering above the island clear cut against a flushing dawn.

Near the fungus mound I saw the broken lump of stuff that I had knocked from the creature's arm. I knew now that salt water would cleanse, and an irresistible curiosity drew me closer to the thing. I stooped and picked it up. It crumbled in my hand's, like the yeasty wings of the giant moth that first night. One part, however, seemed of stronger texture. I rubbed it, placed it in the palm of one hand, and smote it with the other.

Then, in sudden comprehension, leaped to the water's edge and scrubbed it in the crystal fluid. Then stood long and quietly, with heart heavily pumping, staring first at the grotesque and poisonously colored fungus of the fast-lighting forest, then to the incomprehensible, yet in a way horribly illuminating, thing I held in my palm.

I raised a hand to my forehead, and jerked it down again with a sudden cry. My skin had felt as though incrusted with a bubbled grease. My hand was covered again with greenish brown mold. I raised it to my nostrils, cried out again and dashed down the beach to my companions.

One look, and I dared not touch them with my hands. I cried wildly to them to awaken. They came jerkily to a sitting position, wild-eyed in alarm. Then with cries of horror stared upon each other. Faces, necks, hands, exposed feet and wrists were covered with a finger-thick moldy crust. And Mack's hair was a mass of feathery gray.

Madly we dashed again into the salt lagoon. And came from it many, many minutes later, clean, but with skin strangely drawing and tingling. And on Doug's left cheek was a whitish spot, which, as the natural flood of life fluid rushed to the place to rebuild the broken tissue, rapidly became veined with crimson.

Silence then, for there was no need to speak what we now felt was certainty.

Without a word I showed them what I had come upon beneath the crust broken from the creature's arm. Then, at last, Douglas spoke, and his voice throbbed not so much with fear as with deep pity.

"Cloth! Part of a shirt! The things were men."

But Captain Jim amended the statement, with a fear in his voice that doubled the tingling on my skin.

"You mean," he whispered—"you mean they *had* been men."

His eyes seemed to center hypnotically upon the blotch upon Doug's cheek, and slowly my old friend flushed; then turned away.

There is but little use in recounting our search for drift from the wreck. Suffice it to say that before noon time arrived we had made our way completely around the island, only to come at last upon the long mound near which we had spent the night. We held a short consultation, and decided that we must try the material the island afforded.

It was with loathing that we approached the vermilion-carpeted glen upon which we had made our search for water the day before. And at once I caught sight of a flitting figure in the depths, a figure whose gray-mottled dull green and erect posture showed that the manlike things were watching our every move.

The giant trunk of the towering fungus that had first drenched us with its brown cloud of spores was easily pushed over by our combined effort, And the flat head of the thing, its diameter as great as our arms could stretch, twisted off and fell limply flat at our feet.

We dragged the leprous trunk to the water's edge, and, with hope beating high, out into the deeper waters of the lagoon. Then again did our hearts drop, for the fungoid log sank like a plummet to the bottom.

We returned and dragged down the great fluted fan whose hideous green speckled purple brown was so greasy to the touch. It, too, sank.

It was then that Captain Jim began to curse the fire opal that had brought us to this place of horrible and deathly existence.

"Unlucky!" he cried suddenly. "Opals—always unlucky. The curse of the ages is on them, and misfortune they bring to man. I'm through. I'm going back there to find something to eat. I don't care if it kills me now, I'm through. The cursed things are unlucky. We're going to die here, anyway, horribly, and I'm going to eat. Anything! Anything! Those man-things must eat. And I'm going to. I'm *through*. I'm going to eat."

And before Doug or I could stop him, he had dashed up the beach and disappeared.

Go in after him? Doug made a move to follow, and I held him back with all the desperate strength I had left.

"No," I cried. "No, no, no! Doug, in God's name, don't follow! Don't. He'll come to his senses when the—the things in there get after him. He'll come to his senses after their first touch. He can get out again. No; no."

Doug slumped to the creamy, clean sands.

"We must get off this island. We must."

Then without a word he jumped to his feet, and tearing off his shirt, dropping his trousers, he started for the lagoon.

"Wait!" I cried. "What are you going to do? You can't swim to safety."

"No," he returned calmly. "But I can swim out to the reef and bring back some parts of the *Emerald Spray* from which we can make a raft."

In my desperation I followed him to the strand. Then gripped his arm again.

"You can't," I whispered. "Look."

The great triangular dorsal fins of sharks cruised in the quiet waters.

"You can't," I repeated. "They're surer death than Jim has gone to. You must not go."

"We must get off this island," he muttered, staring out at the green combers battering the distant reef.

From behind us came the rising wail we knew so well. At once came an answering call.

Spellbound, we turned and watched, expectant of I know not what.

Closer and closer came the calls. Rising in hopeless wail, falling again with that shuddering sob of hopelessness and despair.

Then suddenly rose a cry that was different, a scream of fear.

As one we started for the vermilion trail.

Yet before we had gone ten steps a figure broke through the purple bloating undergrowth and rushed down to us, howling with fear. At our feet it fell to its knees, raising arms trailing with leprous growth—a face on which was sprouted the moldy, green-brown nodular excrescences we had seen the night before.

But the voice was different. Clearer. Somehow familiar. It pleaded with us, and a word or two of blurred English came to our startled ears.

The trailing arms gesticulated. Pointed back at the forest. Then to us. To the sea. Back to the fungus.

With a sudden oath Doug seized the mold-odored creature by the arm and dragged it toward the water.

"Doug!" I cried.

"Help me!" he snapped. "Help me! He knows something. To the water—to the water! Maybe then he can speak."

VIII

The creature was—or, I should say, had been—the Kanaka boy.

In terror he came to us, terror of something that had come upon him in the midst of the island's haunting growth. But it was with cries of desperate fear that he tried to fight Doug and me off when we dragged him to the waters.

I know now why this was.

I know now that the fungus stuff had so worked into his very flesh that the action of the salt water was nothing less than torture. I know now that while the fringing crust of the stuff sloughed off his skin almost instantly under the decomposing action of the saline fluid's chemistry, the growth had already, in these two days upon the island, worked in its horrid development so as to penetrate the skin and spread out into the living red flesh beneath. And I know that, though we saved the lad from the living death that would have been his upon this fearful bit of land, nevertheless we almost took away that life in the process of salvage.

At last his frantic strength gave way to exhaustion, and when we finally bore him from the lagoon and laid him upon the glistening sand, he collapsed in a wilted, sobbing heap.

And Doug and I looked at each other now with a full comprehension of the doom that was ours with horrible certainty, were we to sojourn longer in this place. There was but one kind of life upon the island—fungoid. The only creatures natural to the island, the giant moths, were all but fungoid. The things that had visited us during the night had once been men even as we—but they, too, were now all but fungoid. During the nighttime, when we slept and our own resistance was at the ebb, we ourselves had fallen beneath the power of that malignant life. And this Kanaka lad, with but two days in the midst of that hotly teeming life, had all but succumbed.

And Jim, Captain Jim—he had fallen to the cries of his body for food, and even now was somewhere, somewhere—we stared into the violently poison color of the stuff—in there.

We recalled the battle we had had with the living stuff that, even as we tramped it down and tore off its clinging growth, had leaped up with renewed vigor, with relentless persistency, diabolic menace.

Doug, wide-eyed, took his eyes off the exhausted boy for a moment, and voiced my own thought.

"The damned stuff all but beat us down, Clarke. Filled our throats, our lungs, our bodies. It would have killed. But this lad here—is still alive. And those other poor devils—they're still alive. Is there something that—that kills the human in a man, kills the clean animal of him, and yet allows his body, in its form at least, to still keep on? To still, in its ghastly way, live on?"

I shook my head. How did I know? It was unbelievable, and yet in that creature of the night, and in the Kanaka, did we not have something of proof? And on our own bodies, the same? That grayish blotch on Doug's own cheek. I found myself staring at it, and dropped my eyes guiltily only when the sudden flush rushed to it, and my partner covered it with a quick flash of his hand.

"But why," I demanded, speaking more to myself than to him—"why, when these other—men—found themselves falling beneath the influence of the stuff, did they not get off the island?"

Doug stared out into the placid emerald crystal of the lagoon. My own eyes followed his as they watched the tacking dorsal fins of the great sharks.

Then he gave a short cough.

"I choose the water and the sharks first," he suddenly cried.

"I, too."

Yet, why, if they had been men, had these others not chosen the quick, clean death themselves? Did they take the chance here because of hope—hope for a rescue?

Then, if that were true, I argued, why had they not come to us at once, as soon as they discovered the presence of clean men upon the shores, and on their mold crusted knees pleaded for deliverance?

"They didn't do it," I insisted; "they didn't do it."

Doug watched the slow breathing of the brown lad, the blotched leprous discoloring of his once sleek skin.

"They came to us last night," he suggested. "They tried to speak to us. They wanted to tell us something; and, fools that we were, we scared them off."

"I know that," I cried. "But if they really feared the life here, if they really wanted to get off this devilish place, they must have known that we were their best bet. Why did they run from us, back to—back to that?"

Then in Doug's eye, steadily fixed upon mine, I saw his answer. And it was even as I feared. The horror of it, the pity! It was the only answer that could be, the only answer that could clear these things that had been men from the charge of mental and physical cowardice. A great rush of emotion rose to my throat, and I choked back a gulping sob. Captain Jim—in there—now—even now—in the beginning of his—

"The boy here had been in there two days," he cried. "He rushed out from it to us in some great fear. Yet he had been in there two whole days—eating—drinking. Yet, in sudden fear, with those cries behind him—rushed out to us—"

I touched the lad with my foot. He did not stir. His long, labored breathing told the story of a complete exhaustion.

"He will stay here for some time," I said. "Come, friend. We must follow Captain Jim. We must save him. We must get him, and then the four of us, while we are men, must get away. Away, Doug. You hear me—we must get away. We—"

And suddenly I came to a full halt, my face hot with the rush of shame. For my own voice had wailed in my ears with a note of hysteria.

Then Doug seized my arm again, and we walked steadily up the sands, over the vermilion carpet of the tiny glade.

An involuntary shudder shook me from head to foot as we passed the giant puffball into which I had crunched and all but buried myself when first we had sought for water. And the feeling came strong upon me again that the bloated purple that covered the ground as far as the eye could see was watching us, creeping out to inclose us, and I came to fear a glance to our rear lest—I should find we were already cut off from the haven of the beach.

The huge gaunt stalks of the fungus soared again about us, and the sickening stench of the hotly palpitant life force of the stuff steamed in our nostrils once more.

Twice there came a sudden, shadowy movement over our heads, and each time followed the drenching discharge of a suffocating cloud of brown spores.

But on we marched, Douglas and I, in the vain hope that before we succumbed we might find Captain Jim, and drag him, even if it be against his will, back to the clean chemistry of the waters of the blessed life-saving lagoon.

IX

How long we tramped through the silent fungus I do not know. Hours, I suppose, and not a second of the time were we free of the feeling that the stuff was watching our every move, waiting for us to get deeper within its hot heart, breathing upon us its dankly soporific breath, gathering to itself an overwhelming potential of life strength that this battle might be our last. Then, quite suddenly, and almost upon us, it seemed, came the wailing cry of the man-creatures.

Instantly a deep, guttural curse.

We wheeled about, and there, squatting on his hams
beneath a great fluted fan—specked with a thousand eyes
of arsenic green on its leathery brown surface—was Captain Jim. In his hands he held a broken chunk of the stuff,
and over this he peered with glaring eyes at our intru-
sion. Glared, then ducked his head into the horrid mass of
the thing he held and ate. Raised his face again, chewing
voraciously.

"Jim!"

The word burst from both of us.

With an oath he leaped to his feet.

"Get away! Get out!"

The voice was hardly his. The eyes were hardly his. The
action was that of a maniac.

Before we could say a word, he had dropped to a squatting position again, and with his eyes gleaming balefully
over his crust of fungus began to feed once more.

My partner's grip on my arm again.

I looked where he silently indicated, and started. But
a step from where Captain Jim squatted lay one of the
man-creatures, sprawled awkwardly, motionless, silent.
And I knew in my heart that the thing was dead. Dead—
and Captain Jim—

Doug whispered in my ear.

"Those cries just before the Kanaka boy rushed out to
us— Had they— those things—attacked Jim?"

Hardly had he spoken when again came the sobbing
wail, from close at hand. And just beyond Captain Jim
we made out four of the grotesque fungoid figures. Their
own coloring was that of the lower growth, and it was
only their sudden movement that made us aware of their
presence. They were not watching us, however. Their eyes,
half hidden in the horrid nodular and befringed growth on
their faces, were on Jim.

"They don't mean any harm to us or him, Doug!" I whispered. "They want to help. And yet;—yet he's killed one of them, killed one."

"Come on!"

And we leaped upon Captain Jim.

He seemed to have gathered a triple strength from the food he had eaten. Down the three of us went, with the fungus stuff crunching beneath. I sensed a shadow pass over us again, and even as I fought awaited the downpour of brown spores. Then wondered that it did not come.

For a moment then my eyes were held by the glaring orbs of Captain Jim as he cursed and struggled to throw us off. Then a movement beyond us caught my glance again, and I saw that the four man-creatures had approached in a group, and were watching intently, hopping, in uncanny watching of the battle, from one foot to another. And above the cursing came the furry calls again and again.

"Fools!"

The word came in a veritable shriek from Jim.

"Fools! Eat the stuff, eat it. God! You've never eaten the like before. Stop this. Cut it. There, damn you, take that! Will you let me alone? Will you try to stop me from eating this—"

And his voice trailed off in a sobbing curse.

Doug, struggling with the madman's right arm as was I with his left, cried above the mêlée:

"The stuff's got him, too, Clarke. Fight for his life now. For his life and ours."

Ah, I cannot tell of the battle there in that ungodly place, with the feel of the utterly damned about us. The sense of a life force holding itself in until the most propitious moment for onslaught, watching us, menacing— The hellish coloring, the nightmare forms. The warm vapor, life-laden, sodden. And those four pitiful things that had been men, grouped there, hopping about in excitement as they watched, calling with their furry voices as we fought.

Twice my bare foot broke through the leathery surface of the purple bloat beneath us, and the tiny, vermilion tongues of the palpitant fungoid beneath leaped forth, flickered, spread in a living mat under our heaving forms—warmly, dankly, horribly alive.

Again and again the shadows crossed and recrossed over us, as the giant umbrella heads of towering stools peered down, as though watching the progress of the struggle. And my fears ebbed and flowed each time, yet each time the shadows passed and the dread drench of spores did not come. What are the things holding off for, I wonder? Did they know? Were they certain now that their turbulent, though silent, life force would in the end have its way? Did they know that Captain Jim already had partially succumbed, and that if he defeated my partner and me, we, too, would become as those man-creatures peering at us there? Did this fungus life know? Could it reason?

Strange thoughts, you may say. Aye, they were strange thoughts. Yet had you been there— Had you been struggling in that warmly steaming hell, feeling with every resistant sense of you that that steaming hell itself was alive with evil purpose and malignant desire—ah!

"*Eat!*" screamed Jim again. "Stop. Eat it yourselves. Then—damn you!—then, you'll know. Then, *then,* you'll stop. *Eat—*"

"You fool!" stormed Douglas. "Be a man—a *man,* Captain Jim!"

The words seemed to penetrate some undrugged part of Jim's mind. His eyes slowly changed. His struggles ceased. He lay back in our arms, and gasped in great gulps of the warm, throbbing, sodden air. Then, quickly, he brushed his eyes with his arm.

"Doug! Clarke! In Heaven's name—where—what—" He stared about him. He covered his face with his hands, and sobbed. "Take me out, take me out. Before it comes on me again. You don't know. You can't know—"

We held him between us, and taking our bearing by the sun, dipped in the west, started for the distant beach.

A furry cry came then from the pitiful man creatures, and I swung about with a knotted fist ready to fend off their attack. But they took the lead before us, and hopped on in their peculiar gait, turning now and again to beckon us on.

And Captain Jim groaned aloud. "One of them—back there—the Kanaka boy was eating the stuff. Said it was good. So I tried it—was coming back to you. Forgot. I—*forgot*. Then they came—and one of them—tried to stop me. The boy was with them. They seemed to know—tried to stop me. I went mad. The boy ran, screaming. I didn't think—I ate, *ate*—"

"We know, Jim," Doug whispered. "We know."

Then the sun was suddenly blotted out. The purple bloat beneath our feet arose, furrowed, and broke. The stream of released living vapor enveloped us. And with a silent, but palpitating rush, the living fungus leaped again to hot, lustful life.

The weird hopeless call came distantly.

"Keep together!" cried Jim. "Fight! Fight! Fight!"

X

The trailing tatters of gray stuff grew on the beach where we flung them. Spread. Carpeted the coral sands with a shroud of spongy fungus that filled the air with the warm stream of its diabolically effervescent rush into life, and more life, and yet more. Reached out, arose in great cloud-like masses until, overtopped with its own weight, it fell

with a sickening crunch and a puff of steaming spores that
brought forth new masses.

Shapes arose in it, nodular, spherical, huge soaring
forms that burst into great umbrella heads, matured, and
drenched the lower masses of stuff with the brawn clouds
of their fertilizing dust. Huge fan-shapes of the hideous
green-specked brown leaped up in our very path. The gray
underfoot took on the purplish tinge of the-bloated quilt-
ing of the main forest.

Our lungs were filling. Great masses of the gray stuff
choked my very throat, the warmth of its generation burning
the membranes, the steamy mold of it dulling my senses.

But one thought—the lagoon—

We plunged in.

To the very water's edge that tremendous life energy
beat its way—gray masses of it, huge stalks of leprous
yellow, pale purples and fishbelly greens—slowly, as we
fought there in the salt waters for life, changing to the
deeper colors of the more hideous shade. Sickening miasmic steam spread low and seeking.

Spore heads burst—giant puffballs —great roached
mounds—and all ebullient with the terrific life force of a
malignant fungus that owed its super-generative powers to
the torrid tropical sun and the steaming tropical down-
pours. And perhaps to some strange seed fetched out of
the depths of the sea from a prehistoric continent long
submerged—brought to the fertilizing, heat and moisture
of the equatorial belt by the tiny coral insect that builds
great lands. And here—rushing at us, great things peering out over the very water upon us, bursting in a brown
stench of spores—then, one of them, overbalanced in horrid eagerness, fell into the sea.

With the speed of its growth it disintegrated, dissolved,
disappeared. We gave a feeble shout. The salt lagoon was
our refuge—in the water we were safe.

Then a sudden cry from the Kanaka boy, who had come to life again during our absence. And sailing in upon us, tacking to right, tacking to left but approaching with relentless certainty, was the great dorsal fin of a shark.

We stared at the baffled fungus, and out to that white and gray messenger of quick doom. If death were to come, the latter were the better way.

Came a cry from the beach, far down to our left—the shrill sobbing cry of the man creatures, of the things this teeming life had resolved to make of us. We had come out of the forest far to the southward of the vermilion carpeted glade—the great mound of growth near which we had slept the night before was close to the western curve of the beach. The cry came from it, and high upon it we could make out the figures of the fungoid men.

"By Heaven, they're calling to us!" cried Doug. "They can't mean us any harm. They didn't harm you there in the island, Jim. They must mean something. That shark—jump!"

The great fin had veered from its angular course and the water seethed before it. Madly we tore into the fringing rot of the fungus and splashed through the lapping shallows down the beach. The force of the growing stuff seemed momentarily to have spent itself, and a clear sweep of the clean sands spread before us.

The man creatures leaped up and down in their excitement as we approached the great mound near the water's edge.

Once more they began to tear at the stuff on the lower surface and to beckon us to do the same.

And in sudden comprehension as I stared at the peculiar shape of the hill-like mass, I started to tear the stuff away myself. Then, though quivering with the thought of the thing, the terror of land and sea forced me, and I plunged my hand arm-length into the mass. Abruptly, not

an elbow's depth beneath the crusted surface, it crashed
against something hard. I gave a cry of excitement, and
dashed to the lagoon. Coming back I showered a cupped
handful of salt water against the hole I had made. Another
and another, then finally, when the light of day penetrated, gave a whoop of half hysterical joy.

"*Wood!* It's wood, fellows, it's wood—a ship—a ship!"

With what cries then did Doug and Captain Jim and
the Kanaka boy dash water upon the enshrouding fungus.

And how the man creatures hopped awkwardly about,
ever dodging the falling spray themselves, but ever tearing
at other parts of the mound, disclosing more and more
that what we had all at first taken for a huge mass of fungoid material was but a fungus-hidden wreck.

Then came a curious call from Captain Jim, who had
been working at the vessel's stern.

"Fellows! Look at this."

One glance at the exposed transom of the schooner,
and we turned our eyes upon the man creatures hopping
behind us.

"God pity them!" breathed Douglas Gordon. "Punishment they deserved, but never this."

The name of the wrecked schooner was still apparent,
gleaming dirty white against the molded teak of the vessel's transom. It spelled the fate that had come to these
unfortunate creatures, it spelled the end of our chase, it
spelled too, hope that we might evade the horror that had
come to these men who had stolen our great fire opal and
fled before our vengeance in the schooner *Black Moth*.

Truly had their punishment been a dreadful one. Yet,
truly, too, did they realize their own condition, and that
that same condition would be ours did we dally overlong
upon the Fungus Isle. They had seen us, they must have
recognized us as men at least, even if their brains were too
far gone to know us as the rightful owners of the treasure

stone. And as best they could, though fearing our very touch, they had conveyed to us the information that in this molded mound lay our salvation, and our only one.

The moon rose, and still the things worked with us as we cleaned the wreck. And toward dawn, Captain Jim came upon the hatchway aft, and despite our remonstrances declared he was going down below decks.

Evidently during the storm the hatchway had been closed. It took our united effort to slide the door forward in its swollen grooves, but our hearts beat gladly again when we saw that the necessities imposed by the storm that had brought the *Black Moth* to the coral sands had also kept her cabin clear of the island's horrid growth.

The schooner was canted over on her side as though beached for a cleanup of her bottom, but we scrambled madly down the short ladder, slipping and falling over each other in our efforts each to be first to find the thing that had suddenly again become uppermost in our minds. Water, and food—of which we had had none for forty-eight hours and more—were things for the future. Fear of the fungus was gone—the planks were here about us wherewith to build a raft and sail for a cleaner, saner land. And a shark was naught but a fish in the sea.

But now—at last, with a whoop of joy, we came upon a small blackwood chest. Caught it up, bore it topside, set it down in the angle of deck and cabin bulkhead, opened it—and the slanting rays of the sun just peering over the eastern horizon, over the mad, soaring forms of the fungus forest, were broken into the thousand and one gleaming flames of the great block of fire opal.

Water beakers we discovered in the hold, and tinned food. Sparingly we ate, with the hopeless, but nodding things that had been the rapers of our treasure, silently watching.

We called them to us. But they shook their heads quickly, and with their peculiar hopping movement, turned as one, and disappeared up the vermilion carpeted trail.

And Captain Jim, turning to us, told us why they would never again come out.

"I ate some of the fan stuff," he said. "In the first days here they must have sampled it, too, perhaps in curiosity. You saw how the stuff affected me—drugged, gentle swaying joy—bliss beyond words; more, and more, and more—they *cannot* leave. They lost all that made them man, they took on the life of the fungus—and God help them, they became half fungoid themselves. Yet—"

And Douglas Gordon finished for him.

"Yet they knew somehow what their fate must be, and ours. And somehow, heaven alone knows, they knew they must warn us. Whatever they were, and whatever they have become, there still is something in them that makes them men."

I stared from the growing warmth of our returned mass of opal up the vermilion carpeted trail, at the silently waiting forms of poison color, at the gray mass of stuff that had pursued us in our last flight to the cleansing water of the lagoon—and in my mind I saw with full clarity the fate that, but for them, must also have been ours. And I dropped my head.

"God help them!" I muttered as had Doug and Captain Jim. "God help them. And may they soon pass to a cleaner, sweeter life than that of Fungus Isle."

MANDRAKE

Adam Hull Shirk

"Fallon, you've got to help me!"

Dr. George Burton laid one hand, which trembled, upon the arm of his friend, the eminent psychologist, Professor Fallon, and fixed his tired eyes upon the latter's calm face.

"Of course I'll help you, George," said the scientist, reassuringly, "but first you must tell me just what is the matter."

Dr. Burton sat back in his chair and nodded slowly:

"Yes," he said, "I will. But—I don't understand it all myself."

"Never mind—go ahead—"

"You remember my writing you last Fall that I hoped to be married before so very long? Well, that hope may never be realized. This is the story: A couple of years ago, Power Marbury and his wife and two daughters came to Cranways. Six months later, Mrs. Marbury died. You may recall the case. The husband was convicted. It was murder, and though the evidence was purely circumstantial, there was never a doubt of the outcome. Power Marbury was sentenced to pay the extreme penalty and did so, unconfessed."

The physician rose and took a turn across the room before reseating himself. The psychologist said nothing. Presently the younger man continued:

109

"Can you imagine the effect on those two girls—Alice, not yet sixteen and Marjorie just two years her senior? Is it any wonder that they were stricken, almost driven insane? It was fortunate they had one friend in this narrow, hell-fearing community. Old Squire Broadman had been their father's executor, to care for the considerable property left to the two girls, but remaining in his hands until they should marry when it reverted to them automatically. He it was who defied the pious citizens und took them in, to share his bachelor home, like daughters of his own. Had it not been for him, Fallon, God knows what would have become of those two helpless orphans."

"What followed?"

"Fate seemed to be relentless," pursued the doctor, "and after a while Alice fell ill. I was called in. But in spite of all I could do, she faded, just as a flower transplanted to alien soil will wither and die. I exerted all my slight skill. The malady was apparently impervious to drugs. And in the end she—died. . . . That left Marjorie—alone.

"In the days when I had attended her sister, I learned to love her. I have never met a girl who was blessed with a sweeter disposition and how she bore up under it all, no one will ever understand. I had not spoken to her, of course, but some day I knew that I should do so; and that she would receive my proposal favorably I had good cause to believe. . . . This brings me up to recent events—events that have resulted in my sending for you, Fallon, my old friend!"

"You are welcome to my help—but you have not yet told me what the present difficulty is."

The physician sighed:

"I'm coming to that," he muttered "It was about three weeks ago that I learned Marjorie had taken to visiting the cemetery where her mother and father and sister were buried. It lies just outside the village. I remonstrated with her, because I saw it was a means of keeping the tragedies ever before her mind. But it was of no avail. Then, about ten days ago, she was stricken—"

"Stricken?" The scientist looked sharply at his friend. "What happened?"

"She was found on her doorstep in a dead faint, a look of absolute horror frozen on her face. I was called, and it took me several hours to revive her. When she came to, she confessed to having been frightened, but that was all she could or would tell. Then I learned she had been to see a charlatan who has lately come to town and established himself in offices here—Valdemar is his name, and he claims to be a hypnotist, psychometrist, or something of the kind."

"I know the breed," nodded Fallon. "Go on. She saw him?"

"Yes. I deduced that this might be the cause of her collapse and visited him myself. He admitted her consulting him, that she seemed obsessed regarding her father's possible innocence and had asked his advice. He said he had been unable to help her. Indeed, he seemed so fair spoken that I could find no cause to blame him. But Marjorie grew worse. She has become morose and seems to have lost confidence not only in me, but even in her guardian, who is as deeply anxious as I am.

"Fallon, she is secretly worried or frightened, and it is driving her slowly mad. That's why I've sent for you. Can you help me—by helping her?"

The savant sat for a moment immersed in thought. Finally he nodded:

"I feel certain I can," he declared, "and I suggest that we call on the young lady at once. Can it be arranged?"

"Certainly—I was about to suggest it—"

"Introduce me as a brother physician visiting you—nothing more and—"

Fallon's speech was interrupted by a knock at the office door, and in a moment the attendant announced that Peleg White wanted to see the doctor urgently.

Burton turned to his friend apologetically: "He's a sort of half-wit I've befriended—it won't take a moment."

"Bring him in," suggested Fallon.

The old creature came haltingly into the room, a malformed, hesitating parody of mankind. His story was quickly told, however, and, strangely enough, bore upon their present problem:

"It's about Miss Marjorie, Doctor," he said. "I know she's a friend of yourn. Well, last night I slept out in the old hollow tree near the buryin' ground, and I seen her come steelin' in like a ghost. I wasn't afeared, though, an' I followed to where her father was buried. She kneeled right down by his grave, and I thought she was prayin'—"

"What was she doing— ?"

"She was pullin' something up outen the ground— looked like a weed or somethin'. And just as it came 'way, they was the most awful onearthly shriek I ever heard in all my born days. Miss Marjorie she yelled out, too, and started to runnin' away. I run, myself. And then I knew you'd oughter know."

"Thant you, Peleg," said the doctor with a look of dismay on his face as he glanced at Fallon. "Here's a dollar for you. Don't say anything about this to a soul."

Mouthing his thanks, the half-wit hastened away. Burton, turned to his friend.

"What does it mean?" he asked.

"It means," said the psychologist, "that the sooner we see Miss Marjorie, the better. Come along."

They found the girl alone, pale, indicating by her manner lack of sleep and a condition of extreme nervousness.

To their questions as to her feeling, she answered listlessly. The psychologist said little, but observed her every move and gesture.

Back at Burton's office, the latter asked:

"Have you formed any conclusion?"

The other shook his head negatively.

"Not as yet. But I can assure you of one thing. There is a cause for her malady that is not altogether pathological. It goes deeper, my boy—we've got to locate it."

On the following day, while the two men were seated again in the doctor's consulting room, Peleg White put in his appearance in a state of extreme agitation. Admitted to the office, he plumped down on the table a grotesque object that resembled nothing the physician could remember having seen in his experience.

"I just come from Miss Marjorie," panted the half-wit. "She wanted I should sell this durn thing for forty cents or less. Said I mustn't take as much even as half a dollar cause she'd paid that for it. Told me not to tell nobody she give it to me, but I reckon I kin tell you. Anyway, who'd give me even a penny for the thing."

"I will," said Fallon, before his friend could speak. "Here's exactly forty cents. Take the money right back to the lady and don't tell her who bought it. Here's a quarter for yourself."

When the creature had departed, Burton turned to his friend with the pain he felt written plainly on his face.

"In God's name," he cried, "what is it?"

Fallon took up the thing and examined it with deep interest. It was a vegetable of some sort, of a sickly flesh color so far as the root was concerned; black mould still clung to it, and when viewed from a certain angle, the root portion bore a most uncanny resemblance to a human body.

"This," said the psychologist, slowly, "is a mandrake. One of the first I've ever seen!"

"Mandrake?" Burton repeated in a puzzled tone.

"Exactly. The one plant concerning which superstition is almost universal. Many books have been written about it. Even Shakespeare refers to it—I think in 'Romeo and Juliet,' where he speaks of 'Shrieks like Mandrakes torn out of the earth'."

The doctor shook his head, shudderingly.

"I can't understand—"

"This much," said the scientist, quickly, "I do understand—we must get back to Miss Marbury at once."

Dr. Burton stared at him in sudden alarm.

"You mean she is worse?"

"I don't think so—but something must be done immediately. I suppose," he added, "you trace the connection between my quotation from Shakespeare, and the story of Peleg about Marjorie at the cemetery?"

"You mean the shriek—that she was pulling this thing from the earth—?"

"It seems likely. But let us be going."

They found Marjorie so greatly improved on their arrival that Dr. Burton, at least, was overjoyed. His friend, however, seemed less impressed by her greater vivacity and the improved color in her cheeks. Seeking an excuse for their return so soon after the previous visit—though the doctor himself was in the habit of calling almost every day—Fallon observed that he had wanted to look at some of the Squire's books which he had noted when they were there before.

"I'm sorry," said the girl, "the Squire is out. But you can make yourself at home there, anyway—in the library."

Fallon smiled at her as he expressed his thanks.

Dr. Burton followed him to the door.

"She's better, don't you think?"

"She's seen Peleg," murmured Fallon enigmatically, and left them together.

In the library, quite an extensive one, he browsed among the books, looked at several, rubbed some of the upper edges gingerly with his forefinger and read a few lines from certain volumes. He also examined the contents of a Japanese card tray on a table, slipped one card into his pocket, and made a note on a slip of paper.

When he returned, Marjorie was smiling happily, but, as he gazed into her face, he noted the sudden alteration in her expression. She was staring with increasing horror, past him at the doorway. Dr. Burton noticed the change at the same instant, and rose with a question on his lips. But Professor Fallon, seizing a stick from the corner of the room, slashed viciously at a small pinkish object that was crawling along the floor and through the draperies at the entrance.

The scientist followed, leaving Burton to care for the girl, who had sunk back on the couch, one hand at her heart:

"He lied to me," she whispered, "he lied—"

Then she fainted. As the physician set to work to revive her, sounds of a struggle from the hallway came to his ears and his friend's voice calling his name. He laid the girl gently on the couch and tugged madly at the bell rope. As he tore the curtains aside and rushed out a servant came screaming down the corridor—

"They're killing one another," she cried.

"Go to Miss Marbury," he ordered, and hastened to where Fallon was struggling in the grasp of someone who, in the dim light he could not at first recognize: then he caught a glimpse of the white hair and beard of Squire Broadman, just as the scientist cried out:

"Hurry, for God's sake! Can't you see he's crazy?"

Together they overpowered the maniac and bound him with a cord from the portieres.

"He was in a niche of the wall," explained the psychologist, as he regained his breath. "He jumped on me as I came out."

"What does it mean?" asked Burton.

"First 'phone for an ambulance to take him away. Then get an order for the arrest of that fellow Valdemar. After that I'll explain. How is Miss Marbury?"

"Fainted—but she will be all right. Wait for me—I'll use the 'phone downstairs."

A few moments later he returned.

"That's attended to. The ambulance is coming, and they'll get Valdemar—it seems they've got enough to hold him on, anyway—obtaining money under false pretenses or something."

Marjorie had fallen into a deep sleep under the ministrations of the psychologist, and Burton drew his friend into the library.

"For heaven's sake," he begged, "tell me what it means."

The other removed from his pocket another of those ill-favored vegetables and laid it on the table: "There," he said, "is the root of the whole matter. You see tied about it a bit of silk thread? I broke it with my cane. The other end was in the hands of the madman. Briefly it is part of a diabolical plot to drive Miss Marbury insane or to the grave. It's God's justice that the one responsible suffered the fate he intended to inflict on another."

"Squire Broadman?"

"Of course. He would have lost control of the estate when Marjorie married, would he not?"

"Yes."

"That's it. Probably he has speculated with the money he held in trust. Now as to the Mandrake—and Valdemar: The cemetery story and the business of selling the plant were my first rays of light. In the library here I found, among other books, Thomas Newton's 'Herball to the Bible.' It had been much used—lately. No dust on it such as the other books showed. This passage was marked:

> "'It is supposed to be a creature having life en-gendered under the earth of the seed of some dead person put to death for murder.'"

"In a more recent work, Skinner's 'Myths and Legends of Flowers,' I discovered a dog-eared page on which I read this: 'The devil has a special watch on these objects and unless one succeeded in selling one for less than he gave for it, it would stay with him till his death.' How does that strike you?

"But now we come to Valdemar. Here is a card I found in the Squire's card tray there. It's the charlatan's, you see. On the reverse is a memo in the Squire's writing—'See V. tomorrow and get more mandrakes.' You see, he was a benevolent old fiend. Of course, it was he who shrieked in the cemetery as she tore up the mandrake. It's hellish—that's all. Now let's see Valdemar."

They found the eminent psychometrist in the city jail, much perturbed and decidedly crestfallen. He told them, under methods not far removed from the third degree, his part in the transaction: Broadman had been working on the girl's mind, telling her she ought to vindicate her father's memory if she could, and sent her to Valdemar, whom he had previously hired to help in the nefarious scheme. He told her to go home and if anything happened to tell him.

As she reached the door, a white figure rose in the dark hallway—as prearranged—and commanded her in sepulchral tones neither to rest nor sleep till her father's memory had been cleared. She swooned.

Then she told the Squire, but he cautioned her not to speak to the doctor about it and again to consult Valdemar. Broadman had read the mandrake stuff, and the charlatan had arranged to secure some of the plants—goodness knows where—and suggested to Marjorie that she plant one on the grave of her father. Later, if she pulled it up, and the thing shrieked, she would know her parent had been justly punished. It had merely to be planted one day and torn up the next, they told her, to attain the desired results.

She had paid fifty cents for the thing, it seems, and naturally threw it from her when she heard the awful cry. Returning home, she found what she believed to be the same mandrake somewhere about her room, for as Skinner's book had further said: *"Throw it into the fire, into the river. . . . so soon as you reached home, there would be the mandrake, creeping over the floor, smirking human fashion from a shelf or ensconsed in your bed!"*

She told Valdemar, and he assured her that if she sold the thing for less than she had paid for it, the curse would be removed. She tried this, but again one of the dread plants crept across the floor. Then the end had come swiftly. Doubtless, Valdemar admitted, the squire was himself half demented for years. Burton, putting two and two together, believed that in some subtle way Broadman had brought about the death of Alice, as he had hoped to encompass that of Marjorie, or at least to drive her insane, so that she might not marry and thus automatically expose his own guilt in the matter of the money.

"Which proves," remarked Fallon, as he bade his friend good-bye at the station the following day, "that it pays to read abstruse matter sometimes. I knew the legend of the mandrake long before I refreshed my memory of the thing in Squire Broadman's library!"

SI URAG OF THE TAIL

Oscar Cook

Dennis sat on the verandah of his bungalow and gazed meditatively around him. He could not look at the view, because there was none to speak of since the house was built on an island in the middle of the Luago River. On all sides of the island grew the tall rank elephant-grass and nipa-palm. Here and there a stunted, beetle-ridden coconut tree just topped the dense vegetation, a relic of some clearing and plantation commenced by a native, then left to desolation and the ever-encroaching jungle.

Dennis was bored. He was two years overdue for leave; also the day was unusually hot. The hour was about four, but though the sun was beginning to slant there was no abatement in the fierceness of its rays. After lunch he had followed the immemorial custom and undressed for a short siesta, but sleep was denied him. The mechanical action of undressing had quickened his brain. The room seemed stifling; the bed felt warm. He bathed, dressed and betook himself to the verandah. Here he smoked and thought.

And his thoughts were none too pleasant, for there was much that was troubling him. Throughout the morning he had been listening to the endless intricacies of a native land case—a dispute over boundaries and ownership. He had reserved his judgment till the morrow, for the evidence had been involved and contradictory. He had meant to go over the salient points during the afternoon, and instead, here he was seated on his verandah smoking and thinking of an entirely different matter. Try as he would, his mind would not keep on the subject of the land, but roamed ever and ever over the mystery that was fast setting its seal of terror and fear on the district.

From a village in the *ulu* [source] of the river, strange rumours had come floating downstream. At first they were as light and airy as thistledown—just a passing whisper—a fairy story over which to smile; then they passed, but came again, more substantial and insistent, stronger and sterner and not to be denied. Their very number compelled a hearing; their very sameness breathed a truth. Inhabitants from the village had gone forth and never returned; never a trace of them had been found. First a young girl, then her father. She had been absent six days, and he had gone to look for her. But he looked in vain and in his turn disappeared. Then a young boy, and next an aged woman. Then, after a longer period a tame ape, and finally the headman's favourite wife.

Fear settled on the village; its inhabitants scarce dared leave their houses, save in batches to collect water and food. But fear travels fast, and the rumours reached Klagan and came to Dennis's ears. In the end the mystery caught him in its toils, weaved itself into his every waking moment and excited his interest beyond control.

An idle native story: the tale of a neighbouring village with an axe of its own to grind. He was a fool to worry over it. Such mare's nests were of almost daily occurrence, thus Dennis argued; and then from two other villages came similar tales. Two little girls had gone to bathe in the height of the noonday sun. At moonrise they had not returned. Nor in the days that passed were they ever seen again. Two lovers met one moonlight night and waded to a boulder in midstream of the river. Here they sat oblivious of the world around them. They were seen by a couple of natives passing downstream in their boat and then—never again.

Down the river crept the cold, insidious Fear like a plague, taking toll of every village in its path. In their houses huddled the natives, while crops were unsown and pigs uprooted the plantations; while crocodiles devoured untended buffaloes, and squirrels and monkeys rifled the fruit trees. From source to mouth the Fear crept down and in the end forced Dennis's hand, compelling him to action.

Thus as he sat on his verandah and cursed the heat of the sun and the humidity of the tropics, unbidden and unsought the mystery filled his thoughts; and he began to wonder as to if and when his native sergeant and three police would return. For he had sent them to the *ulu* to probe and solve the meaning of the rumours. They had been gone three weeks, and throughout this time no word had been heard of or come from them.

In the office a clock struck five. Its notes came booming across to Dennis. Then silence—not complete and utter stillness; such is never possible in the tropics, but the silence of that hour when the toilers—man and animal—by day realize that night is approaching; when the toilers by night have not yet awakened.

Lower and lower sank the sun. In the sky a moon was faintly visible. Dennis rose, about to call for tea, then checked the desire. From afar upstream came the chug, chug, chug of a motor-boat. Its beat just reached his ears. He looked at his wrist-watch. In ten minutes he would go down to the floating wharf. That would give him plenty of time to watch the boat round the last bend of the river. In the meanwhile . . .

But he went at once to the wharf after all, for mystery gripped him, causing him feverishly to pace up and down the tiny floating square. Chug, chug, chug, louder and louder came the noise; then fainter and fainter, and then was lost altogether as the dense jungle cut off the sound as the boat traversed another bend of the river. Chug, chug, chug, faintly, then louder and stronger. A long-drawn note from the horn of a buffalo smote the air, and the boat swung round the final bend. Only a quarter of a mile separated it now from Dennis.

As the boat drew nearer he saw that she was empty save for the *serang* [helmsman] and boatmen. Then the Fear gripped him too, and he quickly returned to the house. With shaking hand he poured out a whisky-and-soda, flung himself into a chair and shouted for his "boy."

"*Tuan!*" The word, though quietly spoken, made him flinch, for the "boy" had approached him silently, as all well-trained servants do. Quickly, too, he had obeyed the summons, but in that brief space of time Dennis's mind had escaped his body and immediate wants to roam the vast untrodden fields of speculation and fear.

With an effort he pulled himself together.

"The motor-boat is returning. Tell the *serang* to come to me as soon as he has tied her up. See that no one is within earshot."

"*Tuan.*" And the boy departed.

Scarcely had the boy left than the *serang* stood in front of Dennis. His story was brief, though harrowing, but it threw no light upon the mystery. For two days, till they reached the rapids, they had used the motor-boat. Then they transhipped into a native dug-out, leaving the motor in charge of a village headman. For three days they had paddled and poled upstream till they came to the mouth of the Buis River. Here the sergeant and police left them, telling them to wait for their return, and struck inland along a native track. For sixteen days they waited, though their food had given out and they had taken turns to search the jungle for edible roots. Then on the sixteenth day it happened—the horrible coming of Nuin.

The boatmen had gone to look for roots. The *serang* was dozing in a dug-out. Suddenly it shook and rocked. Something clutched the *serang's* arm. It was Nuin's hand. Startled into wakefulness, the *serang* sat up; then he screamed and covered his eyes with his hands. When he dared look again Nuin was lying on the river bank. His clothes were in rags. Round his chest and back ran a livid weal four inches wide. His left leg hung broken and twisted. His right arm was entirely missing. His face was caked in congealed blood.

As the *serang* looked, Nuin opened his lips to speak, but his voice was only a whisper. Tremblingly, haltingly, the *serang* went to him and put his ear to his mouth. "Sergeant—others—dead—three days—west—man—with—big—big—others." The whisper faded away; Nuin gave a shudder and was dead.

They buried him near the river and then left, paddling night and day till they reached the rapids. A night they spent in the village, for they were racked with sleeplessness, and they left the next morning, reaching Klagan the same day.

Such was the *serang's* report.

The Fear spread farther down the river till it reached the sea and spread along the coast.

In the barracks that night were two women who would never see their men again; was born a baby, who would never know his father; wept a maiden for the lover whose lips she would never kiss again.

As the earliest streaks of dawn came stealing across the sky, the chugging of a motor-boat broke the stillness of the night. Dennis himself was at the wheel, for the *serang* was suffering with fever. With him were nine police and a corporal. They carried stores for twenty days.

The journey was a replica of the *serang's,* save that at the village by the rapids no friendly headman or villagers took charge of the motor-boat. The village had fled before the Fear. On the fifth day Buis was reached as the setting sun shot the sky with blood-red streamers.

On the banks of the river the earth was uprooted; among the loosened earth were human bones and the marks of pigs' feet. Among the bones was a broken tusk, sure sign of some fierce conflict that had raged over Nuin's remains.

Dennis shuddered as he saw the scene; his Murut police, pagans from the interior of North Borneo, fingered their charms of monkeys' teeth and dried snake-skins that hung around their necks or were attached to the rotan belts around their waists, that carried their heavy *parangs* [swords].

Occasionally throughout the night the droning noise of myriad insects was broken by the shrill bark of deer or kijang. Sometimes the sentry, gazing into the vast blackness of the jungle, saw the beady eyes of a pig, lit up for a moment by the flames of the campfire. Sometimes a snake, attracted by the glare, glided through the undergrowth, then passed on. Once or twice a nightjar cried and an owl hooted—eerie sounds in the pitch-black night. Otherwise a heavy brooding stillness, like an autumn mist, crept over the jungle and enveloped the camp. Hardly a policeman slept; but dozed and waked and dozed again, only to wake once more and feel the Fear grow ever stronger. Dennis, on his camp-bed under a *kajang* awning, tossed and tossed the long night through.

Dawn broke to a clap of thunder. Rain heralded in the new day.

"Three days—west." This was all Dennis knew; all he had to guide him. For this and the next two days the party followed a track that led steadily in a westerly direction.

On the evening of the third day it came out into a glade. Here Dennis pitched his camp. The tiny space of open sky and glittering stars breathed a cooler air and purer fragrance than the camps roofed in by the canopy of mighty trees. Thus the tired and haunted police slept, and Dennis ceased his tossing. Only the sentry was awake—or should have been. Perhaps he too dozed or fell fast asleep, for a few unconscious moments. If so he paid a heavy penalty.

Dennis awoke the next morning at a quarter to six to see only the smouldering remains of the campfire.

"Sentry!" he called. But no answer was vouchsafed. "Sentry!" he cried again, but no one came. Aroused by his voice, the sleeping camp stirred to wide and startled awakeness.

The corporal came across to Dennis, saluted, then stood at attention, waiting.

"The fire's nearly out; where's the sentry?" Dennis queried.

The corporal looked around him, gazed at the smouldering fire, counted his men, then looked at Dennis with fear-stricken eyes.

"*Tuan!*" he gasped; "he is not—there are only eight men!"

"Is not? What d'you mean? Where's he gone?" As Dennis snapped his question cold fear gripped his heart. He knew; some inner sense told him that the man had disappeared in the same mysterious fashion as those early victims. Here, in the midst of his camp, the terrible, unseen thing had power!

"Where's he gone?" Dennis repeated his question fiercely to quench his rising fear. "What d'you mean?"

For answer the corporal only stood and trembled. His open, twitching mouth produced no sound.

With an oath Dennis flung himself from his bed. "Search the glade, you fool," he cried, "and find his tracks! He can't be far away. No, stay," he added as the corporal was departing. "Who is it?"

"Bensaian, *Tuan*," gasped the terrified man.

Dennis's eyes narrowed and a frown spread over his face. "Bensaian!" he repeated. "He was Number Three. His watch was from twelve till two."

"*Tuan!*"

"Then he's never been relieved. From two o'clock at least, he's been missing!"

"*Tuan!* I must have slept. I saw Auraner relieve Si Tuah, but I was tired and—"

"Search for his tracks," Dennis cried, breaking in on his protestations, "but see no man enters the jungle."

In that tiny glade the search was no prolonged affair, but no traces of the missing man were found—save one. A brass button, torn from his tunic, lay at the foot of a mighty billian tree. But where and how he had gone remained a mystery. Only the regular footprints as he had walked to and fro on his beat were just discernible, and these crossed and recrossed each other in hopeless confusion.

Over the tops of the trees the sun came stealing, bathing the glade in its warming light, but Dennis heeded it not.

"Three days—west." The words kept hammering in his brain as he sat on the edge of his bed and smoked cigarette after cigarette. Up and down the glade a sentry walked. Round the fire the police were crouched cooking their rice; over another Dennis's boy prepared his *tuan's* breakfast.

At length, when ready, he brought it over to him, poured out his coffee and departed to join the whispering police. But though the coffee grew cold and flies settled on the food, Dennis sat on, unmoved, deep in his distraction.

This was the fourth day! For three days they had journeyed west, following Nuin's almost last conscious words. The glade was hemmed in by the impenetrable jungle; no path led out of it save that along which they had come. It formed a *cul-de-sac* indeed! And Bensaian was missing!

As Dennis sat and pondered, this one great fact became predominant. Bensaian was missing. Then what did it mean? Only that here the thing had happened, lived or breathed or moved about. Here, then, would be found the answer to the riddle! In this little glade of sunlight must they watch and wait. Into the trackless jungle he dared not enter, even if his men could hack a path. To return the way they had come would make his errand worse than fruitless. Watching and waiting only remained.

So they waited. Day turned to evening and evening into night; the dawn of another day displaced the night; the sun again rode over the tops of the jungle. But nothing happened. Only the policemen grew more frightened; only Dennis's nerves grew more frayed. Then once again the night descended, but no one in the camp dared really sleep.

Up and down walked the sentry, resting every now and then, as he turned against the billian tree. A gentle breeze stirred the branches of the encircling trees, bearing on the air a faint aromatic smell, that soothed the nervous senses of the resting camp, as a narcotic dispels pain. One by one the police ceased whispering and gently dozed, calmed by the sweet fragrance. Dennis ceased his endless smoking; stretched himself at ease upon his bed. The sense of mystery seemed forgotten by all; a sense of peace seemed brooding over them.

Midnight came and the wakeful sentry was relieved. His relief, but half awake, railed at his fate—the half-unconscious dozing was so pleasant, and this marching up and down the glade, while others rested, so utterly to his distaste.

As for the fortieth time he turned about at the base of the great billian tree, he lowered his rifle, rested for a few seconds with his hands upon its barrel, then leaned against the dark ridged stem; just for a moment he would rest, his rifle in his hands—just for a moment only, then once again take up his beat.

The wind in the trees was gradually increasing; the fragrance on the air became more pronounced. The camp was almost wrapt in slumber. On his bed Dennis sleepily wondered whence came the pleasing, soothing odour, that seemed to breathe so wondrous a peace. Against the billian tree the sentry still was leaning; his rifle slipped from the faint grasp of his hands, but he heeded not the rattle as it struck the ground.

Peace in the glade from whence came so much mystery! Peace while the dread, though unknown, agent drew near apace!

Down from the top of the billian tree it slowly descended, branch by branch; slowly, carefully, silently, till it rested on the lowest branch still thirty feet above the sentry.

The bark of a deer broke the stillness of the night. From afar came an answering note. Somehow the sound awakened the sentry. He looked around him, saw the fire was burning bright, picked up his fallen rifle and commenced to walk about.

Down the far side of the tree a bark rope descended till its weighted end just rested on the ground. Down the rope a man, naked save for a bark-made loin-cloth, descended till he too reached the earth. Then, pressed flatly to the great tree's trunk, he waited.

Across the glade the sentry turned about. With listless, heavy steps he was returning. Nearer and nearer he approached. At the foot of the billian tree he halted, turned and leaned against its trunk. The tension of his limbs relaxed. The rifle slipped from his grasp, but hung suspended by the strap that had become entangled over his arm. A light unconsciousness, hardly to be designated sleep, stole over him. From the camp there was no sign of wakefulness.

Slowly a figure crept noiselessly round the tree and stood gazing at the policeman. Naked indeed he was save for the *chavat* [loin-cloth] of bark; his thick black hair hung over his neck and reached beyond his shoulders, framing a face out of which gleamed two fanatical shining eyes. His body to the waist was covered with tattoo. From each of his breasts the designs started, spreading to waist-line and round to the back. The nipple of each breast gleamed a fiery burnished gold, while from their fringe spread outward, like a full-blown flower, five oval petals of wondrous purple hue. From the golden centre of each flower ten long pistils spread, curving downward and round his body. At their source they too were of a purple hue, but as they reached the petals their colour turned to gleaming gold which slowly changed to glistening silver as their ridged ends were reached. These ridged ends were circular, and their silver rims framed brilliant scarlet mouths, shaped like the sucking orifice with which the huge and slimy horse-leech gluts its loathsome thirst for blood.

The man's arms were unusually long; his finger-nails had never been clipped; the splay of his toes, especially between the big and the next one, uncommonly wide.

One hand still clutched the bark rope; the other hung loosely at his side. Though he was tall, standing five feet ten inches, and heavily built, he moved as lightly as a cat.

Lightly he let go the rope and extended his two long arms toward his unconscious prey. The cry of a nightjar sounded close at hand. The somnolent sentry stirred as the sound just reached his brain. With a spring the man was upon him. One hand upon his mouth; one arm around his chest pinioning his arms to his side. With a swiftness incredible he reached the far side of the tree, let go his grasp upon the sentry's mouth, and using the rope as a rail, commenced to climb step over step with an amazing agility.

"*Tolong!*" [Help!] The cry, laden with overwhelming Fear, rent the stillness of the night. "*Tol*—"

All further sound ended in a gurgle as the relentless pressure round the sentry's chest squeezed out all breath from his body. The camp at that sudden cry of human agony and fear awoke to life. Instinctively the police seized their rifles; the corporal blew fiercely on his whistle. Dennis hurriedly pulled on his mosquito boots and picked up his revolver from under his pillow.

"Corporal!"

"*Tuan!*"

"*Siapa itu?*" [Who's that?]

The cries rent the air simultaneously. Then came silence for the fraction of a second, as everyone stared hopelessly at one another as they realized the glade was empty of the sentry.

"Si Tuah! Tuah!" Dennis's voice rose in a long cry, breaking the sudden silence that followed the camp's awakening. "Tu-ah," he called again.

Somewhere from among the trees came a sound—a kind of muffled sob—a choking, gurgling cry of fear. To the edge of the jungle close to the billian tree Dennis and the corporal darted.

"Look, *Tuan, a* rope!" the latter gasped.

"My God!" Dennis whispered. "What does it mean?"

"It's made of bark and—" began the corporal, but the rest of his words were drowned by a loud report.

"*Jaga! Tuan, Jaga!*" [Look out!] he cried, as a jumbled shape came hurtling down from the branches of the tree and the frayed ends of the rope came writhing about them.

The snapping of a twig overhead, and a smoking rifle fell at their feet.

As the shape reached the ground with a sickening bump, two figures fell apart and then lay still.

"Seize that man and bind him!" Dennis cried, pointing to the naked form, as he bent over the prostrate figure of Si Tuah. "Gently, men, gently," he added, as four police picked him up and carried him over to their *kajang* shelter.

His left arm hung loosely by his side, two ribs were also broken, but his heart still faintly beat. Dennis poured a little brandy down his throat. Slowly Si Tuah came to. He tried to rise to sitting posture, but fell back with a groan of pain.

"He came upon me from behind the tree—I must have dozed," he muttered. "He picked me up—the pressure of his grasp was awful—and then commenced to climb the tree, holding the rope as a rail and walking up step by step. I struggled—just as we neared the branches his grip slackened—I could not cry—I had no breath—I only groaned, I struggled once again—my foot kicked the butt of my rifle—my toe found the trigger and I pressed and pressed—there came a report—we fell—and—"

Si Tuah had fainted again. Dennis's eyes met those of the corporal. "The shot must have severed the rope," he whispered.

"*Tuan,* his *nasib* [fate] was good," the corporal answered, and they crossed to where the human vulture lay, one leg twisted under him, his *chawat* all awry. As the policemen rolled him over on his face to knot the ropes— they showed but little pity for his unconscious state—the *chawat* came undone and slipped from his waist.

"Look, *Tuan,* look!" the corporal gasped, and pointed with shaking finger. "Look, he has a tail—it's not a man— it has a tail!" And feverishly he fingered the charms that hung around his neck.

Dennis looked, following the pointing finger, then bending down, looked long and closely. It was as the corporal said. The man possessed a tail—a long, hard protuberance that projected from his spine for about four inches.

"Bring him to the camp," he ordered. "Place two sentries; one over him, one on the camp. He is only stunned; there are no bones broken. In the morning when Tuah's better we'll learn some more."

Dennis walked across to his bed. The Fear was gone, but the mystery was still unexplained. The camp-fire burnt brightly, giving out a smell of pungent wood smoke. The soothing aromatic scent of an hour ago was no more. From the police came intermittent whisperings; from the man with the tail naught but heavy breathing. On his bed Dennis tossed and wondered.

As the early dawn first faintly flooded the sky, shriek upon shriek rent the air. Si Tuah had become delirious. The man with the tail awoke and listened. From a group of police squatting over a fire their voices reached him. His eyes blinked in perplexity. Quietly as he lay, he dug with his nails a small round hole in the earth about five inches deep. Then gingerly he moved, and in spite of his bonds sat up. From his bed Dennis watched him. Into the hole he fitted his tail, then looked at his bonds and the group of police: He opened his mouth, but no sound came forth. His tied hands he stretched out to them. His face expressed a yearning. It was as if their voices brought a comfort or recalled a past. Then tear after tear rolled down his cheeks.

Calling the corporal, Dennis crossed to the weeping man. At Dennis's approach he looked up, then with a cry buried his face in his bound hands and rocked his body to and fro. He was afraid—afraid of a white man, the like of which he had never seen before.

"Peace, fool," the corporal said roughly, speaking unconsciously in Murut; "stop your wailing, the *tuan* is no ghost but a man, albeit all-powerful."

Slowly the tailed being ceased his weeping and looked up. "A man!" he muttered. "A man and the colour of the gods!" He spoke a bastard Murut and Malay that caused Dennis to start and the corporal to frown in perplexity, for his meaning was clear, though many of the words, akin to either language, were yet unlike either. But they understood him.

"And your name?" Dennis asked in Malay, but the being only shook his head in fear, extending his hands in supplication.

"Loosen his bonds," Dennis commanded. "Ask him his name and tribe and village."

The corporal obeyed, and then translated.

The man's name was Si Urag. He came of a Murut race that years ago had captured some Malay traders. All had been killed except the women. These had been made to marry the head-men. Then came a plague and nearly all died. The remnants, according to custom, moved their village. For days and days they walked in the trackless jungle. Then from the trees they were attacked by a race of dwarfs who lived in houses in the branches. All save him were killed. He lay stunned; when he recovered consciousness he saw that the dwarfs had tails and that they were disembowelling the dead and dying and hanging their entrails round their necks. Fear seized him. He tried to rise and run away. He staggered to his feet, tottered a yard or two and then collapsed. Terrified, face downward, he waited for his foes. With a rush of feet they came. He waited for the blow. It never fell. Suddenly he felt a gentle pull upon his tail—the tail over which all his life he had been ridiculed; then came a muttering of voices. From the face of the moon a cloud passed by. He was in a glade and lying near a pool. Over the air a heavy scent was hanging. Suddenly the waters stirred. Out of their depths a flaming gold and purple flower arose. Ten tentacles spread out with gaping, wide-open, blood-red mouths. Shriek upon shriek of utter agony rent the air. Into the flaming golden centre each tentacle, curving inward, dropped a dwarf. Into the depths of the pool the flower sank down. All was still. Si Urag was alone.

That night he slept in a house among the branches of a tree. The surviving dwarfs had fled.

In the morning he collected the corpses of his friends and placed them near the lake. That night from his tree-house he watched. The moon was one day off the full. When at its highest point in the sky, the waters of the pool became disturbed. Again the golden-purple flower arose from its depths and the soothing scent spread over the jungle. Again the red-mouthed tentacles spread over the shore and sucked up the corpses, curved themselves in toward the golden centre, dropped in its bell-shaped mouth the stiffened bodies. Once again the human-feeding flower sank beneath the waters. Once again all was still. Gradually the narcotic smell grew less; slowly the moon sank in the west. All was dark and silent.

On the next and two following nights the flower appeared. Each night the hungry tentacles sought for food—human or animal. Then with the waning of the moon the flower rose up no more. Still in his tree-house Si Urag watched and lived. Where else was he to go? His tribe was killed; the dwarfs had fled, and of them he was afraid. On account of his tail he was shy to intermingle with other humans, even if he knew where to find them. Here was his house, safe from wild beasts that roamed at night; in the pool were many fish, in the jungle many roots and fruit. Here was the wondrous flower that fed on men, that spread its wondrous scent, to whom he felt he owed his life. Here, then, he would live and consecrate his life in a kind of priesthood to the flaming gold-and-purple orchid.

The corporal ceased and his eyes met those of Dennis. There was no need to answer the unspoken question in them. The mystery of those disappearances was explained.

"And that?" Dennis pointed to the tattooing on the prisoner's body.

Si Urag understood the gesture, if not the words.

"Is the picture of the flower I serve," he answered, looking at the corporal. "Two nights ago I fed it with a man clothed like that"—and he pointed to the police. "A night ago I caught a pig and deer; last night I caught a man"—he pointed to where Si Tuah lay in his delirium—"but a magic spoke from out a tube that flashed fire and the rope was severed and . . ." He shrugged his shoulders with a world of meaning, then, "I am hungry; give me some rice," he begged.

For a while he ate his fill. Then when the sun rose high over the little glade Dennis questioned him further, and from his answers formed a great resolve.

The glade of the golden-purple flower was but a few miles away. A little cutting of the jungle, and a hidden path—Si Urag's path—would be found. That night the moon would be but two days past its zenith, the wondrous flower would rise for the last time for a month—or rise never to rise again, hoped Dennis.

Si Urag was complacent. Was it fear or cunning? Who could tell? His face was like a mask as he agreed to lead the little party to the pool where dwelt the sacred flower. The hour was after midnight. In the camp three police watched the delirious Si Tuah. Along a narrow track that led from the jungle to a pool, silently stole eight men. In the west a clipped moon was slowly sinking. Out of the jungle crept the men, into a glade silvered by the light of the moon.

"To the right ten paces ex—" Dennis's whispered orders faded away, giving place to a breathless gasp of surprise.

There in the middle of the pool was the great golden-purple flower, its centre flaming gold, its petals deepest purple, its ten pistils curling and waving about—curling and waving toward the little group of men as they emerged from the track; the blood-red, silver-rimmed mouths opening and shutting in hungry expectation. Over the glade lay the heavy aromatic scent.

Speechless, spellbound, the little party looked at the wondrous, beautiful sight. The deadening spell of that narcotic scent was spreading through their veins. Lower and lower slowly sank the moon.

Si Urag fell upon his knees, covered his face with his hands and commenced to mumble a prayer. His action jerked the rope with which he was attached to Dennis and the corporal. With a start the former awoke as from a trance. All the waving pistils were pointing and stretching toward the huddled group. The moon was nearly touching the farther edge of the sky. Soon—soon . . .

"To the right ten paces extend!" Like pistol shots Dennis's words broke in upon the night. Unconsciously, automatically, the police obeyed. Si Urag remained in prayer. "Load!" The one word cut the stillness like a knife. The waving pistils changed their curves—followed the extending men, stretched and strained their blood-red mouths.

"At point-blank—fire!" Six tongues of flame; one loud and slightly jagged report. Four pistils writhed and twisted in an agony of death. In the flaming golden centre, a jagged hole. The heavy aromatic scent came stealing stronger and stronger from the maimed and riddled centre. The moon just touched the far horizon. Slowly the wondrous flower began to sink, the waters became disturbed, the pistils seemed to shrink.

Si Urag rose from his knees and prayers; uncovered his ears, over which he had placed his hand at the sound of the report. From Dennis to the corporal he looked in mute and utter supplication. From head to foot he trembled.

Slowly the moon and flower were sinking. One pistil, bigger, stronger, fuller-mouthed than the rest, seemed reluctant to retreat, but pointed and waved at the silent three.

Into his *chawat* Si Urag dived his hand. Quick as lightning he withdrew it. A slash to the right, another to the left, and he was free. A mighty spring, a piercing cry and he hurled himself, as a devotee, into the great ravenous, blood-red mouth. Slowly the pistil curved inward. Over the golden bell-shaped centre it poised. Then it bent its head; its silver rim distended and then closed. Si Urag was no more.

The moon sank down out of sight; the wondrous flower with its maddened, fanatical victim slipped beneath the waters of the pool. The stillness of the jungle remained; the scent of dew-laden earth arose. Darkness—and a memory—surrounded the group of seven.

The tropic sleepiness of 3 p.m. hung over Klagan. Suddenly the chugging of a motor-boat was heard coming from afar upstream. Down to the tiny floating wharf the populace descended, headed by the *serang*. Round the last bend swung the motor-boat, drew alongside the wharf and came to rest. Out of it silently stepped Dennis and the weary police. One of them carried two rifles, which told the wondering people of a death. Two of them supported Si Tuah, which told them a struggle had taken place. Over his features spread a smile as his hands met those of his wife. "'Twas a near thing, Miang," he murmured, "and it happened at the dead of night. A man with a tail and a golden-purple orchid which he worshipped."

From the people rose a gasp of wonder and cries of disbelief. Then Dennis raised his hand.

"Si Tuah speaks the truth," he said, "but Si Urag of the Tail no longer lives, and the flower no more can blossom. The Fear is dead."

Then unsteadily he walked to his house.

THE GRAY DEATH

Loual B. Sugarman

Unwaveringly, my guest sustained my perplexed and angry stare. Silently he withstood the battering words I launched at him. He appeared quite unmoved by my reproaches, save for a dull red flush that crept up and flooded his face, as now and then I grew particularly bitter in my tirade.

At length I ceased. It was like hitting into a mass of feathers: there was no resistance to my blows. He had made no attempt to justify himself. After a moment of silence, he spoke his first word since he had entered the room.

"I'm sorry, my friend, sorrier than you can imagine, but—I couldn't help it. I simply could not touch her hand. The shock—so suddenly to come upon her—to see her as she was—I tell you, I forgot myself. Please convey to your wife my most abject apologies, will you? I am sorry, for I know I should have liked her very much. But—now I must go."

"You can't go out in this storm," I answered. "It's out of the question. I'm sorry, too, sorry that you acted as you did—and more than sorry that I spoke to you as I did, just now. But I was angry. Can you blame me? I'd been waiting for this moment ever since I heard from you that you had come back from the Amazon—the moment when you, my best friend, and my wife were to meet. And then— why, damn it, man, I can't understand it! To pull back, to

shrink away as you did; even to refuse to take her hand or
acknowledge the introduction! It was unbelievably rude. It
hurt her, and it hurt me."

"I know it, and that is why I am so very sorry about it
all. I can't excuse myself, but I can tell you a story that
may explain."

I saw, however, that for some reason he was reluctant
to talk.

"You need not," I said. "Let's drop the whole matter,
and in the morning you can make your amends to Laura."

Anthony shook his head.

"It's not pleasant to talk about, but that was not my
reason for hesitating. I was afraid you would not believe
me if I did tell you. Sometimes the truth strains one's cre-
dulity too much. But I will tell you. It may do me good
to talk about it, and, anyhow, it will explain why I acted
as I did.

"Your wife came in just after we entered. She had not
yet removed her veil or gloves. They were gray. So was
her dress. Her shoes—everything was gray. And she stood
there, her hand outstretched—all in that color—a body
covered with gray, I can't help shuddering. *I can't stand
gray!* It's the color of death. . . . Can your nerves stand the
dark?"

I rose and switched off the lights. The room was
plunged into darkness, save for the flicker of the flames
in the fireplace and the intermittent flashes of lightning.
The rain beat through the leafless branches outside with a
monotonous, slithering *swish* and rattled like ghostly fingers against the windows.

"The light makes it hard to talk—of unbelievable
things. One needs the darkness to hear of hell."

He paused. The *swir-r-r* of the rain crept into the stillness of the room. My companion sighed. The firelight

shone on his face, which floated in the darkness—a disem-
bodied face, grown suddenly haggard.

"A good night for this story, with the wind crying like
a lost soul in the night. How I hate that sound! Ah, well!"

There was a moment of silence.

"It was not like this, though, that night when we started up the Amazon. No. Then it was warm and soft, and the
stars seemed so near. The air was filled with the scent of a
thousand tropical blossoms. They grew rank on the shore.

"There were four of us; two natives, myself and Von
Housmann. It is of him I am going to tell you. He was a
German—and a good man. A great naturalist, and a true
friend. He sucked the poison from my leg once, when a
snake had bitten me. I thanked him and said I'd repay him
some day. I did—sooner than I had thought—with a bullet! I could not bear to see him suffer."

The man sat gazing into the flames, and I listened to
the dripping rain fingering the bare boughs and *tap-tap-
tapping* on the roof above.

My friend looked up.

"I was seeing his face in the flames," he said. "God help
him! . . .

"We had traveled for days—weeks—how long does not
matter. We had camped and moved on; we had stopped
to gather specimens—always deeper into that evil undergrowth. And as we moved on, Von Housmann and I grew
closer; one either grows to love or hate in such circumstances, and Sigmund was not the sort of man one would
hate. I tell you, I loved that man!

"One day we struck into a new place. We had left the
tracks of other expeditions long before. We trekked along,
unmindful of the exotic beauty of our surroundings, when
I saw our native, who was up ahead, stop short and sniff
the air.

"We stopped, too, and then I noticed what the keener, more primitive sense of our guide had detected first.

"It was an odor. A strange odor, indefinable and sickening. It was filled with foreboding—evil. It smelt—*gray!* I can not describe it any other way. It smelt dead. It made me think of decay—decay, and mold, and—ugly things.

"I shuddered. I looked at Von Housmann, and I saw that he, too, had noticed it.

"'What is that smell?' I asked.

"He shook his head.

"'*Ach,* dot is new. I haf not smelled it before. But—I do not lige it. It iss not goot. Smells is goot or bat—und dot is not goot. I say, I do not lige dot smell.'

"Neither did I. We went ahead, cautiously now. A curious scent pervaded the air. It puzzled me. Then it struck me: *silence.* Silence, as though the music of the spheres had suddenly been snuffed out. It was the utter cessation of the interminable chirping and chattering of the birds and monkeys and other small animals.

"We had become so accustomed to that multitudinous babel that its absence was disturbing. It was—eery. Yes, that's the word. It made that first impression of lifelessness more intense. Not death, you understand. Even death has in it a thought of life, an element of being. But this was just—lifelessness.

"The gray odor had become so strong that it was wellnigh unbearable. Then we saw our guides running back to us. They rebelled. They refused to go beyond the line of trees ahead. They said it was *taboo.*

"That ended it. No promise, no threat, nothing would move them. Do you know what a savage's *taboo* is? It is stronger than death. And this place was *taboo.* So we left them there with our stuff, and Sigmund and I went on alone. We reached the farthest line of trees and stopped on the edge of a clearing.

"I can't describe that sight to you. But I can see it— good God, how I can still see it! Sometimes I wake up in the night with that nightmarish picture in my eyes, and my nostrils filled with that ghoulish stench.

"It was a field of gray; almost, I might have said, a field of *living* gray. And yet it did not give the impression of life. It moved, although there was not a breath of wind; not a leaf on the trees quivered, but that mass of gray wriggled and crawled and undulated as though it were a huge gray shroud thrown over some monstrous jelly-like Thing. And that Thing was writhing and twisting.

"The gray mass extended as far as I could see ahead. To the right the sandy shore of the river stopped it, and to the left and in front of us it terminated at a distance of a few yards away from the trees where a belt of sand intervened.

"I don't know how long we stood there, my friend Von Housmann and I. It fascinated us. At last he spoke.

"'*Heilige Mutter. Was kommt da?* Vot in der name off all dot iss holy do you call dot? Nefer haf I seen such before. Eferyvere I haf traffeled, but nefer haf I seen a sight lige dot. I tell you, it makes my flesh crawl!'

"'It makes me sick to look at it,' I answered. 'It looks like—like living corruption.'

"The old German shook his head. He was baffled. We knew we were looking upon something that no living mortal had ever gazed upon before. And our flesh crawled, as we watched that Thing writhing beneath its blanket of gray.

"We walked slowly and cautiously across the strip of sand to the edge of the gray patch. As I bent over, the pungency of the odor bit into the membrane of my nostrils like an acid, and my eyes smarted.

"And then I saw something that drove all other thoughts from my mind. The mass was a moss-like growth of tiny gray fungi. They were shaped like miniature mushrooms, but out of the top of each grew a countless number of antennae that ceaselessly twisted and writhed in the air. They seemed to be feeling and groping around for something, and it was this incessant movement that gave to the patch that quivering undulation which I had noticed before.

"I stared until my eyes ached. 'What do you make of it?' I ask my friend.

"*Ach,* I do not know. It iss incombrehensible. I haf nefer seen such a—a t'ing in my whole, long life. It iss, I should say, some sort off a fungoid growt'. Ya, it iss clearly dot. But der species—um, dot iss not so clear. Und dose liddle feelers; on a fungus dot iss new—it iss unheard off. See, *die verdammte* t'ings iss lige lifting fingers; dey svay und tvist lige dey vas feeling for somet'ings, not? I am egseedingly curious. Und I am baffled—und, my friendt, I do not lige dot.'

"Impatiently, he reached out a stick he was carrying, a newly cut, stout cudgel of dried wood. He stirred around with it in the growth at his feet. And then a cry broke from his lips.

"*Ach, du lieber Gott—gnädiger Gott im Himmel! Sieh' da!*'

"I looked where he was pointing. His hand trembled violently—and little wonder! The stick, for about twelve inches up, was a mass of gray!

"And as I watched, I saw, steadily growing before my eyes, that awful gray creep up and surround the wood. I'm not exaggerating; in less time than it takes to tell, it had almost reached Von Housmann's hand. He threw it from him with an exclamation of horror.

"It fell into the gray growth and instantly vanished. It seemed to melt away.

"Sigmund looked at me. He was pale. At last he sighed.

"'So-o-o! Ve learn. On vood it grows. I might haf guessed. Dot iss der reason dot no trees are here. It destroys dem. But so *schnell;* ach, lige fire it growed. My friendt, I lige dot stuff lesser *als* before. It is not healt'y. But vot vill it not eat?'

"I handed him my rifle. He took it, and poked the growth with the muzzle. Man, my hair fairly stood on end! Do you know anything about fungi? No? Well, I have never known or heard of any vegetable growth that would attack blue steel. But that stuff—I tell you, that rifle barrel sprouted a crop of that gray mass as quickly as had the wood!

"I grabbed the gun and lifted it out of the patch. Already several inches of steel had been eaten—literally *eaten*—off. I held it up and watched that damnable gray crawl along the barrel. It just seemed to melt the metal. It melted like sealing-wax, and great gray flakes dropped off to the ground.

"Nearer and nearer it came—to the rear sight, the trigger-guard, the hammer. It was uncanny—like a dream. I stood there, paralyzed. I could not believe what my eyes told me was true. I looked at Sigmund. His mouth was open and his face was white as death. I laughed at his face. That seemed to tear away the mist. He yelled and pointed, and I looked down.

"Not two inches from my hand was that mass. I could see those feelers reaching out toward my hand, and I was sick. Instinctively, I threw the gun from me, aimlessly, blindly. It fell on the sand belt outside the gray mass.

"Hardly had it struck the sand before the growth had readied the butt, and then there was nothing to be seen but a tiny patch of that gray, poisonous Thing. And as we looked, it began to melt. Gradually, steadily, it was disappearing.

"'Quick, quick,' shouted Von Housmann, and we ran over to the spot. By bending over, we could see what was happening.

"The feelers, or antennae, which we had noticed before, had vanished, but instead, at the base of each individual plant, there were similar tendrils, but more of them—thousands and thousands of them all feeling and groping frantically about. And as they swayed and twisted and brushed the sand, one by one they shriveled up and seemed to withdraw into the parent body.

"Gradually this nucleus itself shrank and withered, until it was no more than a tiny gray speck on the sand. Soon that was all that was left: a lot of tiny whitish particles, much lighter in color than the original plant, scattered around on the sand.

"I looked at Von Housmann, and he looked at me. After a long interval, he spoke, slowly, almost as though it were a painful effort.

"'Ant'ony, ve haf seen a—miracle. From vot, or how, or ven, dot hell-growt' sprang, I do not know. I do not know how many, many years it has stood here; maybe it has been here for centuries. But I do know dis: if dot sand was not here—vell, I shudder to t'ink off vot vould be today.'

"I stared.

"'You do not understand? Ach, so! You haf seen vot happened to dot stick? Und to dot gun of steel? So! Look, now.'

"He took off his hat and went over to the border of the patch. He touched— just barely touched the brim of the hat to the gray matter and held it up. Already a growth was moving up the linen. He nodded, then threw it away, onto the sand. Speechless, we watched it fade away under the merciless attack of that horrible stuff, and then, in turn, the gray fungoid growth wither and disappear.

"'Now do you understand? Do you see vot I meant? Vood, steel, linen—eferyt'ing vot it touches it *eats*. It grows fast—like flame in dry sticks—all-consuming. *Aber—siehst du?*—dot sand, ven it touched dot, it died. It starved. Und see! Look close—more closer still—at dot sand. Do you see anyt'ing odd about it?'

"I shook my head. It looked very fine and light, but I could not see anything unusual.

"'No? Iss it not glass, dot sand? Look at it und at der sand vere dot Ting has not been, and see if it is not so different.'

"I picked up some sand from under my foot. And then I saw what he had seen at once. The sand in my hand was coarser, dirtier—in short, like any fine-grained sand you may have seen. But the sand where the gray stuff had fallen was clear, glass-like. It was almost transparent, and I saw that what was there was a mass of silica particles. I nodded.

"'Yes,' I said. 'I see now. That stuff has eaten out every particle of mineral, of dirt and dust, but not the silica!'

"'Egsactly! Und dot iss vot has safed us from—Gott only knows vot! I do not know vot dot stuff vill eat, but I *do* know it vill not eat silica. Vy? I do not know. Dot is yet a mystery. So, it starts; *ach,* dot too, I do not know—but it starts somewhere. Und it eats und grows, and grows und eats, und eferyt'ing vot it touches it consumes—egsept sand. Sand stops it.

"'It eats out der stuff in der sand, but not der silica, und starves und dies. It is a miracle. If der sand vas not here—ach, Gott!—it vould keep on going until—vell, I do not know! I haf nefer seen dot before. I am intrigued, und I am going to take dot stuff-—oh, only a liddle bit! und I shall not rest until I haf learned somet'ing about it. Und because I haf seen it does not lige sand, I vill make for it a

cage—a liddle box of glass, und study it lige it vas a bug.
Not?'

"We returned to where our natives still stood with our
packs. We quickly fitted together some microscopic slides
into a rough box and bound it about with string. With it,
we returned to the edge of the gray patch. Von Housmann
knelt down and carefully scooped up a bit of the fungus
with a glass spatula. He dumped this into his box and
waited. In five minutes it had disappeared. He looked up
blankly.

"'You forgot, Sigmund,' I said, smiling at his woeful
expression. "It starves on silica. It won't live in glass.'

"'*Ach, Dummkopf!* Of course! I haf forgot dot. But ve
vill fool dot hell-plant. He goes yet on hunger-strike—no?
Ve try now dot forcible feeding.'

"He took out his knife and cut several small splinters
from a near-by tree.

"'Ve vill feed him, so. Dot vood, it vill be for him a
great feast, und he shall eat and eat, und ve vill study him
und see vot ve vill see.'

"Laughing, he bent over and shook out the tiny gray
residue which was in the box. He dropped in a sliver of
wood and was bending over to refill his box when I felt a
sting on my foot. I looked down, and my heart stood still.

"On my shoe, just in between the laces, was a spot of
gray. I could not move. I was cold. I can not describe how
I felt, but I seemed turned to stone. My flesh quivered
and shrank and I was sick—very sick. Sigmund looked up,
startled, and then he looked at my feet.

"The next thing I knew I was on my back, my foot in
his hand. One slash of his knife across the thongs which
laced my boot, and he jerked it off.

"The biting grew worse. I heard him gasp, and then I
felt a sharp pain. My head swam and I must have fainted.

I regained consciousness—I don't know how soon after—
and I found myself back under the trees. I looked at my
foot, which was throbbing and burning like fire. It was
swathed in a bandage that Von Housmann had taken from
his emergency kit and was wrapping around the instep. It
was deeply stained with blood.

"I moved, and he looked up. He smiled when he saw I
was conscious.

"'Dot vas a close shave—yes? It had just eaten into der
shoe as I pulled it off, und one spot—lige a bencil-dot—
on your skin vas gray. So I cut it out and all around it, und
so you haf a hole in your foot, but—you haf your foot.
Now so! You lie here, und I get der men and ve take you
to bed.'

"A tent was soon erected and I was carried into it. For
two days I lay there, delirious much of the time. Sigmund
never left my side. He even slept there. He was insistent
that it was his fault. He said one of the apparently dead
fungi had dropped on my shoe and had revived there. That
is, the plant, instead of dying, had shriveled up, but the
life-nucleus was still strong. I shudder even now when I
think of what might have been.

"At the end of the third day I was able to hobble about
a little with the aid of a cane. That afternoon Sigmund
came to me and asked if I would care to go with him to
fill his little glass box. I refused, and he laughed. It was
the last time I ever heard him laugh. I begged him to leave
that stuff alone.

"Still laughing, he made some light reply and left me. I
lay in my cot. I was filled with forebodings. The heat was
intense, and I must have dropped off to sleep. I dreamed
horrible, troublesome, weird dreams. I awoke, bathed
in a cold sweat. I felt sure that something was wrong,
that someone was calling for me. I got to my feet and
left my tent. No one was in sight. I tried to laugh at my

premonition. I bitterly regretted that I had allowed my friend to override my persuasions.

"Hurrying as much as was possible, I started toward the clearing. My wound throbbed and ached. Once I stumbled in my eagerness. It was horrible—like a nightmare.

"I must have covered half the distance when I heard a scream. What a shriek it was! I wake up nights even now hearing it. It was unrecognizable—like some unearthly animal. Just that one scream. My stick hindered me. I threw it away and ran.

"My blood was cold in my veins, but I felt not one twinge of pain in my foot. At last I came to the edge of the clearing. And there—God, it makes me sick even now to think of it."

The speaker paused. His face was chalky, and he shuddered and buried his face in his hands. I think he was crying.

Outside, the wind still howled, dully, monotonously, eerily. Sometimes it would shriek and scream. Then my friend's voice again—level, dead, cold.

"I looked out, I saw Sigmund standing on the sand. I can see him as plainly as though he were here now. His face was ashen. He was looking down. At his feet were the fragments of the glass box he had made.

"He was holding out his hands, looking at them. They were gray. And they writhed and twisted, but his arms were still. He was not even trembling. My tongue clove to the roof of my mouth, and my throat was dry—but at last I called to him.

"'Sigmund! Sigmund!' I cried. 'For God's sake—'

"He looked up, and, I tell you, I never want to see such a face again! I can never forget it. It was the face of a soul in torture. He looked at me and held out his arms. His hands were gone—flaked off in large gray, writhing drops to the sand at his feet!

"He tried to smile, but couldn't.

"Another gray blob dropped off. I was dizzy with sickness. It was unbelievable. And then he spoke. His voice was well-nigh unrecognizable. It croaked and broke:

"'Done for, my friendt. I feel it eating to my heart. Be merciful and help me. *Shoot*—quick, through der foreheadt!'

"His words beat through the stupor clouding my brain, I started toward him, my hands outstretched. I could not speak.

"'*Um Gottes Willen, bleibt da!* Stop! Stop!'

"His words halted me.

"'Sigmund! My friend! What—'

"'Do not come near me! Vould you also be so tormented? Vot dot Gray touches it consumes. Do not argue, I say, but shoot! *Heilige Mutter!* Vy do you not shoot?'

"His voice rose into a shriek of agony. What was left of one arm had sloughed off, and the other was almost gone. A little mound of gray grew larger at his feet. His flesh was consumed, skin, blood and bone absorbed by that vile gray Thing, and he shrieked in agony and prayer. Both arms were gone, and the stuff at his feet had already begun to eat through his boots.

"I shot him, between his eyes. I saw him fall, and I fainted. When I came to, there was only a mound of tiny gray fungi, greedily reaching their hellish tentacles for sustenance and slowly shriveling into tiny light gray specks of dust on a glossy patch of sand."

THE MAN-TRAP
Hamilton Craigie

The laboratory of Professor Pordenone was a strange and curious place. Entering it, you were immediately sensible of an odor that was like an emanation, rising, head-high, in an almost overpowering perfume, sickish-sweet; it was like the close smell of a hot-house, but magnified, as if a giant had dealt there in his strange garden of distorted smells.

For it was a place of giants: out of the loam, that was like a thing of life, there rose, gigantic, plants that towered to the height of a tall man, and beyond it; in the green gloom of a perpetual twilight they rose up, monstrous, misshapen, like a forest of fantastic shapes seen in the dim shuttle of a dipsomaniac's dream.

And there was this about it: you could hear the silence, if you were there to hear it, for it was like the silence of a vault, a singing silence, a silence as of waiting, heavy, like a weight upon the ears, until—you opened the door.

Then—as if at the quick whisper of a sudden wind, there would come a rustle, a murmur, a *movement* in that greenish gloom—but there would be no wind, although the sound followed always upon the opening of the door.

Now, with the opening of the door, there was revealed a grinning, hairless head, three-pointed; the eyes chill, with a fixed, unwavering, unwholesome brightness, like a painted flame. A moment it peered and grimaced in the doorway; then, sidling inward like a crab, Professor Pordenone surveyed his grim garden with a mirthless smile.

And now, as he stood there, the forest of viscid green seemed welcoming him; it swayed and rustled; head-high, at the height of a tall man, the giant fronds writhed and twisted as in a wind invisible, bending and swaying as in a dance of death.

But there was no wind. The air of the place, dead, heavy, lifeless, seemed brooding in a changeless calm as Professor Pordenone stood smiling and rubbing his palms. In the humid air the flame from the lighted taper in his hand rose upward in the dimness like a painted sword against that dim green background to right and left; like a licking, hungry tongue, it forked upward now as the professor turned, lean head thrust forward like a pointer at gaze.

Now his face seemed touched with a sudden, sly malevolence; his thin, spatulate fingers, reaching, had extended the taper with a little, flicking motion against a tall plant at his right.

Upon the instant, as if it had been a thing alive, the trifoliate frond had bent as a steel blade bends double; then, as a bayonet thrusts, soundless and swift, its spike-tipped lance had sprung level with his eyes.

Professor Pordenone chuckled, moving as a cat moves, for all his bulk. An inch—and the great spur had reached him, thrust in carte. The plant—*Hecate triformis*—was a hypersensitive, of course; heat acted upon it as the needle to the pole; but for a moment, fantastic as it might have been, it seemed as if it had been almost humanly endowed with motion, malevolent and swift.

The professor, moving forward, the taper still in his hand, halted now before a row; gigantic, dark-green they were, shading almost to black; ugly, as a toadstool is ugly,

ten feet in air rearing their crested hoods like cobras—
and like sleeping cobras, nodding their heavy heads with a
slow, swinging motion, to right and left.

The professor, taper held in his fingers like a baton,
seemed like a man who walked now with wariness and
care. Still with that secret smile edging his thin lips, he
faced forward now, bowing as an orchestra leader bows
before the curtain.

"My children!" he whispered, low. "Your time will
come—even now is it at hand! I, Udolfo Pordenone, have
promised you! And then—ah, then, we shall see!"

One, peering inward at that curious chamber, would
see, but he would not have believed. For, indeed, as might
be seen in any hot-house, there were foxglove, starwort,
narcissus, orchis, crane-fly and cipripedium—but hideous, distorted, monstrous beyond all imagining, thrust-
ing aloft with filaments that had grown to cables, stamens
that were like writhing columns, pistils that were like
gigantic swords.

The thing that had become a bayonet was fantastic and
dangerous enough, but it was before a curious monster
that seemed a cuttlefish rooted in black loam that the professor paused and gloated.

Beneath its soaring antennae, quivering like the sentient fingers of a giant squid, there was a flat, white disk, a
dead white, like the belly of a snake. Now, as the professor
halted before it, this curious disk quivered, shook—moved
of a sudden like a hungry mouth, subsided, as the professor, stepping backward a pace, extended the thin taper's
flame, like the flicking of a whip, which in effect it was.

"Ah—not yet, my friend!" the low voice murmured.
"Not yet awhile—but—patience—and it shall be a fact
accomplished."

2

Professor Pordenone was in his way a genius, though a
perverted one. That plants could feel, that they could even
see, he was aware, just as a schoolboy is casually conscious
of the inevitableness of two and two. The East Indian sage
who had, by an almost miraculous devising, been able to
observe with his super-delicate instruments, the death
throes of a flower [a fact; featured in the newspapers of
May, 1923], stood merely at the threshold, where the professor had passed onward through the door.

Now, as he went outward from his laboratory, he smiled
thinly as if in anticipation: an indwelling, secret smile
that lingered as he closed shut the heavy door with its
patent spring lock.

He stood now in a lofty, dark corridor leading to his
bachelor quarters, a study and a bedchamber, where, alone,
he slept and ate, poring over his formulae like another
Faustus, delving in the dark secrets of life and of death.

Passing, with his swift, silent step, into his study, and to
an elaborate escritoire in the corner, he snapped on the light,
for it had come on to evening, and took up a small vial from
the desk. In a large, square tub to the right of this desk
there was a plant; it was little more than a seedling; but
even to its infinitesimal, flat disk, it was a perfect replica
of that Gargantuan horror in the dim garden just beyond.

The professor, holding the vial to the light, shook it
gently from right to left, removing its glass stopper, in
his eyes a queer, greenish light seeming to be mirrored in
the contents of that vial, milk-pale. One drop—a milli-
gram of that candescent liquid—and, as he was wont to
say, he could grow trees from grass-blades. That seedling
now—well, in the morning he would—give it new life.
Meanwhile. . . .

Propping the vial against a corner of the desk, he took
from a cellaret at his elbow a goblet of old Faience, and

with it a decanter. He drank, once, and again. . . . The vial, unheeded, tilted sidewise, so that, unseen, perhaps three drops of its potent liquid spilled over upon that Lilliputian seedling in its tub. Tomorrow—ah, tomorrow, as he had planned it from the first, he expected a visitor: Gammage, the orchis-hunter—Gammage, who had laughed at his assertions, laughed at him, Udolfo Pordenone, the great, cited innumerable precedents for his confounding, snapped his fingers at him, belittled him, scoffed at him times without number.

And tomorrow Gammage—would pay.

But first he would show him the proof; after that his enemy would disappear, and by an agency that was neither beast nor human; an agency terrible in its swift, silent vengeance that would indeed leave no trace.

Stoppering the vial with fingers that trembled in their eagerness, he rose, stumbling against the seedling in its tub. A large green-bottle fly, its motion swift as summer lightning, its drone loud in the stillness, evaded the slow sweep of his hand to dip in a bewildering, swift spiral downward across the tub.

Upon the instant there came a furious, frantic buzzing, and then—silence. The fly was gone. But the windows and doors were closed; it could have had no egress from the room. But if the professor had glanced downward at that tub he would have seen that that flat, white disk had strangely broadened two diameters even as he had sat there at the desk.

But he did not look. Those giant monsters in that garden of grim shapes had once been seedlings, some of them, indeed, scarce older than from sun to sun. . . .

The professor, snapping out the light, moved slowly, with a slow, noiseless chuckle, outward to his bedchamber, while behind him as he slept, separated from his bedroom by the width of a single door, there grew and continued a

slow, stealthy rustle: Life, hideous, malformed, rising like
a dim tide ceilingward, there in the murmurous dark.

3

Professor Pordenone, awaking at his usual hour, dressed
in a queer, fumbling haste, departing presently upon an
errand which was to occupy the best part of his day.

He had been upon the point of returning to his study
when, upon an impulse, he had wheeled, his hand upon
the doorknob, in a curious, sudden indecision, which, if
he had been superstitious, he might have called a presentiment—a premonition of a something felt but unseen, hidden yet half-revealed. The liquor that he had drunk had
been potent; that must be it; and his errand could not wait.

And so he had turned backward, striding from the house,
to return at evening, an evening, after rain, of windy dark,
with the wind like a lost soul wailing among the trees, the
road like a ribbon of pale flame between black walls of
ebony, along which his tall, dark figure with its flapping
coat-tails went onward to that rendezvous with death.

The house of Professor Pordenone stood alone on a little rising ground about which was the marshland and the
river. Now, as the lean scarecrow, with its veiled glance
like a cobra's searching in the dust, went forward, there
sounded close at hand the brool of the rushing river, like a
sound heard in dreams; the cry of a loon sounded from the
marshland; the melancholy boom of a bittern answered it.

The traveler's shadow in sable silhouette cut sharp beneath the soaring splendor of the moon that was like a
leprous-silvered finger beneath the low-hung curtain of
the dark; a little wind, pattering in the dust like the feet
of an invisible army of the dead, followed him forth upon
the way; it seemed to voice, a whisper, a summons, a command—but the dark figure was oblivious.

And then, between the nightfall and the night, he beheld a black shadow in the door.

It was Gammage.

The orchis-hunter moved forward as the Italian came up.

"Ah, professor!" he said. "You are on time, I perceive.
I was a little early. I've been waiting . . . five minutes . . .
but—no matter; we've time, and to spare."

Professor Pordenone observed his visitor under lowered
brows.

"Ah, yes," he made answer, with a precise, hissing sibi-
lance. "Quite so, my friend: you have—all the *time* there is."

The accent upon the word was of the faintest. He
paused, his face a white, glimmering oval against the background of the night.

"What is it your Shakespeare says?

> Time hath, my Lord, a wallet on his back
> in which he puta alms for oblivion.

"Is it not so, my friend?"

His dark, Italian face, with its high cheek-bones,
showed in a darkling glimmer beneath the tall, shapeless
hat; with his wide, foreign cloak, and the white, slender
hands moving against the black, there was about him a
sinister air, a something hooded and malign, his glance
upon his visitor as if the very soul of the man had arisen,
deep down, to peer for a moment out of his cold eyes in a
sudden, sardonic flicker of unholy mirth.

The orchis-hunter may have been aware of it; perhaps
something of this may have been reflected in his look, his
tone. Moving outward from the doorway, he shivered slightly in the humid air, for it was not cold. Yet it was as if a
bleak wind of the spirit had touched him, and passed on.

"Ugh! Someone's walking over my grave!" he muttered,
turning aside as Professor Pordenone moved forward to
unlock the door.

The wind, rising, clamored at eave and shutter as the door fell open with a slatting clatter; it shrieked in the chimney on a rising note as the two men, the professor in the lead, went inward to the house.

Here in the bedchamber all was darkness and silence, save for the measured ticking of the hall clock, like the beating of a heart; the squeak and scurry of rats in the wainscot; else was it a silence upon which these empty sounds beat and were lost as rain-drops upon velvet.

The professor, his finger upon the wall-switch, snapped on the light, pointing forward to the closed door leading to his study.

"In there, my friend," he said, "I have a surprise for you; it will take but a moment; through the study, and into my garden; for you must see—you must—ah—*feel* before you will believe. But—*che sara sara*—what will be will be, my friend; is it not so?"

He ceased, and the long, wild laughter of the winds fled past the dripping eaves. Under the lights his face, with its high-arched, broken nose, showed in a Rembrandtesque shading of high light and shadow, like a Savonarola debased.

Then, with his hand upon the doorknob, he paused. Under the light his face, stripped for a moment of its mask, showed for a fleeting instant, like the face of a satyr, satanic in its ultimate suggestion of sheer, feline malevolence; the words purred in the silence like a cat's:

"Now—my friend—in a moment now—you will see. Have I not promised you?"

He flung wide the door to a black velvet wall of Stygian dark, out of which there came on a sudden a rustling as of invisible pinions, and with it an odor, strong and almost fetid; it swept out upon them in a dim tide of soundless flood.

The professor hesitated, wrinkling his nose with a delicate pinching of the thin nostrils, an odd look of surprise upon his face. But the darkness was like a wolf's throat; the single light but emphasized it; it was smothering, opaque, like the thick darkness of a vault.

Then—he disappeared into that velvet black even as Gammage, following, heard his quick foot-falls pad-padding in the dimness of the study just ahead.

The orchis-hunter froze suddenly in motion. There was a light-switch at the door; his fingers were reaching for it even as, from that midnight black, there came a sound inhuman, beastlike, such as nothing he had ever heard, or would hear, by God's grace, while he might live. Once, on a stricken field, he had heard that sound, or something near it: the scream of a horse in its last agony; it rose now even as he fumbled for the light-switch—died to a choked gurgle, a long, shuddering sigh.

Then—he snapped on the switch, and as the light sprang to full flower, at what he saw or thought he saw a weakness seized upon him, and a quick horror turning his bones to water. For there, towering to the lofty ceiling, uprose a thing, monstrous, unbelievable, a thing that, with its waving tentacles of viscid green, stood like a giant squid, rooted in black loam. And then, beneath the flat white disk that was its mouth, the orchis-hunter saw, and seeing, fled outward, trembling, blind and dumb, to the clear air of heaven.

For the thing that he had seen, agonized, contorted, ere it disappeared forever, sucked downward in that insensate maw, had been—the face of Professor Pordenone!

The Fly-Trap, magnified ten thousand diameters; the seedling, grown overnight to the monster that it had become; the fleshless Frankenstein had found its victim.

The Man-Trap had made its kill.

THE PLANT-THING

R. G. Macready

"This morning, Dick, I have something special for you," said Norris, city editor of the *Clarion*, as I approached his desk. "Interview with Professor Carter. You've heard of him, of course?"

"Certainly," I replied. "There are some rather weird stories concerning him."

"Exactly. And the latest of these stories is that Carter is conducting wanton vivisection on a prodigious scale. Holder, of the local Society for the Prevention of Cruelty to Animals, went over yesterday to investigate but was turned away at the gate. He laid the matter before me and I promised to try for an interview."

"Who started the vivisection story?"

"Several farmers, according to Holder. During the past four months they've sold Carter more than a hundred and fifty pigs, sheep, and calves. It is well known that the professor is a scientist and not a stock raiser; ergo he dissects the animals. . . . Can you start now?"

En route to the Carter home I stopped at a hardware store and bought a thirty-foot length of rope. I foresaw difficulty in securing admittance to the professor's domain.

While driving, I brought to mind everything I knew about him. Four years ago he had bought the old Wells

163

place, ten miles west of town. No sooner had it passed into
his hands than he commenced the construction of a high
board wall about the five acres, in the center of which the
house was situated. The wall completed, he had moved
in with a young lady, apparently his daughter, and eight
Malay retainers. From that time on he and his household
might have been dead for all the town saw of them. Our
tradesmen made frequent trips to the place, but all their
business was transacted with a Malay at the gate.

I drove rapidly and soon came in sight of my destination, which stood on a hill a half mile back from the road.
Five minutes later I drew up before the gate, and in response to my hail the Malay appeared. He was a nice-look-
ing young chap, dressed irreproachably, and spoke excellent English. I gave him my card and after a perfunctory
glance at it he shook his head.

"I am sorry, sir, but it is the master's order that no one
be admitted; and if you will pardon my saying so, least of
all, representatives of the press."

"But my business is urgent. Serious charges have been
laid against him, and it is possible that I may be the
medium by which these charges are refuted."

The Malay's ivory teeth flashed in a smile.

"Thank you, sir, but I do not doubt that the master
is able to take care of himself. Good day." This last was
spoken in a tone of polite finality as he turned on his heel
and walked away.

I entered my car and drove back to the highway. However, I was determined to get that interview by crook if
not by hook; if I may say it, this policy of mine had made
me star reporter of the *Clarion*'s staff. So I continued on
down the road a few hundred yards and parked the car in
the grove, where it was hidden well. I then took the coil of
rope and made my way through the grove, which swung in

a huge, narrowing semicircle up the hillside to the north-west corner of the Carter grounds. Arrived there under the fifteen-foot wall, I looked cautiously about me. So far as I could see, I was unobserved.

Just within the wall grew a great oak, one of whose major branches extended well outside. Quietly I flung one end of my rope over this limb, fashioned a running noose, and drew the rope tight. Then slowly I wormed up the barrier.

From the top I gazed down upon a glory of wonderful, luxuriant flora. Stately ferns waved gently in the stirring air, beautiful flowering shrubs were interspersed here and there, while everywhere in the emerald grass, still wet with dew, nodded strange, exotic plants. Ever a lover of flowers, I forgot my mission as I looked. There came to my nostrils odors more fragrant and elusive than any I had heretofore known.

Suddenly I crouched low. On noiseless feet there passed beneath me a Malay, who had emerged without warning from a clump of ferns. He paused for a moment to brush an insect from a shrub, then disappeared from view in a thicket of high, green bushes.

Stealthily I slid to the ground and started toward the house, guiding myself by the observations I had made while on the wall. It was very likely, indeed, that the professor would kick me forth the instant he discovered my presence, but at any odds I should have something to tell the readers of the *Clarion*. Too, my audacity might count in my favor.

I had not gone far before I became conscious of an odor utterly different from the others. It was vague, but none the less disquieting. A feeling of loathing and dread pervaded me, a desire to clamber back over the wall and return to the city. The scent came again, much stronger, and I stood irresolute for several minutes, fighting down a sense of faintness as well as the longing to take flight. Then I advanced. In thirty seconds I came to the edge of a small, open space. At what I beheld, I put out a hand to a large fern to steady myself.

In the middle of that tiny clearing grew a thing that, even now, I shudder to describe. In form it was a gigantic tree, unspeakably stunted, fully twelve feet in diameter at the base and twenty-five feet high, tapering to a thickness of two feet at the top, from which depended *things*—I cannot call them leaves—for all the world resembling human ears. The whole was of a dead, drab color.

Dreadful as was the appearance of the thing, it was not that which made me reel as I looked. It was writhing and contorting, twisting itself into all manner of grotesque shapes. And *eyes* were boring into me, freezing the current of my blood.

Something rustled in the grass. I looked down and saw an immense creeper snaking toward me. For the first time I observed that it was joined to the trunk of that frightful thing, and so near the ground that I had not seen it for the tall grass. With a cry of horror I turned to run.

The creeper leapt at me and fastened around my middle with horrible force. I felt something in me give way. Frantically, I struck and tore at the ghastly, sinuous girdle that encircled me, undulating like the tentacle of an octopus. Fruitless, fruitless! I was drawn relentlessly forward.

I screamed. In the trunk of the thing there had appeared a mighty, red-lipped orifice. The tentacle tightened and I was lifted off my feet toward that orifice.

A beautiful girl was bending over me when I opened my eyes. She spoke, in a musical voice: "Please do not move. One of your ribs is broken."

A tall, gray-haired man who had been standing in the background now came to my bedside.

"I am glad that I came in time, my boy. Otherwise . . ."

He was Professor Carter. He presented the girl as his daughter Isobel.

Here one of the dark-skinned servants entered with some articles, which he deposited upon the center table.

"I am going to set your rib," announced the professor. And forthwith he took off his coat and rolled up his sleeves. When the job was finished to his satisfaction, I besought him to telephone to town for a taxicab.

"I shall certainly do no such thing," he said. "I insist that you remain our guest until you are recovered."

Isobel Carter proved a wonderful nurse during the three days that followed. Indeed, the moment I had first looked into her deep black eyes, I knew that I loved her. I should have liked to remain in bed indefinitely with her to care for me, but was ashamed to do so. On the third morning I was moving cautiously about the house, she supporting my steps, although there was no need of it. The professor joined us.

No mention had been made of my weird adventure in the grounds, but at my request he now told me how I had been saved from the hideous creature.

"Your first cry reached my ears as I was walking toward the house and I immediately dashed in its direction. You were about to be swallowed when I arrived. I gave a sharp command, and my travesty released you."

"It obeyed your command?" I exclaimed incredulously.

"Precisely. It acknowledges me as its master. For six months, its period of life so far, I have superintended its growth and ministered to its needs.

"But *what* is it?"

A dreamy look came into Carter's eyes.

"For many years my brother scientists have sought for the so-called 'missing link' between man and ape. For my part, I dare to believe that I have discovered the 'link' between the vegetable and animal kingdoms. The creature out there, however, has, to my mind, not as yet passed the initial stage of its development. Whether it will attain the power of locomotion remains to be seen."

He paused, gazing out of the window, then continued.

"Twenty years ago, in Rhodesia, I chanced upon a carnivorous plant that gave me my clue. Since then I have labored unremittingly, crossing and recrossing my specimens, and you have seen the result. It has cost me three fourths of my fortune, and countless trips to Asia and Africa." He indicated a vast pile of manuscript on the table.

"The life history, precedents included, of my travesty. It will form the basis of a work that, I do not doubt, will revolutionize science."

Glancing at the clock, he rose to his feet.

"It is feeding time. Do you care to accompany me?"

I assented, and we went out.

The thing remembered me, for the huge tentacle swept out in my direction, curling impotently in the empty air. I shuddered, and kept my distance.

A Malay appeared leading a calf. It was lowing piteously, for it had sensed danger.

The tentacle thrashed about, endeavoring to clutch the animal, which lunged back, wild with terror. The man wrapped his arms about it and hurled it forward. It was seized. A loud cracking of bones broke the momentary silence, and was followed by an agonized cry. Six feet from the ground the great orifice gaped wide. The calf disappeared. A fleeting second and the mouth closed. There was no sign of its location; the trunk was smooth and unbroken.

A nausea had gripped me during the scene. The professor and the Malay were apparently indifferent. They conversed briefly. Then, linking his arm in mine, Carter led the way back to the house. As we walked thither, I broached the subject of departure. He would not hear of it, insisting that I stay until Saturday.

While in his study I had noticed an elephant gun in a corner. I asked him whether he had done any big-game hunting.

"That gun? Tala had me get it. He asserted that he could foretell tragedy in connection with the creature; that a day would come when I should lose control of it. I scouted the idea, but to humor him purchased the weapon, which stands there loaded in the event need of it arises. Still, it would assuredly break my heart if anything necessitated the slaying of my travesty."

At the door of his study he excused himself and went in. Isobel carried me off to the veranda hammock. As we talked, it was inevitable that the subject of the plant-thing should come up, and a shadow crossed her face as we discussed it.

"Tala says that Father does not know how dangerous it is. He is right. But Father will not listen."

The next morning I again went with Professor Carter to the little clearing.

It was a sheep this time. The poor beast was paralyzed with fright, and stood passive, waiting for death.

The tentacle shot forth, wavered a second, then encircled, not the sheep, but Professor Carter, who seemed stricken by surprise.

He ripped out an order: "Off!"

The tentacle only tightened. Agony settled upon Carter's face. I sprang forward to drag him back. The tentacle released its hold for one lightning flash, then seized us

both. We strove in vain against the vise-like cable. The
Malay, with a wild cry, turned and rushed down the path,
shouting as he ran.

The thing was playing with us as a cat plays with mice
it has caught.

It could have crushed us effortlessly, but the tentacle
tightened by degrees. In spite of all we could do, we felt
that we were being dragged forward to where the frightful
red mouth yawned. Our eyes bulged, and I could see that
Carter's face was taking on a greenish tinge. I extended my
free arm and our hands clasped. Then there was the roar of
a gun at close quarters and the tentacle gave a spasmodic
jerk that flung us twenty feet. We rose, staggering.

Tala stood by, the smoking elephant gun in his hands,
staring at the thing. Following his eyes we discerned a
large, ragged hole in its trunk, from which a stream of
blood was flowing and forming a great pool on the ground.

Even as we looked, the travesty went into the death
agonies. And as it writhed it emitted a sound that forever
haunts me. Presently its struggles ceased. The professor
buried his face in his hands.

I had not noticed Isobel's presence. Now I turned and
saw her beside me, gazing with horror-filled eyes at the
terrible drooping form. I took her away from that tragic
spot, for I knew that Professor Carter wished to be alone.

DORNER CORDAIANTHUS

Hester Holland

From the time of his leaving college when I first met Dorner, his whole life was given up to research work.

He was an ardent palæobotanist and his passion for delving into the history of bygone plants was as keen as that of an archæologist among mummies. Like them, he was prepared to go through any dangers for the sake of new discoveries and I received letters from all parts of the world where he was digging among the rocks in the hope of finding fossils of unknown prehistoric plants.

His house in Surrey, where he lived with his old servant, contained the cabinets where he kept the magnificent collection of curiosities and relics of ever-growing interest. Apart from these botanical treasures the rooms were a museum for rare shells, weird insects, precious stones, idols and whatnots. I would spend happy weekends browsing among these curios, and I'm afraid I envied him the job, which seemed infinitely better than my stockbroking one.

However, at forty Dorner had still not attained his ambition. When I could get down from town for the evening, we would potter round his charming garden and discuss his pet scientific points.

'I am positive,' he would say, 'that some day they will discover a fossilised seed in which a fertile embryo will be

found. Then we will really be able to know what a prehistoric plant was like.'

We argued this point so often, I used to tease him.

'How can you expect a seed that has been embedded for
millions of years to sprout? You might as well hope to find
a sleeping Dinosaur. Besides, seeds germinate upon the
ground, not on the plant, and in that time of great heat
they germinated at once.'

He would put forth the instance of the toad that had
been imprisoned in a stone for centuries and was still alive.

'A reptile,' I said. 'We are talking of vegetables.'

Dorner had a theory that the missing link between human beings and the rest of the living world would eventually be established through plants. He argued that the
functions of plants are identical with those of men.

'They have never gone on their bellies like animals, I
believe there is a direct connection between them and us.'

'Well, how did we manage about our roots?' I would
put in.

'It is hardly necessary for some plants to have roots.
They exist chiefly by air taken in by their leaves.'

Sitting in his garden one evening on the day before
his departure on a long tour of research, he broke silence
by saying, 'You know, I think the legend of the mandrake
must have some truth in it.'

'The Mandrake was supposed to squeak, wasn't it?' I
asked.

'It screamed when it was uprooted and the roots had
a human shape. Don't you see a connection with Dante's
story of the free people in Hell and the Maya symbol of a
branching body?'

'I can't quite see what you are driving at. Those were
allegories.'

'There is truth at the bottom of all allegories and legends. The fact has been proved time and time again. Why,

there are meat-eating plants now, plants that move, that have digestive powers as we have.'

'Well?' I asked.

'Millions of years ago, in some great geological up-heaval there may have been destroyed a plant which had become free of the soil. Which lived by oxygen as we do.'

'A kind of emancipated cabbage?' I suggested.

It was impossible not to poke fun at Dorner. He was like a child when he got on to his pet theory but he took my chaff in good part.

Next day I saw him off on his expedition to India, where he was to lead a research party to the lesser-known portions of Gondwana Land. This region they knew to be rich in species of Permo-carboniferous flora. Dorner looked like a plant himself as he stood on the deck, waving goodbye. His thin little body was rigid, whilst his arms brandished a walking-stick and two green-topped butterfly nets. After a few months I began to have letters from him. They had found some excellent specimens of Glossopteris flora, relics of some hitherto unknown plants. They had had exciting adventures with snakes, and so on.

After that I heard no more until one morning I received a telegram from a remote station in India. It was like Dorner to wire. In his excitement he couldn't wait for the post to impart his news. What he had to say thrilled me, though I was not so keen on Palæobotany as my friend.

'Returning at once. Discovered apparently fertile seed. Sail Sinai June 26th. Dorner.'

I realise the importance of the discovery. None of these embedded seeds had so far shown any powers of germina-tion. If this seed should quicken it would mean the re-cre-ation of a plant which had its being in those past ages that we can only guess at.

I met Dorner on his arrival in England and we went
back to his house. He seemed smaller and thinner than
ever, but wild with excitement and enthusiasm. We sat
up late in his little sitting-room, while he described his
adventures and exhibited his trophies. The wonderful seed
was displayed with the reverent pride of a young mother
displaying her first-born. It had been discovered among
several other fossilised seeds in the Talchin boulder beds.
Why it had not germinated was a mystery but it was still
fertile, and Dorner had decided to plant it under the conditions he thought would be most natural to it. In appearance it had the fleshy consistency of a nasturtium seed,
with the same crinkled skin. But whereas that is generally
green or brown, this was a sickly yellow. But one should
be lenient with a complexion when it is a few million years
old. What I could not forgive was the seed's strong resemblance to a dried maggot. I pointed this out to Dorner,
hiding my repugnance as best I could.

'You don't think you have got hold of a fossilised grub
by mistake?' I asked facetiously.

He was hovering tenderly over the curled, blackheaded
little body lying in its bed of cotton wool, and answered
with great lack of humour. 'Don't be an ass. This may prove
my theory. I wonder what sort of temperature a specimen
of this sort would require.'

For the next few weeks I believe his spirit lived in the
Palæzoic Age while he tried to emulate its climate with
what scientific aids he possessed. During this time he
was very mysterious about the seed and allowed no one
near the greenhouse where it had been planted. However,
I turned up one evening at his house, and he took me
down the garden with Tim, his fox terrier, dancing at our
heels. The little dog was no more excited than his master.
Dorner was positively trembling. The only words he said
were, 'It's sprouted. Come and see!'

The conservatory was stacked with electric heaters, artificial light and, in fact, every appliance he could think of to give the plant a better chance. He would not allow Timmy in. He might get entangled among the wires and things. We both adored Timmy. Leaving him to bark dolefully outside, we advanced into the holy of holies.

I found Dorner had arranged a kind of barricade among the seed beds. Evidently winds were not allowed to blow upon it or the sun to beat too fiercely. It might have been an Emperor's couch which we approached; but though I smiled to myself I could not but feel awe-stricken. Here was the descendant of plants which had flourished when our world of man was not thought of. When enormous and grotesque reptiles walked the oozy earth and fought with each other for the mastery. And now nothing remained of them but a few hoarded bones. Dorner switched off an electric battery which was doing its best to persuade the Embryo that it was back in the Dark Ages, and presented to me a large pot full of earth.

'I noticed it this morning,' he said in a whisper.

Bending cautiously over the earth, I saw a small white object protruding above the surface.

'Oh, is that the seed?' I asked.

He nodded, 'I've been to endless trouble getting the right chemicals for the soil. I wrote to Edgar for particulars. He is an expert on what soil was made of at that time. Judging by the result, I must have got the right ingredients.'

I looked more closely at the tiny plants and as I gazed it seemed to writhe upwards like a worm does as it presses its way through the ground. I felt suddenly sick.

'It's moving!' I said.

'Yes,' gasped my friend. 'That's the most marvellous thing about it. It shows my theory was true. It moves of its own accord.'

We went out of the stifling greenhouse to meet the joyous bounding Timmy. After that there was no doubt about the seed having germinated. To give it more freedom—there were no pots in the *Palæozoic Age*—Dorner moved it into a specially prepared bed in the greenhouse. When it was large enough to receive visitors, scientists called upon it. Reporters waited for interviews. It was photographed. Botanical papers wrote long articles about it. It was christened *Dorner Cordaianthus* as palæobotanists earnestly agreed it belonged to that family. Dorner himself considered it more of a *Cycadean* type, but subsequent events proved him wrong. I was much too ill-versed in the technical knowledge of these things to argue the point, but I was very proud of being one of the first to see it in its infancy.

It certainly grew at a tremendous pace. This may have been due to the artificial aids received. A fortnight after my first visit I inspected the plant again, and was astonished at its rapid development. The *Cordaianthus* now had the appearance of a tree and was nearly two feet high. Branch-like shoots protruded from the upper part of its stem or trunk, which measured about two inches in circumference. White in colour, it was lined all over by a network of brownish veins that evidently formed some part of a system of circulation. The whole growth was covered with fine hairs as one sees on a poppy stalk. These hairs became sharp hard points or thorns when approaching the end of the shoots. The shoots did not develop from the ends like ordinary plants. There were no budding leaves or flowers. They were in the nature of suckers, each having a worm-like heart surrounded by the thorns, while the branch body grew from the parent stem, becoming broader and longer, but never losing its original shape. These sucker-like heads expanded or contracted as the plant swayed. For it swayed like seaweed in a swell. But there was no current to sway it. As if in some unfelt wind it writhed up and down with a horrible rhythm of its own. The word growth adequately expressed the impression the plant gave me. It had the decayed appearance of a fungus, rather than the freshness of a shrub. Also, there was none of that roughness of texture one sees on the bark of shrubs. The main stem from which the branches grew was smooth as they were. The joint was invisible like the arms of a body. That was what it reminded me of. But not of a human body. More like an attenuated octopus, with its sucker-like tendrils growing out and lengthening as the thing got bigger. And it always kept up that slow, horrible swaying movement. The thing was alive like an octopus.

I turned to Dorner, who was watching it with adoring eyes.

'Have you ever tried to kill it?' I asked.

'Kill it?' he exclaimed in horror.

'Yes. Have you ever tried to find out whether it will die like an animal, I mean? Some plants are harder to kill than animals,'

'For instance?'

'Well, the ordinary convolvulus is pretty hard to eradicate from a garden. At least I find it so. Chop it off at one end, it will come up in bunches somewhere else. It has wormlike roots, rather like this!'

'Fancy comparing a common thing like that with *Cordaianthus,*' exclaimed Dorner.

'It grows nearly as quickly as this,' I answered. 'I could swear it has done some growing while we were here.'

He swelled with pride. 'Isn't it marvellous? And we are practically the first who have ever seen it.'

It certainly was wonderful, but I thought as I watched those undulating suckers moving in this blind rhythmic way that before the climate in that long past time got too hot or too cold for it, the *Cordaianthus* could not have been nearly so decorative as our simple little convolvulus.

Dorner stepped forward and touched one of the ten-drils. Instantly, as though an electric message had passed through the whole body, all the suckers turned to the one his hand rested on.

'Take care!' I cried.

A thorn had pricked him. There was a drop of blood on the whitish surface of the plant. Dorner took out his handkerchief to wipe the stain away but I stopped him, saying, 'Leave it there. It will be gone tomorrow!'

'But why should it go—and it looks beastly!'

I pointed to the sawing heads which were bunching together round the red splodge. 'They will suck it up. It's blood they want.'

Dorner stared at me. 'You mean it's insectivorous, but it's quite a different sort of plant.'

'I think it's carnivorous,' I answered. 'You'll have to give it something to eat. Those worm things want something more than carbon dioxide.'

Just outside the greenhouse door, on our way in to tea, was a small white object pressing its way through the turf.

I showed it to Dorner. 'You needn't have worried about all those electric contrivances. Our *Cordaianthus* seems to be making itself very much at home.'

My friend was on his knees examining the tiny shoot.

'It must have sunk its roots right under the greenhouse,' he said in an awed voice.

I laughed. 'The climate of England seems to agree with it. You'll be having it popping through the drawing-room carpet next. I believe it gnaws its way up.'

'Rot!' said Dorner. 'It's funny it hasn't any leaves, though, perhaps there will be some kind of bloom. Well, let's hope it will be a nice looking one whenever it thinks fit to come out.'

We went in to tea.

I was right about the plant's growth. In a week or so Dorner's lawn was punctuated with its writhing tendrils. Evidently it grew faster under ground than in the air. Dorner was obliged to destroy some of them. He even dug down and cut the roots away, but this was as useless as destroying a convolvulus. He said it was like cutting worms in half and made him sick. Then the neighbours who at first were anxious to have cuttings from the new plant began to complain. The *Cordaianthus* was sprouting all over their gardens.

'And I don't like the look of it,' said the vicar's wife. 'I've never seen a tree that moves without anything to move it. Please take it away, Mr. Dorner. It's coming up all among my vegetables.'

There began a regular campaign against the *Cordaianthus* in Dorner's garden as well as others. His lawn presented a mass of sprouting worms, to which weed-killer and the spade were vigorously applied. He was content to keep one specimen, which grew outside the greenhouse. The one inside had died of a mysterious disease. We were at a loss to know what had killed it. Dorner thought the heat had been too great, but I harboured the view it had starved to death. We watched the emaciated body quiver in a last agony like an animal.

'It wants meat,' I said, nauseated by the sight.

Dorner would not believe it was carnivorous. 'How could it get meat in the *Palæozoic Age?*' he argued. 'I'm giving it a special sort of water with chemicals in it which Edgar sent me.'

Suffice it to say, the thing died.

One evening we were sitting in the garden discussing the surviving plant. There had been a stream of complaints that morning from the houses round about. People could not eradicate the roots from their land.

'The cartloads of weed-killer they must have bought would sink a ship,' said Dorner, sighing. 'I believe they are afraid of the thing.'

'Afraid or not,' I answered. 'It's not jolly to have it hanging about in flower beds.'

My friend stroked Timmy's soft coat tenderly. 'I think there will be a flower soon, now it's got into the right environment. The greenhouse was evidently too hot. As we know it must have existed in the Permo-carboniferous strata when things were getting a bit cooler owing to glaciers. The reason for this seed having been fertile but never germinating was a sudden catastrophe of some kind— flood, earthquake or landslide, which submerged it.'

'It certainly possesses the vitality which would account for its tenacity to life,' I commented.

Dorner seemed to have dropped his theory of plant and human connection. Once or twice I caught him looking at the tree with aversion in his eyes. It stood now about four feet high, and in the full light of the afternoon sun presented a particularly white and uncanny appearance. The crowd of suckers which formed its branches curled and uncurled gently in the summer air. A vigorous extermination of all subsidiary shoots had left it for the moment the sole survivor on our lawn.

'I suppose it will die in the winter,' said Dorner presently.

'I hope so,' I answered. The remark did not cause the flare of temper I expected.

'I don't believe I should care,' he said, with the naivete of a child. 'Not since this morning.'

'What happened this morning?'

'I went up close to have a look at it and one of the suckers twisted round my arms. It took quite a time to get it off. It showed extraordinary strength.'

I stopped to pat Timmy, who lay by our feet 'Why don't you cut it down?'

Dorner looked apologetic. 'It's such an extraordinary thing; seems a pity to destroy it, but if it dies a natural death, I shan't mind. I suppose it would have to be killed sometime simply because it shows a propensity to live. I expect in the Dark Ages, or whenever the thing existed, there was plenty of room to spread. No back gardens there.' Dorner smiled. 'How keen Rayland would have been to see it. He reconstructed the *Cordaianthus,* you know, although I have never agreed this had the slightest resemblance to that family.'

As Dorner spoke, a bird fluttered on to one of the slowly moving branches. With the swiftness of a snake the bough it rested on lapped round the struggling body and crushed it to death. I sprang to my feet. If a hatchet had been in my hand instead of a stick, the tree would have been hacked to pieces. I struck furiously again and again.

Dorner came to the rescue. 'It's no use doing that. The bird's dead. There will be another cause for complaint among the neighbours if it starts eating the livestock. Evidently that's what it has been needing.'

I saw the scientist was transcendent in him, or I would have pleaded for the venomous thing to be destroyed. Dorner however was obsessed by the idea of seeing a possible flower, and would not give up that hope without a struggle.

Business kept me in town a good deal and I did not see much of him. He wrote that he was in trouble again with the neighbours. They threatened to take action against him for still keeping the plant. Then I had a heartbroken letter saying that poor little Timmy was dead. He had been found curled up in the tree with the suckers massed about his body like a swarm of bees.

'I killed the *Cordaianthus*,' wrote Dorner. 'Dug it up
and burnt it. People can't grumble any more, but it wasn't
for their silly sakes I killed the thing. I was so mad with
rage about Timmy. It might have spared him. I used to
give it hunks of meat, too.'

Poor Dorner. But one might as well bring an *Ichthy-
osaurus* into our civilised world and keep it as a pet. I
hoped he would plan another expedition soon and forget
his disappointment

I was away in Paris for a month and when I came back
I rang him up. As a rule he came to the telephone himself
and I was surprised when his old servant answered.

'The professor is not here, sir. We have been trying to
find you to ask if you knew where he had gone?'

'When did he go?' I asked.

'He's been away three days sir. I don't know what to do.
He's not left any address.'

Evidently the responsibility of his vanished master was
proving too great and the man was anxious I should come
down.

I did not feel anxious as I knew Dorner was upset about
his plant and had probably gone off for a change, not
wishing to be bothered with letters. However, things began to look serious when I found that no luggage had been
taken, and my friend had not said anything about going
away. I rang up the police. Why his man had not done so
before was a mystery to me, but I suppose he did not wish
to do so for fear of annoying Dorner. He had just gone on
from day to day, hoping his master would turn up.

The police arrived and questioned old Standish as to
when he had last seen his master. It was after tea three days
ago. He had seen Dorner go down the garden smoking a pipe.

'Did the gentleman say anything to you before he went
out?'

'Yes, sir. He said he was going out to get some weed-killer.'

'Why did he want weed-killer?'

'I don't know what he wanted it for specially, sir; he used it a good deal lately.'

'What on?'

'For that queer plant of his, sir. It kept coming up in odd places.'

'I see. And where did he keep the weed-killer?'

'In the greenhouse at the bottom of the garden.'

'And are you sure Mr. Dorner didn't come back to the house again?'

'I couldn't be sure of that, sir, because I went back to the scullery after I saw him leave the house.'

'Could you see the garden from the scullery?'

'No, sir; it's at the back.'

'And when did you begin to be disturbed at your master's absence?'

'I had supper ready for him, sir, and rang the bell, but he never came in.'

'Was he generally punctual for meals?'

'Not as a rule, sir. I've known him stay out till twelve or one o'clock in the morning. That's why I didn't worry as much as I might have done.'

'But in the morning when he was not in his room, what did you think then?'

'I didn't know what I ought to do, sir. I didn't like to ring up Scotland Yard in case he'd come in and find the place full of policemen.'

The sergeant bore this well, 'But you should have got into communication with us before this, you know. I suppose you searched the house?'

The old man had looked everywhere. The greenhouse and surrounding shrubberies were examined and the local ponds were dragged. The excitement became intense. People forgot their quarrel about *Cordaianthus* and became full of solicitude.

'Such a charming man! I do hope nothing has happened. He was so eccentric, wasn't he?'

For myself, I wished I had not left Dorner at a time when he needed a friend. I was afraid his disappointment about his plant must have affected his brain. All the same, there seemed no particular reason why he should have been so upset. I noticed several little white shoots coming up on the lawn, which showed the *Cordaianthus* was still throwing out hostages to fortune. But from where? Leaving the inspector and his men to ferret among the bushes in their search for footprints and so on, I retraced my steps to the house. A member of the Force was at the front door talking with Standish.

'And the cellars?' I heard him say. 'Did you go through them?'

There was only the wine cellar and the coal hole, but I remembered another room which Dorner always kept locked, and which the old man with his limited intelligence would not have thought of looking in. This cellar room was very dark and was used for storing certain specimens Dorner brought home which required a damp atmosphere. I did not remember it having been opened lately and suddenly understood what had been in my friend's mind when he got the weed-killer. I beckoned to the sergeant and he followed me down the cellar steps.

'I don't think Standish will have searched this part of the house,' I explained. 'Mr. Dorner generally kept this room locked. Hallo! The door's half open!'

We had come to the door and I tried to push through. It resisted me strangely, as if some soft pliant body leant against it on the inside. Then, as I persisted, the door gave way and we saw a crowd of white, slowly-moving arms stretching out towards the light. A spectral tree was growing from the damp earth floor of the cellar, its trunk long and attenuated, with branches which stretched up till they crushed against the low ceiling. In the midst of them, and close in their white embrace, was the body of Dorner. It was wrapped and locked in a mass of suckers. He must have come down here to find out where the roots came from and touched one of the starved things, by mistake. It had wound about his throat, a rooted octopus. I and the sergeant hacked it to pieces, but Dorner was dead. On some of the hairy tendrils something had grown. It was a kind of scarlet fungus, blotching over the sickly branches. The *Cordaianthus* had flowered at last—whether before or after Dorner's death no one could tell. I will not describe the condition he was in. The plant *was* carnivorous and it had taken what it could get.

THE DEVIL-PLANT
John Murray Reynolds

The public will recall the disappearance of Jonathan Darrowby, about four years ago. A noted explorer, he went alone into the jungles of Brazil and never returned. Nothing was known of him until the so-called "Darrowby Manuscript" was found, a little less than a year ago.

At first that strange document, "The Darrowby Manuscript," was believed to be a hoax. What it related was so weird, so horribly unbelievable, that it was thought to be a practical joke or the product of a diseased imagination. But now that the handwriting has been definitely established as that of Jonathan Darrowby, and Professor Briggs has located the site of Palaos, there is no longer any doubt of the authenticity of the papers.

The manuscript, or rather diary, is written in a small, leather-covered note-book. It was found on a shelf in a junk store in Para, still wrapped in the oiled silk that had protected it when found floating down the river three years before, tied to a piece of wood. The first part contained valuable but technical and rather dull notes on the author's explorations, but the last few pages are here reproduced exactly as written. J. M. R.

187

FEBRUARY 18. Arrived at Palaos today. Came here just after noon, a little mud flat at the junction of the Orinoco with a smaller stream. Desolate little place. Dark jungle walls crowding close on each hand, the muddy river flowing by, and then the delta—with half a dozen miserable hovels raised on shaky piles above the mud and a larger house (this one) standing alone behind. One of these inexplicable little settlements, fungus growths that spring up in out-of-the-way places and drag out monotonous existences. It's damp and unhealthful and fever-ridden, but it is like heaven after weeks of the jungle alone.

Natives had told me that a white man lived here, but I hadn't really believed it till I saw this house. Then I knew it was true; you could tell at first glance no native had built it. I wanted to shout aloud at the prospect of some-one to talk to after weeks of lonely silence.

As I stood there on the river bank a moment, just be-fore splashing through the shallows of the smaller stream and crossing to the village, there came a faint breeze. It was blowing *from* Palaos, and it brought a mixed odor of garbage and wet bamboo and unclean humanity. Then a new smell came down on the strengthening breeze. The odor was faint and undefinable, but it was definitely un-clean—evil. A phrase once used by an old river boatman recurred to mind: "The Devil breathes behind Palaos, *Sen-hor!*" The Devil's Breath! The thing is well named, whatever it is. Then the breeze died and the smell was no longer perceptible. With a shrug I waded through the shallows and came to Palaos.

When near enough to this house I shouted, and the owner walked out on the porch and waved his hand.

"Hello, friend," he called cheerfully in English. "Come on in. Glad to see you."

He is a queer little man, my host, this dweller in the heart of the jungle. He is fat and rotund, but he cannot be

over five feet two or three inches in height and his frame
is so small that his actual bulk is not great in spite of his
stoutness. The lower half of his face is hidden by a bushy
and unkempt black beard, and he wears the thickest spectacles I have ever seen. The heavy lenses give his eyes a
distorted look. At least, I think it's the lenses. Sometimes
I'm inclined to believe there is something a little queer
about the eyeballs themselves.

In such far-flung sentry posts as this there is little that
is artificial. The man with the beard did not even invite
me to stay: it was a foregone conclusion that I would share
his house. As I slipped the pack from my shoulders he took
it from me. He carried it in here and laid it on the floor
beside one of the two cots in the bedroom.

The little room has a floor of rough boards covered
with a coarse matting, and the walls are of smooth poles.
Beyond the netting-filled window this afternoon was a
world of sunlight with the river a brown smear across the
green of the jungle; now it is a patch of warm blackness
with insects buzzing ineffectually against the netting.

"Make yourself comfortable, friend," my host told me.
"There is water, and you will find a towel hanging on the
nail. You will wish to change your clothes, no? Somewhere
I have a suit that is for me a little big; perhaps you can
wear it. I will search."

What a relief to wash up and shed my travel-stained clothing! The white duck provided by my host is tight across
the shoulders and very short in the arms and legs, but it
can be worn. When finished, I found him out on the wide
porch, sitting in a long chair with a palm-leaf fan in one
hand and a long-stemmed amber and meerschaum pipe in
the other. He was reading a French scientific book.

"Well, friend," he said when I appeared, "how do you
feel now?"

I started to thank him, but he only made spluttering noises and refused to let me. Seems to be one of those people who are embarrassed by gratitude. Incidentally, I can't quite place his accent. It seems predominantly German, but at times it holds certain peculiar undertones I have noticed in the speech of Russians. He has not told me his origin and I have not asked. It is always better not to.

"Well, friend"—he inevitably addresses me that way—"my name is Wanless. You have not heard of me, no?"

I had to admit that I hadn't, and he laid down his pipe and slapped his plump thigh and laughed uproariously. Seemed to consider it a huge joke. At last he subsided into quiet chuckles, then added:

"No, friend, not yet. But you will. A time will come when the whole world will know the name of Wanless. I have patience. I can wait, and it will not be long now."

We sat talking all afternoon. Not for many dragging weeks have I seen a white man, and it must be years since the last one visited Palaos. Wanless tells me he has not been over a hundred miles down the river in more than ten years.

A girl came at his call and brought us drinks—necessarily warm and without ice, but refreshing for all that. I was rather surprised to see the girl. Wanless hadn't struck me as a man who would go in for that sort of thing. She is some kind of a mixed breed, part Portuguese and part Indian. Tall and slender and rather good-looking. She wore a shapeless dress of very dirty white cotton and had a square of scarlet silk tied over her head and knotted at the side. Her hair is black and straight, quite fine and silky, evidently a heritage from her Portuguese blood. Wanless calls her Lucia.

The relationship between the two is rather puzzling. Wanless tells me he bought the girl from a passing trader,

a man who abducted her from some down-river settlement and then tired of her unsubdued hatred. He also says
he keeps her because she seems contented and is useful
around the house, but the instinctive and unthinking con-
sideration he shows the girl convinces me that his feeling
really goes deeper. As for Lucia, it is evident that she wor-
ships him.

Wanless has gone to bed and is snoring loudly; I stayed
up to get these notes in shape. God! What a relief it will
be to sleep in a bed again, even a little iron cot, after
weeks of the jungle!

FEBRUARY 19. Loafed around and rested up most of the
day. It is pleasant to sit in a chair on the porch and do
nothing at all. In a day or so, after a little rest, I will move
on.

Wanless and the girl puzzle me more all the time. There
is another factor in their relationship, one more difficult
to understand. It is fear. That Wanless is unaffected by
the fear is evident; that he is not the immediate cause of
it is equally so. But I hadn't seen Lucia half a dozen times
before I was convinced that the girl lives in mortal terror of—what? Something. It shows in her eyes; there is a
latent horror in their depths that is never entirely absent.

In the middle of the afternoon Wanless joined me on
the porch and we yarned till twilight began to dim the
outlines of the mud flats before us and the jungle behind.
We spoke of the jungle and its ways, of the million unan-
swered mysteries of South America's dark interior, and of
the fascination and repugnance of this Orinoco country.
But mostly we talked of the varied life that teems in these
muddy waters and throughout the fever-ridden thickets
behind. I know a good deal about them myself, but Wanless' knowledge is extraordinary. He has a keen faculty of

observation, and an immense fund of scientific knowledge. It was just before sunset that he showed me his garden.

That man is a botanist! I firmly believe he knows more about flowers and plants and their ways than any man who has ever lived. And his garden is superb. He has a wonderful assortment of growing things, ranging all the way from giant orchids that would set any flower show crazy to miniature *nyctoginaceae* that are marvels of delicacy. I begin to realize that the man is a genius. Such of his chubby face as showed above the black beard beamed with delight at my enthusiasm.

Not all the plants in that garden are beautiful, however. Some are a little too queer for that. They are crosses. There is a whole section full of new varieties which Wanless has obtained by crossing and recrossing existing species. It is evidently the branch of his work in which he is most keenly interested, but I can't share his enthusiasm. It might be different with someone else, but I have never liked the idea of trying to set aside nature's laws in that manner. It is dangerous.

Somehow I don't think I shall ever forget that moment—the two of us standing there in that misplaced garden, with a red sun setting behind the jungle and the old Orinoco slipping muddily by. On one side the beautiful flowers with the giant orchids above them, and on the other those queer, perverted plants.

Then there came the faint stirring of a breeze. The underbrush swayed slightly, a few ripples ran across the stagnant ponds in the hollows of the mud flats, and an occasional palm frond rustled softly. Then the breeze quickened, and with it came the smell. Vile, unclean, revolting, it was the same that had greeted me when first I looked on Palaos.

The words of the old river-man again came back to me: "The Devil breathes behind Palaos, *Senhor!*" Hastily I turned to Wanless.

"What is that?" I asked.

"What is what, friend?"

"The breeze, that unholy smell!" I said impatiently.

Wanless looked at me for a long moment. Almost he spoke, then he seemed to change his mind and it was as though the shutters of his brain had closed. He shrugged.

"Who knows? The jungle has many smells, none of them pleasant!"

"Isn't that what they call 'The Devil's Breath'?" I persisted.

"Who knows?" he repeated. "I listen to no legends. Shall we go into the house?"

Whatever he knows, and I am certain he knows something, he is evidently determined to say no more at the time.

FEBRUARY 22. There is something strangely vivid about this place. The raw colors, the varied smells, the steaming noonday, the chill mists of dawn, all leave strong and not too pleasant impressions.

Nothing particular has happened, but Palaos is getting on my nerves very badly. I just get comfortable in a chair on the porch, when all at once the palms along the jungle edge begin to quiver with moving airs and the Devil's Breath comes down on the wind. Then I jump to my feet and restlessly pace the long porch, sucking on an empty pipe, till the breeze dies.

Today Wanless showed me his laboratory. I don't know the source of his income, but it must be quite substantial. That laboratory is a marvel of completeness—all the more remarkable because it is way up the Orinoco and back of nowhere. Everything in it has been transported for thousands of miles. My eye happened to be caught by half a dozen glass domes that stood against one wall. They were about the shape of the old helmets policemen used to wear, but two or three times the size.

"What are those used for?" I asked.

Wanless smiled. "Well, friend, I do not use them at all in my work any more. Some day I will show you what I did with them, but not now."

FEBRUARY 23. Have definitely determined to leave and move on in a day or so. Wanless can spare enough supplies to fit me out again.

I may even turn down river. The decision to go is a great relief, lifts a great weight from my mind. Yet I don't quite know why.

Wanless is busy in his lab or garden most of the day, but several times I noticed him walk back and disappear into the jungle behind the house. On these occasions Lucia always stands by the window without moving till he returns, stands staring at the dark wall of vegetation with the fear strong in her eyes and her face pale. Once I asked her,

"What do you fear, Lucia?"

"I fear the *thing, Senhor.*"

"What thing?"

"The *thing* in the hut, *Senhor,*" she replied, and refused to say more.

"The Devil's Breath?" I hazarded.

She threw me a frightened glance, but did not reply.

FEBRUARY 24. Wanless took me into his confidence to-night. He had been on the verge of telling me that first evening in the garden. Whether he held back because he was afraid I might be spying on him, or just what his reason was, I don't know. Probably it was only natural caution. At any rate, he told me all about it tonight as we sat in his laboratory.

It was stifling hot, but the hordes of insects had driven us inside and we sat there in the little room with a single oil lamp for light and the long rows of bottles and jars looking down at us from the shadowy shelves.

Lucia sat unobtrusively on the floor in the corner. Now that I'm no longer a novelty she has abandoned the dress donned in my honor and reverted to her favorite household costume—a red waist-cloth and several strings of beads.

"Friend," Wanless started off with his usual form of address, "did you ever hear of the *Zoophyte giganticus wanlessi?*"

Lucia started suddenly and I heard her beads rattle, then she bent her head and began to play with an anklet.

"No," I replied, "I never did."

Wanless chuckled as at a huge joke.

"No, friend, not yet. The world does not yet know of my great work. You are the first I have told, and I only tell you because my work is almost completed. Tomorrow I will show you."

That is what he calls the thing: *Zoophyte giganticus.* Almost anyone scholarly enough to understand the implications of the name could understand from that what Wanless has been doing. For myself I became distinctly uncomfortable. Never have I liked taking liberties with nature. There was a long moment of silence, while Wanless leaned across the table with his eyes seeming to bulge more than ever behind his glasses. It was so still that I could hear Lucia's quick, nervous breathing, and a cougar crying somewhere far off in the jungle, and a rustling under the floor of the house where a pig was rooting in the refuse. After a minute Wanless went on:

"You are not a botanist, friend, but you know much of such matters and can understand what I am about to tell you. As you know, the animal kingdom is one form of life and that of the plants is another. Along different lines have they developed, but their basic principles are the same. And in the lower forms it is often difficult to tell them apart. There are plants which move about, and there are animals which are fixed in one place. There are plants which feed on bugs and insects, and there is an animal which contains chlorophyl. It is simply that these are two divergent lines of development. Do you see what I mean, friend?"

Of course I saw what he meant, I had not forgotten those perverted plants growing in the garden. Also, I began to understand something of Lucia's fear. But I only nodded.

"For years I have been doing this thing," Wanless continued, "doing it experimentally, here in my laboratory. Trying to cross an animal with a plant. Under those glass domes against the wall did I see my first zoophytes survive and grow. That was five years ago. Since then I have experimented with generation after generation of my plants. And I have succeeded, friend, I have succeeded! Out there, in a hut on the edge of the jungle, is a full-grown specimen of my giant animal-plant. Tomorrow I will show you."

When he finished I glanced at Lucia: the girl's face was positively haggard. She did not know much English, but she had understood enough to know what we were talking about. I have now this explanation of the latent terror that never leaves her eyes. Not that I feel any too comfortable myself. Somehow I don't think I shall sleep very well tonight.

FEBRUARY 25. Wanless was true to his word. This morning early we started off to a little clearing that lies about a quarter-mile back in the jungle. He explained that he had been afraid the natives might idly interfere with his experiments, but has found they never go near the place. I am not surprised. We perceived the odor known as the Devil's Breath before we had left the mud flats, and by the time we were within a hundred yards of the clearing the

air was poisoned by the vilest, most horrible smell I have
ever known.

In the center of the open space stood a hut about ten
feet square. It is an ordinary thatch and mud cabin, but
windowless and with a door supported on leathern hinges.
Wanless tells me he built it alone and unassisted.

As we neared the place the stench became almost overpowering. God, that odor! Will I ever forget the taint of
it? I can't compare it with any other; it beggars description. Primarily it's a stench of rottenness and decay, of
putrefaction and death. The odor of long-dead carrion,
the smell of a slaughter-house, the vile gasses of stagnant
marshes, all are mild compared to what emanates from
that unholy place. It was almost more than I could bear.
Made the senses reel, and I think it could easily drive a
man mad.

"Ah yes, the odor!" said Wanless with a chuckle when
he saw me gasping. "It is unpleasant, no? But I have become used to it. Not that I enjoy, but I no longer notice."

"But what in God's name does it come from?" I asked
him.

"From within the hut, friend. The zoophyte feeds
entirely on carrion. Come."

He opened the door and we entered. Only half the hut
was roofed over, the rest being open to the sun. The shadows in the covered part were deep and disturbing, but the
other half was light enough.

Growing in the hut was—well, a plant. It can be called
that for lack of a better name. The central mass was about
eight feet high, grotesque, shapeless, and evil. It seemed
tortured, distorted, and the many short, thick branches
were twisted as though in pain. The thing looked as if
its first ancestor had been a Venus flytrap, one of those
carnivorous flowers that feed on insects, but it was greatly changed. There was one central cavity, lined with stiff

hairs to entrap anything within reach—a cavity of death with a ghastly, dead-white, silky lining, like the skin of a corpse. I can see it yet! Crimson and white and brown, with that silky cavity yawning below and the yellow pollen sticks above, it was like a figment of madness.

As I said, we entered the hut. And I swear to God that the damnable plant turned and *looked* at us. Looked isn't quite the word, for of course it has no eyes. Perceived is better. In some way it indefinably sensed our entrance and seemed to inspect us, and I felt the hair bristling all across my scalp.

I have heard before of giant plants of the fly-catcher species, but this is far worse. The thing has—well, it has personality. It is menacing. There was no breeze within the walls of that hut, yet the misshapen branches were continually in motion. The opening of the central cavity suddenly closed; it was like a huge, malevolent mouth.

On the floor of the hut was the vilest imaginable collection of rotting, loathsome carrion. Portions of the torn carcasses of various small animals lay about in all stages of decay. Around the foot of the thing these fragments formed a solid carpet of filth. The air was rank and foul, and a faint miasmatic mist seemed to be rising from that revolting mass of rotting flesh. The very sunlight that came through the hole in the roof was different and somehow unhealthy. This was the thing that for years had poisoned the wind behind Palaos, and had given rise to the legend of the Devil's Breath.

We stood there a while, Wanless beaming with a childlike pride and I simply staring. The thing has a ghastly fascination. Then one of the lower branches reached down, seized on half a young pig, and tossed it into the suddenly opened cavity. The jaws closed again with a snap, and I had seen enough. I turned and charged out of the hut, and Wanless followed more slowly.

Not till I was back on the river bank did I pause. The fever-filled air of this Orinoco jungle is like the breath of heaven after what I had just been breathing.

"What was it?" I asked when Wanless had caught up with me.

"My zoophyte, friend, my giant animal-plant. Born of my years of experiment, developed from a Venus fly-trap, and sired by half the animal kingdom!"

"But good God, man," I almost shouted at him, "why did you have to choose a plant of *that* sort to start with?"

"Because I wanted one as nearly animal at the beginning as I could get it. By that much did I make my task easier."

After we came back to the house Wanless gave me the details of his experiments. Some of them are pretty horrible. Most things sprout almost at once in this climate, and by intensive fertilization he has speeded up growth so that he has raised as many plant generations in the last five years as would normally grow in thirty or forty. Gradually he has trained the *thing* to feed on carrion. The rest of his methods are better forgotten; they are not pleasant.

As we came back I noticed that Lucia had, as usual, been keeping her vigil at the window.

FEBRUARY 26. By now I am thoroughly convinced that, like so many geniuses, Wanless is slightly mad. No ordinary man could have done what he has done. The most normal thing about him is his treatment of Lucia. It seems remarkable that the cold-blooded sponsor of the zoophyte could be so kind and considerate toward a mixed-blood native girl. I believe that in his own queer way he really loves her.

Tomorrow I move on. Thank God for that!

MARCH 3. Move on? Not for a week yet—if then. The fever has me. An hour after I wrote the last entry above I was flat on my back with the local variety of malaria. And have been ever since.

Somehow I think the foul air I breathed in the hut of the zoophyte may have something to do with this. That may not be medically possible; I'm not much of a medico. Whatever the cause, here I am, and almost too weak even to write.

MARCH 5. A little better now. Lucia takes care of me, administering suitable doses of quinine and keeping me supplied with water from the big canvas cooler that always hangs from the porch roof. I've grown quite fond of the girl. She is a primitive creature in many ways, but she's kind-hearted and means well. She sits cross-legged on the floor beside my cot for hours, with a water jug between her knees and her eyes fixed on vacancy. Perhaps she thinks; perhaps not. One never knows.

MARCH 7. Am convalescing now. Wanless is seldom in evidence, but he did have a talk with me today and I learned the reason for his absence. He is quite jubilant.

"Progress, friend, progress!" he said, and beamed till his beard quivered. "I have again tried feeding my zoophyte on living flesh instead of on carrion. This time it is greatly a success—the plant becomes almost human. Now I range the jungle and trap small game for it. Soon it may hunt for itself—who knows? The roots are shallow, and it moves them. What do you think?"

I guess the fever must have soured me, for I snarled at him: "Since you ask me, I think you ought to let the damn thing starve to death."

"No, no, friend," he laughed; "to science it would be too great a loss. But you speak of hunger. Always is it hungry now; since it has tasted living flesh it will not touch carrion. And I cannot seem to trap food fast enough.

You should see how it snatches at anything I bring it! And it is strong, too; today I held out a stout stick I was carrying, and it snapped it like kindling. When you are well I will show you."

"Like hell you will!" I answered, and turned over to try to sleep. It seemed impossible to make the man angry.

MARCH 9. God! What a day of horror this has been! But to go back to the beginning:

I was quite a bit better this morning and sat propped up in a chair on the porch. Wanless had disappeared before I awoke, but Lucia was busy about the house. It struck me that she was even more silent than usual, and when she looked out the door for a minute I received a distinct shock. The girl was terrified! If ever I saw stark, primitive fear on a face it was then. I called to her, but she turned away without answering. The sense of menace that has been with me ever since I arrived in Palaos increased, and I grew restless and irritable.

It was sometime after noon that Lucia finally came out on the porch, walking with a slow, mechanical tread. There was an air of fatality about her, of resignation. In one hand she carried a chicken, its legs tied together with a cord.

"What is the trouble, Lucia?" I asked her in the bastard Portuguese she used.

"It is that I must go to the *thing* in the hut, *Senhor*," she told me, and I noticed that little beads of perspiration were standing out all over her tawny hide. "The Master is hunting, and he told me to feed this chicken to the thing at noon."

I tried to dissuade her, but she shook her head. She was terribly afraid, but Wanless had said something must be done and there was no stopping her. Finally I let her go. God forgive me for it! At that I don't know just what

I could have done to stop her, for the fever hasn't left me much strength. Down the path she went, winding back across the mud flats toward the jungle, walking with a slow and lagging tread. Then the first bushes swallowed her, and she was gone.

For perhaps twenty minutes I was not particularly worried. I did not exactly forget about the girl, but I did manage to dismiss her from my mind. And then suddenly came the realization that half an hour had passed without her return. I felt cold all over, and my hands began to shake. I remembered what I had seen in the hut, and I remembered what Wanless had told me of the new hunger of the *thing*. At the end of forty-five minutes I could no longer sit still.

Throwing aside the thin robe that covered me, I swung to my feet and started to cross the wide porch to the open door of the house. The fever has weakened me even more than I realized, for my knees were unsteady and tremulous and I fell prone on the floor before I had taken half a dozen steps. Slowly and laboriously I pulled myself to my feet and tried again. The result was the same. I was still lying full length on the splintery boards of the porch floor when Wanless appeared, making his way back between the native huts. When he saw me he threw down the small game he had been carrying, and came running up to the house.

Wanless was strong, for all his small frame. With scarcely an effort he gathered me up in his arms and dumped me back on the chair where I had been sitting. In my haste I choked on the words, but finally I gasped out what had happened. His face darkened, and without a word he turned on his heel and hurried away down the path to the jungle. As he went there came a faint puff of wind that bore with it a trace of that never-to-be-forgotten stench. It was almost as though the *thing* knew of his coming, and mocked him.

For a while nothing happened. It seemed that the sun paused, that the earth ceased its movement, and that time slumbered; and then at last Wanless came running back. He ran at full speed, looking at nothing, his face set in grim and terrible lines. Most of his clothing was ripped from his body; strange red welts covered his arms and shoulders; and one side of his head was crimson with blood where his ear had been nearly torn off and hung dangling from a single flap of skin.

I called to him, but Wanless never noticed me. He was past all thought or reason, and intent on only one idea. Across the porch and into the house he charged like a maddened boar, and I heard him throwing things around in the store-room. An instant later he reappeared, ran out with a long-bladed machete gleaming in each hand. Leaping down the steps in one bound, he ran back toward the jungle. His torn clothes fluttered behind him and the blood from his wound left a scarlet trail across the bushes.

This time he did not return. Time passed, with nothing disturbing the sultry calm, and when I could bear it no longer I again tried to stand up. This time I seemed a little stronger. Holding to the chairs and then to the walls themselves for support, I managed to enter the house. From a bottle on the table I poured out half a tumbler of brandy. The fiery spirits seemed to give new strength to my weakened legs.

With an energy born of desperation I commenced to dress. I slipped on my trousers, and a pair of high boots. My Colt lay on a chair, but I did not even take it—how can one shoot at a thing without vitals? Instead I went to the store-room and found another machete. With this, and a heavy staff to keep me upright, I started toward that ill-omened jungle clearing.

It took a long time to make that journey of about a third
of a mile. God knows it seemed like ages! It was as though
I struggled against unseen currents, and every movement
was sluggish. Fever is a weakening thing, and I fell frequently in spite of my staff. When this happened I would
lie still for a moment, fighting for breath, then once again
stagger to my feet and start forward. At last there came
that ghastly stench of decay, and I knew I was approaching
the clearing.

The place was silent and still under the glare of the
afternoon sun. An ominous silence. The grass seemed to
undulate and quiver in the heat, and even the trees around
the edge of the clearing drooped listlessly. The door of
the hut was open and a severed branch lay athwart the
entrance. It had been cut off by a stroke of a machete and
was covered by a slimy yellow liquid, a sort of blood. And
then I looked inside the hut. . . .

I will not attempt to write what lay therein. God knows
it will be long before I sleep well at night, for the memory
of it. The girl had nursed me, and Wanless had been my
friend. Yet the culminating horror was not their fate but
the fact that the *thing* was gone. Even now, right at this
minute, it must be somewhere at large.

For minutes on end I stood staring, unable to move my
eyes. At last I uttered a strangled cry and staggered out
into the clearing. Many dry bushes and shrubs lay near
by, and I piled them high around the walls of the hut and
set the whole thing afire. I think I was slightly mad just
then—and I am none too sure of my sanity even now. A
great column of greasy black smoke mounted up into the
air as I began my painful journey back here to the house.

It is now evening, with the last light fading, and I am
feverishly working to finish up these notes. I have ready
a large square of oiled silk and a block of wood, and if

anything happens I will wrap the book in the silk and throw the whole thing out the window into the river.

Later. Something is coming! I can hear a slow splashing in the puddles out on the mud flats. A moment ago a dog was howling furiously; he ended with one ghastly scream and has since been silent.

I have a machete, and the door may hold. If not—? The porch is creaking as though under a weight, I think I will . . .

[The manuscript ends abruptly at this point, and the above may be regarded as Jonathan Darrowby's last words. Professor Briggs located the site of Palaos after some difficulty, and found that the few natives had moved away and the jungle had reclaimed the place. The big house had evidently been destroyed by fire, perhaps from an overturned lamp. There was nothing to be gained by staying, and Professor Briggs left that same night.]

THE GAS-WEED
Stanton A. Coblentz

In all respects but one, there was nothing unprecedented about the ball of fire that startled the western hemisphere toward the end of the year 1968. A meteor of exceptional brilliancy, it was first observed somewhere far above the Arizona desert, traveling westward at a prodigious speed; and a few seconds later, after terrifying the natives of Southern California with its baleful red light, long phosphorescent trail and ominous hissing, it went to its rest on a forsaken beach of the Pacific. For ten or twelve days it was not even known where it had struck; observers generally were of the opinion that it had plunged into the ocean; and while newspapers bore a flaming account of the event and even the scientific journals took some note of it, astronomers were agreed that phenomena as spectacular had been observed before: as witness the records of innumerable fireballs, beginning with that declared by Plutarch to have fallen in Thrace as far back as the year 470 E. C.

Had it not been for a chance observation, the theory that the meteor had vanished beneath the waves might long have remained current. But it happened that Clifton Herrick, an aviator flying low over the coast in the Intercontinental War, noticed an enormous mound or crater of earth reminding him of the shell hole made by an

exploding projectile, except that it was incomparably
vaster than any shell hole he had ever seen. Though its
depth was not more than a score of yards, it measured
between a quarter and a third of a mile from rim to rim.
Herrick's first theory was that it indicated some previously
unexplained volcanic action; and this view was apparently
confirmed by the seething heat that drove him away when
he attempted to approach closely, and by the scorched
and withered state of the once abundant beach grass surrounding the place. Military experts, however, when told
of the discovery, were of opinion that it represented some
nefarious device by the foe; and only after the cautious
investigation by the War Department did the astonishing
truth reveal itself. A scientist of the investigating party,
attracted by scattered masses of iron of a telltale composition, proclaimed that the eruption incontestably was of
meteoric origin: the largest meteorite ever seen to fall by
man lay buried here on the seacoast!

Even so, the announcement occasioned no great flurry.
The world at that moment was engaged so busily in the
practice of war, that scientific observations of a nonmil-
itary nature aroused but passing interest. Little did men
dream of the transcendent importance of this particular
bit of scientific news! Little did they suspect that it was
to prove more momentous than any war that man had ever
waged! There were none who foresaw the gruesome, unthinkable events that were to convulse the world within
the next year or two; for there were none who, at that
day, could have known of the one respect in which that
meteorite was different from all its predecessors, and of
the tragic significance of the single point of variance.

Ignorant of the peril that they were releasing upon
their fellows, a small group of scientists began a minute
investigation of the meteorite. As soon as it had cooled
sufficiently to permit them to work in comfort, they

undertook their excavations, burrowing on all sides and even beneath the enormous mass, and at the same time blowing off some huge fragments by means of dynamite. These they subjected to chemical analysis, finding them to be composed of the same alloy of iron and nickel as that of countless smaller meteorites. It was only after they had penetrated deep down into the fallen mass that they discovered anything of scientific note; and then the observations, while unusual, did not seem in any way significant. At a depth of about forty feet, the dynamite of the excavators revealed a rich vein of some quartzlike rock—not precisely like any terrestrial quartz in appearance, yet of a flinty hardness and of the same chemical composition as quartz. What was more important—but what the observers, in their haste, did not note until later—was that thousands of minute black specks were embedded in the quartz, no larger than pinpoints and presenting under the microscope a smooth polished surface and a shape not unlike that of the common bean. Had any of the scientists at that time taken notice of the black particles, he would probably not have been impressed, for they would have seemed to him to be mineral matter of no extraordinary nature; and no steps, accordingly, would have been taken to prevent them from escaping in their myriads into the world at large. And this is profoundly regrettable, for it means that, once the dynamite had released the unsuspected peril, no human agency would be able to check it at its source, or prevent its spreading.

Weeks went by. The world, unaffected, hastened fiercely about its other affairs. The Intercontinental War was blazing more hotly than any other conflict in history; the great trans-Pacific invasion was being undertaken, with the loss of a hundred million lives in India and China; airplanes were laying waste the leading cities of the Pacific seaboard, and poison gas was annihilating whole populaces in Australia and western Europe; and mankind, with one half of the white race and one half of the yellow race ranged against the other half of the white race and the other half of the yellow, was waging a desperate and apparently losing battle for existence. Had any one suggested that, while the guns were flaming and the shrapnel bursting, the most powerful arbiters of all lay strewn about a Pacific beach in the shape of some microscopic black particles, the idea would certainly have met with wholesale ridicule; yet the simple truth, which we of today realize all too bitterly, is, that each of those black specks contained more diabolical potentiality than a thousand tons of high explosive.

It was little more than a month before the first portents of disaster appeared. A party of chemists and astronomers, returning by airplane to conduct a fresh investigation of the meteorite—which had lain unheeded for several weeks—were startled to observe the altered appearance of the beach where it had fallen. All of them were sober men of science, yet all, as they afterwards confessed, rubbed their eyes and gaped and wondered if they were dreaming—it seemed almost as if the beach had disappeared! Or, rather, the sands of the beach had disappeared; and, at the same time, the crater caused by the meteor had almost vanished! But for hundreds of yards where the sands had been, and for other hundreds where the crater had gaped like a ghastly sore, there was a thick reddish growth of some mysterious vegetation! Weirdly translucent, and dense as the foliage of a tropical jungle, it fringed the ocean to a height of twenty feet, and, unaffected by the brine, stretched out into the water for well over a quarter of a mile!

It would be pointless to describe this strange vegetation in detail, for it has since grown familiar as grass to every child. Let it suffice to state that it was then in a half developed, sprouting stage, somewhat like a leguminous plant with the cotyledons[1] still clinging to it. But even so, it presented an appearance sufficiently fantastic and imposing. It can be most nearly likened to a gigantic fungus, since it possessed no leaves at all; it consisted merely of a mass of tendrils, weaving and interweaving like a pile of intertangled cotton yarn; and its feelers, sprouting out in all directions as thickly as bristles from a brush, showed a tendency to curl like a corkscrew, and in many cases ended in clawlike protuberances that have been compared to the talons of eagles.

But as if these points of novelty were not sufficient, the plants showed other and still more striking peculiarities. The first of these was that, here and there among the wilderness of tendrils, there was an opaque round mass double the size of a man's head, deep purple in color, and surmounted by a growth of shoots and stems that bore a remarkable similarity to hair. And, to complete the likeness to a human head, there were several orifices corresponding remotely to mouth and eyes; and these were seen to open and contract for no known reason, giving the illusion of a face grimacing with the most horrible, distorted malevolence and mockery. Scientists were afterwards to explain that these were mere centers of growth, corresponding roughly to the trunk of a tree; but there are thousands who, to this day, remain unconvinced, and contend that the supposed plants were really not plants at all, but represented some inexplicable cross between vegetable and animal life. . . .

---

[1] These are the so-called seed leaves, which are what we eat in the leguminous plants. If you see a bean seedling just pushing up its head you will see the two cotyledons, which have protected the tender leaflets on their way through the soil.

Subsequent events developed numerous arguments to support this view. One of them was to be found in the second
marked peculiarity of the plants. This was discovered—and
in a most unfortunate way—by the members of the scientific party upon their investigation of the curious growth.
For, after they had alighted from their airplane and started
on foot toward the plants, they encountered an unexpected obstacle. When they were within a hundred yards of the
fringe of vegetation, a queer odor came to their nostrils,
vaguely sweet, pungent, indescribable and as distinctive as
the odor of ether, and more subtly unpleasant than they
could explain. They had no thought, however, of possible danger, and continued on their way until the foremost was within twenty yards of the plants. Then suddenly
an extraordinary thing happened. A pale greenish-yellow
cloud, of the color of chlorine gas shot toward them from
the plants, as though forced out of nozzles under high
pressure. Before they had had time to retreat, the gas was
drifting all about them. And the foremost of the scientists
reeled, gasped, and sank with a deep sigh to the earth.

Two of his comrades, a little to his rear, likewise gasped
and staggered, then wilted like men who have been shot,
and dropped to earth. The remaining five members of the
party, not quite in the line of attack, coughed heavily and
felt their heads dizzily swimming, but somehow remained
on their feet. Stumbling like drunken sailors, they struggled forward to aid their companions—only to succumb
to a new wave of the gas, which leapt forth in a vehement
burst from the tendrils of the plants. And when the second
wave had passed, seven silent forms lay strewn about the
beach.

But in the form of the eighth victim, still prostrate
upon the sand, there might have been observed some signs
of life. One man, a little further than his fellows from the
reddish growth, might have been seen to move his limbs

in random, feeble gestures, somewhat like a beetle that has been trodden upon. Gradually, in the course of what may have been hours, his movements began to take on a little force and direction; and there came a time when, with a sick sensation in the head and the unsteadiness of one who walks a hurricane swept deck, he precariously regained his feet, and by turns stumbled and crawled away from the plant toward the waiting airplane. . . .

He it was who, in a condition halfway between life and death, appeared on the following day in the western offices of the War Department, stammering forth a story of some incredible new poison gas contrivance, which resembled a reddish plant and lured one on to destruction. Such were his ravings and mutterings that many were inclined to believe him a madman, although he spoke in the manner of one who has actually survived some appalling catastrophe, and was eventually identified as none other than Sherman Crass, the world-renowned chemist. But it was only because of the outstanding name and influence of the man, and not because any one believed there could be a particle of truth in his fantastic story, that a small party was sent to investigate the patch of beach of which he gave such lurid warning.

When, after three days, no member of the investigating party had returned, the War Department began to take a somewhat more serious interest. And when, after another three days, still another investigating party had gone forth and remained unreported, it came to be recognized with alarm that possibly there was more than a shadow of truth to Kris's narrative. Rumors that the foe had seized the coast in force now began to circulate; it was common gossip that they had found a base for their poison gas attacks somewhere along the California beaches. And it was for this reason that the War Department, now thoroughly aroused, commissioned a fleet of sixty air scouts and ten

dirigibles, well equipped with guns and gasmasks, to fly
to the alleged military base and attack the enemy in mass.

The experiences of this expedition are among the most
memorable of which our records tell us. Few persons have
ever received a more bewildering surprise than did the
crew of the great air fleet when, approaching the spot indicated in Krass's report, they found the beach overgrown
for half a dozen miles with translucent reddish shoots. But
the plants were not twenty feet high, as Krass had indicated; they averaged forty feet or more! And the great purple
masses that stood out here and there among them were
each as large as half a dozen human heads!

The fleet alighted at a distance of several hundred
yards; and a dozen volunteers were ordered to approach as
nearly as possible to the vegetation. Their fate, however,
might have been foretold; they were still far from touching distance when there was an eruption of the greenish
vapors, and the men staggered, toppled groaning to earth,
and were still. Thenceforth, upon the orders of the com-
mander, every member of the expedition was required to
wear his gasmask.

Even with this precaution, however, they found their
task no easy one. They did not, it is true, succumb to the
gas attacks, for their masks were of the latest style, and
were proof even against the recently developed sulpho-
cyanide vapors, one whiff of which would kill a man; but
they did find themselves the targets of an attack, even
more direct and unexpected in its nature. For, when they
strode within the shadow of the reddish vegetation, the
invisible seemed to open up its arms against them; long,
spinelike blades shot out with amazing speed from concealed scabbards amid the undergrowth. It would be impossible to give an idea of the swiftness and suddenness
of the assault; before they had had time to defend themselves, half a dozen men had been pierced and slain. Some

with thorax and abdomen ripped open, others with heads broken and shattered, they toppled to earth, where they lay in crimson masses that quivered for an instant, and then were still. And meanwhile the blades, with poniard thin edges, curved and gleaming like scimitars, flashed back again into their hidden scabbards.

Thunderstricken, the remaining troops stopped short barely in time to save themselves. Some fled screaming, as though pursued by demons; others remained rooted to the ground, their hair fairly bristling in their fright. To one and all it was apparent that no ordinary enemy confronted them. And to the commanders, observing the horror from safe vantage points in the rear, the conviction came that the fibrous wall before them was not a wall of vegetation at all, but rather some deathtrap contrived with diabolical ingenuity by the foe. For had any such plants as this ever been known before? And had any plants, however strange, ever been seen to strike out like human beings? The idea was unthinkable, preposterous! Accordingly, with the belief that human enemies lay unseen in ambush behind the reddish screen, the leaders ordered a wholesale attack by means of aerial bombing guns, small field artillery, bayonets, and hand grenades. And, as a preliminary to the assault, they directed that the men be all arrayed in those steel coats of mail and helmets which had come to be part of the paraphernalia of modern warfare.

It was the massed attack of several thousand men that brought the greatest surprise of the day. The plantlike growth, though apparently soft and flexible, proved to be actually hard and impermeable as granite! Again and again the attacking bayonets struck with a clatter as of iron against rock; again and again the blades were warped or broken. And the hand grenades and the aerial bombs exploded without causing any visible damage; the shells of the field artillery made only narrow gaps, which closed almost instantly, leaving all as before! The supposed plants were really stronger than steel!

But no sign of a human enemy was discovered by any of the assaulting party. And at length the commanders, turning from the attack in a sort of dazed astonishment, were forced to admit themselves defeated. When finally, baffled and bewildered, they returned home, it was with the report that the enemy had contrived some inexplicably powerful, destructive mechanism, infinitely superior to any previously known.

Now it was that the world was really aroused. Now it was that scientists and militarists alike began to recognize that the bristling reddish growth represented a discovery of major importance. The idea that it was not a thing of human contrivance, that it was something strange, unearthly, sinister beyond all reckoning, was already beginning to gain credence in certain quarters; and the demand for a thorough explanation and investigation was growing louder and more insistent. The American government, throwing open its treasury, in alarm that was daily deepening, offered a reward of one hundred thousand dollars to whoever would satisfactorily account for the red plant. And at the same time it provided unbounded facilities, in the shape of military equipment and scientific apparatus, to all who desired to participate in the investigation. Meanwhile, from all sections, a cry of "Make haste, make haste!" began to arise. For an appalling fact was coming to light, a fact that argued incontestably against the human origin of the spiny reddish thing. The "gas-weed," as it was now popularly called, was still growing with phenomenal speed, and had already attained a height of one hundred feet. Worst of all, it was spreading, not only along the beach, but inland, wiping out every other plant as effectively as a prairie fire wipes out dried grass. An area estimated at over forty square miles had already been conquered by the spreading peril!

It was through the efforts of that celebrated chemist, Sherman Krass, that the world gained its first partial solution of the mystery. Ever since his narrow escape from death at the hands of the unknown, Krass had devoted himself unsparingly to the investigation of the gas-weed. And he it was who first traced its definite connection with the fireball of 1968. Remembering that its first appearance had been in the vicinity of the crater caused by the meteorite, and that it had originally been observed not long after the meteor's fall, he conceived a daring theory which he at once set out to demonstrate scientifically. Tearing apart small fragments of the meteorite and examining them beneath the microscope, he discovered the tiny bean shaped particles; he also discovered how, when split apart, they displayed curious lines and veining, not unlike the veining of a leaf. Next he subjected some of the black dots to qualitative analysis, and in so doing discovered them to be exceedingly complex in structure, composed primarily of a silicon compound, but with the inclusion of quantities of oxygen, hydrogen, carbon and various other elements to be found in organic substances. And yet the silicon was so abundant that, as Krass afterwards confessed, he doubted for a while whether the resemblance to anything organic could be more than superficial. He did not, however, refrain from making a final experiment— and to this experiment the world owes the first great stride toward the mastery of the unknown; he distributed a few score of the black dots in flowerpots filled with a moist sandy soil, covered them with a thin coating of earth, and resolutely waited.

He did not, however, have to wait long. On the following day he observed something red and fibrous just beginning to peep above the earthen surface of the flowerpots.

At first he thought it was perhaps merely some chance
weed; but he was swiftly to be disillusioned. Even as he
watched, he saw translucent shoots pushing themselves
out of the soil with movements so rapid as to be perceptible to the attentive eye!

There could be no further doubt. The discovery was nothing short of revolutionary! Wild-eyed with amazement,
Krass rushed off to broadcast his secret. He had penetrated the enigma of the gas-weed! He knew now that it
was not of this earth! Its seeds had been borne to us by
the meteorite; it had issued from some other world, some
other universe!

Such was the startling fact that Krass proclaimed. But
mankind at large, with its customary skepticism when the
unusual is concerned, did not share in his enthusiasm.
Many at first smiled incredulously, and declared themselves unwilling to accept a tale that so flatly contradicted
all previous experience. How, asked the critics, could a
meteorite come to bear seeds within it? How preserve
them, so that they were capable of germination after
possibly millions of years? And how, even granting their
existence, could they sprout upon the earth, in an environment probably totally different from that known to
their kind?

To all these questions Krass listened patiently, and to
each he offered an answer. Torn from the surface of some
remote planet by some tremendous cataclysm, some volcanic eruption, some collision of worlds, the meteor could
easily have borne within it a portion of rock or soil containing seeds awaiting germination; and these, if small
enough and if fortified sufficiently by ancestral adapta-
tion to extremes of pressure and of cold, might be preserved within the meteor's iron heart, proof against any
change of temperature and unaffected by the passage of

years. And finding on earth a propitious environment—
which is to say an environment that included sunlight, air,
and a moderately warm soil—they at once were brought
to life, and developed as readily as though on their native
sod. In all this, as Krass took pains to make clear, there
was really nothing extraordinary, any more than in the
importing of an Australian plant into North America, or
of a North American plant into Australia; the real marvel
was that such a transplanting had never happened before,
unless, indeed, it had happened a thousand times without
our knowing it, and was one of the obscure causes of the
origin of species.

Within a few days, a number of other extraordinary
facts about the gas-weed had been made public by Krass.
For one thing, he had conducted a chemical analysis of the
young shoots, when they were still relatively soft and tender and had not attained anything of that steel-like rigid-
ity characteristic of the developed plants. He had discovered that, in common with the seeds, they were composed
of a silicon compound, so highly complex that its chemical formula defied analysis, and differed fundamentally
from any other substance ever known on earth. Krass's
theory—based, it is true, upon incomplete researches,
but later thoroughly substantiated—was that the gas-
weed had a totally different chemistry from any terrestrial
organism: instead of the chlorophyll common to all green
plants, it had a reddish pigment which enabled it to uti-
lize the sunlight as a source of growth; while, in place of
the well-known protoplasm, with carbon and nitrogen as
its basis, it had a molecular construction equally elaborate, but with silicon as the essential ingredient. This, in
Krass's belief, explained not only why the weed throve so
well in the sandy soil of the beach, where silicon dioxide
existed in inexhaustible quantities, but why it was able to
build up walls of the flinty construction for which various

silicon compounds are noted. Such are the feldspars, trap rock and others. And this also explained, in the view of scientists, why it was a thing so difficult to compete with, a thing inimical to human life. For that it was inimical to life, as much in the role of aggressor as when deliberately attacked, was fast becoming manifest. Apparently thriving upon success, the plant had continued to develop at a rate that would have been deemed impossible had not the sober facts forbidden denial. From occupying forty square miles of territory, it had come to spread over eighty, then over a hundred and twenty, then over two hundred, then over five hundred, then over a thousand square miles! And this vast conquest was accomplished within a period of weeks! No army known to history had ever subdued territory so utterly and so indisputably. Advancing away from its first field of attack, it was spreading inland, was moving over cultivated ground and crowding out orchards and vineyards as easily as forest trees crowd out grass. Even houses and small towns were not immune to its attack; they disappeared before it as mysteriously as though they had been but phantoms; the translucent ruddy shoots would weave their way through brick and wood, seizing all in a strangle grasp and grinding it to fragments; and when the advance guard had once arrived, in a few days there would remain only a tall reddish tangle, with here and there a purple head shaped mass, uplifted like the face of some inscrutable sentinel watching and warning. . . .

The worst of the matter was that the devastation did not confine itself to a single area. Bad as it was to see a section of the fertile California seaboard succumbing to the invader, it was inconceivably worse to find a dozen, twenty, fifty spots falling victims. How the terror could spread into widely separated districts was not at first apparent, but ultimately an explanation did come. The plants, as

Sherman Krass discovered, were already putting forth seeds; and these minute black particles such as he had already investigated, were equipped with tiny downlike wings, much like the wings of dandelion seeds, except that they were lighter and might blow even further field. Thus, as the facts incontestably showed, they had been borne fifty, a hundred, in some cases two hundred miles from their point of origin; and, in widely scattered regions, among the orange groves of Riverside and in the fig orchards and vineyards of Fresno County, the gas-weed had lifted its rank growth, laying waste some of the richest agricultural regions of the State, and spreading, spreading, spreading, always silently and malignantly spreading.

It was less than six months before the intruder had ceased to be recognized as a matter of merely local concern, and in many quarters had come to be regarded as a worldwide peril. In some way that has never been positively ascertained—whether due to the chance passage of the seeds on the person of some traveler, or to their deliberate transportation as a means of military aggression—the gas-weed gained a foothold first in Europe, then in Asia, then in Africa, then in Australia. Before long there was no part of the world, civilized or uncivilized, that did not know its baneful presence.

It showed itself able to thrive equally well in any climate and in any soil containing silicon; it began scrambling up the arid mountains of Southern California and Arizona, apparently indifferent to the scarcity of water, and was even reported in the saline waste of the Great Salt Lake desert, and among the dunes of the remote Sahara; it flourished on the sides of stony mountains, sending its roots deep down into quartz and flint; it inhabited the clayey valleys of rivers, and among the tundra of Labrador it began to lift its head as though it were in its native habitat.

Slow as the world in general was to appreciate the scope
of the menace, the second six months brought warnings
not to be resisted. For there are some pleas which speak
more forcefully than words, and which no man has ever
been known to deny; and one of these was to be found in
the famine that slowly, stealthily followed in the wake of
the reddish invader. The world's food supplies, depleted
by the most exhausting war in history, would barely have
proved adequate in any case; and the drain caused by the
added destruction proved as decisive, as would a sack of
lead placed on the back of a tottering laborer. Starvation,
already threatening to descend, suddenly reached its bony
hand over all realms; wheat and potatoes rose so sharply
in price as to be beyond the range of the common man;
meat, because of the extensive destruction of grazing land,
soared until it had become a luxury of luxuries. And now
only the well-to-do went their way without feeling the
hunger pangs, while in every city on earth the poverty
ridden thousands, standing in line for a plate of soup or a
scrap of barley bread, cried out in vain for that with which
to appease the clamor of their gaunt and shriveled babes,
of their worn and weeping womenfolk.

"End the war! End the war! End the war!" was now the
cry in all lands. For while Hunger, with its accomplices,
Looting and Riot, went rattling its skeleton fingers about
the earth, the lords of empires, themselves with ample
bread in their pantries, were still urging their underfed
minions forward with bomb and bayonet. And meantime
men of science, debating behind locked doors, whispered
the opinion that the war must automatically come to a
close; but that, even so, only heroic measures could save
the human race.

It will be needless to comment upon the further events
of those tragic days. There would be no object in enumer-
ating the hundreds of thousands that perished of starvation

in China, in Soviet Russia, in England, in India, in the
United States; neither would there be any gain in outlining
the course of that great pestilence which attended the famine, and which for a while converted the surface of whole
continents into a purgatory defying description. Better to
pass over these unhappy events, beside which the Black
Plague that once depopulated Europe would seem like a
backwoods epidemic; better also not to detail by what steps
the predictions of the wise were fulfilled, the man automatically had to abandon the war upon man, in the throes of
the still more desperate war for racial survival.

The all-important fact is that the time did come when
all the remaining energies of our kind were directed toward the problem of the gas-weed. But how attack that
problem? How compete with a foe whose armament was so
impregnable, whose methods of combat so different from
anything previously known on earth? The heads of the various nations, in a conference wherein for once political
bickering were forgotten amid an atmosphere of terror and
despair, agreed upon every possible agency of international cooperation: chemists and botanists in large numbers
were to study the gas-weed; enormous prizes were to be
offered for every important discovery: the laboratories of
all lands were to be thrown open to research workers, and
the results of their studies were to become the property of
all nations alike. So far, so good!—but what if there were
to be no results from their studies? So some of the pes-
simistic inquired, for still the days went by and nothing
encouraging was announced, and still the gas-weed, with
its prodigious fecundity, kept spreading over garden land
and desert alike, devouring, devouring, devouring, insa-
tiable in its greed for prey.

It is impossible to estimate how many brave men,
venturing forth to study the gas-weed, perished of its
poisonous exhalations or beneath its spiny sabers. It is

impossible to compute how many others took their lives in despair, how many died in madness, how many succumbed to pestilence and famine. There is no means of gathering such statistics, for mankind, in its deathly grip with the invader, could no longer give a thought to the mere numbers of the casualties. All that we can say with certainty is that no less than nine-tenths of the human race had been extinguished, and no less than one-half of the world's arable lands had been laid waste, before chance brought that solution which no man's ingenuity had been able to contrive.

In an obscure laboratory connected with an eastern medical college, a young physician, Francis Leighton by name, had been conducting researches into the cause of cancer, a disease which had been gaining in virulence of recent years and still seemed far from being vanquished. At the time of the appearance of the gas-weed, Leighton had been gathering cancer cultures in various tubes and jars and artificially feeding them in preparation for microscopic study. But, upon the worldwide development of the new menace, he had turned reluctantly from his cancer researches into the still more difficult research into the nature of the gas-weed. He had acquired a few flowerpots filled with the young plants, whose seeds and translucent shoots he had laboriously studied; but within a few days, like so many investigators, he had found that his laboratory specimens were fairly running away with him, were threatening literally to eat him out of house and home! Being inexperienced, he had not taken the precaution of destroying the young plants with nitric acid during the first three or four days of their growth, when they were still too tender to resist that devouring reagent; and after the first three or four days, when neither fire nor water nor any chemical known to man had any effect upon them, the gas-weeds dug their clutching roots through the clay of the flower-pots into the wooden floor of the laboratory and the stone foundations, and, drawing nourishment from that difficult source, expanded so rapidly that they seemed likely soon to fill and destroy the building. It was no trifling matter.

But young Leighton, watching in horror as the pest spread uncontrollably, could hardly have known that for once the very rapacity of the foe was to betray it. In his consternation, he did not remember the cancer cultures, which stood unnoticed beneath glass cases in a dozen parts of the laboratory; but the gas-weed, whose hungry grasping arms could overlook nothing—and least of all the silicon-bearing glass—was not slow in finding out that which Leighton had forgotten. The tough reddish tendrils, reaching the first of the glass coverings, forced their way through it as though it had been made of straw, bursting it into a thousand fragments, and proceeding greedily to devour it.

But for the first time the intelligence of the gas-weed—if the uncanny force that guided it can be called intelligence—had been guilty of a miscalculation. And the results of that miscalculation were soon to become apparent. No one at first even remotely surmised the cause; yet a change, an extraordinary change, had come over the plant. Within a few hours the ends of the tendrils, though immune to attack by dynamite or steel, began to crumple up and wither; enormous green black swellings commenced to appear at a hundred points among the wilderness of shoots; the huge purple head like masses sagged and contracted, and faded to a pale, sickly yellow; faint, scarcely discernible noises, like a low moaning, could be heard as the writhing reddish arms threshed one against the other in what observers declared to be like the death agony of some sentient creature.

And a death agony it surely was! Within twenty-four hours, every evidence of life had vanished from the gas-weed. In a fallen, shriveled, blackening heap, loath-some but harmless, it lay upon the floor of the laboratory it had come so close to annihilating.

What had happened to the terrible weed? Leighton, observing in amazement, was at first too bewildered to understand; and it was only by slow degrees that the explanation dawned upon him. The cancer cultures! They had been his saviors! In some unaccountable way, they had attacked and conquered the unconquerable!

Leighton's first impulse was to proclaim the news from every house and hilltop. But, being naturally of a cautious, scientific turn of mind, he restrained his impatience until he had hastily conducted other experiments. Securing new cancer cultures, he deliberately exposed them on the path of the gas-weed—not one time, but fifty! And in every case he got the same result! Within half a day the plants would begin to wither, would develop enormous, hideous swellings, then they would blacken and die!

But why did the change come about? Leighton could not answer, nor could any of the scientists who studied the question. The most that they could state was that the cancer cells, possessing some peculiar property inimical to the life of the gas-weed, had found in the plant an excep-tionally fertile soil; while the plant in its turn, having an inherited immunity to all perils except this alone, had not the necessary resistance. One circumstance only was easily explained: the fact that its incredibly hard exterior did not protect it; for its surface, as observers discovered upon investigation of the remains, was covered with a multitude of tiny breathing places or pores through which the cancer cells might readily have entered.

But whatever the complete explanation, the signifi-cance of Leighton's discovery was clear enough. The an-cient enemy of mankind had become its deliverer! With the aid of our old foe, cancer, we might strike down the invader!

And with the aid of that old foe, we did indeed strike down the invader! Like wildfire the news of Leighton's findings spread around the earth; and, for the first time in history, cancer patients came into big demand. Operations were performed wherever possible upon victims of the disease; and the cells, dropped from airplanes among the vast jungles of the gas-weed, were scattered far and wide to do their deadly work. And never once did they fail! The plants, withering and blackening, began to recede as rapidly as they had appeared; over areas of thousands of square miles they were exterminated, until not one living trace of them remained!

Five years have now passed since the appearance of the pestilence. Today no gas-weed survives, except in a few mountainous and desert regions, and among the frigid wastes of the Antarctic Continent, where their destruction is of but slight importance. But even these, it is believed, will be blotted out within a few more passing years.

And meanwhile humanity, left gasping and bewildered on the very verge of extinction, has been courageously husbanding its few remaining resources, still trembling at the doom it has avoided, and yet daily offering up prayers that the heavens shall not open again to cast down some new freight of terror that man may not be able to resist.

UP IRRIWADDY WAY

Lieutenant Edgar Gardiner

It had all been a tremendous mistake. From the time we had left Singapore on what was to prove such a terrible chase, I had felt that it was a colossal blunder. But the others had overruled my halfhearted protests, inflamed as they were by money madness and treasure lust. But one thing could they think of—that tremendous heap of rubies, of wealth incalculable, the secret of whose whereabouts was at last in their hands.

What did it matter to them that this was the treasure-house of a god? They didn't believe in heathen gods— not they! Nor in the supernatural. Trickery—that's what it was, nothing else, and this talk of a god of destruction whose very name the natives feared to utter was rot; while the tales about the many who had gone to seek this hidden loot never to return—that was nothing but ignorant superstition—native fancy with no basis in fact. Stuff and nonsense!

What did it matter that as far as they knew its devious trail, their information had come a blood-spattered deadly way? That but gave added proof of its genuineness. Men have ever killed for far less than this dazzling pile—history was full of such cases; and it would be so again.

They were positive of the truth and reliability of their map with its ugly brown stains. They were just as sure of the information that had been gasped out by that native priest as his life slowly welled from his body, so terribly mutilated by native vengeance just when he had almost won clear away. And that information had fired them with a madness there was no staying, even while it chilled me with grim foreboding. Perhaps I had been in the Orient too long, had seen too much that could not be explained away; perhaps too much sun and raw native liquor.

I was overruled, browbeaten, bulldogged, until I gave in against my better judgment.

The trip up-river had been—well, not exactly a pleasure, but then, not so bad, either. I had done worse many times. Things had gone smoothly—too smoothly, I could see now. We had been led on like rats into a trap.

Step by step we had followed the trail as shown on that gruesome map, and as each item proved correct the hopes of my comrades had risen the higher while, oddly enough, my own spirits had sunk the lower; for I was scared—I, who had shot my way out of some mighty tight places and through some pretty rash adventures—I, who was never so cool as when the odds looked hopeless—here I shivered with dread while things went so smoothly—too smoothly.

We had cut our way through the jungle after leaving the last outpost of civilization, so called, the six of us: white men all; as brave and fearless a crew as you ever saw—and as unprincipled. We had come upon the ruined temple, almost swallowed up by the ever-encroaching jungle, with little or no trouble. It lay just where the map had indicated. And while the rest had jubilated over the easy conquest, I had known nothing but sick dread, a vague terror that was none the less real, oppressive, impending.

Our campfire gleaming redly over the ruined moldering idols ranged round that great room, and on the red-lacquered beams above, seemed to me oddly symbolic. That greatest stone monstrosity of all, seated above us in its

niche, seemed a live and sentient thing. It leered at me
through the flickering shadows, its one eye following me
wherever I moved until I was almost mad.

I begged and pleaded with my comrades to get out
while there was yet time, but they only jeered and shouted
ribald comments. Forego the loot they had come so far to
get? With success just around the corner? Never! To my
entreaties that we push on then at once, rifle the cache
and go while the night was with us, they turned a deaf ear.
Tomorrow was time enough, they argued. No hurry now. It
was much the best to wait until daylight before descending
below ground in this venerable relic.

At last we lay down, the six of us, and their snores
soon proclaimed the others asleep, but the longer I lay the
more wide awake I became. Restlessly I tossed and tumbled; then in desperation I got up and crouched above the
dying embers. Malevolently that evil image glared down
upon us. So sinister it was that I shuddered. When I could
stand it no longer I picked up a brand, swung it vigorously
overhead until it blazed, and with this torch I clambered
into the niche.

What I intended to do up there, I had not the remotest
idea: perhaps there was a wild desire to hurl that stone
image into the dust—I don't know. What I did instead,
was to thrust the blazing brand into the corners and cran-
nies, seeking everywhere for I know not what.

Across the face of the idol I swung the smoking flames,
illuminating every hollow above, but saw nothing save the
dust of centuries, patched and discolored by the mold of
tropic damp. Then, my sanity returning in some measure,
with a muttered curse I turned and was about to throw the
brand back to the hard-packed earthen floor, but instead,
thought better of it and thrust the torch, with a sardonic
humor, into the figure's clasped hands, into a hollow made
for the burning of incense.

There! Let him sit once more as he had sat in the heyday
of his popularity, with the smoke curling about his Satanic
features. But now no devout throng of worshipers groveled
on the ground before him. Instead lay five hard-bitten
adventurers sleeping the sleep of the just until the morrow, when they would wrest from him his treasures, gathered through the centuries and left behind when his might
had declined into obscurity.

A blood-curdling scream broke through my musings. One
of those five figures raised with a convulsive start and fell
back writhing in agony, while the others came to frenzied
life with a bound and gathered about him. I came tum-
bling from the niche in a hurry.

"Wot's th' matter, hi syc?" growled Jeremy Sykes, while
the others babbled in excitement not unmixed with fear.
The sufferer, however, was beyond answering. A bloody
froth flecked his lips, drawn back from his teeth in an
animal-like snarl; his limbs threshed wildly as those horrible agonizing tremors passed over him; his face turned a
mottled, livid hue.

One glance I took and knew the worst. Of all venomous
snakes—and they are myriad in that land—the smallest of
them all is the most deadly. Scarce six inches long and red
as hell-fire, his bite is the agony of centuries of the pit
compressed into a short half-hour: agony so great that sufferers have been known to choose the merciful quickness
of the steel in preference, though too often they had no
such chance, but bent and writhed in tortures unutterable
until the slow, dreadful end came. And, stop! did not the
natives give him the same name as this fearsome image
above us?

But Jack's paroxysms were growing more violent and
his entire body was turning an ugly mottled purple. His
eyeballs seemed straining from their sockets and his back

bowed as if it must break, while from his lips burst the noise of a soul in torment unutterable. The cold sweat of horror stood damply on my brow and I was sick within.

Another unearthly scream, broken short by a harsh grunted oath as Jeremy Sykes dropped beside him: a flash of steel shone redly up, then down in a shining arc and cheated that dreadful grinning monster behind us of his last full measure of payment.

"God!" breathed Bill Callaghan, passing a shaking hand before his eyes while he drew a shuddering breath. "What hit him?"

I pointed at that grinning image above.

"Hell's bells!" growled Jeremy Sykes. "Nowthin' of the sort. Snake-bite. A little red devil. No cure for it; but an hour or so of what you saw Jack going through. Often enow I've seen it, and twice it was Gord's mercy to pass th' steel between the ribs to end it. Ugh!" And he turned unsteadily away while the others looked at me.

"It's the truth," I affirmed. "Steel is quick and merciful and no less sure. I'd thank anyone for that choice if it ever came to me. Jeremy did the best possible thing."

There was no more sleep for us that night. We sat instead about another blaze which we had built at the other end of the room, furtively eyeing every moving shadow and studiously avoiding the dreadful figure that lay in the half-gloom staring sightlessly up into the niche.

One gone, I ruminated. One. So soon and so terribly. Who would be next? For that more would follow him I was sure. Deep within me I felt that as surely as I knew that I was still alive. And those deaths, I felt, would be just as terrible as this first one, whatever form they might take.

The others laughed at my forebodings. It was an accident, such as might occur to anyone, anywhere. These old ruins, they pointed out, were overrun with vermin. This land saw frequent violent deaths in strange guises. Why,

one in every ten died from the bite of poisonous snakes! I
was an old granny, a superstitious fool.

The quick dawn put an end to our arguing, and as the details stood out more and more plainly in the grayness of
that dim interior, the night seemed more and more like a
fantastic dream—except for that horrible thing that lay,
putrescent already, offensive and swelling, at the far end
of the idol room. With the light came the first bit of the
day's humid heat and in contrast our trip underground
promised relief. We got out the map again and studied
it carefully. Above all things we must not get lost in the
labyrinth beneath us. How extensive it was we could not
tell, nor did we want to know, save as it led us to the treasure we all felt was there.

"Le'see: we go down back of that big idol," said Peter
Drew, his stubby forefinger on the map. "We must. They's
no other place in this room that fits the plan," he argued
as we objected.

"There's no opening there," I protested. "I was up there
when—when—"

"Yeah, I know. But it was dark then. You couldn't see
nothin'. The mouth of that underground passage just must
be there."

To settle the argument I led the way into the niche, and
after looking and prodding everywhere, they agreed with
me that save for a little grille leading upward toward a dim
light no other opening existed.

"Damme, it must be here," Peter insisted.

"Where?" I began. "We have tried everywhere."

"Maybe in the ceiling," he began, and jumped up on
the idol's spacious lap to investigate.

"Oh, nonsense!" I began.

"Hey, look out!" shouted Jeremy as the huge stone idol
tilted slowly forward.

Peter dropped off to one side, catlike, on all fours, and the idol swung slowly back again.

"You've found it," I shouted in triumph.

"Found what, you fool?" growled Jeremy.

"The opening of the labyrinth. It's under the idol, of course. That big stone god tilts on a balance, and under it is the mouth of the treasure-house. I saw the steps leading down."

"Aw, what bally rot!" from Jeremy again.

"Not at all. It had to be hidden, you know. What better hiding-place than under several tons of stone?"

"But how—"

"You saw how it worked. A man's weight out on the knees of the idol opens the way—"

"And its own weight shuts it again, eh?"

"Certainly it does. One of us has to stay outside to work it while the rest go below. Or perhaps there is some way to move it from the inside. Here, Peter, open it again and I'll go down and try to find out."

Obediently Peter climbed up on his perch again, and slowly the idol tilted forward once more. Down, down, till Peter could stand upon the floor and hold his weight about the figure's neck, leaving a yawning hole through which we might easily enter.

Three times we tried the rocking stone to make sure it would work without sticking before my companions let me go down gingerly into the darkness. I counted fourteen steps before I reached the bottom, and the matches I lit showed me the corridor sloping slightly downward before me. By their feeble flicker I saw something else—something that made me shout aloud.

"What is ut, Jock?" and Jeremy's shaggy head was thrust into the patch of light that marked the entrance.

"Two skeletons, Jeremy," I returned. "The poor devils must have come into this place and the idol closed behind them, shutting them in to a miserable death," I called as I bent over them. "And wait—"

Into my voice crept such a note of excitement that all but Peter Drew came scrambling down to me. No doubt he, too, would have been there had it not meant the closing of that massive door.

By the flickering light of a candle or two that they had brought with them, my comrades saw the proof that the treasure we had come so far to find was still there.

How long those two had lain there could not be told; a hundred years perhaps, maybe three times that long—long enough to rot away almost every vestige of clothing. Yet one of those two had brought with him from those treasure rooms below indubitable proof that what we sought was still there. Tucked into his girdle perhaps, or in a purse long since gone to dust, he had brought a dozen or so of splendid rubies that now gleamed redly from about the pelvis bones where they had fallen. Each of them was worth a king's ransom. No wonder we shouted and scrambled for the precious bits of living flame.

A hoarse shout broke on our ears—that was Peter Drew! It brought us up those steps in a panicky run, sent us scrambling into the idol room around the base of the idol that even now was settling slowly into place. I felt its cold rough edge graze my shoulders as I scrambled out with Jeremy close behind me.

A muffled curse, and in my swift backward glance I saw that Jeremy had dropped one of his rubies. He swept it up again almost without pausing and was scrambling over the edge. But that momentary pause was fatal. The huge block of stone was swinging downward now at a terrific rate.

"Hurry, Jeremy," I shouted, and grasped his shoulders to drag him from beneath that impending doom. Too late! There was a soft thud as the idol swung into place. A spasm crossed Jeremy's face. I looked in dazed horror at the swift red spot that grew and grew from about his waist where he protruded from between the stones.

Where was Peter Drew, and why had he not held the stone god down away from the opening? I wondered even as I heard the sharp crack of Bill's heavy revolver and something flashed past my shoulder in a vivid streak of light. My swift glance showed Bill lying flat on the floor of the niche as cool as though he were at tiffin, the while he pumped an occasional shot into the light-shot gloom of the big room beyond.

And Peter's failure to keep the idol in place out of the opening was explained by the same glance, for I saw him lying on his face before that grim deity in an attitude of supplication, arms outspread. Poor Peter! His last act in this life! From his back protruded the handles of two of those terrible throwing-knives of which I had seen a few specimens down river.

Poor, poor Peter! *Semper Fidelis* was the motto tattooed upon his massive chest, and that he had been. Always faithful, yes, faithful unto death! With his last breath as his dying grip had loosened he had uttered the warning shout that had enabled us all to escape from that death-trap.

All? No, not all. There was Jeremy Sykes pinned under that loathsome stone, still alive, still conscious, as I was surprised to discover.

Too well I knew what had happened when that stone settled into place with Jeremy only partly through the opening. How long can a man live when he is mashed into two pieces, I wondered? I had thought perhaps a few moments—surely not as many minutes. Yet Jeremy seemed almost normal in spite of that terrible thing, in spite of that gruesome spreading red flood about him.

"I'm done," he muttered thickly as he caught my eye. "Get these stones—to my wife—you know—address."

I nodded. "If I get out of this alive I'll do it, Jeremy,"
I promised. The filming eyes lit up joyfully.

"Thanks, old top," he whispered.

A deathly grayness was creeping over his features and
consciousness was fast departing. Death was coming almost like sleep.

"Get down, you fool," shouted Bill as another streak
flashed past me, and once more Bill's service revolver
spoke. It was followed by a blood-curdling scream.

"Gutted him. That's two," Bill grunted in satisfaction.
"I wish I knew how many more are out there," he added as
I crawled up beside him.

"Mois?" I questioned.

"No. We're too far north for their range. Bandit loot-
ers from beyond the northern border most likely. Damme,
I missed him," as he pumped another shot at a half-seen
figure.

A sibilant hiss drew my attention to our rear. Fergus
was there beckoning to me and I crawled swiftly backward.

"I think we can get out through here," he whispered,
pointing at the little grille to which I had paid such scant
attention on our first inspection. Fergus had thrust it partly aside and he now crawled through it into the gloom. I
hesitated to follow into that dimly glowing opening that
had swallowed him and now reflected the dim light as he
crawled forward, lighting matches as he went, or a candle
perhaps. Then the light faded out entirely for a few moments, reappeared once more, and then grew brighter as
Fergus' head came into view, disheveled and dirty.

"It leads beyond the temple wall into a thicket," he
grinned. "I don't think there is a soul about outside,
either. They must all be in here. Tell Bill about it and we'll
get going."

"And leave all our outfit?" I began.

"We get away with our lives, perhaps," he pointed out. "Our outfit isn't much good to us if we are all dead, is it?"

He crawled out to Bill's side and they conferred earnestly together for a moment. Then he was back again.

"Come on," he whispered. "Bill will hold them off for a few moments before he follows us."

As I edged around the idol again I bethought me of my promise to Jeremy and took from his stiffening dead hands the jewels that had cost him his life, slipping them into one of the pockets of my shorts.

How silent was the festering jungle, as we crawled out into the light once more! Behind us we heard the muffled reports of two shots, sullen and hollow, and a few moments later Bill rose beside us.

"Got another," he commented briefly. "Now let's get out of here."

We moved as silently and as swiftly as possible toward the river, but we had gone only a few hundred feet when we heard a yell of baffled rage.

"They rushed the niche and found us gone, I guess," said Bill as he increased his pace. "And in mighty scant time those devils will be swarming after us. The trail is plain."

Five minutes passed—five long eternities while we made our way as swiftly and silently as might be toward where we hoped the river lay. Behind us the jungle lay quiet and empty.

"They must have missed us," whispered Fergus.

"Don't ever think it," I retorted. "Those fiends are on our trail, never fear. They're slipping along as silently as shadows and not far away right now. Perhaps they've even got ahead of us, some of them, trying to ring us in." I cast an apprehensive glance through the sun-splashed gloom.

We stepped abruptly through a leafy tangle into a path or animal run.

"Thank God!" muttered Bill as he quickened his pace. Fergus and I followed closely on his heels. "We might get away now," he continued.

"If it's an animal trail, yes," I began. "If this leads to a village, no. For it might be that the villagers are the ones who attacked us."

"Speed is what counts now," snapped Fergus, "not talk," and he pushed past Bill.

"Something else counts most of all—something that neither of you has got," I growled as I jerked Fergus back and took the lead myself. As swiftly as possible I moved forward, yet cautiously, too. Our attackers might be ahead of us and it would be an ideal trick to ambush us, slipping the steel into our defenseless bodies as we brushed past some leafy covert. Not a pleasant thought, that.

Yet, somehow, I didn't think they had passed us. Something within me warned me of danger, yet I was sure that any danger from them was in our rear. But if this path led indeed to a village, there was before us a silent danger more to be dreaded even than that other. So as I slipped along, my eyes were darting everywhere. I stopped at last, so abruptly that Fergus and Bill, crowding me closely, bumped into each other.

"What's the matter?" growled Bill, his voice a mere whisper. I pointed at the trail before us. "I don't see a thing but a leaf or two," he added and tried to push by.

Roughly I pulled him back and, stooping, I carefully lifted a large leaf from the path while they eyed me intently. Carefully I picked up the thorn concealed beneath it, with its gummy message of violent death.

Carefully I searched the ground for more. There were no more. It was alone.

Bill's face was white, his eyes incredulous. "God! Suppose we had stepped on it," he whispered through stiff lips.

"Death, eh?" Fergus' voice was steady but a glance at his eyes showed that he thoroughly understood the situation.

I nodded none too cheerfully as I went on again more cautiously than ever. Soon the path forked.

"Which way?" asked Bill.

Almost without a pause I turned to the left. "The other path goes to a village," I whispered. "And it isn't friendly. They want no visitors."

"How do you know?" Fergus was frankly curious.

"You saw that little bamboo lying across the path, didn't you?" I asked, never turning my head. "That is a plain warning. The path is closed to strangers. Beyond it—"

"More poisoned thorns, eh?" he finished quietly.

"Yes, or worse," I promised.

"This path, now," began Bill.

"Probably runs to the river," I cut in. "And if it's not a game trail there may be a boat. If not—"

"If not," Bill interrupted brusquely, "I've got four more clips of ammunition. How many have you?"

"Six." My eyes never left the trail ahead.

We crossed a glade, and as we entered the jungle again Bill stopped.

"Go on," he directed. "I'll join you in a few minutes. I've had a feeling we were being followed."

"So have I. It's been getting stronger and stronger," said Fergus.

The place was ideal to stop those we were confident were so hot on our trail should they cross the glade openly. Should they skirt it, however—but I did not let my mind dwell on that. Bill was a sharpshooter, and in any event he would not go on the long trail alone.

The path was leading downward into a valley. We must be almost to the river. Our luck was still holding. If there were a boat, now—I heard the crack of Bill's pistol—once—twice—three times—then silence. Fergus stopped.

"I'm going back," he snapped. I laid my hand on his arm.

"No use, lad," I soothed. "Bill's all right. He stopped them, at any rate, whether he got any or not. And they haven't got him, I'm sure. He will be streaking it to us now. If he doesn't—"

I didn't finish, but Fergus' face grew grim as he nodded.

"You're right, Jock. It wouldn't do any good. But if he—" And then Bill was with us again.

"Got another," he jubilated. "Eight between the eyes. And pinked another, I think. They're Mongols, just as I thought—raiders from the North."

My face lighted. "Fine," I exclaimed. "And they have a hostile village behind them."

"By Jove, that's right," Fergus grinned. "And this racket is more than likely to bring the villagers out, too."

I nodded as I swiftly took the trail again.

Perhaps our good luck made us careless; certainly there was little excuse for our running into that ambush. The first I knew of it was seeing one of those flashing throwing-knives streak past me. I ducked instinctively and so escaped the withering shower of slugs and scrap-iron discharged by an old smoothbore muzzle-loader that let go almost at the same instant. Fergus, just behind, was not so fortunate. His hissing indrawn breath told me he was hit, no less than his stagger. Bill's gun and mine exploded at the same instant, and a shriek answered their reports, but whether it was a death cry or not we couldn't tell.

Fergus sank slowly to the side of the trail and a red tide dyed his tattered shirt. Quickly I stooped and got his arm about my neck, then lifted him bodily the while I swung my gun in my left hand in wide arcs covering the jungle before me.

Bill's eager glances stabbed the green gloom about us, but the jungle was still as death. He moved forward close beside the trail like a shadow, taking advantage of every bit of cover while I followed with my burden as well as I could. Fergus' breath came in painful gasps, but he gritted his teeth and doggedly kept on.

It was utter foolhardiness for us to advance so, but with enemies ahead and behind, desperate measures were necessary. And such a desperate play might succeed through its sheer unexpectedness.

So it proved. Bill got in one more shot at a half-seen figure that was gone again in a flash, and, though we crawled along at a snail's pace, we saw no others. Perhaps we had been ambushed by so few that they had no chance in the face of our bold move. Perhaps our one hit had destroyed their desire for combat at close quarters; at any rate we saw no more of them just then.

The ground beneath our feet was becoming a quivering jelly, a swampy quagmire that betrayed the river's proximity. The gloom was even more pronounced, with an oppressive quiet in the air, a sullen foreboding. Despite the heat I shivered.

On such treacherous footing I was hard put to go on with Fergus, and after several hundred feet of it I was almost exhausted. But the gloom was lightening; the jungle was changing; we must be almost to the river.

I could go no farther. Rest I must; my breath came in whistling gasps; I streamed perspiration. Chase or no chase, I could go no farther.

Close beside the path was a round rock about waist-high, and a short distance away a number of others offered an ideal resting-place as well as shelter should we

be attacked. Bill stopped on the path, his glance darting
incessantly about, every sense on the alert, and I carefully
eased Fergus onto the nearest rock—not a rock after all,
but some kind of spongy vegetable growth such as I had
never seen before. Warily I rocked on my feet, too spent
to take the few steps that separated this growth from the
others. Bill dropped back to us and the lines in his face
smoothed themselves momentarily as he smiled.

"We'll make it, old things," he encouraged. "It can't be
far now."

Fergus' chin slumped forward onto his chest; his body
sagged slowly toward us as I jumped for him. He was per-
ilously close to a collapse, though the Lord knows he had
gone through enough to try even a well man. His face
was gray, his eyes closed. My arm about his shoulders, I
strove to raise him, but he seemed made of lead. Again I
heaved—no result. Bill stepped to the other side and we
tried together with no better luck.

Then the terrible truth struck home to both of us.
Fergus was held fast by that strange vegetable growth on
which he sat. His legs seemed half embedded in its rub-
bery substance. But that was not the worst. All about him,
through those plant tissues, was a red stain, deepest close
to him and fading gradually away.

I think I was the first to understand. Some few carnivorous plants I had seen before, but not of such a size or
shape; my experience having been confined to Venus fly-
traps and pitcher-plants back in the dim days of my youth.

"We've got to free him from this thing. Bill," I said
rapidly. "It's not only holding him fast but it's drawing
every drop of blood out of him," and I pointed to that
darkening stain.

"God!" gasped Bill as his nimble mind took it all in at
a flash. He heaved and tugged till his mighty thews and

sinews cracked. As well have tried to pull down a vine-entangled jungle giant bare-handed as to pull that yielding form from the plant's tenacious grip.

"Cut him free with your knife, Bill," I suggested.

"I can't," he groaned. "I lost it crawling out of the temple through the passage."

"I lost mine, too," I admitted hopelessly. Oh, for one of those throwing-knives that had flashed past me not so long ago!

But Bill was heaving and tugging again in a frenzy. In desperation he jumped upon that spongy mass, stooped, and then lifted Fergus with a firm grip under his arms. Just such a heave had I seen him make in Singapore one day when he had lifted the end of a great teak-wood timber so they could take the crushed body of a coolie laborer from beneath it. But all in vain: though he heaved and tugged till I feared for Fergus' body, he never raised him an inch; he merely sank his own feet into the spongy mass to his ankles. And Fergus' legs, I noticed, were now almost buried in that frightful plant, while the red stain had spread through its entire bulk. And Fergus' face and arms were turning a sinister bluish color.

Oppressed by a sudden fear, I thrust my hand within his tattered shirt. I groaned. Fergus was dead. Not the slightest tremor rewarded my exploring fingers pressed over his heart. It was stilled forever.

"He's dead, Bill," I shuddered. "One of those slugs must have got him worse than we thought and he bled internally, or—"

"Or this devilish plant killed him," and then Bill's face became a tragic mask of terror. "It's got me, too," he screamed, while he struggled wildly to free himself from that deadly grip about his ankles. But each violent struggle only sent him the deeper into that yielding mass.

Fergus' legs had vanished entirely into that horrid thing. He was engulfed almost to the waist and sinking slowly ever deeper. Bill had sunk ankle-deep before he discovered he was trapped, and his struggles to free himself speedily sank him almost to his knees.

Helplessly, sick at heart, I watched the hopeless struggle, unable to help in any way. There was nothing I could do bare-handed; no one to whom I could appeal for help. The brigands behind us, the natives behind them—all hostile, all seeking our death.

Bill was the first to recover his nerve. Face to face with a terrible and certain death that had already taken his brother and was about to claim him, he nevertheless refused to yield after his first momentary lapse.

"Go on, Jock," he urged. "You can make the river, perhaps. Take Fergus' gun and ammunition and his rubies. Here's mine." He tossed me three flashing bits of flame. "They're yours, and welcome. I'll hold those devils back when they come as long as I—"

He shuddered. I knew what he meant by that unfinished sentence. I shook my head in negation.

"Go on, you fool!" he raged. "There's none to mourn me. Good riddance to bad rubbish. The world's the better for me leaving it," and he grinned wryly. "Perhaps I can do a little bit of good now to offset all the bad. Go on, old top, and good luck." So in the end I was persuaded.

Heavy-hearted I went forward, carrying with me the loot of two dead men and that of another who faced horrible death and hopeless odds as I may someday hope to face them, unafraid and smiling. A gun in each hand, I crept slowly along that shaking, sucking path that threatened each moment to dissolve into abysmal ooze beneath my feet—onward to I knew not what, I knew not where. Death, certain and terrible, was behind me where it had already overtaken all of my comrades in most horrible forms. Would it get me too, I wondered? Would the powerful long arm of that long-forgotten, long-neglected god of destruction reach out even to me? In my heart was a sick dread, and a determination to do my best, whatever the odds.

I made my way through the gloom, my eyes ever ahead, my ears turned backward to where that grim, terrible thing was happening—or was it all over? What a cowardly fool I had been to leave! Yet, perhaps I would have been a greater one to have stayed.

No, it was not all over yet. I heard Bill's pistol cracking spitefully—half a dozen times; then after a pause, another string of shots.

Good old Bill! A man at the last, whatever his faults. Going down like a hero, game to the very last, never giving up, even though the odds were overwhelming.

My mind was engrossed over what was behind me when it should have been most concerned with what lay ahead. That is my only excuse for what happened. The path dissolved suddenly into nothingness; I scrambled madly for another precarious foot-hold; half turned, and began sinking slowly into that deadly muck—sinking to a death no less terrible, no less certain than those others had been.

I felt the muck creeping slowly and steadily upward. Already my thoughts pictured its constricting clutch about my chest, its deadly entry into my throat and lungs. Ugh! What a way to die—unseen, unheeded!

But wait! Perhaps there was a more merciful death even now creeping along that path behind me. I strained my eyes through the semigloom, hoping to see the skulking forms of the bandits. Better the merciful crash of a destroying bullet or the stabbing pain of one of those deadly knives than this slow, sucking horror about me.

Knee-deep already, I made no useless moves that might drive me down the faster. Though death seemed certain, I would not give up hope until the last. My guns in my hands, I would go down shooting if the enemy came. If not—well, I would go down anyway, perhaps with a last mercy bullet from my own hand.

What was that movement back there along the trail? Had they caught up so soon? Yet, it couldn't be. It might be monkeys, perhaps, in the trees above the trail; humans were hardly likely to come so.

Dimly through the oppressive gloom I made out a round, brilliant blue globe swaying at the end of a slender stalk and gathering to itself the faint light of that dense growth until it seemed to glow like a monster jewel. While I watched, several more of them appeared, rising above the lush jungle growth and bobbing gracefully above the path I had come. Odd how such trivial things should register on my mind in this extremity.

Slowly I sank into the slime—waist-deep—then more slowly yet until that filthy mess was up about my chest. But so slowly now was I sinking that I could scarce tell it. The minutes dragged endlessly by; each seemed like an eternity.

Would they never come, I wondered, after what seemed years of waiting? Had Bill's last fusillade beaten them off for good? I think I really hoped for the bandits' coming; anything was better than this slow, horrible approach of death, alone and unheeded.

Again and again I twisted my head around to view that path along which I had come, but it was utterly without movement save for the swaying and bobbing of those lustrous blue globes above the rank, steaming jungle growth.

Ten more minutes passed—or perhaps it was an hour—I don't know. The ooze had risen no higher. Though I felt nothing solid beneath my feet, I had failed to sink any deeper; I must be floating in that semi-fluid mess. My heart rose at the discovery, yet my reason told me that it meant nothing: I was helpless unless assistance of some sort arrived. Though I might not suffocate under that filthy ooze, I was doomed no less surely.

I felt, rather than saw, a movement beside the path; my quickened senses warned me that my pursuers had arrived. By straining to the utmost I could swing my arm around so that my gun commanded the path. Carefully I sighted into the thick of that dense growth; blindly I pressed the trigger, and the spiteful crack of my revolver broke through that brooding oppressive silence, to echo and re-echo against the thick leafy growth that hemmed me in.

I saw the bullet shatter one of those bobbing blue globes; saw the shattered shards drop, followed by a blue smokelike cloud of dust that settled slowly. Again I fired, aiming blindly, and yet a third time, but the only tangible result was the shattering of yet more of those odd things, followed by other clouds of that blue dust that sank slowly out of sight behind that luxuriant jungle growth, spreading as it dropped.

Had I imagined the presence of an enemy? Were my senses giving way under the strain of this terrible ordeal? It would seem so. The jungle was as motionless as ever. Not a sound, not a movement betrayed the proximity of man. Ah, I had it! They hadn't seen me yet; they were trying to locate me.

A scream rang out—wild, inarticulate with fear, with agony. And hard on its echoes the jungle woke to life with a chorus of them; the death-still growth sprang to motion as half a score of frenzied figures broke out into the path.

It was the end, I told myself grimly, the last desperate charge that must surely overwhelm me. Very well. Let them come. It was at least a relief after all these horrors. I was ready to die. But I would not go alone. I would hold my bullets until I could make them all count. There would be plenty to join me as I took that last long trail.

But it was not the rush of an attack after all. These ter-ror-stricken Chinese half-castes were too utterly demoral-ized to think of anything but blind flight—flight in any direction in their frenzied efforts to get away from that accursed spot. While I watched I saw two of them pushed headlong from the path into that morass that hedged it so closely, to sink into its depths still struggling madly and screaming eerily at the top of their singsong voices.

In God's name, what had happened there? Another dropped across the path, writhing in agony, and yet an-other. In all directions they sprang, colliding blindly with the jungle growths, slipping heedlessly off the path to sink into that deadly slime, or dropping in their tracks to lie threshing with pain. One huge, half-naked fiend sprang directly toward me, dropping into the ooze only a few feet away, where he twisted and clawed blindly.

As I watched his death agonies my dazed mind dimly grasped its stupendous horror. My bullets had not gone so wild as I had expected after all. True, I had hit no human body, but I had loosed upon these cutthroats something more deadly for them than mere bullets. Those slowly sinking, spreading blue clouds had dropped upon their naked bodies, unnoticed perhaps, but only so for a few moments.

Dustlike spores they must have been, of some gigan-tic fungi unknown to science, growing in that almost un-known land; another of those terrible carnivorous plants such as had laid hold of Bill and his brother a short while before—or was it ages ago?

The gleaming yellow body so close to me was stilled now; its struggles were over. Even as I watched, a terrible change was going on—a change that my mind refused al-most to believe. Swiftly its color was changing from yellow to blue. Its outlines grew indistinct. The upper part of the torso seemed dissolving into a mass of little tentacles that grew rapidly and stretched upward in a compact group. Higher and higher they rose until they stood a foot above the level of the morass—two feet—three—. And now from among them were pushing up colorless spikes that gleamed whitely as they rose swiftly. Up, up, up, until only by straining my head backward with all my might could I see their tips.

Their upward growth was stopped, yet they seemed still in motion. The rods were becoming more slender, the tips were thickening rapidly. Now the whiteness of them was changing to a deep glistening blue and the thickened tips were becoming those glistening blue globes I had seen rising above the jungle growth, while the compact mass of tentacles at their base was assuming a wilted, shriveled appearance, to fall over at last, a putrescent mass, upon what had once been a human body vibrant with life. Only upon the path I saw the leg lying of what had so short a time before been a man.

Dimly in the back of my mind some memory was struggling toward the surface of its consciousness. In my school days, in my youth I had watched slimes and molds under the high-powered microscope and had seen those tiny infinitesimal growths complete their life cycle so. But they had been tiny growths, fractional parts of an inch in height—never such monstrosities as these. And their similar upthrust sporangia held in their shells the dustlike spores of another such life circle, even as these blue globes that bobbed about in the air above me.

So far I reasoned, when like a flash, my own danger came to me. These spore-cases bobbing above me so lazily held another such cycle within their gleaming shells. In the fullness of time they would open, dropping another slow-floating, blue, dustlike cloud to settle down, down, down upon me held fast by the ooze beneath them.

In that moment I think I went stark, raving mad, screaming curses at the top of my voice, beating wildly at the viscous unresisting filth that held me there, until at last reason fled.

What happened after that I could dimly reconstruct when, I know not how long after, I woke once more to reason within the high latticework hut of a native village. So weak that the slightest move took prodigious effort, I opened my eyes to the blazing sunlight and stupidly watched a native woman busy at her mud hearth preparing a meal. She turned and smiled as she saw my eyes upon her, calling in her musical voice while the hut shook as someone climbed the ladder without and a man entered; a golden-hued native like the many I have met in that upland country.

For many days I dwelt with them, slowly regaining strength under their ministrations, until at last I could travel again. From that hut, one of the pitiful few that formed the village, under the guidance of the native, I made my way back to the Irriwaddy and the trader's landing.

Of the scene on that jungle path or the ruined temple with its forgotten treasure they could not or would not tell me. Nor would they talk of my rescue. I surmised that the man had come along that path of sucking, treacherous death and had plucked my unconscious body from its slimy embrace, bringing me to the village. Of my guns or the rubies there was no sign; they must have been sucked down into the ooze.

Back once more at the river's edge, I loaded my guide with what was to him a veritable treasure of brass rings and armlets, smiling a return to his thanks while my eyes traveled over the breast of that tawny stream that would carry me away forever from that still powerful though forgotten god whose arm had so nearly taken me.

MOSS ISLAND
Carl Jacobi

Fifteen miles off the New Brunswick coast, to the south of Marchester yet north of Lamont, lies a great timber-covered rock which has become known as Moss Island. With its endless chain of reefs, its frowning sheer walls, and its bastions of dense underbrush and giant trees, the island has remained untrespassed and primeval. Fishermen fear its jagged sides and keep well away. And as far as I have been able to learn, I am the only human being, or at least the only one for years, who has cared to visit its Eden shores.

For the sum of ten dollars, a little fishing smack had brought me out, had carefully threaded its way to a bit of beach on the western side.

"You're a darn fool," the rather deaf owner of the boat had growled when we arrived. "I'm givin' ya fair warnin'. I'll keep my part of the bargain and come back for ya at five o'clock, but only if the weather permits. I'm not so crazy about the looks of that sky over there, and if there's anythin' stronger'n a breeze comes up—well, you can figure on stayin' here 'til it calms down. I ain't a-goin' through that bunch of saw-teeth in a wind for the fun of it. Not with my boat. Anyway, what's interestin' here? Nothin' on Moss Island but trees and rocks. Not even any moss no more. Somethin' killed it," and he pointed to a smooth expanse of black rock, in places covered by a mass of last year's vines, dead and brown colored. One slab high above me looked like a woman with long, flowing hair, a great embossed Medusa, it seemed, when the wind ruffled the withered grasses.

"That's Mape vine, not moss," I corrected him. "There's probably lots of moss farther in where there's damp shade." I picked up my hammer, my chart-drawing board and my knapsack and stepped from the boat, adding in explanation: "I'm going to do a little geological survey work, examine the rock formations, you know; and I don't think we'll have a storm. The weather report didn't say so."

He gave a derisive humph, whether at the nature of my work or my remark about meteorology I was left wondering, for without another word he shoved off. For a while I watched the boat bobbing away through the white caps, the little sail growing smaller and smaller and showing clean white in contrast to the green water and the blue sky. Then I turned to my surroundings.

I was still below the island proper, the cliff running some thirty to fifty feet up to the edge of the woods. In some places the wall was almost perpendicular, and I looked about for means of climbing it. Farther on along the beach I came upon a break and a series of jags which, with a little manoeuvring, would serve as a staircase. I began my ascent. It was hard, slow work. Gulls whirled about me at my interruption, filling the air with their clamor. Ensnarled Mape vine impeded my progress, and clumps of scarlet bush, which seemed to thrive on the scant nourishment it found in soil-filled crevices, dug its thorns relentlessly into my hands. Upon a little jutting shelf I saw a dead snake, its head hanging into space as though watching something below.

At length I reached the top, which I found to be flat as a plateau, the surface from the edge of the cliff quite void of vegetation for a distance of about five yards, when abruptly began a wall of trees, the outer ones bearing evidence of the ravages of the elements. Peering off to sea again, I tried to catch sight of the boat that had brought me, but though I looked until the air before my eyes appeared porous, I could see no sign of it.

Striving to throw off a growing feeling of depression, I broke out into a loud whistle, following any tune my lips desired. The whistle seemed to travel for miles in the clear air. It rose above the trees and went far over the island. There was no echo. Only the waves swashed over rocks below me, and as I walked along the screaming cries of a solitary gull fell perfectly into the rhythmic cadence of my steps.

I kept close to the edge of the cliff. To have attempted penetrating that jungle of growth would have been foolhardy. So I watched for a place where the trees might thin down, reflecting idly that the glacial drift must be of a considerable depth to support such extensive vegetation. About half a mile onward I found some pieces of shale with a few shell fossils and a small slab of limestone with remarkably clear impressions of crinoids. These ancient forms of marine life I determined to be of the Mississippian geologic period.

But for some reason I lost interest in my work. The very solitude of the island seemed to have crept into me and dulled my senses. Occasionally I was forced to enter the wood to circle a mound of larger rocks that defied ascent. Occasionally I caught the glint of the sun shining upon the bloated body of a dead fish lying far below on the little stretch of sand. And although I had gone only a short distance, all the while the weight of my knapsack seemed steadily increasing.

By three o'clock I had almost reached the opposite side of the island. It was there on the eastern exposure that I came upon a sheer wall, a rock formation that would have delighted the most experienced geologist. Here with the Pennsylvania strata folded and resting upon the eroded edges of the Mississippian was a great sedimentary history of geologic time.

For a long while I examined the wall—from its base upward as high as I could reach. At length, taking my hammer, I began working on a rather peculiar outcropping vein or rather a slight discoloration on the rock. Strange enough, as I went deeper the color changed: from a dark brown at the surface to a reddish brown and from a reddish brown to a deep scarlet. If this were oxidation . . . but no. . . . And then suddenly my hammer broke through— into a cavity in the limestone, a large hole which had been hollowed out by the ground water slowly filtering through the rock crevices and in the course of time dissolving the soluble parts. Such cavities are common to limestone, I knew, but sometimes rather interesting phenomena accompanies them. And so with a feeling of expectation I went to work with a will, enlarging the aperture until it was wide enough to thrust in my hand.

I extended my arm into the opening gently, clawed air for a moment, and then reaching downward, felt a cold, sticky liquid touch the fingers. Hastily I drew my hand to sight. It was dripping with a brownish, viscous solution that had a musty odor. I stared in amazement. Pockets of mineral water are not uncommon in this district, but always it is clear and transparent. Never had I come upon any liquid formation in such a mucilaginous state.

The thought of oil flashed across my mind. I cast it aside with a sheepish smile. There is no oil on the New Brunswick coast nor for thousands of miles in any direction. And this brownish mass in no way resembled crude petroleum. It was very odd.

And then quite suddenly I remembered a recent conversation with Professor Monroe at the University of Rentharp, where I am doing graduate work in geology and mineralogy.

"Phillip," he had said when I came upon him in one of the laboratories before a table of vials, tubes, and instruments, "Phillip, I believe I've made a discovery." And while he worked he had told me in his short, jerky, nervous manner about muscivol, the name which he had given to his find. "It is very rare," he had said, "rarer than radium."

I have always been interested in botany and I have a fair knowledge of the subject, but I confess some of his scientific explanation went over my head. This much, however, I roughly gathered:

In northern climates, under favorable conditions, can be found a rare moss which resembles and yet fundamentally differs from the common *Saelania* moss. After living in great luxuriance for a number of seasons, this *Musci* plant will suddenly die. If the diseased plant is examined just before its death, it will be found that almost a reversal of the natural processes of growth is going on.

A month earlier a small blister or pouch develops just above the rootlets. And for some unknown reason most of the food elements which the plant obtains from the soil and from the air, instead of serving to nourish the whole plant, gather and centralize in this pouch in liquid form. The rest of the plant is thus robbed of its food; it can no longer live healthily, and growing in damp places as it does, it is slowly overcome by rot.

The decay affects the contents of the pouch. The liquid goes through a process of fermentation, though that is hardly the correct term. At length, however, the pouch bursts and the liquid soaks into the soil.

If a large number of these diseased moss plants are present, the ground will be almost saturated with the liquid.

In time—always under favorable conditions—the liquid will soak down until it reaches and becomes a part of the ground-water—that is: the water in the solid rock below the surface which one taps when digging a well.

Limestone is full of subterranean cavities. The water carrying this plant-liquid in solution may find one of these, enter it, and become stagnant. Gradually the cavity deep down in the rock will be filled with the pouch-liquid of hundreds of these diseased mosses. And what is equally important with it will be certain amounts of mineral matter which is always present in the ground-water.

"Nowhere can it be found in the same intensity," Professor Monroe had said, "and in no two places is it really the same, for the mineral matter in the solution will always vary."

"Well, what good is it?" I had asked, rather bored by his long explanation.

The professor had put down his test tube, leaned across the laboratory table and said slowly: "I have discovered by accident that sometimes this liquid—Muscivol, I have called it—sometimes it contains all the elements of growth."

"What do you mean?" I asked, puzzled.

"I mean that if I apply a small quantity of it that has the right amount of mineral matter in solution to the original moss plant, one in healthy condition, its rate of growth will be speeded up tremendously. I mean that the few drops of Muscivol I have been able to find when placed on the stalk of a moss plant caused it to leap upward to twice its original size in a few seconds."

And as I stood there on the cliff, staring at my dripping fingers, it all came back to me. With a start I realized that this must be a vug of Muscivol, that rarest of liquids, the essence of moss growth. In haste I emptied the coffee from my thermos bottle and, using the cover as a cup, carefully reached into the cavity and with the utmost care began the process of capturing as much of the sticky fluid as I could. I smiled to myself as I pictured Professor Monroe's surprise and delight when I brought him this find. The most he had been able to discover was a few drops, while here was almost a quart. True, I did not know as yet if it contained the necessary mineral matter to make it potent. That I must leave to the professor and his test tubes. When I had filled the thermos bottle, I carefully closed it and placed it in my knapsack.

The next hour I spent in making a rough chart of the sedimentary wall before me and writing in notebook a brief geologic description of the island, this, of course, was part of my university work, length, the brief survey completed, it occurred to that I still had time for further exploration before boatman would return, and so shouldering my knapsack, I headed into the interior.

In a moment, as though a mighty door were shut, the woods closed dark upon me, and I found myself in a jungle of growth that discouraged further penetration. Gradually, however, as I struggled forward, the underbrush, finding insufficient sunlight to exist, thinned down until there were left only trees and moss. The strange, luxuriant abundance of the latter accounted, I saw, for the island's name. Fern moss, Long moss, Urn and Cord moss, *Catharinaea angustata*, *Polytrichum strictum*, and tree moss—in every division common to the northeastern United States the *Musci* order here was represented.

On rotting logs, at the foot of trees, in parasitical clumps upon the trunks, and on the ground as a soft carpet of damp green—everywhere was moss. With its perpetual damp and shade and its moist sea air, the island seemed to present strangely perfect conditions for this plant.

The wood was silent about me now, and only occasionally, when the tessellation of verdure above became less dense, could I see the light of the sky. As I went deeper, the trees seemed to take definite positions in the forest about me, to form long, dark corridors with winding turns. The mosses lost their dark greenish hue and developed into a bluish yellow, a sickly yellow in the morbose gloom. The air was moist and warm. It weighed heavily upon my lungs and seemed to throw a great torpor over my body. I wiped the perspiration from my forehead and went on. The island, it appeared, was infested with blue jays, jays strangely fat and overnourished. Great flocks of them rose up at my approach, their screaming cries filtering slowly through the sodden air like the death wails of a thousand drowning cats.

But as I went farther and farther, even they disappeared, and I was left with only the walls of trees, the floor of moss and the gloom. I saw more varieties now: Shaggy moss, Hooked moss, and Hair-capped moss. Yellowish plants, they were, sickly and flaccid in the half light.

At random I chose one of the corridors through the trees and made my way slowly forward, my steps velveted in the soft grasses. Winding, yet ever going deeper into the interior, the walled lane stretched before me like a living gallery. The intertanglement of foliage far above was heavy and dense, admitting no light but only a strange green glow. An odor of rot rising from the earth crept into my nostrils, and I began to breathe with difficulty.

It was a quarter after four by my watch when I reached a point where the trees opened abruptly onto a little glade. Roughly estimating this to be about the heart, the center of the island, I was about to turn and retrace my steps when a mass of white at the far side of the open space caught my eye. I stepped forward and found myself gazing at a great circle of densely packed *White Moss*. For some moments I stood there, looking down at the cushion-like tufts as a wave of loathing slowly rose within me.

The species I had recognized as what is technically known as *Leucobryum glaucum*, a *Musci* plant common enough in moist woods, but for some reason, whether because of its contrast to the green and yellow moss on all sides or the anemic pallor of its gray whiteness, I viewed it here with a feeling of utter revulsion. There was something repulsive about the very way it sprawled across the glade.

During all this time, with the enthusiasm of exploration, I had almost forgotten my finding of the liquid in the limestone cavity. Now, however, I felt a sudden desire to prove to myself beyond a doubt that the solution really was Muscivol, by observing how this moss plant would react to a few drops. Quickly I unfastened my knapsack, drew forth the thermos bottle, and unscrewed the cap. Then carefully tilting it over the matted circle of white moss, I let a small amount of the brownish liquid fall.

The result was amazing. The plant quivered a half moment, then shot upward with terrific growth rate. Unconsciously I jumped back. My foot caught in a bramble. I lost my balance and fell full length. The thermos bottle bounced from my hand, rolled across the ground straight into the White Moss plant, and there the viscous contents began to pour forth.

With a cry of dismay I realized what had happened. A quart of Muscivol was upon the plant, a quart where a few drops had been multipotent. A great shudder ran through the moss. A sobbing sigh came from its grasses. And then with a roar, the rootlets gouged down into the ground, tore at the soil, and the plant with a mighty hiss raced upward, five feet, ten feet. The tendrils swelled as though filled with pressure, became fat, purulent, octopus folds. Like the undulations of some titanic marine plant the white coils waved and lashed the air. Up they lunged, the growth rate multiplied ten thousand times.

A tentacle in its mad gyrations brushed my face. I screamed in horror, turned to the wood and ran—down the long corridors, the lanes, the galleries, through the trees. Behind me the roar rose into a great thunder; the hissing stabbed the air like escaping steam. On through the dark woods I raced, a wave of wild fear surging over me. Looking over my shoulder, I could see the white moss with coils like cables now, climbing over the trees, advancing with frightful velocity. Muscivol! What fiendish chemical was this that could destroy the very laws of nature? The black boles of the trees like shrouded phantasms leered at me in mocking answer as I lunged by them. A great wail rose up as a thousand terrified blue jays flapped away in a mad hegira for safety. The forest was endless. Miles I seemed to have run, but with a heart pounding triphammer pulsations I tore on even faster toward the cliff.

At length I reached it, emerged into the open air, but found the day not as I had left it. A heavy fog had rolled in from the sea, had thrown a veil over the entire coast.

I did not stop. To the rear the wall of white was lunging over the island now like a tidal wave. Came the repercussions of the crashing of trees, snapping under the great weight of the moss. The growth fulminations pounded against my ear drums until they seemed ready to crack. Along the cliff, through the thickening fog, I ran. And suddenly a fearful thought came to me. Suppose the boatman had not returned? Plangent and insanely insistent, the question beat through my brain. I could see myself being crushed, strangled, smothered in those white folds.

Again I looked back. Again I screamed in stark horror. With frightful rapidity the advancing moss was gaining on me. Like an octopus the tentacles were clawing the sky, engulfing the whole island. And now the ground beneath my feet, torn and ruptured by the distant moss roots, began to shake in cataclysmic convulsions.

But at length I reached the break in the cliff where I had made my ascent from the beach. I ran to the edge and peered over. The boat was there! Through the haze of the fog I could see it drawn up on the sand, the boatman placidly smoking his pipe, waiting. Never was a sight more welcome, and with a prayer of thanks I leaped to the jags in the rock sides and began my descent. Going down was harder than coming up. Twenty times I saved myself from falling only by grasping the Mape vine coils. The thorns of the scarlet bushes stabbed to the bone.

How I ever reached the bottom safely I don't know. I remember running wildly across the beach to the boat, climbing in, and shouting something unintelligible to the astonished boatman. And then we were out on the water, heading into the fog, the cool salt air fanning my face.

I came to my senses finding the old man chafing my wrists.

"What in thunder happened?" he asked. "What's the matter?"

I stood up in the rocking boat. Vaguely, indistinctly through the haze I could see the great bulk of the island a half mile to our lea.

"That moss!" I cried, "that wall of white moss! Don't you see it?"

He stared over the water, squinting his eyes.

"Moss?" he repeated slowly. "Did you say moss?" and he turned to me with a queer look.

"I don't see no moss," he said. "All I can see is fog, white fog."

THE GIANT PUFFBALL

Eugene Stowell

Professor Hoff was one of those rare men who was both a "pure scientist" and a keen business man. Every schoolboy, I suppose, knows of the many hybrid plants of which he was the originator. In the field of theoretical science he is well known for his work in regeneration and micro-dissection—those two very fascinating problems of modern biology. Many times have I gone into his laboratory at the State University and surprised him at his microscope, busily engaged in taking apart a single cell or injecting into the cell some chemical. More often, however, one could find him in the university greenhouse, working in a shaded section on his special hobby, the giant puffball; *Calvatia gigantea,* it is called by the botanist.

The giant puffball is the grand prize of the mushroom hunter. It is an excellent edible species, abundant, growing on lawns, pastures, and meadows. One of the most impressive features of this giant of its class is its tremendous size. It has been found in nature to grow to enormous dimensions; sometimes it has been found with a circumference of six or seven feet. But its size is not the most interesting feature of this freak of nature. It has great powers of regeneration. That is, the plant has a great propensity to reproduce any part of the huge oval sphere which is its edible part. This huge structure, which resembles a great snowball in color and shape, can be grown in the shade for a long time without turning black and shedding its millions of minute spores or single celled "seeds." This is accomplished by cutting part of the puffball off each day and allowing the plant to regenerate the removed part.

How the professor ever made his great mistake, I do not know. But make it he did. So great was his mistake that the reputation of the man for a long time was in the balance. The welfare of the community, itself, was, and still is, in danger. Perhaps the great man was so engrossed in the idea that he forgot the consequences which might follow. However that might be, it still remains that the unpleasant events which occurred in the greenhouse on Chapel Hill have not been accounted for up to the time of the publication of this article.

My first inkling of the experiment, the first inkling anyone had—for I was a great man's best friend—came to me in the following manner. I had been invited to the scientist's home for supper. This meal consisted of a dish made from a few slices of the giant puffball, on which the professor spent most of his time. After supper, the scientist invited me to his private laboratory in a most mysterious manner. It is unusual for Dr. Hoff to show any emotion, so that I had reason to be exceedingly curious about my trip to the laboratory with him that night. On his table was a wonderful research microscope with full dissecting equipment and a very unique injecting pipette, which could be used to inject small quantities of chemicals into the single cell. It was with this equipment that the great cytologist had made his contributions to the knowledge of the cell.

Dr. Hoff, who is a very small man, looked up at me with his pinpoint eyes on fire behind his great nose and said in a solemn voice, "You are now going to see something that no other man except myself has ever seen."

The doctor was right. With a movement, which would have put Napoleon to shame, the little man adjusted the microscope, turned on the lights, and then stepped back with a grand gesture. I believe that the importance of the discovery had gone to his head. I took one look and then another. What I saw seemed unbelievable. In the field of the microscope there could be seen two or three cells which had just emerged from the spore of the giant puffball. This was not the important thing, however, for the cells were in an actual state of division. One could see the nuclei in the cells break up into small particles; see these particles divide, and then watch half of them go to the opposite ends of the cell. A cell wall was then formed between the two groups of particles. These divisions followed one after the other until I saw a mass of cells, where there had been but two or three before. Not only were the cells dividing at a great rate, but the cells were of an enormous size.

Everyone is familiar with the rapid growth of the common mushroom. They often grow from a very small size to a full-grown toadstool within a few hours, but this spore of *Calvatia gigantea,* had it been given enough nourishment, would have developed into a giant puffball before my very eyes. I turned to the professor for an explanation. With a triumphant smile he gave his answer to the question in my eyes. "I have been working for years on this problem," he said. "By a careful study of the cell I have been able to discover a chemical which will increase the rate of cell-division a hundred times and at the same time increase the size of every cell. Had the cells you saw been given the right kind of nourishment, this division would have gone on until the puffball would have reached the size of a house. That is what I propose to bring about."

I did not see the Doctor for several weeks because of an extended business trip I was forced to take. Nor did I hear from Dr. Hoff, for, like many men, he is a poor letter writer. When at last I could find time to call on him at his greenhouse, he greeted me as we greet a friend whom we know we can trust with a real secret. Without saying a word about his problem, he took me into the greenhouse and into the part of that structure which was shut off from excessive light and prying eyes. There stood the monster, for I know not what else to call it. One could see it expand and move as new cells were constantly being added to the bulk of the huge oval thing. At that time the structure must have been at least ten feet in diameter and slowly but visibly it was expanding. Over the greenhouse there hung a sickly musty odor. The scientist explained that he had injected his chemical into the spore of a giant puffball and had given it nourishment and shelter in the greenhouse. He had, from time to time, taken some of the growing tissue off of the white, oval structure, and had thus prevented it from turning black, or rather brown, and sending out its spores.

So great was my awe of the enormity of the discovery and so overcome by a fear of this creature was I, a fear, which I could not explain, that I slept but little that night. In the morning a new fear came to me with a suddenness that left but one purpose in my mind. I must warn the professor before it was too late. But the professor did not need the warning. When I arrived, I learned that the poor fellow had also been up all night, watching the monster grow, until he had reached the same conclusion which I had come to.

"Doctor, you must get rid of this terrible thing," I said. "If you do not stop its growth, it will become so enormous that it will destroy the building, perhaps other things—maybe even human life!"

But the Doctor was far ahead of me. He looked at me with those disconcerting eyes of his and said, "My dear friend, you do not begin to see the terrible situation in which I have unwittingly placed myself. Come to the greenhouse with me; you will see for yourself."

The poor man had been very busy that morning. Around the glass walls of the greenhouse he had had erected what seemed to me to be much the same thing as a circus tent. We walked inside. All was dark, but everywhere there was that nauseating odor. When I became accustomed to the poor light, I could make out the outline of what had been the greenhouse. Here and there the glass was broken and a grey white substance protruded into the opening. The monster had grown too big for the building over night! And now and then the glass could be heard to crash and the ominous silence was broken. What terrible forces the scientist had let loose! Two men had been working at one end of the huge oval all the morning. But to no avail. Every shovel full removed was at once replaced by the thing.

A thought struck me, "Why not let the monster mature and send forth its spores? If it is left alone it will soon do that and the danger will be over." The professor looked at me as a drowning person might look at another giving well-intentioned, but impossible advice.

"My dear fellow," he said, sadly. "If the thing is allowed to shed its spores, the trouble will only have begun. Each spore will develop one of these monsters and these millions of plants will develop millions of spores just as quick in development as this monster is. To keep the thing growing will mean that it will grow to such a size that the buildings will be destroyed one after the other, that the whole town will be in danger. To let the thing shed those spores means a great danger to all of mankind. Think of the power exerted by a blade of grass which grows through a cement walk and then think of millions of this thing all over the land!" The poor fellow had tears in his eyes.

Still the monster grew. Steam-shovels, men with hand-shovels could not remove it. Like a flow of lava it expanded day by day. And underneath the ground the monster was at work. Those thread-like structures, which are to be found in the ground and which supply nourishment to the part of the puffball above ground, were stealthily pushing their way among the soil particles in search of food. Yards and yards the mass of strands grew each day. The soil itself—at least the part on the surface which contained decayed matter—became a mass of thread-like strands of living matter. The monster continued to grow so rapidly that at the end of the week the matter was known to the police and they at once took control of the thing. It was now necessary to close in the entire block which, before the advent of the terrible discovery, had been the location of the greenhouse and the biology building. These buildings were no more. Just as the slow progress of a lava flow goes over or through the things in its path, so the Monster, or Thing, as it was now called, went over or through everything in its path.

But the Thing was not solid as the stream of lava. Only grudgingly did it exert its power when it was necessary to force its way through a window or some other opening. Mostly it was content to go around trees and other ridged things in its path. But it was capable of exerting great force whenever necessary. Its density was not great, a fact which made it more powerful, as the police would soon find out.

From the beginning it was decided to keep the news away from the townspeople. It was for fear of a panic that the police forbade the people of the town to come up Chapel Hill. In reality, Chapel Hill was an island surrounded by the great river which wound about the foot of the incline on which greenhouse and biology building were built. As the entire island was the property of the university and as everyone knew of the peculiar experiments which sometimes were performed on the island, no one gave the recent isolation of the island any thought.

The police naturally thought of explosives as a means of ridding the world of this pest. And so it was that charges of T.N.T. were placed about the Thing and set off. But that availed nothing. The explosions merely tore holes in the soft tissue, which immediately closed up with a sickening sound.

And the thing grew.

By this time the Monster had practically covered the island and Dr. Hoff was at his wits'-end. The police became more disturbed. But the Thing continued to grow until it had the entire island covered with the mass.

There came to the minds of some of us the question whether or not the Monster would not send forth his spores in spite of our efforts. For, as the Thing approached the water, it gradually ceased to respond to the cuts which were given it.

It was the professor who finally solved the problem. He came rushing into my office in the city with news that he had been relieved of his worries. For a moment I thought that he had lost his mind, but his words convinced me that he had really been relieved of the responsibility of having brought the Monster into the world.

It was a simple matter. The Thing had merely used up all the food on the island and was even then at the mercy of the authorities. For years, however, it has been necessary to keep a close watch on the island and exterminate all puffballs which appear upon it. There is still danger that one of these may come from the thread-like portions of the Monster left underground.

But the real cause for uneasiness lies in the fact that the formula for the chemical which was invented by Dr. Hoff was stolen from him. He is not certain just what plants or animals can be made to regenerate from cells in which this chemical has been injected. Owing to the danger involved in the experiment, he had never tried it out after the experiment which nearly proved so disastrous.

AT THE BEND OF THE TRAIL

Manly Wade Wellman

They stood at the bend of the trail, young Bruce Armstrong and white-haired Hubert Whaley, conversing while their black bearers raised their tent and built a cooking-fire. The sun was low on the African horizon and they whiled away the minutes before supper by conversation.

"As I was saying," Whaley told his young friend, "the natives invest every unusual object—rock, hill or what-not—with a supernatural personality and give it a wide berth. Look at this sharp curve in the trail. For years they've been dodging out to one side, just to avoid that root."

He pointed to a strange growth in the lush grass. It was long and crooked, lying in the shape of a letter S. If straight it might have been ten feet long, and it tapered from the size of a man's ankle at the point where it sprouted from the ground to a whiplash tip. It might have been the root of a tree, but there was no stem within yards to which it might attach.

"Rum thing. Looks as if a tree must be growing upside down," commented Armstrong. "Branches in the ground, root in the air, what? A chap could write books and books about uncatalogued plants in these parts. And you say the boys won't touch it?"

"Not one of them," replied Whaley. "Can't say that I blame them. It looks uncanny enough."

"What utter rot!" cried the younger man. "Come now, Whaley, do you mean

to say you give a minute's serious thought to their superstitions?"

"I mean to say that Africa's full of strange beings and doings," was Whaley's sober response. "When you've been here as long as I have—"

"I'm turning missionary this moment," cut in Armstrong. "I don't begrudge the blacks their ideas, but when a good friend and Englishman gets a touch of their religion I have to do something about it.—Hi, you Johnnies!" he cried to the bearers on the other side of the curved trail. "Tumble over here. Tell 'em, Whaley, I don't speak their lingo yet."

At Whaley's call a score of plum-colored men gathered, eyeing the whites with respectful interest.

"Look here, you chaps," said Armstrong. "What's all this about roots and spirits and such like? It's a lot of foolishness, you know.—Pass that on to 'em, Whaley, will you?"

When Whaley had translated, the headman replied that their tribal beliefs had been taught them by wise old men, who must have known the truth.

"Rot!" cried Armstrong when Whaley had rendered this into English. "Rot, I say, and I'll prove it. You're afraid to touch this root, are you?" He stepped close and set his boot-heel on the growth. "Well, then, suppose I show you that it's perfectly harmless."

A cry of alarm went up from the bearers—a cry echoed by Whaley.

"Look out, Armstrong! Look out, man, it's moving!"

The free tip of the root was swaying to and fro, like the head of a blindworm. Even as Armstrong stared in chilled amazement it writhed up from the ground and curled back toward his foot. With a startled exclamation he jumped away. The root-tip sank quickly down and lay motionless again.

Whaley and Armstrong looked at each other, at the root, and at the retreating bearers.

"I call it odd," said Armstrong after a moment, in a voice that quivered ever so slightly. "Something to tell about back home, what?"

"Best leave it alone, old man," counseled Whaley. "Suppose we see what's for supper."

They ate in the gathering gloom, ate silently. In silence they smoked their pipes. The usual singing and laughing of the bearers were subdued also. Whaley noticed Armstrong's nervous fidgeting, wondered what to say, and said nothing. A dry rustle in the grass attracted their attention.

"What's that?" demanded Armstrong sharply. "A snake?"

"Let's have a look-see," suggested Whaley, taking the lantern from the tent-pole. "Dashed unpleasant things, snakes. Bring along the gun—it might be a big one."

But they found no snake, and the bearers, called to help look, said that there were few snakes in this part of the country. Finally the two whites returned to the fire to resume their smoking. Armstrong muttered, twitched and finally broke the silence.

"It's all nonsense, and I say it once for all."

"What's all nonsense? What do you mean?" asked Whaley, though he knew well enough.

"This beastly root business. It gets on my nerves. I can't forget it. When it writhed under my foot—ugh! My flesh crept."

"Don't try to worry it out," Whaley said. "You'll only go batty trying to explain it."

At that Armstrong jumped up, reached into the tool-box just inside the tent and grabbed a hand-ax. With this he strode away toward the trail.

"Don't be a silly ass, man," called Whaley, following him. "What are you going to do?"

"Going to cut that root out," flung back Armstrong. "I've bothered about it quite enough. I shan't sleep to-night, not while the thing's there."

"It's just on your nerves, Armstrong," said Whaley. "I tell you, it's nothing. Just a funny-looking plant that rustled when you kicked it.—Hm! What's this?"

They had come into the bend of the trail. The last rays of light showed them that there was no root there, no growing thing larger than a blade of grass, not even a hole to show where it might have been. The ax drooped in Armstrong's hand. The two stared at each other as the night rode down.

"Wood's scarce hereabouts," said Whaley in a low voice. "Perhaps the boys cut it up and used it for a fire."

Armstrong shook his head. "No, Whaley. You said yourself, and so did they, that it was a thing not to be touched."

They walked back to their camp. The brightness of the lantern shed a little comfort on them as they again sat in silence. "Bed?" suggested Whaley at last, and they entered the tent. "Now, forget—"

"You're a topping fellow, Whaley, but I don't need ba-bying," said Armstrong, sitting on his cot to pull off his boots.

"Of course not. Go to sleep now, there's a good chap, and don't dream of roots."

"Dash it all, who's going to dream about 'em?" said Armstrong as they put out the light and lay down.

Silence yet again, and after a minute or two Whaley could hear Armstrong's deep, regular breathing. The young man was asleep, probably had dismissed the queer adventure of the evening as a trifle, But Whaley, as he himself had said, had lived too long in Africa to banish all strange things so lightly from his mind. He pondered long before he, too, dozed off.

He woke suddenly with a wild shriek splitting his ears, the shriek of a man in mortal terror. He sprang out of bed, shaking the sleep from his eyes. Moonbeams came through the half-opened flaps, showing Armstrong struggling on the ground between the cots. He was fighting somebody or something—Whaley could not see his antagonist. The older man dropped to his knees, reaching out to help. His hands fell on a quivering band that circled Armstrong's chest. He recoiled from it with a cry. He had touched wood, wood that moved and lived like flesh!

"Whaley—the thing—it's choking me!" gasped Armstrong in a rattling voice. "It has a spirit—it's after revenge—"

He writhed along the ground and half out of the tent, then collapsed. In the light from the moon Whaley saw a sight that stirred his white hair. A writhing, cable-like thing was grappling with Armstrong. It had wound twice around his body and arms, and the two loose ends were lashing to and fro like flails.

Whaley flung himself forward again. One of the flailing ends fell on his head, knocking him back into the tent. He went sprawling, half stunned and almost out of the fight. His hand fell into the open tool-box. A single grab found the handle of the ax that Armstrong had picked up earlier in the evening. The feel of the weapon seemed to restore Whaley's strength. Once more he charged into the battle.

Armstrong barely quivered now. Only the nameless attacker moved. Whaley put out his hand and clutched the larger coil that crushed his friend's chest. Sinking his nails into the coarse, splintery skin that coated it, he dragged it

a little free of its hold and struck with the ax. The blade
sank deeply into the tough tissue. He wrenched the ax
free, and the moonlight fell upon the gash, as white as
fresh-cut pine.

The floundering coils churned with new, hostile energy,
loosening their hold on the fallen Armstrong. Whaley
dragged at them, and they leaped and twisted in his hand
like a flooded firehose. The smaller end glided across the
ground and whipped around Whaley's ankle, climbing
it in a spiral. Another loop snapped on his wrist like a
half-hitch, almost breaking it. He grunted at the crushing
agony, but with a supreme effort, drew a length almost
taut between arm and leg. With all the strength of his
right arm he drove the ax. He felt the steel edge bite deep.
The grip on wrist and ankle relaxed and he freed himself
with a sudden struggle. The two sundered halves of the
thing flopped and twisted on the ground, like the pieces
of a gigantic severed worm.

Whaley's mind whirled and he yearned to let himself
drop and swoon, but he lifted the ax and struck again and
yet again. His chest panted, his brow streamed sweat, but
he chopped and chopped until only pulsating fragments
lay around him. He dashed them all into the half-dead
fire, which blazed quickly over this new food.

Then for the first time he realized that the native bearers were gathered, watching in frozen horror. He looked at
them, then at the silent form of his partner. He knelt and
passed his hands over the still body.

"Broken arm—three cracked ribs," he said aloud. "Not
bad for an evil spirit." He called to the headman. "Build
up the fire, heat water. Bring a bottle of brandy. You other
boys, carry him into the tent. Lord, what a country!"

SEEDS FROM SPACE
Laurence Manning

It was blowing half a gale up Broadway, and when I turned along the side street, the rain started. Before I reached the Stranger Club, I was drenched. Inside, the rooms were warmly glowing and the silence made it seem like another world. It was nine in the evening and no one was sitting in the lounge except Colonel Marsh. He raised his bushy white eyebrows and his eyes glanced at my wet clothing like a trainer judging the condition of an athlete.

"Hot toddy!" he said sharply.

"Eh?" I replied, rather startled.

But he made no reply—merely crooked a finger at the steward and, in less than no time, I was ensconced beside him in a comfortable chair sipping the warm stuff. As usual, the Colonel had been right. The toddy was exactly what I needed. My toes began to tingle with warmth and the trophies on the wall over the huge fireplace seemed suddenly cozy and homelike.

"Bad night outside," grunted my companion. I nodded pleasantly. "Reminds me of a curious fellow I once met— and a curious story he told. Just such a night as this," continued Colonel Marsh, and I hitched myself into a more comfortable position and took another sip. But the Colonel had fallen into a reverie and the expected story seemed in danger of never being told. I knew better than to ask

for it—that would get me nowhere. Instead, I racked my
brains for the proper remark.

"I'll bet he didn't offer you a hot toddy," I said at last.

It was his turn to be surprised. "What are you talking
about?"

"This curious chap you mention who told you stories."

"Oh, that," he seemed to bring his voice out of his
chest. "I should say not! I asked for one, though, and he
stared at me as though I had offered to bite him!" After
a moment he sat up in his chair and puffed out his mus-
tache. "I never knew whether or not to believe him. Most
likely he was slightly mad. What do you think?"

"You haven't told me about him yet," I reminded my
companion.

"Eh? Haven't I? Thought I had. It was the trees, you
know. He seemed to think they were alive and could talk
to him, or at least knew what he said. Accused me of murder because I had cut off some spruce branches to make
a bonfire. Asked me how I'd like it if the trees cut off my
arms and legs! Must have been mad, you know!"

"What did you go camping with him for? I should think
you'd have picked better company. Colonel."

"Good God! Who said anything about camping with
him? He came blundering through the woods to my campfire—all excited and waving his arms about. I told him I'd
be most happy to stop burning wood if he'd provide me a
nice warm coal-fire to sit beside. It was a blustery night in
October and it gets pretty uncomfortable up in Maine. So
he hemmed and hawed—dam' fidgety chap, you know—and
invited me to spend the night with him in his camp. So
I did—glad enough, you can wager. His camp was a five-
room house, modern and substantial, but set off all by itself
in as dense a square mile of woods as you have ever seen."

"What were you doing up there in October all by yourself?"

"Hunting. This was years ago when I was a young man. I'd been out after deer and got lost. Figured I'd camp where I was and get back to my party in the morning. As a matter of fact, I did find them the next day. But it's curious how tonight brings it all back—I'd half forgotten. Quite mad, he must have been, don't you think? Had plenty of money and spent it all planting these dam' trees of his. Lived in a shack so he could afford to buy more land and set out more trees. In my opinion he was crazy as a coot—have another toddy?"

I could have brained the man with the ash-tray! Sometimes it's as easy as nothing to get him to spin a yarn—and then, at other times, it's harder than pulling teeth. The worst of it all is, there's nothing you can do to prompt him, for he's as obstinate as a mule. If he thinks he's being pushed, he shuts up like a clam. I suggested a glass of sherry and sighed. When it came there was a silence and the clock struck nine-thirty. I yawned vainly and began to think of going home to bed. And then, all of a sudden, the Colonel was telling his story and I didn't think of bed again for two hours.

"Blenkins!" exploded Colonel Marsh. "That was the name! Crazy as a coot—here's the story he told me. It appears he used to live in a penthouse in Greenwich Village. Had the roof to himself and had fixed it up with great boxes of earth to hold flowers and shrubs. Wealthy young cub, he must have been. Well, one summer he went on a motoring trip through New England and stopped a week at Bar Harbor. He climbed up to the top of Mount Desert and stood there one late afternoon looking down over the ocean hundreds of feet below him and stretching out to the horizon. While he stood there he heard something swishing overhead—a tiny sound—and felt two or three sharp taps on his neck. Something got down back of his collar—a small hard little object—and he fished with his

forefinger and pulled out what seemed to be three seeds.
He glanced up at the western sky and then ducked, for a
scattered handful of the seeds almost struck his face. They
passed overhead at a fairish rate of speed and seemed, he
said, to be going so fast that they would land in the water
a mile away down the slope of the hill. That was all that
happened then. He stayed half an hour but no more seeds
went by and he was afraid it would be dark before he got
back to his hotel in Bar Harbor.

"As for the seeds, he put them in an old envelope in
his pocket and forgot all about them. When he got back
to New York a few weeks later, he found them and, out of
curiosity, stuck them in the box of earth that held a privet
hedge along one side of his roof.

"It was a cold winter that year, Blenkins told me. All his
privet died, but what with one thing and another, he didn't
get around to having new plants put in the box and, when
warm weather came, it was too late and there the privets
stood—dead and lifeless. Some weeds grew in the box, but
he did not bother to pull them, for the dead privet would
make his roof look unsightly no matter what he did. So it
happened that he did not notice how very peculiar three
of the weeds were until late June or early July. They must
have been queer, all right, to judge from his description.
At first they looked like grass, or perhaps onion shoots—
tall straight stems. Then the stem grew rough and knobby
and needles came out on them like a Juniper. He bought a
lot of books on botany and started reading up in the hope
of identifying the things, but couldn't find anything at all
like them in the books.

"I don't know what he did for a living—drew dividends
and drank, I expect, like many another. He used to get
pretty well tanked up by evening and sit in a porch chair
with a glass in one hand staring at the weeds. By mid-

July he had cleaned everything out of the box of earth but the three curiosities—dead privet and all. It didn't strike him that these were growing from the three seeds that had fallen on him on Mount Desert for quite a while, he said. When it did, he didn't get excited—judged they might have been carried by the wind from most anywhere—Asia, perhaps, for all he knew or cared. He did, however, think it curious that of all the seeds he had seen flying past these three were the only ones to reach soft earth. All the others must have just missed the top of the hill—the last hill in North America—and gone on into the Atlantic Ocean. Whatever they were, they were the only three in this part of the world.

"Then the really hot New York weather came and his three weeds changed once more. All the needles fell off and large green leaves came out, like maple leaves, and the plants grew two feet in a week. He stayed in New York that summer instead of going north—he was so interested. And by August the strange plants were five feet high and two inches through and the stems were solid and woody to the touch. He watered them twice a day now—used to pour a little whisky on the earth, I judge—and spread some patent fertilizer around. Babied the things, in fact. When all the leaves fell off, he imagined he must have killed them—that was in August. But new buds opened at the top of the bare trunks, three buds exactly on each one. Out from these there sprouted branches and the trunks seemed to swell and swell as the days passed until finally they looked like nothing on earth—great foot-thick posts with three long whip-like branches growing out of the top and ending in three or four ribbons of leaves. The leaves were thick and firm to the touch like a palm frond. The trunks were thick in the middle, swollen up like a snake that has swallowed a goat, and bulged a bit at the top. The roots acted queerly, too, Blenkins noticed, for three main roots kept heaving up out of the earth, taking the trunk with them up into the air. Finally there they stood, each supported on three leg-like roots and with three arm-like branches trailing from the bulbous top. And toward the end of August all three started budding—huge cancerous-looking buds that glistened in the sunlight, oily as Amontillado sherry in a glass.

"Blenkins, of course, thought they would flower and every morning he used to pop out on the roof before break-fast to look at them, but the buds didn't seem to change any more. In fact the weeds—he called them trees, and they must have been that by now—the trees, then, seemed to have stopped growing altogether. For a week he kept expecting something new to happen, but it never did and he finally lost interest and went on with his drinking in a more serious way—making up for lost time, I expect. Crazy as a coot. I'd say, and drunk to boot. Didn't keep any ser-vants—probably because he liked to do his drinking in private. He had a woman come in every week or so to wash dishes and clean up the apartment. Well, I take it he must have been doing some fancy drinking about then, but this is the story he told—believe it or not.

"One night in early September he was sitting in his living-room when he thought he heard a noise out on the roof. He listened carefully and couldn't hear anything more; decided he must have been mistaken. Besides, how could anything get up on his roof? There was a sheer wall all around it—a drop of fifty feet or more to the street. The only way out there was right through his living-room and out the French doors that he had covered with heavy hangings to keep the draughts away. Any visitor that came through those doors would have to be able to climb like a fly, he thought, and smiled to himself.

"Just as he got feeling all comfortable again, he heard another sound outside—a thump. Couldn't be any mistake about it. Then he began to feel nervous. The janitor was down in the basement and if he shouted his head off no one could hear him. He remembered that he kept a .32 Colt automatic in the closet, though, and he started to get up out of the chair. Apparently he had more of a load aboard than he thought, for he made heavy weather of the course to the closet and his head was dizzy with the effort of thinking all of a sudden. But he got the gun and put it in his pocket and was wondering whether or not to try to get as far as the elevator outside and away to safety when . . . must have been a shock for the poor beggar," mused the Colonel and shook his head doubtfully.

"In Heaven's name!" I demanded, "what happened!" I don't believe I ever knew a more exasperating *raconteur.*

Colonel Marsh looked at me in mild surprise and for an instant I feared I should hear no more that evening. But fortunately he was not offended. "Knocks," he replied, "knocks on the glass doors hidden behind those great vel-vet curtains. Like this," and he struck the table three times slowly and impressively, and peered at me under his white eyebrows. "Must have been a shock to the chap!

"Blenkins could hardly believe his ears—wished he didn't have to, in fact. There was nobody outside on his roof. He knew it the way you know the earth is round or that the sun will come up in the east tomorrow. But there had been three knocks or he was drunker than he ought to be—and as a matter of fact, he could feel himself grow-ing more sober every second. He stood there gawking at the curtains and fiddling with his pistol for a long time. He had begun to believe that perhaps he *had* been drunk, when the three slow knocks were repeated, firmly and un-mistakably.

"Still he didn't move. He was thinking that since some-one was really there, it must be a burglar—but since when have burglars knocked to announce themselves? A wild

idea of aeroplanes went through his head, but his roof was
small—couldn't land an autogyro on it these days, even,
and in those days the Wright Brothers were still front-page
news. Of course he thought of ghosts, night-prowlers,
werewolves, and such things, but only in a kind of vague
panic. He says he was almost ready to go to the doors and
pull them open when he saw the knob begin to turn! Blenkins didn't breathe during the time it took for the catch
to click and the door begin to push inward and when he
saw what stood in the opening, framed by the light of the
rising moon, he just gasped once and stopped breathing
for another spell. There stood one of his strange trees,
holding on to the knob with the long finger-like leaves at
the end of one branch!

"He's not sure just how long afterward he opened his
eyes—probably a second or two—and saw all three of the
creatures standing just inside the doorway quiet and terrifying. He says he knew at once that they were looking
at him—could feel it—though it wasn't until the next day
that he learned what wonderful organs of sight and hearing those ugly, sore-looking buds of theirs really were. He
shut his eyes hard once more and opened them again, half
hoping to banish the horrid sight—but there they stood,
solid and real and one of them reached out a branch and
the ribbony fingers touched a chair and felt over it as
though exploring a new thing.

"Blenkins tried to speak, but his voice was hoarse and
he croaked like a dying fish. Instantly one of the tree-creatures started making sounds with its roots. He finally got
his throat clear and said 'What are you?' and 'Waa *aah* roo'
came grunting out of those roots—like an echo.

"The poor man gasped once more and sat down suddenly in a chair that stood behind him. His nerveless fingers still held on to the .32, but he had no will or strength

left to think about weapons. It suddenly came to him that these trees could walk and see and—were actually imitating what he said! Intelligent trees—well, the man was drunk or crazy or both and trees are no worse than pink snakes, I suppose," said the Colonel. Then after a second's thought, "Yet, with it all, as I said before, I don't know whether to believe him or not. It's all so dam' plausible!

"He tried 'em out—talking, you know. 'Man,' he said, pointing to himself and all three croaked it after him. It was a bubbly, watery sort of voice they had, Blenkins told me. They made the noises through air holes in the base of their roots. 'Chair,' he said, pointing to the article which one of the creatures had been examining. 'Table,' 'floor,' 'walk,' 'light,' 'book'—he pointed out the meaning of each word and they watched him or examined the article with interest. Books interested them most—they stopped the show, in fact. Blenkins had a haphazard library—every book he had ever read. Fairy tales and primers from his childhood and all. Those trees liked the primers and shared them between them and he couldn't get another word out of them. Then he felt weak all of a sudden but didn't dare go to his bedroom to lie down, so he took to the whisky bottle instead and he doesn't remember anything more of that weird night.

"But he remembers waking up the next morning, all right! An awful headache! A mouth like dry soap! He was lying on his own bed fully dressed and when he stood up to look at himself in the glass, he was shocked (so he says) to see that his hair was grayer than it had been the day before. Of course the first thing he did was to creep into his living room to see if the creatures were still there. The room was empty. However, it was simply littered with books. They lay on the floor, the table and the chairs by the dozen and all the lights were burning. The door to the roof was closed and it took a deal of courage for Blenkins

to open it and look out. The first thing he saw were the
three grotesque trees. But he wasn't in the least alarmed,
for they were all three back in their places in the box of
earth with their roots firmly in the ground! So he'd imagined the whole thing!"

"You mean that's the end of the story?" I protested.

"Nonsense!" snapped the worthy Colonel. "Can't you
keep quiet a minute?

"He felt as if an enormous load had been lifted from his
mind, Blenkins said. He walked over and patted those thick
five-foot trunks to reassure himself and stood breathing
the crisp autumn morning. What a fool he was making of
himself, drinking away his life! He'd go out at once—have
breakfast in a good restaurant and spend the day looking
up some of his old friends. He bathed and changed his
clothes and slipped out to the elevator, almost not daring to look into the living room. He didn't take a drop to
drink that whole day and returned, about five in the afternoon, feeling like a new man. He entered the living room
thinking to himself that he might even go out to dinner,
rather than cook and eat his meal all by himself. And then
he noticed the floor—not only books were littered there
but *earth!*

"'Good God!' he said and stepped back, all his horrors
of the night before vividly recalled to mind. And as he
spoke, the light darkened at the glass doors and he glanced
up startled to see the three trees entering the room solemnly in single file. He says that their main roots bent
like knees and the tangle of smaller rootlets slopped down
soddenly as they walked, like a forkful of hay.

"'Welcome back, man!' said the first tree and 'welcome'
echoed the other two as they stood in a line looking at him.

"'What . . . who are . . . I've gone off my head!' muttered poor Blenkins, feeling the sweat start coldly down
his forehead.

"'Have you no greeting to exchange for ours?' asked one of the Things.

"'Are you really *talking?*' he gasped.

"'Of course! Cannot you hear us? But of course you do not doubt your aural senses; you perhaps mean to indicate that you are surprised. You need not be. Your books last night were well enough arranged to teach us how to communicate with you. Your language is quite simple, really. We were thoroughly competent in it long before your star appeared.'

"'Books . . . language . . . simple! But . . . I *can't* be imagining this . . . it was true last night, then! But you are speaking *English!* And last night you were just beginning to learn words!'

"'I have just finished saying that your books were well adapted to teaching us how to speak as you do—it was quite simple and we had the whole night in which to do it. Are you so surprised?'

"Blenkins looked from one to the other and shuddered at the grotesque and intelligent buds that corruscated oilily at the top of the bulbous bodies. The long snakelike leaves wriggled and twisted almost continually and as each spoke, there was a fat blubbery smacking among the roots of the tripod legs—like the sound of gas bubbles rising in a sewer. His mind reeled.

"'What . . . who . . . what sort of Thing *are* you?' he whispered painfully.

"'We are vegetables, in your language. Possibly trees, though we cannot be sure. Your books seem to describe only the lower orders of vegetable life. Possibly we are animals. When we had been through the small primers and others of your books we found the dictionary, which was most thorough and helpful. All three of us read this through page by page last night. Animals seem, according to the dictionary, to be many things—but active and sentient, as distinguished from the vegetables. We are active and sentient, yet the pictures of animals seem quite different from us, and many of the vegetables look somewhat like us—so we are uncertain as to our status.'

"At this point Blenkins pressed his hands to his head in despair. 'I must have a drink after all,' he said as he poured a stiff one.

"'You're trees,' he said at last, slowly and firmly as though he would force them to act the part. 'You're trees—vegetables—and you shouldn't be intelligent—you shouldn't be able to talk, nor even to walk around out of the earth. What does it all mean?'

"'Ah! It is as I suggested,' put in another of the Things. It might be easier if I mention now that later on Blenkins gave them names. One was browner than the other two, who were rather gray of bark, and this one Blenkins called Brownie. Of the other two, the one who had just spoken stood only five feet high on his three roots, as compared to the others' six or six and a half feet of stature. This one he mentally referred to as Shorty. The third, who seemed to do most of the talking, he had nicknamed the Babbler.

"Brownie and the Babbler were silent and Shorty continued speaking. 'It seemed to me that this planet was strange. There are then no intelligent vegetables at all here?'

"'Intelligent vegetables! What are you talking about?'

"'I am talking about trees and shrubs and plants—in fact about vegetables that may be intelligent. But surely you understand your own language?'

"Blenkins said that they seemed only able to understand literal meanings. Tone of voice meant nothing to them. Everything he told them, moreover, as he soon learned, was believed absolutely and completely. The very idea of saying what was not true had never seemed to have occurred to them, and these two facts made the conversations he held with them difficult at times. "'Of course I understand the words,' answered Blenkins. 'What I meant was that there are no vegetables like you anywhere. Such things have never been heard of nor imagined. I do not understand how you can possibly talk or walk—or see or hear, for that matter.'

"'We do these things in much the same way as you,' answered the Babbler after a pause. 'We walk on our roots, as you see.'

"'But . . . how can you move them? And—oh, there are so many crazy points about it!—trees usually die if their roots are taken out of the earth.'

"'Even when they are not feeding?'

"'But they always *are* feeding—except in winter, perhaps.'

"'And in winter?'

"'Yes . . . I suppose that is true. We can take a tree out of the ground in winter and even keep it stored in a shed until spring without killing it. But it isn't winter.'

"'Our feeding period is evidently not the same as with your trees here. We feed only while the star shines.'

"'The star! There are a million shining outside,' for it had grown dark.

"'I mean your star—the sun, you call it. We feed only during the day. At night we are active. Your trees are active, I suppose, only in the winter.'

"'No, no! They are *never* active. They have no muscles to move with. Winter and summer, day and night, they remain in one spot from the day they sprout to the day they die. That is what makes it seem so strange for you to be here . . . walking around.'

"'But how do *you* walk? The tissue cells contract powerfully making one side of your leg shorter than the other, thus moving the entire limb. It is precisely the same with us. These native trees you mention must be very low in evolution. We must be animals, after all. What makes you think us trees?'

"'Your whole appearance . . . besides you grew from seeds. I planted the seeds myself in that box outside. You are trees, all right. That's the only one thing I *am* sure of any longer.'

"'As for our talking,' put in Shorty methodically, 'the air-vents in our roots form words as easily as your mouth seems to.'

"'And our outward organ,' added Brownie, pointing to the sticky bud with an upward flung leaf-finger, 'sees and hears as well or better than your eyes and ears combined.'

"'But after all, it is our place to be curious—not yours,' said the Babbler. 'We are the explorers on a strange planet. You must tell us about yourself. When do you eat . . . and how, for I see that your roots are short and small!' He pointed at Blenkins' feet as he spoke.

"'I . . . I'll have to have another drink,' said poor Blenkins. After a moment he tried to begin an explanation that would satisfy them. 'Trees have roots and live in the earth. They feed on . . . I don't know exactly . . . .'

"'Sunlight and the salts in earth moisture,' put in Brownie. 'Go on.'

"'Well . . . animals have no roots at all. They live on food like . . . well, cows eat grass, for instance; dogs eat bones and meat; I eat bread and meat and eggs and such things. Animals eat things with their mouths—chew 'em up and swallow them—and their stomachs digest them. Trees haven't any mouths or stomachs. That's the big difference . . . but what do you mean when you say you are on a strange planet?'

"'First things come first,' replied the Babbler. 'I begin to understand. Animals are in reality parasites who can support life only on other life. You eat meat—that is, dead animal life—and bread, which is dead vegetable life. Trees and other vegetables are not parasites, but true life. They do not have to kill in order to live, as you do. Their food comes from the sun and the earth.'

"'It is a new thing,' put in Shorty. 'Such a warped and evil form of existence has not been found anywhere else in the Universe.'

"'It is evil,' agreed Brownie.

"'But look at the results,' put in Blenkins, thoroughly warmed by his last drink. 'Without animals there could never have been men.' And he drew himself up proudly and reached over for the bottle, only to misjudge his balance and tumble out of his chair onto the floor.

"The tree creatures looked at him a moment in sober silence. 'You did not even know what food trees live upon,' suggested the Babbler. 'You seem intelligent, but strangely uniformed.'

"'Ah, but I am not a botanist,' answered Blenkins. 'This is the age of specialization. One man knows only one subject.'

"'But your ancestors—some of them at least—must have known botany.'

"'What has that to do with me?'

"'You have, of course, all the knowledge and experience of your ancestors stored in your mind.'

"'Nonsense! Who ever heard of such a thing!' exclaimed Blenkins.

"'I do not understand. Did you not hear my words?'

"'I mean, what our ancestors knew has died with, them.'

"'This is extraordinary! Do you have to learn all your facts over again each time a child is born?'

"'Why, of course! How else can anyone learn?'

"'Among us,' remarked Shorty quietly, 'we emerge from the seed with a precise memory of every thought that ever passed through the minds of our ancestors. I understand

now, however, why you have so many books. It is to preserve the thoughts of one generation so that the next may
learn them quickly.'

"'These men are very poorly constructed and their intelligence is an inefficient thing,' spoke up the tree he referred
to as Brownie.

"'They are perhaps hardly worth our further study, after all,' agreed the Babbler. 'Our course for the future
seems fairly simple. Nevertheless, this man here has done
service in caring for our seeds. If there are further things
he wishes to know, I will take the time to discuss them
with him.'

"At this, the other two turned and began looking among
the books until they found a geography. This they brought
under a light and leaned over it intently. Blenkins said
that they went through it at a furious rate of speed—five
or ten seconds sufficing for them to memorize a page of
type or an entire map. It was at this time that he began
to realize how infinitely above his own intelligence these
creatures towered. He began asking questions of the Babbler and succeeded in obtaining a complete explanation
of their existence there. When we had achieved this, he
says, he could not help feeling that the human race was
doomed.

"Roughly speaking, this is the story of the tree-creatures which, according to Blenkins, he put together after
a dozen conversations at various times. There are, it appears, many other planets similar to ours circling other
suns. Life is very common on them. However, these planets are not in our universe, but a distant one—for all the
stars in the sky are only the separate parts of one universe
out of perhaps countless millions of universes. 'Life' as
it is known on these planets is entirely vegetable. There
are hundreds of types of vegetable life—hundreds of

thousands of species and varieties—but of them all only
one has ever developed intelligence. This breed is that of
the tree-men who were sharing his roof-garden.

"As to how they ever got here, it appears that they prop-
agate by seed and that this seed has the property of great
tolerance to extremes of heat and cold. When a planet
becomes sufficiently populated, these creatures construct
a large gun and fill a shell with seed which is shot violently out into space and bursts. Thereupon the millions of
seeds are scattered at cosmic speed and spread out through
space, never stopping until they by chance actually collide
with some celestial body or enter its sphere of gravitation-
al influence. Should they land on a star, of course they
are instantly consumed with the heat. Should they land
on a planet without the proper natural condition for the
support of their form of life, naturally enough they never
sprout. By far the greater number of such broadcast seeds
never touch star or planet but merely continue through an
eternity of space—potential life destined to remain forever
dormant.

"It's a strange idea," commented Colonel Marsh. I
thought of some of our own seed pods that explode violently to throw seeds great distances through the air. Even
our native pine cones are miniature broadcasters. But I
remained silent for fear of stopping the flow of narrative.

"But the most sensational part of it all is that when
this seed landed on an agreeable planet and sprouted into
a tree, the creature was instantly intelligent, educated,
and trained by instinct—guided by a share in the racial
brain—a brain millions of years old, wise and capable.
Gad! What we humans could do with such a gift!

"The memory of these particular three tree-men went
back to a vague and misty past—billions of years ago. The
most recent thing they remembered was life on a crowded
planet circling a twin sun—one yellow and the other a

dwarf red, soon to be cold. Research in science was carried
on here—that seemed to be all they lived for. Then came
the construction of the colonizing artillery and they remembered nothing more. The Babbler told Blenkins that
at least a hundred thousand light-years must have been
crossed in their travels to this solar system and that their
speed through space might average less than one-ten-thou-
sandth of the speed of light. Fancy that! One billion years
just for the voyage! Of course they remember nothing of
the time they spent in the seed stage.

"With an intelligence of that sort, learning a language
in one evening was child's play, as Blenkins soon realized.
The creatures had no language of their own that he could
understand, though he got some vague idea that they read
each other's mind-vibrations with their roots. It seems
that they must spend half of their time rooted in the earth
and holding their leaves up to the rays of the sun. Otherwise they would suffer from malnutrition. But during this
feeding period their roots are able to vibrate in the earth
in a way that translates ideas as quickly as thought can
originate them. Talking English made Brownie and Shorty
impatient, it was so slow and cumbersome a means of conveying information. But the Babbler seemed to like it, told
Blenkins he did, in fact. He explained that his thoughts
were slower than those of his companions and he liked the
extra time involved in their translation by voice.

"Well, that's enough of an interruption for explana-
tions," said the Colonel. "That first night of conversation
with the Babbler, Blenkins did not go to bed at all. Once
he got used to the shocking idea that such creatures could
exist at all, his brain took fire from the heady nature of
what he learned. Here was matter, he thought, to startle
the world wide awake! He pictured the headlines in the
newspapers and grinned to himself. Just before dawn he
began to get the idea that these tree-men were masters

of enough new and revolutionary inventions in mechanics and biology to change the face of human existence and then he got so excited that he found himself drinking bottle after bottle of liquor and remaining sober throughout."

Colonel Marsh was silent a moment. "Chap must have had an inexhaustible cellar!" he decided, with a vaguely envious tone of voice.

"The Babbler had asked him why men preferred to eat other life instead of obtaining their food directly from sunlight.

"'Why, merely because we don't know how to make food from sunlight,' he answered, surprised. 'Don't you suppose we'd stop raising animals for food—or growing wheat—if we could make food artificially in a factory? Of course we would. It'd be cheaper.'

"Shorty and Brownie looked up. 'But how very simple! That can be shown you.'

"They showed him, too. At least he feels sure that what they told him would work as a process. But, of course, he didn't understand a word of it all. He wasn't a chemist, he explained.

"'Another specialized knowledge?' asked Shorty.

"'Yes . . . I could get a chemist here, perhaps . . .'

"'No,' replied Brownie. 'This is childish talk. Vegetables, says his dictionary, are not sentient. They, however, have mastered the principal formula necessary to life on planets. This man—and all other men—are parasites, lacking the intelligence to solve that simple problem. What can their chemists know? Besides, their books speak too much of things we do not understand—love and hate and murder and war and mercy—what are these things?'

"Blenkins was silent a moment, hoping to think of some way to persuade them to write out the formula.

"'What do they mean by art and music, for that matter?' put in Shorty.

"'Art—why that is making beautiful pictures. Here, like this.' And he brought out a book filled with color reproductions of paintings. The three tree-men bent over it silently and the Babbler handed it back to Blenkins. 'They do not seem very accurate pictures,' he remarked.

"'It's not their accuracy—it's the color and the form and . . . well, of course. I'm not an artist.'

"'Just what *is* your own specialty?' asked Shorty.

"Blenkins, of course, had none and said so. He felt the absurdity of his position keenly. But, as he asked me, who could have told when he was a boy how important it might be to him to enlarge his education? Up in his cabin in the north woods he now has a fine science library—seems to have studied the volumes in it, too. But that didn't help him then.

"'Anyway,' he said to Shorty, '*music* you should be able to understand. I've a phonograph and you can hear some. Art . . . well, art's different. Perhaps ordinary photographs are better than paintings from some points of view. But music . . . .' And they spent the rest of the time until dawn broke listening to phonograph records. The three tree-men said they had never heard any sounds like it before. Shorty decided that the vibrations per second were related mathematically and counted them (apparently their strange bodies needed no instruments to help in such research). The Babbler preferred dance music, but was interested in Wagner. Shorty neither liked nor disliked—merely counted and noted effects. Brownie said that the sounds made his roots tingle and went out to watch the dawn come up, where he was presently joined by the other two. Blenkins saw them climb onto the great box and start wriggling their roots into the earth. In a few minutes they were motionless, standing as they had stood for weeks—looking like freaks of nature, but nothing more. He himself was suddenly struck yawning and staggered to his bedroom where he slept until late afternoon.

"When Blenkins stood, still yawning, on his roof, the three vegetables were back in the box of earth, leaves rustling slightly in the breeze. He spoke to them and received no answer and then felt the Babbler's nearest leaves, only to have them writhe away from out of his hand. He stood then for a time looking down upon the street over the balustrade and thinking. If he could learn how to make artificial food he would be a millionaire—that much was certain. If he could in some way keep these creatures to himself there was no telling what new inventions he might not obtain from them. He would patent the valuable ones and be the most famous inventor in human history. After all, these things—brainy enough—were only vegetables. There must be some way to control them. Why not try heavy rope or chain? On the other hand, might he not do best for himself by merely announcing his discovery to science—let people who knew more than he did handle the whole affair? Discoverer of a new genus—it might be named after him—Blenkinsi, or no—Blenkinsiana, perhaps.

"And while he leaned there, thinking, he heard a noise behind him and turned to see the three creatures pulling their roots out of the earth, shaking them delicately, and stepping down from the box to the roof itself. The sun had set.

"'We have decided that your art and music are merely clever methods of wasting time,' announced the Babbler at once. Blenkins merely gaped without answering.

"'And that all parasitical forms of life are evil—dangerous,' added Shorty.

"'You mean men as well?' asked Blenkins, not yet understanding.

"'Of course! We shall colonize your planet and then things will be very much improved.'

"'But won't you take up a great deal of land—a colony of you?'

"'We shall require the entire planet in a few years. Until that time you men and your other forms of life here are welcome to use it.'

"'Welcome to use it!' Blenkins exclaimed, somewhat nettled at the nonchalant dismissal of the human race. 'Suppose *you* are not permitted to do this colonizing?'

"'Really,' answered the tree-creature he called Brownie, 'this is not edifying. How shall these men prevent us? We are stronger and are more intelligent.'

"By this time Blenkins had fortified himself with a drink or two, as I gather. For some reason he lost control of himself completely and rushed, red-faced, to seize the nearest thing with which to strike at the speaker. It chanced to be a stout steel poker from the great fireplace that faced the doors to the roof. This he brandished and shouted, 'I am a man and I do not permit you!' and then he cursed them and struck at Brownie with his weapon. Up flashed one of the arms and the long green finger-leaves seized the poker in an overpowering grasp and wrenched it from him. Another arm was thought to bear upon the piece of metal and, Blenkins says, the tree-beast proceeded calmly and quietly to bend the half-inch bar into the form of a narrow spiral. 'You see our strength,' it said and dropped the twisted metal on the floor where it rang like a gong. Then the three of them started out the door without a word.

"Blenkins does not pretend to apologize for his next action," said Colonel Marsh. "He was savage with too little sleep and too much alcohol. The gesture of the sentient vegetable seemed suddenly a last intolerable insult. His hatred welled up inside him like a red tide and he pounced upon the table drawer, drew out the automatic, and fired two shots into the back of the Babbler.

"The sharp crash of sound seemed to sober him suddenly and he stood still while the three creatures turned and came back to him. 'You see,' he muttered unsteadily, 'we men have other means of strength than our mere muscles.'

"The three trees stood in a row looking at him, but in complete silence. Blenkins noticed that the Babbler had two holes through his trunk and that a thick yellow liquor oozed out of each and dripped greenly down on the floor. To this the tree paid no attention and in a few seconds the flow had ceased and the wounds glistened stickily. The silent regard of the creatures was more than he could bear. He was in an agony of fear—certain that all three would seize and kill him at once. Sweat stood beaded heavily on his forehead and 'Damn you—oh *damn* you!' he shrieked. 'Kill me if you can!' He brandished the automatic once more, his arm suddenly trembling wildly. Then the Babbler spoke. His voice was quiet and full of the utmost calm.

"'A singular happening,' he said. 'Tell me, man, how was it the part of wisdom to do that? It seems to me to have been ill advised.'

"'You . . . you are going to kill all the animals on the earth!'

"'And what of it?'

"'What of it! Why, only that we will kill you first!'

"'But surely that form of life which is most intelligent is entitled to exist in the place of those less well fitted for life?'

"'We are as well—better fitted than you!'

"'But we should not have destroyed animals violently— that is a savage act. We should merely occupy the land to the exclusion of the animals, a very different thing. Moreover, your intelligence cannot be high. Indeed it is so low that we do not fear the worst you can do. You must have known that you have no power—even with that explosive missile, pistol you call it—to destroy us. You should have refrained from the attempt, knowing its absurdity. Were you more dangerous, we should take steps to prevent you from harming us. As it is—you can see that my sap had ceased to waste away. In an hour the bark will have begun to heal.'

"Blenkins felt a wave of relief that he would not be punished. He had instant recourse to the bottle of liquor and succeeded in quieting his nerves with a pint of the raw stuff. All that night he sat there, sipping at it, and the tree-creatures moved quietly about the apartment conversing, perhaps, but silently. When dawn came. Brownie approached him and silently seized his arms. He found himself propelled toward his bedroom and pushed inside, where he heard the door being closed and fastened behind him. Too stupefied to care, he flung himself on the bed and fell into a profound sleep. It was late afternoon when he awoke and, being hungry, tried to open the door. But it was securely fastened and he fell prey to a thousand imaginations and fears. Then he heard scuffling roots on the floor outside and the door was opened.

"'You may come out,' announced Brownie, and turned away.

"Blenkins slipped into the kitchen and fried eggs and bacon and toasted some bread. After he had eaten, he felt much better. He was thoroughly ashamed of the scene he had made the night before and determined to make every possible effort to obtain information on the making of artificial food from the tree-men. As he entered the living-room. Brownie stood between him and the outer hallway of the apartment, as though to prevent his escape.

"'I am a prisoner, then?' asked Blenkins.

"'Yes. It is possible that many men together might destroy us. We do not wish this to happen until we have seeded and planted the seeds which are to form our future colony.'

"'You need have no fear,' said Blenkins in a mournful tone of voice. 'I am very sorry for what happened last night—I must have taken too much to drink. I wish to apologize to the tree I wounded.'

"'No necessity for that. We knew very well that your action was not intelligent—that is to say, that it was not meant.'

"'Then I am forgiven?'

"'You have done no harm—what is there to forgive? If you mean that there may be no consequences of your action harmful to you, I can assure you there will be none. You must not leave this place until we have gone. That is all.'

"Blenkins poured himself a drink and swallowed it.

"'Why do you poison yourself so much with that liquid?' enquired Brownie. 'You claim to have intelligence—that is not an intelligent action.'

"Blenkins mumbled an excuse and all his hatred of these cold superior creatures returned with tenfold force—but a quiet hatred this time. 'If you would seek to make us perfect, you would help me to understand how to prepare synthetic food from sunlight,' he said. 'I could write it all down if you would explain it slowly.'

"The Babbler entered the room at this point and Brownie turned to him. 'If you wish you might try to explain how to live to this parasite,' he said. 'I have no more time to waste on him.'

"'Why, very well,' answered the tree spoken to. 'Get paper and pencil, man. First it is necessary that you have a complicated organic substance similar to the green stuff your dictionary calls chlorophyll. Then you must have a constant supply of water with salts in solution, carbon, and other substances. Finally you must expose your chemical to sunlight. Now have you that all down . . . and is it clear to you?'

"'Yes, yes!' exclaimed Blenkins frantically writing. 'Go on!'

"'Now for the particulars—first the containers for all these. They should be rock crystal for the chlorophyll and some opaque substance for the salt solution—stone or wood or metal, it does not matter. The crystal vessel should be shallow and fed from beneath by the liquid, rising under pressure. The product of the photosynthesis should escape at the sides of the crystal chamber in the form of liquid or semi-solid carbohydrates. Have you got that?

"'Now there must be a positive method of floating off these carbohydrates constantly as they are formed; there must be a means devised for making this chlorophyll-like substance; there must be some way of preparing the inorganic liquid which is the raw material of our factory. Note those points down and we will take them up one after the other. I find I must again consult your dictionary, for though the ideas I wish to express are extremely simple to me, your language is not designed for their easy expression.'

"Thereupon he preceded to leaf over the pages for a few minutes. 'This is very stupid!' he exclaimed and leafed some more. 'No, it is not here. I did not remember it.'

"Blenkins was watching in an agony of apprehension. 'What is the trouble?' he enquired at length.

"'Only that your language is apparently incapable of scientific ideas,' answered the grotesque creature. 'I am very much afraid it will be impossible to explain the process to you after all.'

"'Ah, but that is not a complete dictionary—it is an abridged one.'

"'What, another of your specializations?'

"'Pretty much so. A chemical dictionary would give you all the words you need—if I could only go out and purchase one . . . I'd be back in ten minutes,' he pleaded recklessly.

"'What you ask is quite impossible.'

"'Moreover,' put in a new voice, 'it is quite useless. These men are not destined to last long enough on this planet to make it worth while to even begin their education. We are now ready to commence preparations for our departure and in another few months we shall have planted millions of our seed all over the earth. In another year each of those millions will be as we are and will have seeded in turn their millions of millions.'

"Blenkins turned to see Brownie standing in the doorway, Shorty behind him. At the sudden picture these words presented in his mind, he found his knees weaken and his resolution and ambition turned to water. He drank a glass of whisky and sat down in a chair.

"'How will you leave this roof,' he asked fearfully.

"'We shall fly. We do not believe that even if all the animals in the street below should band together they could prevent our walking through them. Nevertheless, that would be a slow and foolish method of locomotion.'

"'Fly!' exclaimed Blenkins looking around the room. 'How will you build your machine?'

"'We need none. We shall spend a few days rooted in the soil and grow wings. At the same time, we shall mature our seed, so that when we are ready to depart, we shall have the purpose at hand. The only thing lacking is this, man. The earth out in those boxes is poor and the water supply insufficient for our purpose. We shall not permit you to leave, but that machine on the desk which your dictionary describes and pictures is a telephone and you must speak on it and have fresh soil brought up for our use.

"'You will have it brought tomorrow. The—I believe they are called peasants, or perhaps farm laborers—at all events, the men who bring it shall place it upon the roof and depart. You will be in your room and they must be told that you are not to be disturbed, also that we are valuable and exotic vegetables which must not be harmed. When they have left the new earth, they must go away at once. Then we will release you from your bedroom.'

"'When you give your instructions over the telephone we shall stand beside you and see that you say only what we have directed you to say,' put in the third of the tree-men. Then all three stood still and stared at Blenkins.

"'But they won't leave it until they are paid—I must be here to give them money,' he protested.

"'According to your books, money is only a promise to pay. You can promise them to pay when you are speaking over this instrument.'

"Blenkins laughed hollowly and pulled a bill from his wallet. 'See here! It is a promise to pay—yes! But it must be signed by the Secretary of the Treasury of this country. It has to be on this kind of paper.'

"'Very well. You will leave some of these papers on this table beside the telephone where the workmen can take them in payment for the earth. Now there must be no more objections. Take up the telephone and say what you have been told!'

"'But—oh this is absurd! It is after five o'clock. All the stores are closed. Besides, come to think of it, I never heard of a store that sold earth. I don't think there is one in the whole of New York City.' He opened a cabinet which housed the telephone books and picked up the Red Book and began searching through it, but without success.

'I might try some of these Garden Supply numbers—or perhaps Nurserymen . . . but they'll all be closed now.'

"'Try one,' commanded Brownie. And at random, Blenkins selected a number and dialed it. There was no answer to the first long ring and Blenkins would have hung up, but was prevented by a green and muscular finger-leaf. Then to his surprise a voice answered. Earth? No, they didn't carry it. No. Not in New York City. Have to get it from out of town. Take a week. Wouldn't manure do? Well, manure was available by the ton. Yes, could be delivered tomorrow afternoon early.

"Blenkins glanced up hopelessly at the tree-men leaning over him. 'Will you be there another five minutes,' he enquired. 'Good. Then I'll call you right back.' He hung up.

"'Can't buy earth,' he explained. 'But they have manure to sell. Wouldn't that do just as well? It could be mixed with the earth in the boxes and the resulting soil should be rich enough.'

"'Manure?' asked Shorty. 'That is an excretion from animals, is it not? What use would that be? It sounds rather disgusting.'

"'But . . . it's what we use for our very finest gardens! It makes plants grow better than anything we have ever found—much better than plain earth!' expostulated Blenkins. 'Besides, I can get it for you easily—all put up in bags. Earth would take a week to get here. Suit yourself!'

"'Of course, we cannot tell until we see it—but perhaps it will do. I think we should try it anyway. If it is not suitable, we will have to wait for earth, that is all. Order some.'

"'How much do you want?'

"'How shall I answer—in size or in weight? I am not able to give the weight, but in size—enough to fill those boxes.'

"'Well, they're two feet square and six feet long—say three square yards each. You'll want about nine yards of manure and the man said that a ton was a yard—that's nine tons! At fifty dollars a ton for the stuff delivered—why that's four hundred and fifty dollars! I haven't that much money with me,' and he shut his lips obstinately. 'Besides, why should I give you all that money—just so you can take the world away from me and my kind? No, sir, I won't do it.'

"'This is very trying,' remarked Brownie, reaching forth an arm and seizing Blenkins by the neck. 'I must force you by intimidation, I can see. You fear bodily harm—we have all noticed it Therefore you will either do this or suffer bodily harm. It is very simple.' He released his grip and Blenkins slumped back in his seat moistly and poured a drink with trembling fingers.

"'All right,' he whispered and then cleared his throat. 'All right, I'll do it. They'll take my check—I can mail them the check and order tonight and they'll deliver the stuff tomorrow. Let me up.'

"Feverishly he hunted for his check book, his pen, an envelope, and a stamp. When he had sealed the letter (not before Brownie had made him show it) he asked if it would be all right for him to step into the hall and mail it.

"'I will go with you,' said Brownie, and seized his arm with those thick long leaves that gripped so tightly Blenkins said he still had the marks to show. The mail chute was beside the elevator and Blenkins despairingly hoped that by a miracle the elevator might ascend and the operator see him. But there were no other apartments on the roof and he almost never had a visitor. They dropped the letter and returned. Brownie still holding firmly to his arm. Once inside, the tree-man let go and Blenkins tottered to the table and to further draughts of liquid courage. Feeling rather better after an hour or so, he endeavored to make conversation with the Babbler and asked him how he could grow wings.

"'Very simply,' was the reply, 'by wishing to!'

"Blenkins was in no state of mind to understand such a cryptic remark and asked for further enlightenment.

"'Why, it is related, in a manner of speaking, to the thing your books call creative evolution. Are you unable to change your form?'

"'Change our form?! No man can do that—can you?'

"'That is what I am talking about, you stupid animal! Of course, the changed form must be in relation to what already exists. I cannot grow four arms—only three. I cannot change my fingers in number. But as for their shape, there is nothing easier. In order to fly we will our fingers to become broad and flat so that instead of three arms and hands we have three wings with which to beat the air. You will see it all . . . but no, I had forgotten our new plan. You will not see it.'

"Blenkins licked his lips and his throat felt suddenly dry with a new fear. 'Why . . . why not . . . why won't I see it?'

"'Because you will be shut up in your room during the few days we require to grow wings.'

"'Oh!' Blenkins felt relieved but with a queer sinking feeling in the pit of his stomach. This, then, was the beginning of the end for the human race. Once the manure had arrived he would be shut up and unable to do anything. These nightmare creatures would fly over the world and lay a million seeds each. Men would never be able to find them until they commenced to sprout next year. And by that time it would be too late—besides, three million of the things, scattered through the jungles and the forests of the north! No, the end of his race was in plain sight. Being the sort of man he was, his first thought was to reach for the bottle. In an hour he cared nothing for what

might happen to anyone. The Babbler helped him to bed
and he did not even hear the door fastened on him.

"He awoke with a splitting headache and a mouth that
felt like flannel. The window of his bedroom looked across
two flat roofs at a tall building a block away. The sun
shone flatly against the red brick of it and he realized that
it was midafternoon. He would not be allowed to leave his
room until the tree-creatures came down from their box of
earth with the evening and unlocked his door. He turned
over to try to sleep some more, but could not, so he rose
and took a long, hot shower and felt much better. It was
still not yet four o'clock when he had finished and then,
to his surprise, he heard the door being unfastened. A sudden great hope rose in him. The workmen, perhaps, were
here with the manure and . . . the door opened to reveal
the Babbler's fantastic form.

"'The new earth has arrived,' said the creature. 'You
must show us how it is used. Come.'

"On the roof was a very respectable pile of manure—
blackish brown and with little odor, for it had been well
rotted. 'Usually,' said Blenkins, 'it is mixed with the earth.'

"'In what proportions?'

"Blenkins, of course, knew next to nothing of garden-
ing. But he was so ashamed of being forced constantly to
admit his ignorance that this time he tightened his lips
confidently. 'Half and half!' he stated.

"The Babbler, meanwhile, had thrust a tentative root-
let into the mass and was wriggling it around there. By degrees he proceeded until his roots were entirely immersed
in it.

"'This is very extraordinary!' he exclaimed. 'It is perfectly delicious. I'm in favor of not bothering to mix it
with earth at all.'

"Brownie and Shorty cautiously tested the manure.
Brownie withdrew his roots after a minute or two.

"It may be poisonous—though I admit it gives the proper reactions. But it is so quick-acting! Come, let us withdraw for a time and observe its effects, for they puzzle me.'

"Shorty withdrew slowly. 'It's great stuff! So this is a product of animal life—perhaps we will let some animals share the planet with us after all! Which are the animals that produce this particular manure, man?'

"Blenkins' jaw dropped with surprise. 'Horses and, er—cows, I believe.'

"'And do men value their manure?'

"'Yes . . . for growing plants. Makes 'em grow better than anything.'

"'Ah!' remarked Brownie, the doubter. 'You mean the plants that you grow for your food? Well . . . perhaps that is a sufficient answer.'

"All this while the Babbler had been trying to get his roots out. At last he succeeded and fell down heavily on the roof. He rose to his roots again unsteadily. ''Markable!' said he. 'Very sticky stuff . . . shticky . . . very, very 'markable. What do you others think?'

"'What is the matter with you?'

"The Babbler had by now got himself more in hand. 'Manure clings to the roots. I was well embedded. Besides, the sun is still shining and it makes me dizzy to miss my full day's feeding.'

"'Well . . . let us all three try the new manure for the remainder of the day. Tonight we will decide if any harmful results are apparent and, if not, we will go into our seeding and wing-growing tomorrow.'

"As he spoke, he was clumping methodically into the center of the fragrant pile and the other two were beside him. Blenkins waited until all was quiet and then took a step backward, wondering if his moment for escape had come. But like a whiplash a long green leaf caught at his waist and drew him back.

"'You stay here!' said the Babbler. 'We'll not be long—only until the sun sh-s-sets. Besides I want to thank you—we *all* thank you—for this mosht delish-sh-sh . . . for this *manure!*' and he swayed his thick bulged trunk solemnly and catching at Blenkins' hand with an extended leaf began to shake it up and down and sideways in what he may have believed to be the human fashion of expressing thanks.

"Now you know," said Colonel Marsh, "this fellow Blenkins would be considered a nobody. He had money, of course, but no knowledge of art or science to amount to anything. Yet all the while he was possessed of a profound knowledge which he had never realized he possessed. He was a learned specialist in one subject—perhaps there was no greater in all of New York in those days. To this hidden talent the human race may easily owe its present existence. For Blenkins knew all the symptoms of intoxication as few men have ever known anything.

"It's curious," continued the Colonel, "that at the right moment fate sends the right man to meet any given situation. Suppose a great chemist had been in Blenkins' shoes. It's true he might have learned the secrets that he has been searching for all his life in the laboratory. But would that have prevented these tree-beasts from over-running the earth? Not at all! No, sir, a great specialist was needed and there he was—Blenkins. And after one wide-eyed stare at the Babbler, he *knew!* Here was something he was capable of handling. He warmly pressed the Thing's outstretched leaf and climbed up beside him on the manure.

"'That's fine!' he exclaimed in comradely tones. 'But let me get my fee—er, my *roots* in the stuff, too.' He wriggled his feet about as he spoke until his bed-room slippers were fouled with the mess. 'It certainly is good, all right, all right, isn't it, old fellow?'

"'Besht thing I yev-yev . . . ever! All due to amamas—no thass no' ri'—*an-im- als*. You are animal, too. All animals—all making manure for vegetables . . . great . . . h'mm . . . h'mmm . . . mmmm . . . .'

"Blenkins wondered hopefully, but did not dare move yet.

"'Not much more sunlight today,' he ventured. There was no answer. He pressed his hand around the leaf that gripped it and there was a faint answering pressure. Then the leaf slipped and fell away limply. He carefully loosened the one that gripped his waist and it too fell and hung beside the motionless trunk. Then, hardly daring to breathe, Blenkins withdrew first one foot and then the other, leaving the ruined shoes in place, and slopped down from the manure pile in his socks. Still there was silence and he turned and, white-faced now, raced to the door and the hall outside.

"Frantically he pressed the elevator button and after what seemed many ages the face of the operator showed. 'You're quite a stranger, Mister Blenkins,' said he. Blenkins pushed in, breathlessly.

"'Down! Quick!' he said. The operator seemed to be sniffing in a puzzled manner. When they reached the ground floor he turned to Blenkins.

"'You haven't any boots on, sir,' he remarked in shocked tones. 'And your feet . . . that is . . . they're *dirty*, sir!'

"Blenkins scarcely heard him. 'Open the door quick!' he exclaimed. 'Those trees may start after me any minute! Man! This is life or death!'

"'But, you can't go out on the street that way . . . *oh!*' and suddenly the operator grinned and opened the door. Blenkins rushed out across the hall toward the door. The doorman was staring at him as he approached, but dividing his attention with something the elevator operator was trying to signal to him by tipping his head back and holding his hand as though it held a glass. The doorman was a slow-thinking person. Here was Mr. Blenkins without shoes, his clothes in disarray, wild-eyed, and his trousers and socks slimy with filth. There remained his duty, and he moved forward his whole two hundred pounds to its performance.

"'I'm sorry, sir,' he said. 'We can't let you go out that way. You will have to go back to your apartment and dress properly. Here, Bates, you keep your eye on the door as much as you can and I'll go up with Mr. Blenkins.'

"For a minute Blenkins struggled wildly, but he was a baby in those great hands and half-dragged and half-carried, he found himself back in the elevator, shot up to the roof, and stood in front of the apartment door. His well-meaning captor started to feel in his pockets for keys, but Blenkins in an agony of desperation, pulled these forth unaided and unlatched the door.

"'All right, you dumb ox! Come on in, if you must! If those trees start after you, you'll know that I'm not drunk or crazy!'

"He wanted to peer out at the manure-pile, but was dragged through the living-room and only got a glance that showed the three things standing there. Then his trouser legs were jerked off and the socks with them.

"'I know we shouldn't have let that manure go up here without investigating!' muttered the worthy doorman. 'You'd best wash yourself, sir.'

"Blenkins saw out of the window that the sun was getting very low. As soon as it was gone, he knew, those tree-men would drag themselves out of the soil and come for him. If he hurried . . .

"Ten minutes later, dressed to the satisfaction of his enforced censor, he left the apartment and breathed a sigh of relief as the elevator shot them down to the street. To the elaborate apologies of the two attendants he returned no answer except a brief, 'Well, no harm done after all—sure you meant well.'

"When he had gone, the two looked at each other and burst into a peal of laughter. 'It's a wonder it wasn't pink snakes instead of trees walking after him! You know how big a pile of empty bottles there is up there—scattered everywhere all over the place? Enough to kill you and me, Bates!'

"But Blenkins was hurrying along the streets to a police station a few blocks off. At last he came to it and in the large, well-lighted doorway stood a huge figure in uniform. He could have been the brother of the doorman back at the apartment. The association of ideas suddenly struck home on Blenkins and his hurrying feet faltered. Instead of turning to enter he found himself walking past the station, his mind in a sudden turmoil. What should he say to the police, anyway? Trees walking around on his roof, that were going to seed and overrun the whole earth. Trees that talked and grew wings. We-e-ll. And suppose they went back with him, even though they didn't believe what he said. They *couldn't* believe it! But even if they destroyed the trees, what then? The world would be saved, of course, but he, Blenkins, would spend the rest of his days in an asylum as sure as the sun was setting across the Hudson River.

"And that finally was what settled the matter. He walked the streets for hours under the lamp-light, not daring to go back home. After a while he entered a restaurant and ate some food. Then he walked the streets some more. Finally he went to a saloon he knew where they stayed open all night and managed to forget his troubles over a dozen stiff drinks. But soon after dawn he grew sober all at once and no amount of whiskey seemed able to remedy the condition. About eight he was out walking once more and glancing hopelessly into the windows of the stores, just now being opened for the day's trade.

"Presently he was attracted by a window full of tools and hardware of all kinds. There were wrenches and saws

and drills and axes—the axes gave him the last desperate
notion. He stopped as though he had been pole-axed and
stood staring at them—axes of all sizes, with the steel polished and glistening in the early sunlight. Some had the
back of the head painted red and some green. The green
ones fascinated him; they were almost the color of the sap
that had welled out of the gun wound in the Babbler's
body. Then he entered the store . . .

"When he got to his apartment house, Bates solicitous-
ly offered to help him into the elevator. 'Quite a night of
it you had, sir!' he murmured with secret admiration. 'Let
me stand those parcels over here, Mr. Blenkins.'

"Blenkins thanked him abstractedly and, arriving at
the top floor, stood a moment eyeing the closed door that
led to his apartment. 'Help you in, sir,' offered the operator. But Blenkins refused. This thing would have to be
done by himself without help. The elevator descended
and left him there alone. With a shiver he glanced at his
watch—nine-thirty. If the trees had gone back at dawn
they should by now be thoroughly drunk with manure.
It had taken them less than half an hour last evening. He
cautiously opened the door a crack. The living room was
empty. He tiptoed in and set his purchases quietly on the
floor. Now to cross the living-room and peer through the
French doors. There they were—all three of them—solidly
rooted in the pile of manure! Ah, but would they leap out
at him if he showed himself?

"In great indecision he found a glass—unwashed—and
emptied the last of a bottle into it. His eyes glanced around
the room and he was suddenly struck by the absence of
manure stains. If the trees had walked here last night,
their roots would have made a pig-sty of his living-room—
perhaps they had remained all night where they were!

"Well, that thought gave him courage to open his parcels and bring forward the axe and the saw. A long pull at a fresh bottle of rye gave him the final push that brought him, wild-eyed, to the side of the manure pile. He stood there looking at the quiet branches armed with thick, elongated leaves and a great hatred for these creatures shook him like a fever. Before he had time to think, the axe had bit chunkily into the body of Brownie and the green sap splashed. Now in a panic of fear, he rained blow on blow until the splintered trunk lay in pieces and even the arms were separated from the handlike leaves. He paused to wipe the moisture from his forehead and noticed with horror that the leaves were commencing to wriggle. He chopped at them again and again, but the mutilated pieces seemed capable of separate life.

"The thought of fire came to him and in an instant he had raced into the living-room and thrown newspapers and books into the great fireplace and set them alight—then back to the roof and picking up pieces of the tree to throw on the blaze. The last piece—half an arm—wriggled in his hands and he dropped it with a shudder on the hearth and raked it into the fierce heat with his toe.

"Sobbing with excitement and fear, Blenkins returned to the roof and commenced on Shorty, half expecting him to have been aroused. But he disposed of him as he had the first and broke up two empty wooden liquor cases to add to the fierceness of his bonfire, throwing in books by the armful to help out. When it came to the Babbler, his strength was almost gone and he dragged him from the manure bodily and sawed him in half. The root end went in the fireplace all right, but the branch-end trailed on the hearth and the leaves writhed for five minutes. Blenkins says that he was violently sick for half an hour immediately afterward and then came back to the living room and cleaned things up as best he could before falling asleep.

"Well," remarked Colonel Marsh, "That's the yarn—
take it or leave it."

And, as you see, I have taken it.

THE MOANING LILY

Emma Vanne

When Carl Brense, exponent superior of Harvard, Oxford, Heidelberg and what not, took up botany as his life profession, we, his class-mates, were not in the least surprised. There was something about the man's tall, very thin frame and lean sensitive face that suggested flowers and subjects idealistic. His gray eyes were big and soulful and his features sharply chiseled like those of a Dante. And when he smiled, it was only a fleeting condescension to the distressing materialness of the surrounding world.

For five years after our graduation, I never set eyes on Carl. Then, one day, I ran across him at a flower-show in New York City. He was standing like a sober statue alongside some ravishing roses and sweet peas. I greeted him affectionately, and he was really glad to see me.

"Heavens, man," I enthused wholeheartedly, taking in the marvelous exhibits, "I never saw such exotic colors in flowers before. That purple rose there with its lemon leaves! And those silver sweet peas! No wonder they have won prizes! How do you do it!"

"Oh, everything is simple to him who knows how," said Brense unruffled. "I have made an exhaustive study of plant-grafting and am compiling a book on the subject. I have won thousands in prizes."

"Well, well!" I ejaculated. "You are taking it seriously. Live here?"

"No," answered Brense. "I have a little stone cottage near the palisades in Jersey. There I grow a good-sized garden far removed from city confusion."

Then he took out of his pocket a card, penciled his address thereon, and handed it to me.

"I would like to see more of you, Crale," he said. "I am very lonely."

So, from then on, Brense and I became close friends and I had ample opportunity for seeing how extremely intense he was in his devotion to rare floral specimens.

Then, one raw November day, the man suddenly disappeared. I went to his cottage only to find it shuttered and silent. An old caretaker, his man-servant, was mechanically puttering around Carl's garden and looked up listlessly as I approached.

"Ah, Mr. Crale, glad to see yez," said the old man, hobbling toward me. "Mr. Brense left a letter for you. Here it is."

I took the letter and proceeded to read it.

"I am going to Brazil," wrote Carl, "on the most exciting adventure of my life. The tropical blossoms down there are the most curious in the world, and I must study them. I will produce a flower that will shock mankind—just you see. This uncontrollable ambition has fired me consummately. God willing, I will return and exhibit a peerless super-specimen. Nothing else matters."

Well, that was that. Carl Brense had gone. So I left the stone cottage and returned to my bachelor-quarters downtown. And thus a year passed.

Then, just as suddenly as Brense had left, he came back one day. Driving aimlessly around, I happened to wander on a Sunday to the familiar acorn road near the palisades and found myself, by force of habit, approaching the little

stone cottage. It was May, and through the tall elms that
shadowed Carl's place I could glimpse a sector of his garden already aglow with its multicolored blossoms.

I stopped my car in front of the low iron gate and cautiously walked up the graveled path that led circuitously
toward the cottage. Bobbing tulips of riotous hues caressed
my feet as I proceeded. I was feeling strangely tremulous
because Carl's abode had always seemed like a sanctuary
to me and I never entered his premises without being
curiously affected.

Suddenly I paused in my tracks, for emerging upon
the lawn at the right was a tall, dark apparition of most
indefinite outline. The face that topped the spectre was
that of Carl Brense, but his figure was swathed from neck
to toe in a long voluminous black cape. And he moved
along evenly over the grass without any visible means of
locomotion, his ponderous robe dragging around him and
completely enveloping his limbs.

"God, man," I called out huskily. "You give me the jit-
ters. Are you turned into a monk or something? Why the
long monasterial robe?"

Carl Brense just extended his right hand from the folds
of his cape and tolerantly smiled. He evidently preferred
to ignore my comment concerning his robe.

"And your face!" I continued persistently distressed.
"You look like a ghost! You must be deathly sick!" And I
was truly worried, for the features of the man were a saf-
fron yellow with deep, dark crescents under his cavernous
eyes. His left hand, which I saw for a fleeting second, was
covered with varicose veins, brown instead of blue! The
sight was startling.

"Come into the house," said Carl quietly. "It's good to
see you again. Tell me about yourself."

"Tell me about *you,* you mean," I remonstrated. "If
you have been studying the flowers of Brazil, your efforts

certainly have been doing you no good. Gosh I can't get over the picture you present!"

We were by then sitting in Carl's lounge. I lit a cigarette, but he would not smoke, and though it was a warm day, he kept his clumsy draperies still swathed closely around his body.

"I have found my flower, Crale," said he portentiously, his eyes glittering. "It goes on exhibition tomorrow at the Flower Show. And, mark you, it will take the world by storm."

"You don't say!" I exclaimed. "Let me see it."

"Not now. You will see it tomorrow," said Brense firmly. "I am very sick, Crale, but I have succeeded in bringing back here the most remarkable of specimens. I call it 'the moaning lily'."

"Aw, Carl," I pleaded, "why in heck will you ruin yourself just to show a new flower! And gad, take off that unsightly cape. This isn't the medieval age. You're in New York, man."

But Carl did not respond. He just twitched nervously, his eyes dropping a little. Then he breathed heavily as if in pain while I thought I heard him moan. At the same time, he arose from his seat with a somewhat labored motion and walked toward the door. I felt instinctively that he wanted me to depart.

"You must not fail to attend the show tomorrow," he said politely. "Be there at ten. I will be in booth twenty. Then you will see the moaning lily."

"All right, I'll be there, don't worry," I promised. "But, hang it all, Brense, snap out of it. Be yourself! I can't bear to see you looking like a Franciscan monk. A man of your brains falling for religion! Heavens!"

"I am falling for no religion," assured Carl solemnly. "I cannot explain now, Crale, but some day you will know what this is all about."

So, the next day, I repaired to the flower show and made straight for booth twenty. Brense was already there sitting in front of his exhibits down near the spectator line. Quite a few people had collected about him, and no wonder.

The sight of the tall, gaunt monk was enough to arouse anybody's curiosity, but that wasn't all. Hugged in the hollow of his left elbow, his long bony fingers gently holding the foliage, was a broad, dignified plant. There were three or four large scraggly leaves upon a thick stout stem, and growing out of the latter was a pale pink lily conical in shape like the Easter lily, but the curling lip of the petal was carmine instead of white and the center was the same rich red. Also, the shoot coming up from the center was red and looked for all the world like a long, attenuated tongue. It was a strange sight and all eyes were glued to the spot. I, too, gazed entranced. Never had I beheld such exotic coloring.

Carl's face was sternly immobile as the public gazed, and he just stared solemnly ahead as the barker at his right began orating on the new prodigy, chanting out in stereotyped phrases his dynamic description of the same.

"Here," he barked, "we have one of the strangest flowers of all time. Imagine a white lily with a red top and a red center. It is dazzling! And that is not all! Step up closely and observe that the opening of the lily is remarkably like a human mouth! In fact, it *is* a human mouth! There are distinctly two red lips with a long tongue emerging between!"

The crowd pressed nearer and were properly impressed.

"And *now,*" continued the barker, "come closer and listen everybody, *lis-ten intently,* and you will actually hear this lily *moan!*"

And surely enough!—from the depths of the flower's interior there issued a definite long drawn out wail, and while it vibrated, Carl Brense still sat immobile, his sad eyes looking vaguely into space.

The spectators were spell-bound. There was something about the sight that was gruesome and uncanny. Why, the "lips" of the lily had certainly moved and the red "tongue" protruding from the center had really quivered as the weird sound issued forth.

Repelled and awed, the public slowly drew back. The pallid ethereal-looking monk with, his big sunken eyes looked like some long-suffering saint. His audience was hushed. It was as if the people were intruding on some sort of a shrine.

The barker, with proverbial callousness, invited the crowd to feel of the flower, but it seemed repulsive to them. They instinctively kept their distance like wide-eyed children. Only I approached and stroked the deep ivory petals and the over-hanging lips. They were softly bulbous like the bleeding-heart. A flower's petals had always to me seemed fleshly to the touch, but this lily was especially so.

But I was principally interested in Carl, so I edged toward him.

"Get out of there, Brense," I said almost fiercely in a tense undertone. "Leave your moaning lily and come home. You look as sick as a dog."

But Carl paid no attention to me. Then the barker continued.

"Mr. Carl Brense here is the most renowned botanist of his age. His successful experiments in the grafting of flowers has made him preeminent in this field, and this last wonder of his is undoubtedly his crowning achievement. Therefore, ladies and gentlemen, this moaning lily has won first prize not only for its extremely beautiful coloring, but because of the strange inexplainable sound that comes from its center. In fact, this flower is supernatural, and is so valuable that Mr. Brense will never leave it. He takes it home with him every night and never allows it out of his sight."

Then the barker proceeded to sell photographs of the monk and the lily to the eager buyers. This ordeal over, Carl Brense arose and sided toward the exit of the booth. He was thoroughly fatigued and anxious to get away, but I pressed in on him. His pathetic expression haunted me.

"Don't lug that clumsy plant home," I begged. "Let me take it to my apartment near here. It will be perfectly safe."

But Carl turned on me, a peculiarly wild look in his eyes, and drew himself up with all the dignity of his six-feet-eight.

"Don't interfere, Crale," he said severely. "I must take my plant with me. Don't worry about me. Thank you and good night."

So I left him. "Carl must be beside himself," I thought resentfully. "He is going too far. This is fanaticism."

That night the phone rang. It was the excited voice of Kito, Carl's man-servant. "Come quickly to Mr. Brense!" cried the servant. "He is dying and is asking for you, Mr. Crale."

"I'll be over right away," I answered.

It was a good forty minutes from my apartment across the George Washington Bridge to the little stone cottage near the palisades, but I managed to have patience and keep my wits clear. Brense had a secret to tell me, I knew, probably the mystery of the moaning lily.

Kito met me at the door, his hands twitching and his voice quavering.

"So glad you come!" he wailed.

"Well, what's happened?" I asked impatiently. "Accident?"

"I don't know," panted Kito. "When Mr. Brense got back from the show, he looked like death. 'Kito,' says he, 'go to the butcher without delay and bring me a quart of blood.' As I hurried off, I saw Mr. Brense excitedly writing a letter. Well, the butcher thought I was crazy, but I

got the blood. Then when I got back to the cottage, Mr.
Brense put the blood into a long, black vase. Then he took
the letter he wrote and stuck in his bosom. Then he looked
coldly at me, sir, and ordered me from the room. When I
came in a few minutes later in answer to his call, I found
him—but step in, Mr. Crale, and see for yourself."

So I followed Kito into his master's bedroom. There
on the table was a tall black vase, and in it towered the
moaning lily, while Brense lay prone upon his bed. He had
evidently flopped down upon it dressed as ever in his inevitable cape. Alarmed, I went over to him. There was no
doubt that the man was dead, for his eyes stared up glassi-
ly at the ceiling. I gently closed them. I loosened his cape
in front and the letter fell out. The latter was soiled with
marks of blood coming obviously from a wound in his left
arm. Eagerly I clutched the bit of paper. It was addressed
to me, so I tore it open, and with a cold tremor permeat-
ing my body, I began to read its contents:

"And so, dear friend," said the letter, "I decided to
study that strange carnivorous plant of Brazil, that plant
that drags to itself insects or small animals and then sucks
the blood out of them, a veritable animal bound to the
soil. After I arrived at the spot and began to analyze the
strange properties of the growth, I became suddenly inflamed, God help me, with a most odious impulse. I was
obsessed. Graft! Graft! The word was forever running
through my brain.

"I have always loved animals, so I did not have the heart
to try my experiment on any one of them. Besides, they
might die too soon. But I must graft that carnivorous plant
on to another thing that was also carnivorous. The idea
was burning me up, so I knew then that I would graft it
onto myself. I had read of the amazing physical fortitude
of certain men who were able to cut off their own limbs

to save themselves from death after a poisonous snakebite. So, reasoned I, why should *I* not be able to endure extreme suffering likewise, for a remarkable cause?

"So, with grim determination, and with the skill that years of experiment have given me, I grafted a stem of this carnivorous plant to my upper left arm. As the thing bulged rather inconveniently, I was obliged to conceal it from the public's view, so I covered myself with a voluminous black cape which was loose enough to enable the plant to breathe freely. Thus protected from prying eyes, I proceeded to await developments.

"Soon, with the accompaniment of a deep, dull ache, the roots began to take hold. The plant was actually going to live! And from then on, I was in the paradoxical state of physical suffering combined with intellectual ecstasy.

"Daily, I watched the stout roots spread under my thin transparent skin. They crawled along quite visibly, across my shoulder and under my arm, scrambling outwards like scrawny, greedy fingers. With a twiny, insidious grip, they embraced my left chest, and I knew positively that when they clutched at my lungs or heart, I would die. But I did not care. All I wanted was my new flower, and my only anxiety was that its sprouting stem might not have time to mature into a blossom before my death would end the experiment. But I was allowed to survive, and for that I was exceedingly thankful.

"Then, just two weeks before I knew the blossom would appear, I returned home, for I had timed the full florescence with the date of the Flower Show.

"And how zealously I watched my treasure unfold! The original flower resembled a lily somewhat, so I was not surprised at the *new* lily that finally materialized. But I *did* wince when I discovered that the opening of the lily was a perfect replica of a boneless human mouth. For months, I had moaned and groaned when no one was near, so it was only logical that the new flower should reflect in substance my most materially active organ. And there was the amazing carmine of the lips and the actual tongue bursting from the center! I was thrilled beyond measure!

"Then, one day, when the lily trembled and actually moaned, well, my exhilaration knew no bounds. I hadn't expected anything like that! My fondest hopes were realized. I forgot my physical pains and the desperate impulses I had had to sever the growth from my body. Instead, I fondly nourished it and was terribly afraid to transplant the specimen for fear it might die before thousands could see it and gasp at its super-excellence.

"But my glory was soon to end, for today, when the bloom was at the apex of its beauty, I realized that my death was imminent, that it was only a matter of a few hours. My glorious parasite had sucked me dry! Also there seemed to be definitely ensuing a certain weakness on the part of the lily. Its fate, of course, was linked with my own. Therefore, I could hardly wait to get home and rejuvenate it.

"I quickly procured a quart of blood which I placed in the glass vase. Then I cut the basic stem of the plant from my arm and placed the twig in the vase. I chose glass because I wanted the observer to know that the lily was in blood Instead of water. Thus nourished, the flower may last a week or so.

"So, my beloved friend, take it back to the show. I want thousands and thousands to behold it and sing its praises. Do not fail me, I beg of you. I am failing fast—it is the end."

Such was Carl's amazing revelation concluding with a pathetic apology for having caused me so much trouble. Trouble indeed! The least I could do now for my dear friend was to loyally carry out his last wish.

So, the next day, with heavy heart, I took the moaning lily back to the Grand Central Palace where I placed it in lone grandeur on a table, its majestic splendor flaring conspicuously from the tall, glass vase.

Heretofore, when the monk held the flower, some trick of ventriloquism had been suspected by some skeptical spectators. But now that the monk was dead, all were convinced that the lily really moaned all by itself. And just as Carl wished, thousands came to gaze upon it, to listen and to wonder.

Then, on the seventh day, the flower began to fade. It shrank rapidly in size and the observers drew close, as usual. Then suddenly, while they were watching, the "red lips" opened wide in one last spasm of life, synchronously emitting an unusually long moan, a miserable sound that could be heard for yards distant. The people repelled, instantly drew back, frightened of they knew not what, some of the superstitious actually crossing themselves religiously.

Finally, the flower gave one last quiver and collapsed centrally into a crinkling mass of folds, its whole weight sagging down over its stout brown stalk. The miracle was no more.

But the fame of Carl Brense and his super-blossom spread all over the globe. But of what avail to him who had perished? The Indian fanaticist walking with bare feet over coals of fire and jagged knives had nothing on *him,* my poor demented friend who had plodded heavily about through long tortuous months in his stifling black mantle, zealously guarding his precious moaning lily.

THE GLOWWORM FLOWER

Stanton A. Coblentz

Beware, gentlemen, before you attempt an interplanetary flight! Beware, not because you may not succeed, but because you may succeed too well! The indirect costs of your experiment may be more than it is worth!

Such was the celebrated warning issued in August, 1976, by Dean Cameron Prince, holder of the Tri-Continental Award for Astro-Physical Research. It was in September of that year, as will be recalled, that the Reimers-Bayle around-the-Moon rocket car was to attempt its first flight.

The pronouncement of Dean Prince, coming almost on the eve of the long-heralded excursion into space, naturally produced something of a sensation—although, when efforts were made to pin the dean down as to just what he had meant by "some new and unforeseen peril," he resolutely refused to explain.

Amid the excitement of the preparations for the space flight, Prince's prediction was soon forgotten; nor was it to be generally remembered again for many months. On Sunday, the fifth of September, the rocket car ascended from an airport in Southern California; and, driven by the explosions of a new volatile fuel named hydrogyl, rapidly made its way toward the Moon.

Throughout the flight, the two occupants of the car were in constant radio communication with the Earth, and

never at any time did they report themselves to be in difficulties.

Up, up, up they ascended, to a distance of more than
three hundred thousand miles, then in a wide circle around
the Moon, photographing its farther side, which had never
before been revealed to the eyes of man, then down again to
Earth, strictly on schedule time—so much so that, whereas
the expedition had been planned to last forty-eight hours,
they set foot on California soil precisely forty-seven hours
and fifty-six minutes after their departure.

It was only to be expected, therefore, that Reimers
and Bayle, the successful space fliers, should be feted and
applauded in a manner befitting the Christopher Colum-
buses of a new age. And while they, in the exhilaration
of their triumph, were contemplating an expedition to
Venus, no one could even mention Dean Prince's prophecy
without being laughed into silence. As yet there was not
even an indication of any possible ill effect!

It is true, however, that there was one unexpected,
although interesting result of the space flight. On the
soil of the airport, close to the rocket car—which, for
exhibition purposes, had been allowed to remain where it
descended—a peculiar plant was observed springing up, a
week or two after the completion of the flight.

As the appearance of the plant—later christened the Glowworm Flower—has become familiar to every man, woman
and child on the planet, it will be needless to describe
it in detail. It was composed, as everyone knows, of a
curly mass of spidery, gray-green tendrils, which spun and
twisted themselves into dainty whorls and patterns, no
two alike, yet all as graceful as the curve of the lily.

There were no leaves; but near the end of the tendrils,
as the plant approached its full height of two or three feet,
a dazzlingly beautiful blossom appeared—a flower which,

opening to the width of a large chrysanthemum, displayed
a snowy-white heart, surrounded by innumerable rain-
bow-colored petals, which shimmered and shifted in complexion with every change of light, sometimes appearing
pale-blue or lavender, sometimes delicately rose-colored,
sometimes palely saffron-tinted, sometimes mauve or
coral or faintly green or splashed with opalescent, creamy
lines, but more often than not a combination of all these
hues, and of a thousand others defying description.

Another peculiarity of the blossom was that, instead
of being invisible at night, it glowed with a weird, almost
ghostly phosphorescence—with a dim, silvery, moonlike
radiance that made it visible from a considerable distance,
and produced an effect at once pleasing and a little uncanny. And at times, from the white heart of the flower,
little gleams and sparkles of light would appear, as though
responsive to some intelligent will.

What made the plant even more wondrous to the senses
was the strange, seductive odor it gave forth. There was
something alluring beyond all words in its fragrance,
which had a heady smell as of wine, and yet was sweeter,
more pleasurable than wine—as though honey and ambro-
sia were blended in its composition.

It was observed that bees went almost mad in its presence, buzzing around the flower in wild excitement, until,
sipping of the nectar, they would fall to the ground as
if stunned, and only after the passage of an hour or two
would be able to take to their wings again—whereupon
they would immediately return to the Glowworm Flower.

Whence came this astonishing plant? Before a month
had passed, it began to dazzle even the unobservant eyes
of the airport attendants, one of whom had the good sense
to clip off a fragment and send it for analysis to Professor
Richard Wallen, of the botany department of one of the
leading universities.

The latter, after conducting a microscopic examination, paid a hasty and agitated visit to the airport, where
he sought out the attendant and asked to see the living
plant at once. "Never," he swore, "have I observed anything like it! The microscope reveals a cellular structure
utterly different from anything I have ever encountered!
Neither my colleagues nor I can understand it!"

Upon being shown the growing plants, the professor
became still more excited. "It belongs to no known species," he stated, emphatically.

For the next few days, forsaking his duties at the university, the professor made his headquarters at the airport. Equipped with microscope, scalpel, and test tube, he
investigated and experimented unceasingly in a little
improvised laboratory he had installed with the cooperation of the airport officials; and it was not more than a
week before he had made the announcement that electri-
fied the Earth.

"I have proved," he proclaimed, "that the Glowworm Flower originates from an infinitesimally small
three-pointed spore, of a type never known before. Multitudes of these spores have been found, upon microscopic
examination, to be clinging to the sides and interstices of
the Reimers-Bayle rocket car. The conclusion, therefore,
is irresistible.

"They have been flying through interplanetary space,
and have been picked up by the car on its flight. In what
world they originated we do not know; but, manifestly, it
was not Earth. Thus, for the first time in history, we may
have the opportunity to witness the growth and development of extraterrestrial life!"

The sensation created by this announcement, it is safe to
say, was hardly less than that aroused by the Reimers-Bayle
expedition itself. Newspapers took up and featured the

report; scientists rushed to Southern California, for a personal examination of the new plant; members of learned societies debated its significance, and physicists and biologists weighed the possibility of the survival of spores in outer space; the public was startled into interest, and the Glowworm Flower became the subject of discussion among men who had but the vaguest idea of its meaning.

Had the plant originated on Mars, on Venus, or on the satellite of some remote sun? Through what incalculable eons had its germ cells been drifting amid interstellar vacancy?

Concerning one fact, at least, there could be no doubt; the Glowworm Flower had actually originated outside the Earth. All the investigating scientists—and they were numbered by the hundreds—were at one on this matter, although they had few other points of agreement. The vegetation of the stars had, literally, been transported to our planet!

Had the Glowworm Flower not been curiously beautiful, and remarkable alike for its exquisite fragrance and its luminescence at night, it might eventually have passed out of view, except for the few specimens retained and studied in scientific laboratories. But, like many another treacherous thing, it allured by its loveliness, and soon had worked its way into favor in the salons of the well-to-do no less than in the gardens of common folk.

The cultivation of the Glowworm Flower had become a fad, a craze, a passion with thousands. As fast as the spores could be developed, the young plants were distributed. Special nurseries arose for that purpose; and at any point throughout the length and breadth of the United States, in Canada, in Mexico, and even in Europe, the traveler was likely to be greeted by the interlacing gray-green tendrils and un-Earthly rainbow-hued blossoms of the stranger from space.

Unfortunately—as it ultimately turned out—it throve equally well in all climates, from the sub-polar to the tropical, and seemed to adapt itself to nearly every variety of soil.

It was in May, 1977—after the Glowworm Flower had become fairly well established—that medical journals began to speak of a new disease that had invaded widely scattered localities. The symptoms, it appears, were fairly definite, although they varied in minor details from case to case; always it was the mind rather than the body of the victim that was affected. The sufferer would first undergo a period of ecstasy in which he would call out in wild joy, like an intoxicated man; then he would fall into a deep coma, from which no effort could awaken him for many hours; then, finally, he would come to himself, invariably with a tale of the most astonishing dreams and visions, surpassing those of the opium smoker.

As a rule, the experience would leave the patient greatly weakened, and he would be as long in recovering as though he had undergone a major operation; yet, invariably, his recuperation would be temporary only; after a few weeks, he would succumb again, undergoing a still more dread visitation of the mysterious malady.

A peculiar fact about the disease was that it seemed to affect only the more highly sensitive and intellectual elements of the population. Writers, artists, professional men, scientists, preachers, scholars, philosophers—all those whose innate gifts and minds required the development of a delicate nervous system—these were the ones that appeared most susceptible, whereas common laborers, street sweepers, truck drivers, and the like, seemed totally immune.

Naturally, physicians were alarmed—particularly as the disease was spreading rapidly. It seems incredible to us to-day that they did not immediately detect the cause; but the fact is that they either remained in doubt, or feared—not without reason—that the announcement of the truth would do more damage than good. At all events, it was months before the source of the ailment was openly recognized, and meanwhile it was constantly claiming new victims.

The strangest thing about the affliction, according to all accounts, was the nature of the visions which the sufferer claimed to see. In all cases, he would describe a sensation as if he "had risen out of his body"; in all cases, he would refer to an intoxicating sense of flying through "tremendous spaces," through distances passing all computation. But, beyond this point, no two accounts agreed entirely, although they all had certain points in common: the description of weird far-off worlds, of comet-swept skies, of flaming galaxies and unfamiliar constellations, of suns and moons unknown to man, and of populated countries fantastic beyond belief.

To consider a typical account, here is the story of Dr. Francis Carlson, the British mathematician, who, as a hardheaded practical man, could scarcely have been expected to indulge in any vagaries of the imagination.

"My first feeling," he wrote, "was one of great buoyancy and lightness, as though I had left a weight of scores of pounds behind me. Suddenly I seemed to rise in the air. A shadowy form, which I took to be my own lifeless body, was lying on the couch in my room. I rose through the walls and ceiling as though they did not exist, and out into the air over the house, which I could clearly see, then upward with a rocketlike velocity, until I had passed above the very Earth, and saw it diminishing beneath me like a shooting star.

"It seemed much later when I found myself on the surface of another world. Three suns glared brilliantly down upon me—one, near the northern horizon, of about the color of our own Sun, although less than a tenth as large; another, halfway down from the zenith to the south, of a sultry copperish red, and much less bright than the first, but with fifty times its disk; while the third, of an unbearable pure-white radiance, was rising slowly in the west. There were also, I think, several moons, colored with shifting pinks, mauves and yellows, but these I did not notice particularly, for my gaze was absorbed in the spectacle beneath.

"The entire surface of the globe was covered with a bewitchingly beautiful foliage, with a jungle growth which, weaving its lovely gray-green tendrils in whorls and spirals to the height of great trees, displayed incalculable multitudes of the most resplendent flowers I had ever seen.

"Larger than a man's face, and more fascinating to behold than the most appealing woman ever put on Earth, each of the blossoms revealed shimmering rainbow-hued petals about a core of pure-white; each, like a sentient being, swayed and tossed gracefully, although no wind was blowing; and each exhaled an odor that it was heaven itself to breathe.

"Truly, I thought that I was in Paradise! And so enraptured was I that it was long before I even noticed the resemblance of these fairy blossoms to the Glowworm Flowers that had so delighted us on Earth.

"It seemed that a long time went by, while I floated gently, as if on wings, through long twilight corridors beneath the masses of gray-green tendrils. And there, among branching lanes shot through with shafts of red and golden and silvery sunlight, I encountered the most glorious folk I had ever beheld.

"Never speak to me of elves! No elf could be so blithe and airy, so spry, so nimble, so kindly, so radiant with laughter as these little creatures that, borne on dragon-fly wings, came singing toward me out of the forest of foliage. Only in the remotest way were they human—rather, they were more than human; they were like angels, like gods! Each, wrapped in a shimmering many-colored gown like the robe of a humming bird, had the daintiest of arms and legs in addition to wings; each displayed long, flowing corn-colored hair, and eyes of an intense, an ethereal blue, set amid features iridescent with a thousand changeful tints. And the song that came from them all was to me as a heavenly chorus.

"Yet none of these strange people could have been, I think, over a foot in height. Indeed, judging from the lightness and ease of their movements as they curved and tossed and played and chased one another in air, I doubt if any of them was as substantial as a dove.

"They did not seem surprised to see me. Their melodious cries, as they approached, were as a carol of greeting. With a sense of encountering old and well-loved friends, I mingled among them; and, as I did so, I seemed to have been reduced to their size, and to partake of their qualities, and to dance and flit as one of them, and a sense of infinite well-being was upon me.

"There was one of their number—a frail and fragile creature, with eyes more deeply blue than those of her companions, and features that shimmered more brightly, and a gown of greater iridescence—who kept always at my side, and matched my every movement, until she seemed my breathing counterpart, and I was drawn toward her with a love that was wholly of the spirit. For we had no physical contact, and desired none, but wished only to float forever amid this world of endless light and shadow, of gray-green foliage and ambrosial perfume, and flowers more ravishing than a lover's kiss.

"A very long while seemed to go by; and we were ecstatically happy, and never ceased to glide through the

singing groves. But there came a moment when a sadness
burst upon me, and a weight seemed to press down upon
my shoulders, and something clutched at my heart, and
drew me away. My airy little companion looked up at me
with a speechless sorrow. In speechless sorrow I looked
back. Suddenly all the light and the fragrance vanished,
and I seemed to be far away, dropping back through the
abyss of space.

"After a time, I saw the Earth below, and it rose to meet
me, and I entered the heaviness of its atmosphere, like one
who, from some realm of light and joyousness, suddenly
plunges into a deep, dank tunnel. At first I saw my house
beneath, and passed through the roof, and on a couch was
the shadow that was my body, and with a strange clicking
sound I reentered it, and awoke, feeling very weak and ill,
and sadder at heart than I can say. But they told me I had
been out of my head. None would believe my tale of the
glorious world I had visited, and the word which they gave
to all the radiance and the splendor was 'insanity.'"

If this had been but an isolated story, it might not repay
repetition at such length. But since Dr. Carlson's vision
corresponded with that of thousands, it is important as
showing the type of delusion common to all the sufferers
from the new disease.

Naturally, the victims protested that their visions were
not delusions, that they represented actual experiences.
But it is well known, of course, that no lunatic has ever
been made to acknowledge his own lunacy.

However, the remarkable uniformity of the accounts
was without a parallel in the history of psychiatry—and,
as a consequence, not a few independent observers argued
for a serious basis for the visions. One fact, at least, came
to be everywhere accepted after the period of preliminary
confusion; that the disease had a single cause—a cause

which was eventually identified as nothing else than the
Glowworm Flower.

Soon after the discovery of the plant, it was revealed,
one of the investigating scientists had made the experiment
of tasting a thick, sticky nectar that formed at the base of
the blossoms. He had been the first victim of the disease—
and had been rapidly followed by others, to whom he had
secretly confided the nature of his ailment.

Through underground channels, the news had spread
long before it had become publicly known; hence the victims began to multiply at an alarming rate. Men of a dull
and strictly prosaic turn of mind, it seemed, were not
especially endangered, for, upon sipping of the mysterious
nectar, all that they would feel was a faint nausea; but
the more sensitive and imaginative the partaker, the more
completely he would succumb.

To cure the chronic user of morphine or opium was
less of a task than to rescue the devotee of the Glowworm
Flower; once having tasted, he would have no object in
life except to taste again and again—and, indeed, it seems
hard to blame him, since he had the sensation of experi-
encing a far more exhilarating and beautiful existence.

Nothing, however, could have been more deplorable
than to see keen and creative minds wasting away in a
drugged languor, to observe painters who had ceased to
sketch, poets who had ceased to sing, musical virtuosos
who had ceased to play, chemists who had turned from
their test tubes, physicians who had abandoned their vials
and stethoscopes, and judges who had deserted their law
books—all in order to enjoy the magic trance induced by
the Glowworm Flower.

To the practical and everyday world, the unanimous
protestations of these deluded ones seemed as fantastic as
the outcries of some fanatical religious sect. Who could
believe that the afflicted persons were really transported in

spirit to the planet of the Glowworm Flower's origin? Who
could believe that they witnessed the actual scenes and
encountered the actual inhabitants of some other sphere?

Yet this is what the victims of the disease firmly maintained; and to convince them of their error was impossible. Hence some of them were put behind the walls of
institutions, where, in their madness, they would cry out
for the Glowworm Flower, and would soon die if it were
denied them; and others, permitted their indulgence,
would go off into successively deeper trances, from one of
which they would not awaken. The term of a man's life, it
was found, would not be more than six months or a year,
once he had succumbed to the fascination of the Glowworm Flower.

Public opinion, usually slow in awakening, at last was fully aroused. Men everywhere became alive to the peril of
permitting the ablest and most useful minds to be cut off
by the mysterious invader from space; and it was conserva-
tively predicted that, in less than a generation, the intellectual bloom of the race would be destroyed forever. Yet
all prohibitions, all laws were futile. The curious among
the uninitiated, and those already victims of the Glowworm Flower, could not be deterred by any penalties. In
all countries, the death rate was rapidly mounting; within
a year, the casualties from the new disease were said to be
as numerous as those of a great war.

The only remedy, obviously, was to arrest the malady at
its source: to eradicate the Glowworm Flower. At a hastily
called international convention, representatives of every
nation signed a pact calling for the extermination of the
plant; everywhere the possession of it was made illegal,
under the severest penalties, and tens of thousands of
men were engaged to enforce the law and to see that every
existing Glowworm Flower was uprooted and burned.

But alas, it was not so easy to drive out the invader, once it had taken possession! The plant was bootlegged by profiteers who heaped up fortunes in the illicit traffic—and the most drastic punishments were required to restrain them. Worst of all, even after the law breakers began to be mastered, the Glowworm Flower was found to spring up voluntarily in scattered parts of the Earth— in farm lands and deserts, on mountainsides, islands and beaches. All efforts to control its spread appeared futile. Whether we desired it or not, it seemed to have settled among us to stay!

More than a year had passed before, amid the darkness of the world's despair, the International Investigating Commission was driven to make a radical recommendation:

"Let all interplanetary flights be ended! Each new expedition into space gathers a new supply of the spores, which cling to the car and scatter on reaching the Earth's atmosphere. Therefore the Glowworm Flower will be with us until space flights are abolished."

Naturally, there was a great outcry against so stern a proposal. Since the Reimers-Bayle expedition, space excursions had become popular; scores of parties had voyaged to the Moon and back, and plans were well advanced in their preparations for cruises to Mars, Venus and Mercury. Hence the prohibition of space travel seemed cruel and bitter to contemplate.

Yet the authorities, in their eagerness to stamp out the menace, were ready to accept a lesser evil in return for a greater. With the consent and cooperation of all nations, and in defiance of world-wide protests, the licenses of all space pilots were withdrawn, and all apparatus for space flights was destroyed. And, from that time forth, the fight against the invading plant began to succeed.

To-day, after ten years, not one of the beautiful, strange-ly seductive blossoms remains anywhere on Earth, except

for the few preserved in museums. There are still many
who sigh in remembrance of its divine fragrance, its other-
worldly loveliness. There are many who voice regret that,
because of the plant, space expeditions should have been
nipped in the bud. But, recalling how many of our best
and wisest citizens sleep in untimely graves, we know that
the measures we pursued, however greatly to be deplored,
were the only ones open to us if the race was to survive.

Hence no words are more frequently quoted to-day than
those of Dean Cameron Prince—unfortunately, so little
heeded when first uttered! "Beware, gentlemen, before you
attempt an interplanetary flight! Beware, not because you
may not succeed, but because you may succeed too well!"

Truly, those were words of wisdom more profound than
we could have known!

FOREST OF EVIL

John Murray Reynolds

JUNE 23.—There may not be much point in my trying to keep this diary. Our chances of returning alive from this mad expedition are not at all good. Probably it is the instinct of the professional newspaper man that leads me to keep a record of the trip. My old boss on the *Chronicle* used to say that on the Day of Judgment a good reporter would be taking notes on the ceremonies and trying to interview the angel with the trumpet.

It all started when Clive Mason came back after five years in Central Asia. He sat sprawled by my fireplace, his lean face strangely somber. Suddenly he said:

"I think I'm going into the Devil's own back-yard, Jim, and I want company. There's a fortune in it—for those who live."

"What kind of a fortune?" I asked him.

He took a chamois bag from his pocket and tossed two small objects on the table. "Diamonds, Jim. Uncut diamonds. Those two were in Tommy Reardon's pockets when he died. Did you ever hear of the Dead Forest of Sanaala?"

"Never."

"I thought not. Few people outside of Central Asia ever heard of it, and most of them think it's a myth. I happen to know that it exists."

"Is that where the diamonds came from?" I asked.

345

Clive's eyes took on a haunted expression, the look of a man who thinks of things not pleasant to remember.

"It's where I think they came from. The Forest of Sanaala lies deep in Central Asia, beyond the desert, between two of the spurs of the Kurugh Khan mountains. It is the bare and long-dead skeleton of what was once a fertile belt of woodland. The desert nomads believe it to be terribly haunted. Haunted—probably not! But I have reason to believe there may be something there more horrible than anything we have ever known."

"Why?"

"Because young Tommy Reardon went into Sanaala. I know that for a fact. And I saw him when he turned up in Changor three months later. God knows how he got there, for Changor lies across the mountains, which are unscalable. That was queer, but his condition was stranger. For one thing, he was blind."

"Blind?" I asked.

"Stone-blind. His eyeballs were completely rotted away, and the flesh around the sockets seemed to have been burned by acid. He was absolutely mad, poor devil, raving mad. He died a few hours later. So that was the end of Tommy Reardon—and God alone knows what happened to him, or how he got over the mountains."

There was a lot more to the yarn, of course. Clive hoped that a larger party might get through, that we would find more diamonds, and so on. I thought about it for several days before I decided to go. Now I am writing this in the vermin-ridden main room of an inn in the small and filthy Chinese city of Weh-Li, half across the world from home. The expedition is well under way.

JUNE 24.—Tomorrow we strike out into the desert! We are all ready to leave Weh-Li, five white men and a girl and some twenty Mongol bearers. The girl, Clarice Saunders, should never be with us, but it can't be helped now. She is the daughter of Peter Saunders, who is second in command of the expedition. He had left her with friends in Shensi province, but she showed up in Weh-li alone this morning and now we have to take her along. At least she's very far from being the helpless type.

Pete Saunders, by the way, happens to be a pretty well-known scientist but he is lean and gray and looks more like a soldier of fortune. The other two members of the party are about my own age. Ed Powell is Saunders' assistant, and Larry O'Neill is a young Irishman that Clive picked up in Shanghai because he liked his grin. Larry's idea of heaven would probably be ten drinks, ten fights and ten women every day. Sort of a disturbing element in a civilized place, but likely to come in handy on this journey.

Later in the day—To the list of the obstacles in our way we can evidently add the name of Doctor Paul Schweitzer. He is a big, paunchy man with thick glasses and an arrogant face. Wears faded khaki and a huge sun helmet. He came striding into our inn this afternoon, kicked one of our bearers out of his path, and then stood with his thumbs in his belt and looked us all over. At last he stabbed a thick finger in Clive's direction.

"You are Clive Mason?" he rumbled.

Clive smiled faintly, but did not get up from where he sat on a pile of boxes.

"That is my impression," he drawled.

"I hear that you plan to go to Sanaala. Do not do so! I am on my way there, I have planned this trek for some time, and I do not want you in my way."

"Know any more good jokes?" Clive asked, his drawl more pronounced than ever.

Schweitzer's wide face began to flush.

"*Donnerwetter,* you force me to speak plainly. Keep out of my way, you damned *Schwein!*"

He was really funny, and most of us laughed. I don't
know what Clive might have done next, but O'Neill took
matters in his own hands. He said something under his
breath and heaved his big bulk upright, and then hit
Schweitzer squarely on the point of the jaw. Larry caught
him as he fell and heaved him out into the muck of the
courtyard.

"Shall I sock him again when he recovers?" he asked
eagerly.

Clive shook his head. "You've done enough already. I've
heard of Schweitzer, and he's a bad actor."

JUNE 25.—Tonight we lie camped in a sandstone depression on the edge of the desert, with our sentry standing
silhouetted against the sky above us. I am writing this by
the embers of our fire, while most of the rest of the party
are asleep. There is our little cluster of tents, and then our
twenty bearers sleeping around us in a circle.

These bearers were the only ones we could get who were
not afraid to head for Sanaala. They belong to some no-
mad Mongol tribe and look like bandits, but they'll probably be all right. As a matter of fact, none of them even
speaks Chinese except their leader. He is a big Manchu
named Lao who looks like an unhung murderer but seems
to be a pretty good sort.

The desert nights are cold. Our sentry is keeping himself awake by whistling some plaintive, endless tune with
only three notes in it.

Tomorrow we leave all regular caravan routes and
plunge into the unknown, an unknown so strange that
probably no living man has yet penetrated it and lived to
tell the tale.

JUNE 27.—Yesterday was uneventful, but there was some
trouble just after we woke up this morning. I heard loud

voices, and stuck my head out of the tent just as Pete Saunders was crawling out of his.

"What's up?" I asked.

"I don't know yet. Look at Lao!"

The big Manchu was in a rage, swearing at two of our bearers in a guttural jargon neither Clive nor Pete could understand. Lao was waving his arms, and then he pointed at the ground. As we crowded around then, we saw what it was.

Footprints! All around and through our camp were strange footprints, the marks of bare feet. In the sand they were not noticeable, but on some patches of crumbling sandstone they were well preserved. Saunders and Lao began to talk in clicking Mandarin, and after a while Pete shrugged and turned away.

"Lao claims the men on guard must have slept during the night," he said, "and that there have been strangers in camp. Let's look over the supplies."

A careful check-up showed that nothing was missing. Clive sat back on his heels and scratched his head.

"It's beyond me," he said. "Those bare footprints were never made by any of our men, but nothing has been taken. Well—the guards will keep awake after this. We'll split the night up into two-hour watches for ourselves, and not trust the bearers alone."

"Think Schweitzer had a hand in this?" I asked.

"Perhaps."

June 28.—I'm too tired to write anything, but there isn't much to put down anyway. We marched and made camp, we ate and we slept. We all took turns standing guard. Clarice Saunders claims she should stand watch also—she's really quite a girl. Stronger than she looks. She hasn't held us up any so far.

We are all on strict water rations, for our route is off all regular trails and God knows when we'll find any wells.

JUNE 29.—Same as yesterday—no excitement. It was hot as the hinges of hell all day. Wish we had more water!

We were sitting around the fire tonight, all smoking and not saying much, when Clarice Saunders turned to Clive.

"Just what do you expect to find, anyway?" she asked. "Diamonds, I know, and perhaps something of scientific value—but what else? What do you think lies behind the Dead Forest?"

Clive hesitated a long time, pulling on his pipe and staring into the embers of the fire. At last he shrugged.

"I don't really know what I expect," he said at last. "I'm thinking of Tommy Reardon's ravings just before he died, but all that may have simply been madness. But it's possible that somewhere nature may be perverted, that strange and terrible forms of life exist. We may find something very queer behind Sanaala."

JUNE 30.—We made an extra-long march today, and will probably do the same tomorrow, now that we have become accustomed to the trek. The sooner we reach the Dead Forest the better, for the lonely Kurugh Khan mountains are beginning to bulk along the horizon. There should be water there. We have a very good supply, but still we all feel a little nervous about it.

The camp is a peaceful place at the moment. Our miniature army of bearers sits cross-legged about the embers of their own cook-fire, while one of them plays some sort of funny instrument with only one string. Pete is going over to the guarded pile of water-skins with some sort of purifying, powder. He filtered the water carefully before we left, but it was probably none too good at the start. Typhoid or dysentery would be fatal to our—

Later.—Something disastrous has happened. Or rather, we have only just discovered a thing that was done some days ago. Now we know why there were footprints around our camp after that first night!

Pete was busy with the water-skins when I suddenly heard him call for Clive. Something in his voice, a certain harshness, made me walk over also. Pete was holding an open water-skin, and he looked at us with an expressionless face.

"Smell!" he said.

We both sniffed at the open mouth of the skin, and found an acrid vapor that nearly choked us. Clive and Pete simply looked at each other.

"Chlorine!" Pete said at last, "liberated from the water by the powder I just added to purify it. The chlorine comes from salt!"

"Good God!" I exclaimed. "Do you mean that our water has been salted?"

Pete nodded slowly, his gaunt face suddenly deeply lined.

"Right! Now we know why somebody was prowling around our camp that first night."

"Schweitzer!" Clive said with a grim snap of his jaws. "It must have been one of his men. Don't let the bearers know about this, yet. Let's see how many of the skins are still good—if any."

We found that four of the remaining skins have not been tampered with. Perhaps the intruder was scared off before he finished his work. Anyway, we still have four good skins of water.

"Enough to take us back safely to Weh-Li," Peter Saunders said slowly. "Or enough—used carefully—to carry us about eight days farther. That should take us to the mountains—if we go on."

"We're going on!" Clive said grimly, and his face was harsh.

I think the terrible weight of that decision struck the three of us, for we turned in silence to look at the rest of

our party. Clarice Saunders was chatting gayly with Ed
Powell as they sat on the sand. The slant-eyed faces of our
bearers were contented as they squatted in their customary
circle. Larry O'Neill was cleaning his rifle with meticulous
care. In all, there were twenty-six people whose fate was
affected by Clive Mason's decision. I wonder how many of
us will leave our bones here to whiten in the desert!

July 1.—As I sit here writing this morning, I can see that
a crisis is near. The salted water was discarded before we
started this morning, and the moral effect on the bearers
was instant and disastrous. Most of them refuse to believe
that any ordinary men could have salted our water. We got
them going at last, but they were sullen and stubborn and
we made poor progress.

There is no chatter, no gambling, no joking in camp
tonight. For the most part the bearers sit in sullen silence
with their weapons across their knees. A few are talking
in undertones and casting occasional glances in our direction. One scar-faced man with one eye is staring fixedly at
me. If it comes to a rush, they are four to one against us.

July 2. *Morning.*—The crisis is here. Now! The bearers
have refused to take up their packs, and have gathered in
a compact group. Lao is talking to them. Clive has just
come back for a minute, and told me:

"You and Powell stay here with the girl, Jim. Keep your
guns ready. If they are set on turning back, it may mean a
fight for the water. Lao is trying to convince them that the
best chance is to push ahead."

Clarice is crouching behind a pack with her rifle ready.
She's a cool one, that girl! Lao's talk seems to be falling on
deaf ears. O'Neill is trying to bully—

That evening.—Camp is very different tonight. In the first place we have no light, for our water supply is so desperately low that we dare spare none for our acetylene lamps. Also, we now have only four bearers instead of twenty.

O'Neill tried to browbeat the bearers into resuming the march this morning, which was very foolish. These bandits are not the ordinary coolie. Larry lost his head and poked the nearest man with his rifle butt, and the bearer went for his gun. Larry was a split second quicker.

I still don't know why it didn't start a general scrap, right then. It looked bad, with the bearer dead on the sand and his comrades gathering for a rush.

It finally worked out that Lao and three others have agreed to go on with us. The others have turned back toward Weh-Li, which they will probably never see. We shared our water equally with the deserters, over Larry O'Neill's violent protest. But it was the only way to avoid a pitched battle.

It was nearly ten before we got started this morning, for we had to unpack all our duffle and re-sort it into the number of loads we can now carry. A lot of valuable equipment lies behind us on the desert, but it can't be helped. We have cut everything to a minimum. We are due for a short, sharp race against thirst! I am sorry for Clarice Saunders.

July 4.—Three tortured days lie behind us, as well as a good many more leagues of desert. God—but we are thirsty! We still have a little water left, but we dare not use it up. Still we have found no water, even though one spur of the Kurugh Khan is quite close.

This is being written by moonlight, as we lie on the sand close to the edge of the Dead Forest of Sanaala. We have at least reached the first fringe of our goal, but we

dare not enter it until tomorrow. Perhaps it's just overwrought nerves, but the forest that lies ahead of us seems
evil and foreboding. Well—daylight will tell us more.

JULY 5.—The desert lies behind us at last, but this place to
which we have come is even worse. Now, in the twilight,
there is a desolation that depresses us all. We are well into
the Dead Forest of Sanaala.

The branches of many trees are silhouetted against the
sunset sky, but there are no leaves to give them body. The
gaunt tracery of branches is black against the sky, like
the ribs of a skeleton. This place is dead. Dead! Even the
motionless, musty air seems of the grave.

Everything here has been dead for a long, long time.
The trees and bushes have not lived for years—perhaps
centuries. The wood is soft and crumbly with dry rot. The
ground is covered by a fine brown dust that is almost the
consistency of ashes. Probably it was formed by the decay
of the leaves that once clothed these bare skeletons. The
winds that swirl across the outer Gobi do not seem to
touch this forgotten corner between the two ranges.

Our four loyal bearers sit in a huddled group, talking in
low tones. On their slant-eyed Mongol faces sits a nameless fear. They stare at the shadows gathering around us as
though they expect to see the ghostly retinue of the great
Genghis Khan ride out from amid the dead trees. No man
knows where he lies buried with the sacred yak's tail stan-
dard above his grave. Clarice, poor child, has laid aside
her head scarf and is combing her hair, which has turned
dry and dull. There are deep circles under her eyes.

JULY 6.—Another day gone, and the dead forest still sur-
rounds us on all sides. There cannot actually be much
more of it, but the place seems interminable. Our remaining water-skin is almost flat, and Clive never lets it out of
his hands.

Tonight we held a conference—a bunch of unshaven scarecrows and a haggard girl. Our voices are all dry and croaking.

"We have a short water ration for tomorrow," Clive said, "and that's all. After that—God knows!"

"Tell us something new!" O'Neill snarled, his head in his hands.

Pete turned to Clive.

"Every pound we have to carry makes it harder," he said. "Why not cut our load down to a minimum."

Ed Powell nodded agreement, but Clive looked puzzled.

"We already have done that," he said. "Even our ammunition is down as low as we dare go."

"What about those heavy canvas suits you made us bring along?" Pete snapped.

With his gray hair standing on end and his skin stretched tightly over his bones he looked like a caricature.

"We don't dare abandon those," Clive said slowly.

Pete's voice rose sharply. "Why not? You never did say what they are for?"

"Don't forget that I examined the body of Tommy Reardon, who once went through here before us. There were strange scars on his body that I can't account for. I have a theory, but it's only a guess. The point is that something sinister lies ahead of us if we live to reach it. We must take that canvas armor along."

JULY 7. *Next morning.*—This will probably be the last entry ever made in this notebook. That is why I am hastily writing it now, in the pale light of dawn, while the others make up the loads and Clarice fixes the bandage on the shoulder of Chang—one of the bearers. Poor devil! This will be a bad day for him.

Disaster came to us in the night, and tragedy is close at hand. The others are silent at their work. We all know that we are entering on the last stages of one of the most horrible of deaths—death by thirst.

Sometime during the night Chang, who was on guard, suddenly shouted and we all jumped up. Dim shapes were moving about the camp. We fired a few shots, there was a little confusion, and the intruders ran. But Chang leaned against a tree-trunk with an ugly knife wound in his shoulder.

That was bad enough, but a little later we discovered something worse. Our remaining water-skin lay flat and empty. It had been slit with a knife!

"One more move for Schweitzer," Clive said wearily. "We owe our jovial friend a lot if we ever meet up with him."

We are ready to start. It seems hopeless, for we are already nearly mad from thirst, but we may as well push on as stay here to die.

JULY 11.—Things looked very hopeless that morning a few days ago. With scarcely a word to each other, through lips that were dry and cracked, we picked up our packs and started.

Hour by hour we plodded forward, while the sun rose high and the still air of the Dead Forest became suffocatingly hot. The ashy dust raised by our passing was a choking cloud. Clive plodded in the lead, occasionally glancing at his compass, and the rest of us straggled after him. The wounded Chang lurched along between Lao and O'Neill, his eyes dim and emotionless.

We halted for rest every hour, stretched headlong in the dust, sprawled in whatever positions we fell on halting. Chang died half-way through the morning, so we simply left him lying there and went on.

Near sunset the end came. We had paused for one of our halts, and at last Clive stood up. He spoke to us, a meaningless sound that rasped in his dry throat, but I knew it was the signal to go on. Painfully I dragged myself upright. A few yards away was Larry O'Neill, standing with his thick legs wide apart and his head hunched wearily forward. We were the only ones. The others had reached the end of their trail.

Clarice made two feeble attempts to rise and then fell back. Her father seemed to be in a stupor, and Ed Powell was muttering incoherently to himself. Lao and the two remaining bearers had obviously not the slightest intention of moving. The thing seemed hopeless. Clive stood leaning on his rifle like some gaunt scarecrow, staring ahead with haggard eyes.

To the west the sky was reddening, glowing behind the branches of the dead trees like a fire in a grate. The trees ahead seemed to be thinning out a bit, and as I stared I saw a stone tower standing above them. Of light gray stone, touched with crimson by the setting sun, it could not have been more than a mile away. I pointed, and tried to shout, though the best I could do was a faint croaking.

It was a journey of nearly a mile out through the fringes of the Dead Forest, across some bare fields and up to the stone tower and well that stood beyond. It was unquestionably the worst mile I have ever covered. Larry and I carried Clarice, who had lost consciousness, and the others managed to stagger along. I think we were all afraid that the tower would turn out to be just a mirage.

Those last few events are dim as a nightmare. I vaguely recall that Clive broke out a canvas bucket and lowered it into the well. I know that the water tasted better than anything in my life. We doled it out slowly, a swallow at a time. Then we all rolled up in our blankets right there beside the well and went instantly to sleep.

Later in the day.—I was interrupted by Ed Powell's shout to come and eat. We have stayed here resting for a few days, but will probably push on again tomorrow. This

little stone tower beside the well makes a good halt-
ing-place.

None of us has been able to figure out who dug this well
and built this tower. Its ancient walls are carved with the
face of some forgotten god. Pete Saunders thinks it must
be the work of some offshoot of the Khmers who built
Angkor-Thom, in spite of the distance from Cambodia.

It is near sunset, and I am writing this sitting on the
ground with my back against the westward wall of the
tower. Before me lies the unknown into which we must
plunge tomorrow. The twin ranges of the Kurugh-Khan,
visible like gigantic ramparts on either side, seem to merge
into each other somewhere far off in the heart of the sunset. The valley between them must be triangular in shape.
There is a patch of good vegetation here, and then an
expanse of bare rock that drops sharply for perhaps a half-
mile. Beyond lie dense woodlands.

The desolation that rules in the Dead Forest does not
hold in the valley ahead. It is fertile—but there is something very strange about it. Ed Powell has just raised the
same thought.

"Those woods look queer," he said, "sort of unnatural."

Clive, stretching his long legs by walking up and down
beside us, nodded slowly. "They look abnormal to me, too.
The green is strangely bright."

That is true. There is something disquieting and unhealthy about that lush forest below us. We can see not
merely green, but other bright colors as well among the
trees, and they don't look quite right either. Remind me of
the colors of toadstools.

Pete has been peering ahead through his binoculars.

"I'm no tree expert, but I'll swear there are some new
kinds of trees ahead," he said. "This will be interesting."

"Hope it's not *too* interesting," Clive said grimly.

"What do you mean?"

"I don't know what I mean. I'm simply remembering what happened to Tommy Reardon."

It all makes me think of what I saw last night when I looked down toward that valley just before turning in. The forest below was alive with lights. White and green, constantly in slow movement, they kept up a sort of endless dance. There was no sound on the still air, but the movement of the lights was ceaseless. Pete tried to tell us they were giant fireflies, but I doubt it.

JULY 12.—We are camped in one of the strangest places on earth. We have been through some experiences that make us begin to understand why Tommy Reardon went mad.

Soon after sunrise we gathered our things together and started west, climbing laboriously down over that long and uneven slope of rock. As we neared the edge of the jungle the queer character of the vegetation became more and more evident. We began to notice a peculiar smell. It was something like the stink of kennels on a damp day, like the smell of a hot-house, like the odor of a menagerie—yet it wasn't quite like any of them.

As we got near enough to see what the trees were like, we were even more puzzled. Their bark ranged from an unhealthy light brown to a sort of dirty pink, and on closer look the bark was somehow gruesome. It was more like the skin of an animal than the bark of a tree. It reminded me of the flesh of a corpse—bloated, and soft with an unhealthy softness. The leaves were bright and thick. But the strangest thing of all was this: all the branches of all the trees were in motion, *but there was no wind!*

Those branches seemed to move as though they were searching for something. They were lazy and sinuous, like the tentacles of a drowsy devil-fish. The trees nearest to us were in the most violent motion. Perhaps violent is not the word, for the movement was at all times easy. What

I mean is that the nearest trees seemed to *grope* for us
with their branches! These devil-trees had personality! We
cursed under our breath, and carefully picked our path so
that we avoided contact with them. Clarice had gone very
pale.

Little by little we came to realize that these *things*—I
cannot really call them trees—were conscious of our presence. They did not seem to have any eyes, but they somehow perceived that we were there. It was horrible!

Ed Powell was the first to speak.

"Do you see them too?" he asked.

"We see them, all right," Larry O'Neill muttered. "I've
heard of the Devil's garden, but I never thought to be in
it this way."

"This is interesting as all hell," Pete said. "In this isolated valley evolution has followed a course only hinted at
in the outside world. The animal and vegetable kingdoms
have been crossed. These things are as much one as the
other. Notice that a few of the branches are shaped like
antennae with round knobs on the end? They are probably
phosphorescent, the lights we saw last night."

"Do you mean those hellish creatures can see?" O'Neill
asked.

"I think so, in some way. Look there!"

As he spoke, a flock of birds came by, probably flying
over from one of the mountain ranges. They were low,
just above the tops of the trees. As we watched, a branch
suddenly shot up in the air and caught an unwary bird
that had been a little lower than the rest of the flock. One
of the big leaves closed like a fist around the bird, which
fluttered helplessly. The branch curved down and thrust
its prey into an opening that suddenly appeared near the
top of the trunk. The jaws, if you can call them that,
closed again with a snap.

Clarice Saunders gasped. "Horrible!" she said.

Clive dropped the butt of his rifle to the ground.

"I've heard of giant fly-trap plants," he said, "but these are far worse. Well—we might as well go on. But first we'll all put on these heavy canvas suits that we've carried with us. I had a hunch of something of this sort after I saw the scars on his body and listened to his ravings. Poor devil, he must have had a tough time getting through here!"

We put on the canvas suits, looking something like aviators. We slung our rifles, which probably wouldn't be much good against creatures with the disseminated nervous systems the tree-animals must have, and instead we drew the heavy machetes we had brought along to cut brush. God knows we never expected to have to use them as weapons against such weird opponents!

Then we started forward in a compact group. Clive went first, then Pete and I with Clarice between us, while Lao and the two remaining bearers brought up the rear. Powell and O'Neill acted as flankers. As the tree-animals were only about twelve or fourteen feet tall, there was plenty of sunlight. Now and then we passed scattered clumps of ordinary trees, mostly conifers. They looked very friendly and normal and home-like!

Though the underbrush was pretty dense, the tree-animals were far enough apart so that it was not too hard to keep out of their reach. We drove steadily forward. The branches of the *things* broke into violent motion as we passed, and the central trunks with their blotchy skin swayed toward us. There were plenty of traces of small game, and we forded several streams.

The tragedy came swiftly. We were passing through a clump of strange red fungi when Ed Powell tripped over a creeper and fell. His face landed squarely on one of the big red fungi that looked something like giant toadstools, and the thing seemed to explode. The next instant Ed had commenced to scream horribly and was rolling over and over on the ground. Even as I jumped to help him, he rolled within reach of one of the tree-animals, and a pair of branches reached down to seize him by the legs.

With a swing of my machete I slashed off one of the branches. The stump curled back as though in pain, and a viscous yellow liquid gushed out like blood. Another branch grabbed at me, the spines on its flat leaves catching in my canvas armor. I slashed out furiously with shortened blade, at the same time seizing Powell around the waist. Then the others arrived, and we dragged him clear. It took two of us to get his hands down from his face.

The poor devil's eyes are entirely gone, eaten away! Evidently the fungus on which he fell contained some very powerful acid. His whole face is terribly burned as well. Clive did what he could to ease the pain, and gave him a stiff injection of morphine from our medicine kit, but it was horrible. The rest of the day Ed staggered along between Pete and me, partly supported by us.

We are now camped for the night in the center of a small grove of conifers. It is pleasant to smell their faint fragrance, and to touch the rough and friendly bark! It helps our sanity in this mad place. As the embers of our small fire fade out, the evil lights on the tree-animals all around us seem to grow brighter. Attached to each of the things is a pair of gleaming globes that move slowly, like giant fireflies. There is something terrifying about being thus surrounded by thousands of strange creatures, knowing that they are watching us through the darkness with their sleepless eyes and always waiting for us to come within their reach.

JULY 13. *Morning.*—Ed Powell is gone. He vanished in the night. We do not know what happened. We can only guess.

Lao was on guard at the time Powell disappeared, and he swears that he heard nothing and saw nothing.

Most likely he had dozed off for a while. We do not know whether Ed wandered away, driven crazy by the pain of his wounds, or whether something took him. Perhaps, back of his disappearance, there may lie some nameless horror yet unguessed. We can only go on.

Evening.—Another night surrounded by the tree-animals. We must be getting near the head of the valley now, but there is no trace of the diamonds. The normal life of the past has taken on all the unreality of a dream. So long ago! It is hard to believe that there ever was any other life than this of peril and danger and endless pushing on.

We passed the body of a man today, or rather part of what had once been a man. The gruesome thing lay at the foot of a tree-animal which had probably eaten the rest.

"Probably one of Schweitzer's men," Clive muttered. "The thing must have caught him and torn him in half."

JULY 14. *Morning.*—There are only seven of us left now, for one of our bearers was taken during the night. Probably the same thing happened to Powell the night before. But even though we saw this man go, we are still unable to explain it.

I was on guard. The fire had died from lack of fuel, for there is little real wood in this ghastly place, but there was a fair amount of moonlight. The phosphor-lights of the tree-animals were, of course, all around us. Suddenly I experienced an unpleasant sensation of being watched. I stood up and looked around, but there was nothing in sight. I started to take a slow walk around the borders of the camp.

It was just as I was completing the circuit that I saw the *thing.* It had lingered for an instant in a belt of moonlight. Gross, misshapen, a mass of tentacles surrounding a stumpy body, it was like a shadow from a madman's dream. Unreal and horrible. For a moment I stared, then shouted an alarm. At the same moment I flung up my rifle and fired.

I must have hit the thing, for it gave a sudden yelp. Then, moving with incredible speed, the monster bounded across the camp and seized the nearest sleeper, who happened to be one of the bearers. It vanished in the shadows. We could hear Fan-Kee's screams dying away in the distance, and then they ended with a gruesome abruptness.

There was no more sleep for the rest of the night. A brief attempt to follow the trail of the thing that had taken Fan-Kee was hopeless. We threw what wood was left on the fire, and gathered close around it.

"What do you suppose it was?" O'Neill asked with awe in his voice.

"God knows," Clive answered wearily. "Ask Jim. He's the only one who saw it clearly."

"Well," I told them at last, "the nearest I can say is that it looked like a cross between an octopus and a cactus plant pulled up by the roots—if you get what I mean."

"Probably the final stage in this strange laboratory of perverted evolution," Pete said slowly. "These other things around us are still more plant than animal, but this new thing is evidently more on the animal side—particularly since it cried out when you shot it. It should be interesting to examine one closely."

"I only hope I never come within a mile of one again," I told him sullenly.

JULY 15.—We should sleep tonight. We are camped on a sandy point running out into a broad lake. The neck of land connecting us with the shore is very narrow, and one man can easily guard it against even such foes as we have here. We now know what our enemies look like. In fact, there are two of them drinking from the lake not two hundred yards away at this moment.

They stand perhaps five feet tall, with a round misshapen body and a dozen legs that are tentacles as well. They look something like octopi, or giant spiders. Dark brown hair covers body and tentacles, but it is not a real animal hair so much as fuzz, such as you find on a root freshly pulled from the ground. They have a head equipped with a sort of beak, and a pair of round cold eyes, and a cluster of leaves on top. When crouching down with tentacles folded they look like a pile of rocks and earth covered with vines or creepers. Yet they are capable of great speed.

Behind us the lake—we have christened it Lake Reardon in memory of the poor devil who was here before us—stretches smooth and cool to the base of the sheer ranges that close the valley. The rock seems to rise straight from the water at all points. Those silent peaks still hold the secret of how Tommy Reardon managed to cross them when alone and injured. We have seen no sign of Schweitzer.

Through the glasses we can see an outcropping of broken rock half a mile along the shore of the lake. It looks like a promising spot for our diamonds.

JULY 19—We have been having another quiet interlude. We have built a barricade of rocks across the narrow neck that connects us with shore, but so far it hasn't been necessary. Some of the tentacle creatures often browse near by, but they do not bother us. Most of the trees along the shore are ordinary pines and cedars, perhaps because the sandy soil is unfavorable to the tree-animals.

These tentacle-creatures seem to be just half-way between the plant and the animal. Though carnivorous and free-moving, they will stand for hours with their tentacles thrust deep in the moist ground. The head and eyes are animal, the coating of leaves is entirely vegetable. If I have any nightmares for the next twenty years, those damn things will be in them!

JULY 21.—Well—we're all rich men. And we're likely to die here without a chance to enjoy our fortunes. I suppose it's funny—but I don't feel like laughing.

Among the broken rock of an outcropping on the beach we found volcanic pipes filled with blue clay. In them were plenty of uncut diamonds. It must be the place where Tommy Reardon found his stones, for the initials T. R. were scratched on a smooth slab of rock. We have plenty of diamonds for all of us, but the trouble is to find our way back to civilization.

I have a feeling we could never get back the way we came. The now aroused tentacle-creatures would make our passage back through the jungle far more difficult. Every day they come in increasing numbers to watch us. They seem very curious. They particularly gather at twilight, squatting along the edge of the jungle and watching us with their cold eyes.

The things seem to be simply curious—not hostile—but we remember the fate of Ed Powell and Fan-Kee. Our policy is one of watchful waiting, for we fear they are not highly vulnerable. We dare not provoke an attack by trying to kill them, yet our passive attitude seems to increase their confidence. They come nearer every day, and we are getting nervous.

No one else has expressed the opinions I have written above, but I think they all share them. They all agreed very promptly to my proposal to build a raft to examine at close range the cliffs surrounding the lake. Shadows are gathering—and we may as well try what we can.

JULY 22.—There came an interruption just as I was writing the above last night. A tall man, who looked like some wild prophet with his black beard and fanatical eyes, stalked out of the woods and walked toward our peninsula. It was

Schweitzer. Behind him were half a dozen Chinese with rifles slung on their backs.

We dropped down behind the barricade and leveled our rifles. Schweitzer halted and held up his hand.

"I come in peace," he boomed. "Let us have a friendly talk."

"Come up to the barricade alone," Clive told him, "but tell your men to stay where they are and keep their rifles slung."

Schweitzer leaned on his rifle and grinned at us wolfishly across our low barricade of rock. He was thin and worn, and through his torn clothes we could see ugly red scars on his body. If the six men with him were all he had left, his party must have suffered even worse than ours in the jungle. Probably it was the canvas armor that saved us, for time and again we had been touched by a long branch of one of the tree-animals as we tried to thread our way among them.

Schweitzer was as arrogant and overbearing as ever. The pride of Lucifer burns in that man, and I think he would try to dictate to the Devil at the gates of hell. Clive stood up to talk to him.

"I come as your friend," Schweitzer announced in his deep voice.

Clive's smile was wintry. "We've seen a lot of that in the past," he said.

Schweitzer gestured impatiently. "That was nothing. Mere measures of war. Now the time has come when it is in both our interests to work together. I have found some fossils of great scientific value. You have found—I noticed through the glasses—some diamonds. Either party is probably too weak to win out of this place alone, but we might do it together. What do you say?"

I wondered what Clive would answer. For myself, I was remembering how Schweitzer's men had destroyed our water supply in the midst of the Dead Forest. Beside me, Larry O'Neill was muttering obscene insults under his breath. Then Clive smiled thinly.

"I'll give you one minute to get off this peninsula and take your men back in the woods. Then we open fire."

Schweitzer's face became dark with rage, but he picked up his rifle and turned away.

"You are a pack of swine!" he shouted over his shoulder. "We have more food and can wait. Stay here till you starve."

With his men at his heels, he strode off into the woods and disappeared. We all relaxed, and Larry muttered gloomily:

"I should have shot that baboon as he walked away."

"Might not have been a bad idea," Clive said grimly, rubbing the unshaven stubble on his chin. "We must raise the barricade higher and keep behind it. When our friend gets a little desperate he may try to pot us from the shelter of the woods. And we must rush building the raft—it's our only chance now that Schweitzer blocks escape through the woods."

"We have quite a number of trees cut already," I pointed out.

"Exactly. We'll work all night till we get enough."

We have raised the barricade higher, and are waiting until after sunset to work on the raft. It seems wiser to wait till darkness will screen us from Schweitzer.

JULY 23.—Things are happening fast, and our sands seem to be running low. It is probably foolish to bother to write this journal any further, but there is a lull at the moment and it is a good way to kill time.

At sunset last night we went to work on the raft. Clarice and Lao stood guard with rifles, while the rest of us felled half a dozen of the medium-sized evergreens nearest

the shoreline and began to strip them of branches. Though
we could see the phosphor-lights of the tree-animals dancing their bacchanale a little way back in the jungle, we
were working in almost complete darkness. We did not
dare risk a light. It would have made too good a target if
Schweitzer were near.

When the logs were trimmed, we dragged them out into
the lake to be pulled to the end of the peninsula. We were
standing waist-deep in cold water. Then we came back
ashore and cut some saplings to make into rough oars.
Clarice and Lao stood together, talking in low tones and
leaning on their rifles.

Suddenly dark figures materialized around us. They
had slipped up unseen from the forest. Lao flung up his
rifle and fired. One of the converging shadows faltered in
midstride and went sprawling on the sand, but venomous
tongues of yellow flame stabbed out as the others fired.
Lao's rifle dropped from his hands, and the big Manchu
sagged. A moment later he had fallen forward on his face.

We were completely taken by surprise, and the thing
was over in an instant. Schweitzer had disarmed Clarice,
and the rest of us had laid aside our weapons when we
waded into the water. Now we were helpless under the
guns of the others.

"I offered you peace, my hot-headed friends," Schweitzer rumbled with a sort of heavy geniality, "but you
chose war. So be it! Now we will take your diamonds, and
your canvas suits which we have seen. But first we will
secure you against foolishness."

He took a short length of cord and stepped up to Clarice, who was nearest.

"Please cross your wrists behind you, *Fräulein,*" he said
with ironic politeness.

For an instant Clarice glared at him, standing very
straight with her chin in the air. Then she shrugged, and

clasped her hands behind her back. Schweitzer tied the
girl's wrists securely, and motioned to one of his men to
take her in charge.

When Schweitzer and his men rushed us I had been
a little farther back toward our own peninsula than the
others. While he talked, and while he was binding Clarice's hands, I had slowly been inching backward. Slow
motion is difficult to detect in the darkness. Just as
Schweitzer finished with Clarice's hands I decided it was
time to make a break for it.

Spinning around, I sprinted at top speed up the peninsula toward our camp—and our rifles—a hundred yards
away. Shouts sounded behind me, and an irregular volley
cracked out. Bullets smacked on the sand ahead, but I was
untouched when I tumbled headlong over the barricade.

A moment later I had cocked one rifle, seized two others, and started back toward shore. There seemed to be a
lot of turmoil on the beach, and when I got there I found
the disheveled survivors of our party in possession of the
field. When I broke away and drew the fire of the German's
men, Clive and the others had jumped them. Schweitzer
had almost immediately called off his men—but they had
taken Clarice Saunders with them!

Behind the shelter of our rock wall, we lit a lantern
and gathered for a hasty council. To leave the camp and
supplies unprotected while we went to look for Clarice
might be fatal. And it would probably be playing right into
Schweitzer's hands, since he must expect us to try a rescue.
Surprise was our only chance, and two would probably do
as well as four. Larry and I were to go.

"All right," I said tensely, "shall we start now?"

"Wait until moonrise," Clive told us, "then you'll have
a better idea of what you're doing. Pete and I will make
some noise here and keep the lantern lit."

Larry and I buttoned our holsters tightly, and secured our knives by lanyards around our necks. We smeared our bodies heavily with grease to give some protection against the bitter cold of the water. At last the moon rose over the jagged peaks of the Kurugh Khan and shed a pale radiance on the smooth water of Lake Reardon. Larry and I shook hands with the others, then slipped over the barricade.

We crawled up the peninsula on hands and knees to avoid being silhouetted against the sky. On reaching the pile of logs we dragged one out into the water, then waded till we were up to our armpits.

"God, but it's cold!" I muttered.

"It is that," Larry whispered back. "What wouldn't I give right now for a good drink of whisky! Irish whisky! Well, come on."

Slowly we waded westward, pushing the log before us and keeping our bodies under water. There was a low mist on the face of the lake, which increased our chances of being taken for simply a drifting log if we were seen at all. Watching the shore as we went by, we pushed steadily ahead.

Once we saw a dark blot against the silver of the beach, probably one of Schweitzer's sentries watching to see if we came along the shoreline. My teeth were beginning to chatter, and I clenched my jaws savagely. At last we saw a pin-point of fire gleaming through the trees.

Where that fire was burning must be Schweitzer and Clarice. We went ahead until we were directly in line with the fire, and then moved slowly inshore. We would have to take our chances on meeting any of the tentacle-creatures on our progress from the beach to Schweitzer's clearing.

Our slow journey along the shore had taken longer than we realized, and the moon was setting when at last we crouched in the shadows at the edge of Schweitzer's

camp. A small fire burned in the clearing, and four of
Schweitzer's bearers were dozing around it. The German
scientist himself sat on a log with his chin in his hand and
his strange eyes fixed on the fire. He seemed to be brooding.

Clarice was near by, sitting on the ground with her
back against a small sapling. Her wrists were tightly tied
behind the slender trunk, and her crossed ankles were
lashed together. She looked very tired. For a few seconds I
whispered in Larry's ear, and then we separated.

I crawled as close to Clarice as I could get without
leaving the shadows, and then settled down to wait. Larry
had farther to go, and it would take him some time.

At last a shot rang out across the clearing. Schweitzer
leaped to his feet, and at the same moment Larry's mighty
voice boomed through the darkness. "All right now, boys,
all together!"

I saw Schweitzer leap into action, snatching up his rifle
and plunging out of the firelight into the shadows across
the clearing. In the moment when he stood there I had
the sights of my rifle lined up on the back of his head,
but I could not pull the trigger. It seemed too much like
cold-blooded murder.

There was a great deal of noise from across the clearing. Scattered shots came in quick succession, and Larry's
voice shouting mingled commands and encouragement.
The German's bearers had all followed him, and our ruse
was working. Larry was doing his best to sound like half
a dozen men. I jumped into the clearing and cut Clarice's
bonds.

"Back along the shore!" I whispered to her. "Come on!"

We broke through the underbrush till we reached the
shore, and then ran at top speed down the beach. I had
thought Schweitzer would be too busy with Larry to notice
what was happening on our side of the clearing, but we

had not gone over a hundred yards when we heard shouted orders behind us and then the crash of men charging through the underbrush.

The damp sand dragged at our feet and we could not make very good time. Dawn was near, and there was a faint gray light along the eastern sky. The men behind us were gaining fast, one well ahead of the rest.

"Keep going!" I snapped to Clarice and spun around with my rifle raised. Then I saw that the nearest pursuer was Larry.

"Get along with you!" he panted, and flung himself down on the sand.

Larry's rifle spat viciously back at the shadows behind, and after a moment's hesitation I ran on after Clarice. With Larry to cover the retreat, it was foolish to let the girl go on toward our camp alone. A minute later I saw her running back toward me.

"Jim," she gasped, "one of those *things* is after me and I have no gun."

Close on her heels was one of the fantastic tentacle-creatures, bizarre and terrifying in the pale light of breaking day. As I shot twice at its cold eyes it leaped toward us with a shrill scream. I flung Clarice to one side and jumped myself, snapping a shot behind the creature's head as it hurtled by me. It fell to the ground, writhing and screaming, but was up again before we had taken a dozen strides.

This time I met the thing squarely, jamming the muzzle of my rifle into its open beak and pulling the trigger. Again the monster went down, screaming horribly, and this time it did not rise to follow as we ran off.

There was now a pale gray light that struck coldly through the mists. Our little peninsula came in sight as we ran, and Clive and Pete came running down to meet us.

"Good work!" Clive snapped. "Where is Larry?"

I nodded back toward the strip of mist-veiled beach behind. "Back there somewhere. Let's go get him."

Clive and I trotted steadily along over the loose sand of the beach. Somewhere ahead of us Larry was still alive, for we could hear a scattering and desultory rifle fire. The beach was a narrow corridor between the blackness of the forest and the mists of the lake. Then with startling suddenness, a man loomed up through the fog ahead of us.

It was Larry. There was no mistaking that hulking form, even though he now staggered with unsteady steps. As we ran forward he fell to his knees. His chest was horrible to see, riddled with bullets, and a crimson trail stretched back across the sand the way he had come. With indomitable will he twisted around and emptied his rifle into the mist. Then, just as we reached his side, he fell again.

There was nothing we could do. A man with a less remarkable vitality would have been dead long before. In the grip of delirium he muttered brokenly that Morales was storming San Jacinto. God only knows in what forgotten fight he thought he was at the moment. Then he died.

Clive and I carried Larry's broken body back to camp. He was a heavy load, but we would not leave him there on the beach for the tentacle-creatures to feed on. Sunlight was gilding the peaks of the Kurugh Khan as we buried him under a big pile of boulders by a friendly pine tree on the edge of the jungle. Then we started to complete our raft.

We were not destined to do any work on the raft. Probably it never will be completed. Even as we got our axes from the stores behind the barricade, Clarice pointed shoreward.

"Look there!" she gasped.

A half-dozen of the tentacle-creatures had emerged from the jungle and were slowly crossing the beach. Gruesome and ominous, they settled down in a semicircle at the base of our peninsula about a hundred yards away. Even at that distance we could feel the relentless glare of their cold and unblinking eyes. Three more came out of the jungle.

"Looks as if they mean trouble," Clive said.

Pete nodded. "They seem to be gathering for an attack in force."

"Then we're done for," I told them hastily. "I fought one on the beach last night. I finished him off finally, but they're very hard to kill. If a lot of them rush us at once we haven't a chance."

While we stood there silently, clutching our almost useless rifles, the gathering of our foes steadily grew in size. By twos and threes, a minute or so apart, more tentacle-creatures moved out of the jungle and squatted down on the sand. There were a full score of them when Pete suddenly swore with deep feeling and began to hurl the contents of the packs out on the sand with frantic haste.

"I've an idea!" he snapped. "Where's that box with the gold assay equipment?"

"In the third pack," Clive answered wearily. He glanced at me, and we were both wondering if Pete Saunders' mind had weakened under the strain. "What good will that do us?"

"There's a lot of potassium cyanide in there. Here! You take this file and cut deep notches in the noses of our rifle bullets. Work fast!"

We caught the idea then, and furiously began to file deep notches in our nickel-jacketed bullets. Pete had found the cyanide and added a little water. As we finished each bullet he stuffed the notch with the deadly chemical and smeared it all over the nose. As each was finished he laid it carefully on a piece of canvas.

"It's just a chance," he said hastily. "The nervous system of these creatures must be very abnormal, but there's a bare possibility that cyanide may do the trick. It's our only hope."

As I write this, with all our bullets ready and nothing to do but hope, the attack is imminent. There must be over fifty of the things on shore there now. They have now arisen to stand on their tentacles, obviously getting ready for a rush. Clive is carefully sighting his rifle, about to try the effect of one of our prepared bullets. . . .

Clive's shot went home, but the creature seems unaffected. God help us now!

JULY 24.—We are now floating on a crude raft on the surface of Lake Reardon, we few who still remain alive. It now seems more hopeless than ever to continue writing, but at least it keeps my mind busy. I certainly never expected any of us to survive that mad turmoil at the barricade.

As if Clive's shot had been a signal, the assault began. The tentacle-creatures began to straggle up the narrow peninsula. The soft sand slowed them up, and they could not move as fast as we had seen them do in the jungle. It was a grim sight to see that horde of perverted creatures waddling silently toward them. I moved over next to Clarice Saunders and quietly decided to put a bullet in her brain the moment the fight was definitely lost.

At once we opened fire, shooting as fast as we could work the levers of our rifles and refill our magazines. A chorus of shrill yelps came from the advancing horde as our bullets struck home. I hit one squarely in the eye and saw it go sprawling among its fellows with tentacles twitching horribly. Another went down, and then another, but the main advance continued almost unchecked. They were half-way to the barricade, and the barrels of our rifles were hot to the touch. Those in the front rank, hit by many bullets, were wavering but still advancing. I made sure that my machete was close at hand, and then shifted my fire to the ranks farther back.

Up to the rampart came the tentacled mob, into the very muzzles of our guns. As we were bracing for the final rush that would send them pouring over the rocky barrier, the two things in the lead stopped short. They began to scream horribly. Not the short yelps that had followed each bullet wound, but a long-drawn keening that chilled the blood. Foam dripped from their jaws. All at once they dropped writhing on the sand, and another just moving past them began to exhibit the same symptoms.

"By Heaven, the poison's working at last!" Pete shouted jubilantly. "Those were hit first and oftenest. Let the others have it!"

That was the secret of our salvation. The poison had been slow to work upon the curious nervous organization of the creatures, but it had taken effect at last. As we poured in a new fire, the same thing began to happen throughout the mass of our attackers. The turmoil was deafening, and the length of the peninsula was a hell of twisting, agonized tentacles. Only one of the things actually mounted the barricade—and was cut to pieces by our flailing machetes.

The survivors slowly withdrew. Perhaps a dozen staggered back across the beach. We shouted and laughed hysterically, but then we took stock of our remaining supplies.

Only twenty or thirty rifle cartridges remained among all of us, and we could never survive another attack in force. We hurried to complete our raft, and in about three hours we had finished. The slain tentacle-creatures had grown still at last, looking like a long pile of jagged stumps. There was no sign of another advance from shore yet, but we wasted no time. As soon as we could load all our gear on the raft we pushed off and floated clear on the waters of the lake.

We turned toward the eastern and nearer spur of the range. Our crude oars were not very effective, but we made definite progress. We were pretty well shaken. Clive took a small bottle of brandy from what remained of our medical stores, and each of us took a drink.

It was just at that moment that there came a sudden outburst of screams and shots from on shore. We could see nothing beyond the edge of the jungle, but the sounds that came across the water indicated that hell had broken loose somewhere beyond the fringe of trees.

One of Schweitzer's men burst out through the underbrush. He backed slowly down across the beach, and every other step he paused to fire at something we could not yet see. Other men appeared, Schweitzer among them. All were fleeing from something that was pressing them back from the jungle.

Then the first of the tentacle-creatures came into sight. It ran toward the nearest of the fleeing men, crouching forward and shaking its ghastly head from side to side. Hit squarely, it faltered for a moment but then started forward again. The man suddenly found his rifle empty. With a despairing cry he hurled the weapon at his pursuer and ran toward the water. The thing caught him in the shallows. Clarice averted her head from the grisly sight, but the rest of us stared in a sort of horrible fascination.

Another wave of the tentacle-creatures swept out of the jungle, and Schweitzer abandoned the fight entirely. Hurling away his rifle, he dove into the water and began to swim out toward our raft. Most of the creatures stopped at the water's edge, but two of them plunged in after the fleeing man. With their tentacles splashing steadily, they caught him in a dozen strokes. For a few seconds there was a wild confusion while they pulled him under; then the water grew crimson and the turmoil died.

Clive laid aside the rifle he had lifted. "Exit Schweitzer," he said without flippancy.

It is now the next day, and we have been a third of the way around the lake. The cliffs are as sheer and unscalable as ever. Only the knowledge that Tommy Reardon escaped in some way from this place keeps us going.

August 16.—It is very pleasant here in the hospital at Changor. After all we have been through, it is good to lie still and do nothing at all. My broken leg is healing nicely.

In the late afternoon of the next day after the last entry above, we were paddling listlessly along the far border of the lake where the cliffs were screened by a great mass of vines. For a while we ceased paddling and just let the raft drift. It was a few minutes later that I noticed we were drifting steadily along parallel to the rock wall.

With every passing minute our speed increased, and soon we were speeding along in the grip of a current that gurgled softly against the rock as it went by. We became frightened then, and tried to paddle out of the current.

Our crude paddles had little effect, and we could not get free from the current. Every minute we traveled more swiftly. The raft swung against the rock with a heavy jolt, and scraped along against the cliffs. Then we were spun around, and many trailing vines brushed our faces. A second later we were speeding along in a faint gray light that quickly turned to utter blackness. The roar of the waters was loud in our ears.

"I see it now," Clive shouted. "We should have realized that the lake must have an outlet somewhere, with all those streams running into it. Try to find that lantern, Jim."

A few minutes later I had located the lantern and managed to light it. We were floating on the surface of an underground river that flowed through a natural arched cavern. The waters hissed and gurgled as they flowed, and the raft sped along at high speed. Though the tunnel varied in width from time to time, we found that one man with a steering-oar could keep the raft in the middle of the channel.

"This must be the way Tommy Reardon escaped," Clive said, "probably on a raft like this. Very likely this thing has its outlet across the mountains. We must be making ten miles an hour."

"But what made Tommy go blind? It must have happened near the end of his journey."

"God knows."

For perhaps an hour more we drifted quickly along. Then Clarice, who was sitting beside me, looked up sharply.

"What's that?"

I followed her pointing finger, and saw a black shape that circled above us. Occasionally it dipped down toward the light, then soared up again to the roof of the cavern, which at this point was quite high.

"Some sort of a bat," I said.

"Queer-looking bat!" Pete Saunders was peering up at it. "Not like any I ever saw before."

Even as he spoke, the thing swooped down toward him. With its leathery black wings flapping, it darted straight for his face. He flung up his arms for protection, and I struck at the giant bat with the butt of my rifle. The next instant it had flown away, but Pete had an ugly wound in his forearm.

"This thing hurts!" he muttered, his voice rising sharply. "It burns. It burns like fire!"

Clive had already ripped open the medicine chest and was working speedily. The flesh around Pete's wound was turning yellow. Then Clive poured on a strong alkaline solution. It smoked as it met the acid eating into the wound. Pete went white as a sheet, and set his teeth in his lower lip till a trickle of blood ran down his chin. After a while he relaxed.

"Thanks, Clive," he said. "I feel better now. That thing injected some kind of acid, all right. The funny thing is that it went straight for my eyes. A second slower with my hands and I would have been blinded."

"Now we know what happened to Tommy Reardon. Poor devil, it was a tough break to have it happen after getting this far. We'd better put our canvas armor on again."

We lost count of time. The hours did not seem to exist in that dark, roaring cavern beneath the mountains. For mile after mile we were carried along on the face of the underground river. The swift current kept the air moving, and we had no breathing. Now and then one of the strange bats swooped down to attack us, but they were not so hard to beat off when we were on the watch for them. Clarice slept fitfully, and the fever from his wound seemed to have made Pete drowsy, but the rest of us were able to keep the bats away from them.

Later, a long time later, a tiny spot of light appeared ahead. I was squatting on the raft at the time, with the lantern behind me. For a minute I blinked, thinking it might be a trick of my eyes, but then I was sure.

"Light ahead!" I shouted.

Clive crawled up beside me.

"Right! It must be the end of the tunnel. We have gone far enough to be on the other side of the Kurugh Khan. Wake Clarice up—and get off this heavy canvas. You can't tell what we may find at the end."

Gradually the spot of light grew larger. Before long we could see the rocky opening at the end. As the daylight filtered into the tunnel we had the illusion of standing stationary on the river while the tunnel rushed past us. Blue sky appeared ahead, there came a sudden roaring— and we were out in the blinding sunlight.

Everything fell away from us. Dimly I realized that the raft had gone over a fall. The logs broke apart as they hit the water below, and a searing pain went through my right leg as the bone snapped between two of the churning timbers. With one arm around Clarice and the other clinging to one of the logs I fought to keep our heads above water. When friendly hands pulled us to shore a little later I tried to speak, and in the same moment lost consciousness.

There isn't much more to tell. We lost all our photos and specimens and scientific data. Most of the diamonds went too, but enough stayed in Clive's pockets to make us all reasonably well off. Clive and Pete are talking about going back some other time to try and capture a tentacle-creature alive in the interests of science, but Clarice and I will probably try a little domestic science instead.

SEED

Jack Snow

The potted plants on the window sill should have given me a clue, but they didn't. After all, they were innocent enough—hardy green vines that added a note of coolness and cheer to the spartanly furnished sanitorium room.

Perhaps I wouldn't have noticed the vines at all, but Myra herself called them to my attention. She had not spoken of them. It was only that occasionally when we were talking, her eyes would wander, almost as though against her will, to the plants. She would stare with peculiar intentness at the vines for a few seconds, and then turn away with an effort. Once I thought I detected a shudder as Myra seemed particularly engrossed in the vines. I meant to ask her if the plants annoyed her and she wished them removed from the room, but at that moment she had started a train of conversation that had banished the odd little incident from my mind for the time. Upon recalling it later, I decided that Myra's preoccupation with the window plants could have no possible relation to her illness, and if she wished the vines removed, she had only to speak to Nurse Wilkins.

I hadn't known Myra was returning to this country until that evening in middle May, when, upon entering my home, hot and weary after a stiflingly hot day filled with the round of calls that are the lot of a doctor in a small

383

suburban town, my good housekeeper handed me a note.
It was from Myra, stating simply that she had taken a suite
of rooms in a fashionable rest sanitorium in the nearby
city, and wished me to call on her that night.

Myra Bradshaw in a rest sanitorium! To say that I was
surprised is putting it mildly. Anyone who has read either
the Sunday magazine supplements or the scholarly journals of scientific societies will readily recall Myra
Bradshaw—beautiful and world-renowned as the famous
woman African explorer.

Her exploits were sensational enough to make her a
natural subject for the big-circulation, luridly illustrated
Sunday magazine sections, while her keenly intelligent
monographs on archeology, anthropology and natural history had won her acclaim respect in that comparatively
small circle of men and women who subscribe to the repu-
table journals of geographic and scientific societies.

Myra Bradshaw was a woman of dynamic spirit and energy—a woman who had dared a thousand perils, faced a
hundred jungle dangers and had exposed herself to a score
of dread tropical diseases—and had never been ill a day in
her life! This I had long marveled at from a professional
standpoint, for, it was my interest in archeology and the
fact that our families had been friendly for many years
that had drawn Myra and me together, not my profession.
Indeed, Myra had more than once sniffed that she had as
little faith in modern MD's as in African witch doctors!

Nevertheless, I concluded, Myra's latest African trek
had proved too much even for her, and she had been forced
to retire to the sanitorium for a rest. After a little reflection, I realized this was not too surprising. The years were
taking their toll, that was all. Such adventures as Myra
indulged in were for the young, and while Myra was by no
means old, she was, I mentally calculated, closer to fifty
than forty.

The stars were gleaming with tropic brilliance, as I climbed into my car and drove the twenty miles to the city, after receiving Myra's message. In all my sixty odd years I can't recall a summer to equal the oppressive, unhealthful heat of that one which marked the reappearance of Myra Bradshaw in my life. The heat came early in May and remained with unslackened intensity late into September. Nor was it a summer of drought.

Most crops did unusually well for they were nourished with sunlight of furnace intensity and watered by frequent, sultry, torrential rains that soaked the steaming earth into a jungle-like morass. It was a season of rampant vegetable growth.

That night the heat was only slightly less than it had been at mid-day. In the reflected light of the moon, there seemed to be reflected something of the heat of the sun, from whose direct rays this little patch of earth had temporarily turned. The crickets, suffused with the abundance of heat and earthly moistures, filled the night with the din of their scraping. With a shudder I recalled reading somewhere that for every human being on the earth there are twelve million insects. Although the road was lonely, with almost no traffic, the night seemed suddenly crowded.

Nurse Wilkins, whom I knew from previous visits to the sanitorium, showed me the way to Myra's suite. I stopped short inside the doorway, finding it difficult to believe my eyes. Could this be Myra Bradshaw? The Myra Bradshaw I had known had been handsome and splendidly formed, radiating perfect health. The figure on the bed was that of a thin, gaunt woman, wasted and wan.

With an effort I endeavored to conceal the very real shock I had suffered. I moved toward the bed, stretching out my hand to clasp Myra's. Yes, it was Myra Bradshaw. Her eyes were unchanged, daring, inquisitive, beautiful, their deep hazel flecked with pure gold. They smiled at me now, and from the pale lips came an invitation to make myself comfortable in a chair near the bed.

Myra and I chatted for the better part of a quarter of an hour, but all the while another part of my mind was busily conjecturing. What had happened to my old friend? What had reduced her to her present pitiably weakened condition? Why had her hand been so icily cold when I had clasped it in greeting? Although the air of the room, was constantly, though gently, circulated by several electric fans, and the three large windows were thrown open to the night, the room was stiflingly hot. Yet Myra's hand was cool—cool as—and I recall now with horror and loathing that the homely old simile ran through my mind—cool as a cucumber.

Finally, employing what I fondly believed to be clever conversational strategy, I steered our talk around to Myra and her sudden and wholly unexpected appearance in the sanitorium. Myra laughed, her eyes twinkling with some of their old merriment. "You old faker, you! I know you've been dying to ask me what I'm doing here, and what's wrong with me to put me in a state like this—flat on my back and weak as a cat!"

I admitted I was.

"Well," replied Myra more soberly, "I'm here as a last resort. But I don't want to tell you anything until you have made a complete physical examination. Can you do that in the morning?"

I assured her I could arrange my morning schedule to take care of the examination.

Great as my curiosity was, Myra remained firm in her determination to discuss her condition no further that night. After a few more minutes I realized that any attempt to extract additional information from her was futile, so with a sigh I bade her goodnight, promising to see her at ten the next morning.

As I drove home through the heat of the night, noting the forked prongs of light that darted above the black treetops on the distant horizon, I wondered with mingled curiosity if cooling rain would me sleep enjoyable that night, and what the physical examination of Myra Bradshaw would reveal in the morning. By the time I reached home, it was quite late and the stupor of the heat, combined with the monotony of the night sounds, and the fatigue of the long day, oppressed me with an utter weariness so that soon sank into a deep and dreamless sleep.

II

"I could've told you, Tom, that there is nothing organically wrong with me, but I knew you wouldn't be satisfied until you had made an examination."

It was shortly after noon the following day, and I had just completed my examination of Myra Bradshaw. Myra was right. I had to admit that my thorough check-up had revealed no trace of any disease, nor could I detect any serious organic impairment. I mopped the perspiration from my brow and sat down beside the bed.

"But Myra," I protested, "there must be something that brought you to your present state. Haven't you any idea—how did it start?"

The woman in the bed smiled at me. "Tom," she said, "if I told you what I suspect is wrong with me, you'd hurry me out of here into the nearest mental hospital. So I'm not going to tell you—not now. I will remain here under your care, and perhaps you will be able to help me. I may be wrong, you know, and I wouldn't want you poking fun at me for the rest of my life, if I told you my suspicions—and then disproved them by recovering!"

I didn't press Myra to tell me what was on her mind. I knew she would confide in me, if she believed her story would be of any aid in treating her. And too, I had some idea how full the jungle is of superstition, and I supposed that not even a woman of Myra's fine intelligence could entirely escape being touched by it after spending years in the African wilderness. So I forgot whatever jungle jargon Myra might be harboring in her mind, and concentrated on restoring her health by modern medical science.

The two weeks that followed were ones of continuing intense heat and increasing worry and frustration for me. Nothing that I did helped Myra in the slightest. I visited her daily, and was forced to watch her waste away visibly before my eyes. I consulted with the foremost specialists in America. I investigated, probed and experimented, I forced and ultimately discarded theory after theory, I spent long hours after midnight reading in the sultry, night heat of my library, hoping that in my books I would find some clue that would start me on the right trail to solving the riddle of Myra's steadily weakening condition. As the days lengthened into weeks, I was forced to admit I was beaten. In despair I realized that a doctor must first have a disease, before he can prescribe a treatment. I couldn't find any disease. The only enemy I had to combat was Myra's extreme weakness, which increased progressively and was obviously induced by her apparent inability to derive nourishment from food. I prepared for her every known variety of energy extract, food concentrate and vitamin-mineral compound, but it was of no avail. My patient ate and drank regularly but for all the good the food did her she might have been on a starvation diet. I was forced to the unscientific conclusion that in some weird, inexplicable manner Myra Bradshaw was being robbed of blood as fast as her food was turned into the life-giving fluid.

The case baffled me completely. It was unreal and nightmarish, and combined with the relentless heat, it caused me to endure many sleepless nights, through which I tossed and turned, damp with perspiration and weary with conjecture. In the black of those heavy, sultry nights, my mind flew off on wild tangents, recalling legends of vampires and fantastic blood-sucking creatures of the jungle. This illustrates very well, I believe, just how thin the veneer of modern learning is, and how it can be rendered even more superficial by climate and temperature.

Meanwhile, Myra's condition was growing steadily worse. I could not give up hope of saving her, but my dismay mounted as I was forced to watch her weakness increase. It was early in August when the sweltering heat had reached its peak, that Myra entered that most dangerous stage in which she lapsed into prolonged comas, regaining semi-consciousness only long enough to take a bit of food. With despair I realized that soon she would lapse into a coma from which there would be no rousing. Death would slip up on her quietly as she slept—and there was nothing I could do. Perhaps intravenous injections would sustain her for a time, but even so her life would soon hang on the hands of the clock.

At a few minutes after eleven o'clock, on the night of August fifteenth, I was in my library studying a recently acquired treatise on the diseases of the tropics, when my phone rang and Nurse Wilkins, speaking from the sanitorium, informed me that Myra had regained consciousness a few minutes before and was asking for me. Wilkins stated further that my patient seemed to have more strength than she had shown for weeks, and was asking for me with a strange persistency. I told Wilkins to remain with Myra and I would leave immediately for the sanitorium.

I will never forget that drive to the city. The night was black and velvety, and the air seemed to be composed of a heat that possessed actual substance and weight as it pressed down on the smothered earth. Any gleam of stars and moon was blotted from the skies by a black, shroud of sultriness.

As I drove down the highway, few cars passed me, and except for the night cries of the insects, I was alone in the night. On either side of the road grew fields of corn and truck gardens of tomatoes, cabbages and other common table vegetables. Never had there been such luxuriant crops. The farmer's only problem was insects, which the heat and moisture favored impartially with the crops.

No doubt it was my own weariness, born of the lateness of the hour, the cumulative enervation of the long weeks of intense heat, and my constant worry over Myra that brought on the extravagant fancy as I drove through the deserted night that the world was intent only on vegetable germination and growth, and that for the time being everything else was of minor importance—swept aside, as it were, from the normal, natural course of life. It was almost as if I could hear the faint crenulation of the leaves as they unfolded, and the rustling and crackling of the stalks and ears as they grew. In the pall of the night there was something repellant, grotesque about the great swollen tomatoes that bulged on the creeping vines, filling the air with their unmistakable vegetable reek.

I shivered in spite of the heat, as, my car carried me down the corridor of towering grain. I felt strangely lonely, like an alien being—an outsider in a world of vegetation, where the sole purpose of existence is to grow, grow and grow in the beaming rays of the sun and the secret moistures of the sultry nights.

III

It was a few minutes past midnight when I entered the lobby of the sanitorium and made my way to Myra's suite. Wilkins, who had been sitting by die bed, arose and quietly greeted me as I entered. A green-shaded bed-lamp standing on a table was the room's only illumination. Gently moved by the electric fans, the sultry night air of the room stirred with an almost liquid motion.

The figure on the bed was pathetically wasted. There was almost no resemblance to the handsome Myra Bradshaw who had stirred the imagination of the world with her beauty, bravery and daring. As I gazed at the pale face, the eyes opened and on seeing me they lit up with an animation they had not shown in weeks.

"Come closer, Tom," the bloodless lips whispered. I seated myself on a chair at the side of the bed and brat my head over the still form.

"You sent for me, Myra?" I asked.

"Yes, Tom," replied the thin voice. "I want to tell you my story. It is now or never," she added with a suggestion of the grim, brash humor that had been so much a part of the old Myra Bradshaw's great charm.

"Plenty of time, Myra," I said, patting her emaciated wrist. "You are better now than you've been for days."

"You know that's not true, Tom," the woman replied. "This is only the final flash of light before the darkness. There is very little time left. Let us not waste it. You must hear my story."

"Very well, Myra," I assented. "I'll listen, only don't tire yourself."

"I haven't spoken until now," the woman began, "because I did not believe what must always have been the truth. Tom, you were right when you suspected that the jungle was responsible for my condition; but you were wrong in searching for a disease. It is no malady that afflicts me . . . at least no ordinary malady!" Myra paused briefly and then her pitifully weak voice continued.

"It began less than a year ago. I was in Leopoldville, when I first heard rumors of a strange village of natives deep in the Belgian Congo, who worshipped a flower, periodically sacrificing the fairest maiden of the village to this *fleur de mal.* Theatrical as the story sounded, I knew Africa well enough to suspect that the rumor very probably had a foundation of truth. I determined to be the first white woman to penetrate to this little-known village of the interior, as well as the first white woman to set eyes on this jungle flower of God. Well, it was the old story. The natives were suspicious of strangers; they had not seen more than half a dozen white men in their lives, and I was the first white woman they had ever seen. They resisted our visit, attacking our bearers. We were forced to wound a few natives to make them behave and to convince them of the effectiveness of our modern arms. Later, of course, we treated and healed their wounds, so really we did them no harm."

Myra paused in her recital, a far-away look in her eyes as she relived for the moment that last weird adventure. Gaining strength to continue, she picked up the thread of her strange story.

"We had no difficulty in locating the temple of the Flower God. It was a bower of unearthly beauty, teeming with such riotous colors and growth as only the jungle can generate. It was nature's own Gothic cathedral with towering walls of infinitely foliated leaves, climbing vines, massive pillars of trees and a green filigree of creepers. Its stained-glass windows were woven of thousands of exotically hued petals.

"I had come, bearing in mind the stories of human sacrifices, fully expecting nothing less than a monster, carnivorous plant—a fly-catcher plant on a giant scale. But I was wrong. There was no such plant. Instead, on an altar-like dais of the cathedral blossomed one, small, red flower. At first sight, I was disappointed. It might have been any one of a thousand jungle flowers. But upon approaching it more closely, I perceived that it did not grow from the soil. What it did grow from sent a chill of horror through me. That blossom was supported by a stem that reared from the gaping mouth of a long-dead native girl. Stifling my revulsion, I saw that natural decomposition of the girl's body had never taken place. Her skin hung about her frame like a loose, brown sack that was beginning to fall to shreds. But inside the shell of her skeleton, Tom, I glimpsed the real evil of this devil flower."

Myra paused momentarily, and in her expressive eyes was reflected something of the horror she was recalling.

"That skeleton was filled with an interweaving and interlacing network of tiny green feelers and roots that perfectly and, completely duplicated what had once been the arteries, veins and capillaries of the unfortunate girl's body.

"The high priest of this jungle temple sullenly explained to me that the flower blossomed only once each year, producing but one small seed. This seed, when fully ripened, was given in food to the carefully selected sacrifice. A short time later, the victim began to weaken and waste away as the seed germinated, and spread its tiny tentacles, roots and feelers through her circulatory system; each of the thread-like feelers drinking of the victim's life blood, until at last the sacrifice died, and the flower blossomed miraculously from the mouth of the dead girl.

"The priest informed me further that the flower I was observing was about to go to seed, as the plant had absorbed all the blood of the girl's corpse.

"Horrible as the priest's story was, it fascinated me. I determined then and there to carry that fabulous seed back to civilization and put the tale to test by attempting to germinate the seed in a solution of animal blood.

"But the priest was cleverer than I," Myra continued. "During the night, he or one of his servitors must have removed the flower and its seed capsule. I was disappointed, of course, but I wanted no more trouble with these natives, whose enmity I had already earned by violating their sacred flower temple, and the whole idea of the flower and plant was so alien and repellant, that I thereupon dismissed the seed from my thoughts, and decided to head back to the coast immediately.

"We remained only one more day in the village, making observations and gathering additional data on the customs and beliefs of these remote savages. It was that one day, I am now convinced, that cost me my life," Myra concluded solemnly.

"Only one thing could have happened, Tom," she went on, beckoning me to silence, as I started to speak. "There just is no other explanation. That native priest, lusting for vengeance for the violation of his temple, managed in some manner to place the seed in my food. As a result, I am about to die—a modern sacrifice to a primitive jungle Flower God thousands of miles away."

"Nonsense, Myra!" I exclaimed. "Your mind is overwrought with your illness. This is certainly a strange story you have told, but you know as well as I that what you suggest is incredible."

"Is it, Tom?" Myra seemed to have spent her pitiably small store of strength in her narration, and now that she had finished her words were tired whispers. "Is it incredible, Tom? I wonder. You do not know the jungle as I do."

Myra's eyes closed and she slipped gently into sleep. I took her pulse and found it alarmingly weak. Nurse Wilkins, who had been a fascinated witness to Myra's story, was at my side. "Is there anything I can do, Doctor?"

"No," I replied with a sigh. "There's nothing either of us can do beyond waiting and watching, I think we should both be here, so I will remain for an hour or two."

Wilkins nodded, and with that knack that is a part of a nurse's training, made herself comfortable in a chair, although I knew she had been on duty far beyond the normal span of hours. I settled back into the chair at the side of Myra's bed. Through the open windows drifted the perpetual clamor of the crickets. The window curtains stirred dully in the hot night air.

The torpor of the heat must have caused me to drop off to sleep, for it was more than an hour later when I was aroused by an exclamation from Wilkins. Instinctively I glanced at Myra. She was dead. She had died so gently and quietly as she slept that neither Wilkins nor I had been aware of her passing. Her eyes were rolled back in her head, her mouth slightly opened.

"Ah, well," I commiserated with a pang of real sorrow and regret, "at least she has gone without pain." For that slight consolation, I could be grateful.

I was about to phone to have the body removed, when my attention was drawn by a strange gurgling or rustling sound that issue from the throat of the dead woman. Wilkins heard it, too, for she was staring as fixedly as I.

And then it happened. I shall state it simply with as few words as possible, describing merely what both Nurse Wilkins and I witnessed with no attempt to theorize or elaborate. For when one is describing the impossible—the incredible—

As Nurse Wilkins and I stared, petrified, a red abomination that I at first thought was blood, caused perhaps by an internal hemorrhage, spread from the mouth of the dead woman. Then, even while my senses revolted, I was forced to see it for what it really was. It was not blood, but a blood red blossom, unfolding its petals before our very eyes as it reared upward on a pale green stem. In a few short seconds the nightmare flower had completed its deathly growth and was about four inches in width, while the stem supporting it emerged some six inches from the mouth of the corpse. Had my very life depended, upon it, I don't believe I would have been able to stir a muscle during those seconds that seemed an eternity. I was as transfixed as any serpent charmed by a Hindu's piping. In that brief blink-of-time all my years of scientific training and learning were blasted to nothingness by the impact of the impossible taking place before my eyes.

It was a noise that broke the spell—the noise caused by steely-nerved Nurse Wilkins collapsing in a heap on the floor. She had fainted dead away. Instantly my mind snapped back into action like a spring suddenly released from tension. Thoughts flew through my head at a furious pace; I knew exactly what must be done. Removing a small pen-knife from my pocket, and fighting down an overwhelming revulsion, I stepped to the bed and forced myself to slip the blade of the knife between the lips of the dead woman, while I severed the stem of the flower in her throat. Then I thrust the clammy blossom into my coat pocket and gently and tenderly closed the eyes and mouth of what had once been Myra Bradshaw. When I finished, the body appeared a normal corpse.

Nurse Wilkins' eyes were fluttering open. In a moment more I had her resting in a chair, staring blankly at me, and muttering, "What happened. Doctor? I—I must have fainted." A few sips of water refreshed her further, and in a few minutes she was her old self, if a trifle shaken. But she remembered nothing beyond the fact that she had dozed, then had awakened to find Myra Bradshaw dead. All memory of the hideous episode of the flower was wiped from her mind. The defense mechanism of Nurse Wilkins' mind was functioning in a manner that would have delighted an amateur psychoanalyst. The mind of this practical, hardheaded nurse simply couldn't accept what it had been forced to record. So, it had resorted to the mechanism of a fainting spell to reject and blot out the incident. Nurse Wilkins remembered nothing beyond awakening to find Myra Bradshaw had died. Then she had fainted—because of the heat and the long months of over-work and extra hours, she stoutly asserted. At any rate, the very next day Nurse Wilkins departed bag and baggage from the sanitorium, grimly determined on a long-delayed and long-needed holiday.

To my relief I discovered later that Myra Bradshaw had left specific instructions that her body was not to be embalmed. Instead, it was to be consigned, whole and untouched, to the heat of the crematorium. I shuddered to think of the green horror of tiny filaments and deli-cate lacements the mortician would have found growing through the blood vessels of the corpse.

For by this time I had come to accept Myra Bradshaw's deathbed story in its entirety. Once the incredible had been demonstrated as factual, I found my inborn scientific curiosity re-asserting itself. I wanted to know more about this weird flower—this *fleur de mal,* as Myra herself had so rightfully termed it. After reporting and recording Myra's death, I hurried through the cloying, humid air of the early morning to my home, my mind busily working all the while, revolving about that curious abomination that lay concealed in my coat pocket.

I had determined to carry out an experiment that would prove to me once and for all time, beyond the shadow of the slightest doubt, the final truth or falsity of Myra Brad-shaw's story.

IV

As soon as I reached home, early as it was in the morning, I went to my laboratory and there carefully prepared
a solution of animal-blood in a beaker. In it I placed the
flower, depositing the beaker in an incubator that would
keep the beaker and its contents at blood heat.

That night was five weeks ago. In that time I have re-
plenished the blood in the beaker, keeping the flower supplied with the life-giving fluid it required to remain fresh
and blooming. I have made several deductions regarding
the blossom. It appears to be an ordinary flower, not unlike the common garden variety of poppy. It possesses no
special attributes of motion or action. Unlike the carnivorous fly-trap plants of Africa, it cannot move when excited
by foreign stimuli, not does it sustain itself on flesh. It
appears to be an ordinary plant, except that it grows out
of a bath of blood, instead of a bed of soil. Also, unlike
the flytrap plant, it is not a tuber, but is a seedbearing
plant. The seed capsule was well formed and had almost
readied maturity last week. It was then I noted that the
blossom first showed signs of beginning to fade and wilt.
This morning, when I examined the flower, I found it almost entirely wilted and apparently lifeless. I determined
that tonight I would examine the seed.

Today I could think of little else than the seed, as I
went through my routine calls and duties. The late September sun shone with all the heat of August, to which
was added the brief fury that accompanies the harvest and
brings the final climax of growth to the plant world.

When the day was finally finished, and I had partaken
of a light dinner, I retired to my laboratory and flung wide
the windows to admit whatever stray breeze there be. The
sun had already set and the horizon was alive with wriggling serpents of heat-lightning, accompanied by a continuous cannonade of thunder, the faint rumble sounding

like the approach of a ghostly artillery. Would the coming storm succeed in breaking the relentless grip of the
summer's heat? I hoped so fervently. As a doctor, I knew
full well the toll this unusual summer had taken in my
own small community. Heat prostrations, heart attacks,
sunstrokes—all had been far higher than average during
these past four months. But now it was late September and
the magnitude of the storm that threatened promised real
relief from the ghastly heat.

Then I forgot all about the approaching storm, as I
turned to the wilted, lifeless flower and the dry seed pod
that seemed somehow to epitomize and concentrate in itself all the miserable heat and sultriness of that long summer of torrid sunshine and misty rains. Perhaps it was
my subconsciousness linking the origin of the blossom
with the jungle-like heat we had endured throughout this
strange summer.

Turning from the window, I removed the beaker of
blood and the flower from the incubator. The wilted
petals dropped away as my hand touched them. The firm,
rounded seed capsule was easily detached from the stem.
There it lay in the palm of my hand—a small, brown-
ish-red ovule, not more than three-quarters of an inch in
length. I cracked the protective shell that enclosed the
seed. The fibrous husk fell apart and I discarded it. In
my hand lay the seed. Moving to the lamp, I adjusted my
spectacles and peered closely at the object in my palm.
And then I gasped with shock and amazement. Could I believe my eyes? Did I really see it?—a palely greenish-white
image, a miniature human shape, not more than half-an-
inch in length, and as delicately and exquisitely formed as
a bit of Chinese jade!

The window draperies suddenly whipped aside as a blast
of hot air swept into the room. There was a terrific crack
of thunder and a brilliant dagger of lightning stabbed its

way through the inky black heavens. During the next few minutes the elements stormed their most eloquently. The fury burst with a violence that seemed to shake the very earth. The wind mounted steadily, moaning eerily as it veered around the corners of the house. Great drops of rain were hurled noisily to the earth. It was the prelude of what proved to be an autumnal tempest. But not even the dramatic raging of the storm could distract my attention from the object I held cradled in my palm.

Hastily I shut the windows to close out the ravening wind and the pelting rain. Then I seized a powerful magnifying glass and brought it to focus on the faintly chill and clammy bit of vegetable growth in my hand.

It was then that I saw the ultimate, yet horribly logical terror that finally and completely verified Myra Bradshaw's story. As I trained the powerful lens on the seed, there came a blinding flash of lightning, accompanied by an ear-splitting roar of thunder that seemed to explode in the garden just outside my laboratory. My electric lamp went dark, plunging the room in complete blackness. Then came another, more prolonged flash of lightning, and while I stared I saw in that glaring light, more vivid than any noon-day sun, that the tiny figure in the palm of my hand was a perfect likeness in every minute detail, to every last delineation of feature—a miniature replica of Myra Bradshaw herself!

While I stared in that weird intensity of illumination, just before the chamber was once more shrouded in blackness, the half-inch seed effigy stared back at me, peering up through the thick glass of the lens with blank and soulless eyes that flashed suddenly open revealing hazel depths flecked with gold, while the beautifully formed limbs of the figurine squirmed and threshed about in mindless motion.

Additional titles of cryptobotanical and cryptozoological fiction, along with other thematic volumes of classic science fiction, fantasy, supernatural, and adventure fiction can be found at:

CoachwhipBooks.com
(print)

Coachwhip.com
(epub)

FLORA CURIOSA

CRYPTOBOTANY, MYSTERIOUS FUNGI,
SENTIENT TREES, AND DEADLY PLANTS IN
CLASSIC SCIENCE FICTION AND FANTASY

Stories include: Rappaccini's Daughter (1844, Nathaniel Hawthorne), The American's Tale (1880, Arthur Conan Doyle), The Man-Eating Tree (1881, Phil Robinson), The Balloon Tree (1883, Edward Page Mitchell), The Flowering of the Strange Orchid (1894, H. G. Wells), The Treasure in the Forest (1894, H. G. Wells), The Purple Pileus (1896, H. G. Wells), The Purple Terror (1898, Fred M. White), A Vine on a House (1905, Ambrose Bierce), Professor Jonkin's Cannibal Plant (1905, Howard R. Garis), The Willows (1907, Algernon Blackwood), The Voice in the Night (1907, William Hope Hodgson), The Orchid Horror (1911, John Blunt), The Man Whom the Trees Loved (1912, Algernon Blackwood), The Pavilion (1915, E. Nesbit), The Sumach (1919, Ulric Daubeny), The Green Death (1920, H. C. McNeile).

BOTANICA DELIRA

MORE STORIES OF STRANGE,
UNDISCOVERED, AND MURDEROUS
VEGETATION

Stories include: Lost in a Pyramid, or the Mummy's Curse (1869, Louisa May Alcott), The Man-Eating Tree (1875, Edmund Spencer), The Devil Tree (1883, Anonymous), Carnivorine (1889, Lucy H. Hooper), My One Gorilla (1890, Grant Allen), Lamparagua (1893, May Crommelin), The Flower of Death (1893, Flavel Scott Mines), The Man-Killing Tree of Ceylon (1893, Anonymous), The Death Plant of South Africa (1895, H. B. M. Buchanan), The Guardian of Mystery Island (1895, Edmond Nolcini), The Man-Trap Cactus (1895, Anonymous), A Flesh-Eating Plant (1901, Anonymous), The Gray Weed (1905, Owen Oliver), The Tale of the Scarlet Butterflies (1908, Beatrice Grimshaw), The Black Orchid (1910, Marjorie L. C. Pickthall), The Adventure of the Devil's Foot (1910, Arthur Conan Doyle), Spores of Death (1913, Sax Rohmer), The Thunder Beast (1920, Joseph B. Ames), Orchid Death (1921, James Hanson), Drosera Cannibalis (trans. 1922, René Morot), The Malignant Flower (1927, Anthos).

ARBORIS MYSTERIUS

STORIES OF THE UNCANNY AND UNDESCRIBED
FROM THE BOTANICAL KINGDOM

Stories include: The Giant Wistaria (1891, Charlotte P. Gilman), Kasper Craig (1892, Maud Howe), The Gold Plant (1895, George Griffith), The Story of the Grey House (1898, Kate and Hesketh Prichard), The Flower of Death (1916, A. V. Pankey), The Lure of the Lavender Trees (1917, Maryland Allen), The Warlock of Glororum (1919, Howard Pease), An Orchid of Asia: a Tale of the South Seas (1920, Edna Underwood), "Glued" (1921, H. De Vere Stacpoole), The Tree (1921, H. P. Lovecraft), Through the Crater's Rim (1926, A. Hyatt Verrill), The Blood-Flower (1927, Seabury Quinn), The Devils of Po Sung (1927, Bassett Morgan), White Orchids (1927, Gordon Philip England), Vine Terror (1934, Howard Wandrei), The Devil Flower (1939, Harl Vincent), The Garden of Hell (1943, Leroy Yerxa), and Cactus (1950, Mildred Johnson).

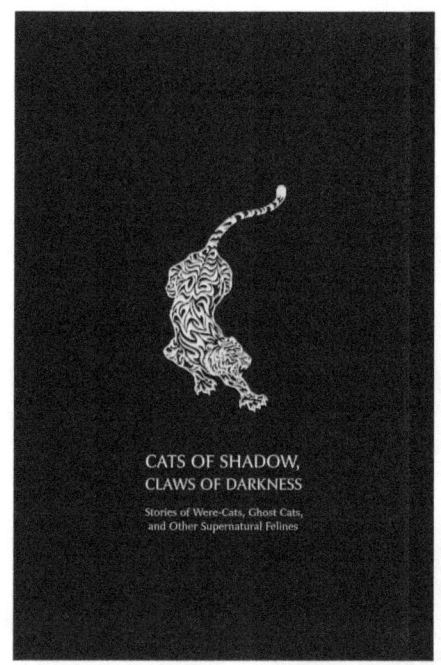

CATS OF SHADOW,
CLAWS OF DARKNESS

Stories of Were-Cats, Ghost Cats,
and Other Supernatural Felines

WULF

TALES OF WOLVES
AND WEREWOLVES

EDITED BY
CHAD ARMENT

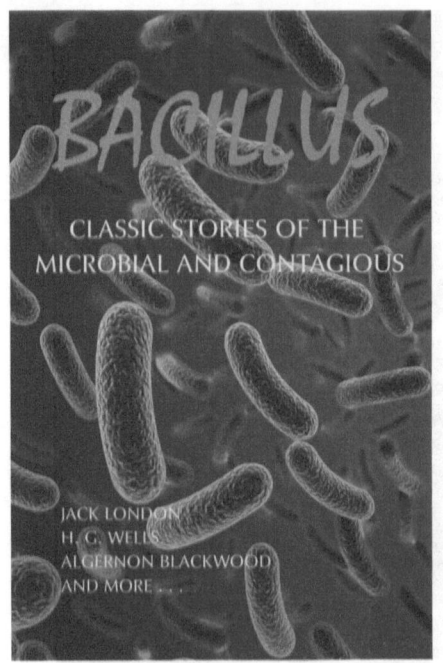

BACILLUS

CLASSIC STORIES OF THE
MICROBIAL AND CONTAGIOUS

JACK LONDON
H. G. WELLS
ALGERNON BLACKWOOD
AND MORE . . .

A SPECTRUM
UNSEEN

Invisible Men, Women, and Creatures in
Classic Science Fiction and Fantasy

zoologica
fantastica

Bestiarium
Cryptozoologicum

Mystery Animals and Unknown Species
in Classic Science Fiction and Fantasy

INVERTEBRATA ENIGMATICA

Giant Spiders, Dangerous Insects, and other Strange Invertebrates
in Classic Science Fiction and Fantasy

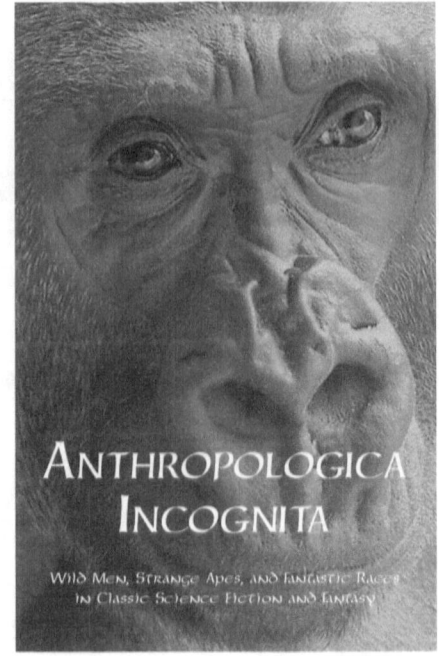

ANTHROPOLOGICA
INCOGNITA

Wild Men, Strange Apes, and Fantastic Races
in Classic Science Fiction and Fantasy

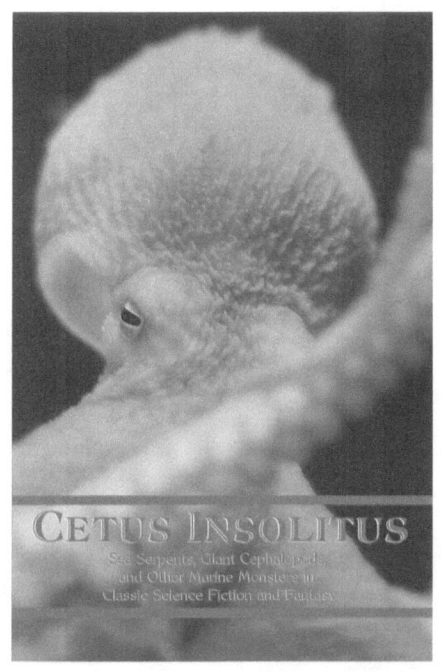

CETUS INSOLITUS

Sea Serpents, Giant Cephalopods,
and Other Marine Monsters in
Classic Science Fiction and Fantasy

OTHER LIFE

An Anthology of
Non-Terrestrial Biology

www.ingramcontent.com/pod-product-compliance
Lightning Source LLC
Chambersburg PA
CBHW020507020726
47493CB00001B/212